RESONANCE

RESONANCE

RAGNAROK TRILOGY
Book Three

JOHN MEANEY

The right of John Meaney to be identified as the author of
this work has been asserted by him in accordance with the
Copyright, Designs and Patents Act 1988.

First published in Great Britain in 2013 by
Gollancz
An imprint of the Orion Publishing Group
Orion House, 5 Upper St Martin's Lane, London
WC2H 9EA
An Hachette UK Company

This edition published in Great Britain in 2014
by Gollancz

1 3 5 7 9 10 8 6 4 2

A CIP catalogue record for this book
is available from the British Library

ISBN 978 0 575 09481 9

Typeset by Input Data Services Ltd,
Bridgwater, Somerset

Printed in Great Britain by
Clays Ltd, St Ives plc

The Orion Publishing Group's policy is to use papers
that are natural, renewable and recyclable products and
made from wood grown in sustainable forests. The logging
and manufacturing processes are expected to conform to
the environmental regulations of the country of origin.

www.johnmeaney.com
www.orionbooks.co.uk
www.gollancz.co.uk

Remembering Anne McCaffrey,
the writer who sang.

Masculine expendability [in war] *proves a part of the cosmic scheme for research and development. And so does the itch of one superorganism to fling itself into battle against another.*

Howard Bloom, The Lucifer Principle

It may now be possible for us to answer the question: How and why do we accept one theory in preference to others? [...] We choose the theory which best holds its own in competition with other theories; the one which, by natural selection, proves itself the fittest to survive.

Karl Popper, The Logic Of Scientific Discovery

You'll see what your eyes will allow you to see.

Muhammad Ali, addressing Joe Frazier

ONE

Call it triumph, following disaster. Say further, that love powered their flight through golden void, as they hurtled past
blood-coloured nebulae amid night-black fractal stars. Conjoined, a single being, a black powerful raptor whose wings
were webbed with red and gold, they flew: ship-and-Roger,
soaring past Mandelbrot Nebula, arcing through breakers of
roiling vacuum, coursing along Calzonni Gap, heading finally
for home.

For Labyrinth, so beautiful, the city-world whose infinite
richness no ship or Pilot could experience in full, knowing
only this: they would die for her.

Old-school powerlifters, like Clayton (now in his prime and
becoming one of Max's best officers) used mag-suits to strain
against induced forces; but Max Gould was older still, and his
methods were primeval, even atavistic. A metal bar, loaded
with three times his bodyweight, was his enemy as he hauled
upwards against a one-*g* Higgs field, his breathing stentorian,
face reddened and arteries ridged: blood pressure through the
roof and Fleming in his mind, the torturer who had gone to
work on Max with such professional thoroughness; and no
one would ever try such a thing again, or Max would tear
them apart.

'Argh!'

He dropped the weights and they banged against the
floor.

Fucking Schenck.

Now Max was in charge and the darkness-controlled

1

admiral, Boris Schenck – make that *former* Admiral Schenck – had fled like the bastard coward that he was, along with hundreds of renegade Pilots; and the best analysis suggested they were headed for the realspace galactic core, where corrupted humans, helped in the past by Schenck's people, had established a huge deep-space base. So Max was vindicated, his power greater than ever; and to prove it, and demonstrate cold self-control, Commodore Max Gould, director of the intelligence service, held back from visiting personal revenge upon Fleming, who had only (in the ancient excuse) been following orders.

Besides, the service could not afford to lose efficient interrogators – *torturers*, let's not mince words – and he could be magnanimous now, with the endorphins of triumph pumping through his blood, while he reconfigured his flowmetal room into the configuration known as *office*, even though the term was deprecated, due for removal from Aeternum in the language's forthcoming upgrade, soon to be published.

The word *renegade*, in contrast, possessed a new prominence in the dictionary.

He used smartgel that smelt like wood-chips – talk about an old memory – and, clean once more, he retuned his jumpsuit to sharply tailored lines, then summoned Zeke Clayton. Less than ten seconds later, Clayton stepped out of a swirling fast-path rotation.

'Sir.' Having adapted to Max's preferred lack of small-talk and deference, he started by saying: 'If we're still due to see Roger Blackstone, then I've got to say, I'm not entirely sure of him.'

Max gestured a flowmetal chair into being.

'Tell me about your doubts.' This was Max playing devil's advocate against himself, for he had doubts of his own, but was always keen to check another's thinking. 'You can't ask for a better pedigree. Carl Blackstone sacrificed himself in a hellflight to save a world.' Ultra-relativistic trajectories along massively non-linear geodesics were a desperate measure and often fatal, as in Blackstone's case. 'Thousands of Fulgidi survivors are his testament.'

In perverse irony, a large percentage had perished more recently when Molsin's sky-cities, the best part of a thousand in number, in close proximity because of a Conjunction celebration, had annihilated each other or committed suicide using seppuku bombs. The violence was born of confusion and deception, initiated and orchestrated by one person: Petra Helsen, creature of the darkness, creator of the Anomaly and now this. A society destroying itself out of fear – itself and the refugees it had taken in, when other worlds rejected them.

'Son of a hero?' Clayton meant Roger. 'Hardly an asset in Tangleknot.'

'An additional challenge to overcome, then.'

'Well, OK, and getting through the training is only the beginning. I understand that, Max. An officer's operational record is everything. But given that he's our most reliable observer for detecting this *darkness* phenomenon, how exactly would you deploy him?'

'Carefully.' Max's voice was mild. 'Wouldn't you say?'

Clayton's mouth puckered in a downward smile. 'Guess I'd better try to stay high in your ratings, boss. I like carefulness. Wouldn't want Control putting me into the field on a whim.'

'Sometimes it's necessary to sacrifice a high-value piece,' said Max. 'Careful calculation is not necessarily to the field officer's advantage.'

'I can't tell you how reassuring that is.'

Max allowed his lips to twitch, acknowledging the ambiguity, as a holo brightened.

'Stay for the chat,' he said.

'Roger's arrived?'

'He's right there.' Max pointed his big hands forward like a springboard diver, and pulled them apart, causing a flowpath rotation to drop a fit-looking young Pilot into place. 'Pilot Blackstone.'

'Sir.'

Max caused a flowmetal chair to rise. Roger sat on it.

Hard-edged. Tough-looking, not like before.

Roger Blackstone was not quite nineteen standard years old, but he was no longer the soft student Max had met during Roger's first visit here from Fulgor, before everything went to hell. Then, Max had determined the lad's extraordinary sensitivity to the darkness; now he had a potential field agent before him.

'Tell us about Molsin,' said Max.

'I was there with Jed Goran, part of our plan' – Roger nodded in Clayton's direction – 'to keep me away from Schenck's surveillance. But Helsen was there, no coincidence, I'm assuming, since that was where most of the refugees ended up. She stole an autodoc, which was a tactical mistake, because otherwise I would never have known she—'

As the debriefing continued, Max analysed Roger and watched Clayton doing likewise, enumerating the changes in the young Pilot. When Roger came to the part of the story where Rhianna Chiang revealed herself as a Pilot agent-in-place – *dear Rhianna, always the best* – and took Roger through an intense mind-body training regime that ended with a total cognitive restructuring, everything made sense: the thousand-metre stare that spoke not of trauma but a heightened reliance on peripheral vision, hearing and smell.

A present from my beloved Rhianna.

Which was to say, a weapon Max had yet to learn how to wield. A weapon called Blackstone. That thought remained as Max picked up the conversation, led the debriefing to its conclusion, and told young Roger to take time out for relaxation and wait for a call. One fastpath summons later and the flowmetal chair was empty, already beginning to melt back into the floor.

Clayton was staring at the ceiling, or rather something in his mind's eye. Without looking at Max, he said: 'You realise he never attended Graduation.'

A ceremony was irrelevant. Max parsed the sentence for unspoken semantics.

'Yet he has a ship. Good point.' Earlier, separately, they had each watched holo footage of a triumphant return to Labyrinth, Roger and his black ship webbed with scarlet and gold: a ship no one had known existed. 'And so very like his father's.'

'Exactly. I don't have a fixation with mindwipe' – Clayton was clearly lying, because the continuing inability of his former partner, Darius Boyle, to regain a normal life following selective amnesia induction that went too deep still burned like acid – 'but we caused Carl Blackstone's wiped memories to resurface, me and Darius, when we questioned him.'

'What are you saying?' asked Max. 'That his ship might have possessed the same memories all along?'

'And couldn't share them because of the mindwipe.'

The amnesia treatment would have affected Carl Blackstone's ability to retrieve the memories in his ship's mind as well as his own: that was a known phenomenon.

'Whether his ship knew already,' said Max, 'is irrelevant when you consider that Carl regained his memories before his last two flights, to Fulgor and back. During one or both of those trips, his ship must have grown a daughter, wouldn't you say?'

Without the guidance and shelter of Labyrinth, parthenogenetic ship reproduction was so very rare.

'If you're worried about the content of those wiped memories,' added Max, 'I can tell you what they—'

'Don't, please,' said Clayton. 'Darius and I learnt them once, and look what happened.'

It was ironic, that their probing had reawakened memories which they themselves, Clayton and Boyle, did not have clearance for: hence the mindwipe, and the neurological side-effects that ended Darius Boyle's career.

'Except that inside the Admiralty, everyone now should know this.' Max knew better than anyone how fast the strategic landscape, and specific needs for secrecy, could change. 'Carl Blackstone saw the realspace base at the galactic core, over two decades ago. The trail led to a young Pilot Schenck, though it took years. That's how my whole counter-operation began, Deke, and I had to keep it buried.'

'Shit,' said Clayton.

It was the first time he had sworn inside Max's office, since Max had officially become director of the intelligence service. But then, Max had never used Clayton's first name before – people rarely did – which signalled that this was an apology, or close facsimile.

Max looked up at the ceiling.

'You could have told us,' he said. 'About the Blackstone ship.'

Both he and Clayton belonged to the minority of Pilots able to perceive Labyrinth's direct communications. But the chances of receiving a reply were millions to—

=Yes.=

Clayton smiled.

'Getting an answer is one thing. A satisfying answer, that's something else again.' Like Max's apology, he implied.

But it was as far as Max would go.

I can't help other people's neediness.

The Anomaly had enveloped Fulgor, Molsin society was gone, and the renegades' massive base at the galactic core seemed merely a bridgehead for an invading darkness whose origins lay so very far away, somewhere on the far side of a cosmic void, itself one hundred and fifty million lightyears in diameter. An invasion was in progress, albeit one initiated aeons ago, and whether its arrival was imminent or a million years away, no one yet knew.

In the face of all this, weak-hearted feelings signified nothing.

Max accepted responsibility because he had to – because no one else had his background or talents, of which the primary one was this: since schooldays he had hated bullies. In the end, his own rotten childhood might help to save humanity; and how ironic was that?

When Clayton left, Max was enveloped in sour meditation, scarcely noticing the man's departure. But Clayton was going to approve Roger's recruitment, officially and on Max's behalf, so that was something: another small piece moving forward a square in the tactical game that was Max's life-work.

Another day at the office, except that soon he would have to find another way to phrase that thought – *office* being deprecated – because nothing remains unchanging, not even the language in which you communicate and think. The ground might shift beneath your feet, but so long as you remembered what you were fighting for, that was enough.

It would have to be.

A fastpath rotation opened before Roger, and Jed's voice sounded: 'Step right in, buddy.'

Roger had called Jed from Erdös Endway, an offshoot of Borges Boulevard, saying only that he had good news. Not that anything was guaranteed: this was the first step into the training programme – one with a failure rate of ninety-something per cent, apparently – and never mind an actual operational career like Dad.

Reality swirled.

'Daistral's warmed up.' Jed held out a goblet. 'For you, mate.'

Roger was in an apartment lounge decorated with holo streamers blaring *Congratulations!* while a lean-faced woman – Clara James, now part of Jed's life – raised her own goblet and said: 'You flew her, Roger. Well done.' She came forward to give him a one-armed hug, drink in her other hand.

'Yeah, well done.' Jed clapped Roger's shoulder.

A three-person party. But who else did he know?

'Thank you both. But that's not all that happened today.'

Jed grinned. 'Guess your balls dropped, old mate. Seems like—'

'Ahem. *Jed*.' Clara poked him in the shoulder with a fore-knuckle fist. 'Behave.'

'Ow. But his voice is deeper already.'

Clara winked. 'I noticed.'

Roger looked at them, his friends, knowing that Jed must have been security-vetted – he and Clara had moved in together, after all – but with restricted clearance, presumably. Only Clara was an intelligence officer.

He looked at her. 'I'm going to be one of you.'

With a muscular grin, Jed said: 'What, a woman?'

Something there?

Roger detected a private joke between Jed and Clara, but no more than that, no hint of what it entailed. As for Clara, her obsidian eyes were focused on him, Roger, her colleague-to-be if he ever graduated.

'Are you willing to pay the price?'

'Maybe I already did.'

Jed let out a melodramatic breath.

'It's like spook central,' he said. 'What have I got myself into?'

'Tangleknot, then.' Clara still looked serious.

Roger nodded. 'Starting tomorrow.'

'Didn't we try that earlier, darling?' asked Jed.

'Oh, for—'

Then they looked at each other and laughed, clinked goblets, and drank a toast. Things were beginning to happen: a career under Roger's control, instead of a maelstrom of events sweeping him up without reason or predictability.

Maybe I can live a normal life.

Except, of course, that was not what he had signed up for; nothing like it.

TWO

It was a year since her last visit to Rupert's office, and this time Gavriela was in a rage, in tears as she stood there, fighting not to slam the *Times* onto the polished desk.

'He deserved so *much*.'

Rupert's pale face tightened. 'I know.'

'Were you ashamed to be seen protecting a *pervert*, was that it, Rupert? Couldn't you have moved to protect him?'

'I'll forgive you that because you were his friend. Because *we* are friends.'

Rupert was the consummate chessmaster, moving spies across the board with whatever degree of ruthlessness was required to win. But he loved men in the same illegal way that Turing had – and in particular loved Brian, father of Gavriela's child – which meant the corridors of Whitehall would grow chilly indeed if they were ever indiscreet. Homosexuality meant openness to blackmail, a lever to crack open a man and produce a traitor; and these days the stakes could rise as far as global war and humanity's extinction: you could never tell where a chain of events – or a chain *reaction* – might end.

'I'm not just talking about stopping the Director of Public Prosecution in the first place,' she said. 'After the trial, your bloody watchers should have been looking after him. Or are you telling me it was suicide, as the papers say?'

Perhaps someone here in MI6 had ordered the killing. Cyanide in an apple, so typically Russian, so perfectly characteristic of the KGB's *modus operandi*, was precisely the kind of thing some Whitehall mandarin might have indirectly suggested, a hint of: 'Who will rid me of this troublesome priest?'

She stopped her thoughts and sat down on the visitor's chair.

'AMT was in a strained state of mind.' Rupert tapped the rosewood desktop, noticed a fingerprint, breathed on the mark, and used a monogrammed handkerchief to wipe the surface clean. 'We did have watchers on him, and they followed him to Blackpool Pier, where he had his fortune told by one Gipsy Rose Lee. When he came out he was white-faced and shaking.'

This was ridiculous.

'He wasn't superstitious.'

'I'm quoting the report,' said Rupert. 'Plus, he had raised the subject of killing himself.'

'With whom?' Normally she would have said *who with?* to annoy him; under stress, she reverted to Teutonic exactness.

'Someone close to Turing. But the point is, when my officers questioned the fortune-teller, she remembered nothing of him. Nothing at all.'

Purely in memory, she heard an echo of nine notes: *da, da-dum, da-da-da-dum, da-da*.

'Tell me there have been no sightings of Dmitri Shtemenko.'

He was her first suspect, when it came to altering minds.

Rupert said: 'Someone who *might* have been Shtemenko was seen at the Institute of Physics. Looking for a Dr Gavriela Wolf.'

'No.'

She *was* registered as a member of the institute, but as Gabrielle Woods, the name that everyone knew her by: the identity created by Rupert during wartime, with a fully backstopped biography. Only someone who had known her earlier than 1941 would refer to the Wolf identity – someone like Dmitri Shtemenko, who saved her and himself from Nazi thugs, back in 1927 when the world was young.

'So, Shtemenko... It's interesting you ask about him, Gavi. Some kind of premonition?'

'I'm Gabrielle, thanks all the same, and no premonition. Do you have any actual intelligence on the man?'

Six years ago, during de-Nazification procedures in Berlin, Dmitri had surfaced using the pre-war German cover identity provided by his Bolshevik masters, and he had slipped away from American and British military police who tried to arrest him. At the time, Rupert had concluded that Dmitri Shtemenko slid across to the East via Checkpoint Bravo, presumably reverting to his real name, to be shot in a courtyard or kissed on both cheeks as the GRU's prodigal son returning. GRU or KGB, they had never determined which.

'We backtracked,' said Rupert, 'to find out he was probably a V-man for the last years of the war' – he meant a Soviet mole inside Wehrmacht intelligence – 'but what he did before that, no one knows.'

'There's no way to justify a manhunt,' said Gavriela.

It was the fear that spoke: a creature of the darkness was on her trail, and if anything happened to her, then what about Carl? Twelve years old, a grammar school boy who had excelled in his Eleven Plus, and whose questions about his father received no satisfactory answers.

'I think there *is* justification.' Rupert gave her the chess grandmaster stare. 'Clearly the real reason has to stay out of the reports – unspoken among friends, as it were – but if our man is back in the field, he'll be a senior intelligence officer by now.'

'Therefore a good catch for Five or Special Branch.'

That was a provocation, because there was no way that Rupert would delegate this outside the family, and never mind that domestic counter-intelligence was explicitly beyond the remit of SIS, alias MI6.

'Europe is just entering a phase of peace,' said Rupert. 'That frees up personnel, cold war or no.'

Fully eight years after V-E Day, that might seem an odd statement to the fabled everyman on the Clapham omnibus; but from her desk in GCHQ, Gavriela kept track of the same events that Rupert did. The past four years had seen – finally! – a decline of the violent anarchy that had ruled most of Europe following the official end of the war.

Whatever the propagandists at home and in America wrote in the newspapers, much of the continent had remained lawless for years, morality dissolved in the need simply to eat. Women and children sold themselves; the concept of personal property did not apply; gang-rape was a pervasive horror; and entire populations died in genocide years after Hitler, in the *Führerbunker* beneath the bombed-out Chancellery, took the coward's way out.

'It will go better if you help,' Rupert went on. 'But I'm willing to use a decoy, if you're not up to it.'

She felt a downward sweep of blood from her face. She had begun by railing about Alan's death; now it was turned around, with Rupert Forrester once again about to shift her where he wanted. Pawn to whatever, check and mate; and never mind the sacrifices on the way.

'Decoy,' she said, knowing she would, after arguing, give in.

Everything else was detail.

Old Joe (or Big Joe, depending on who you asked) projected high above the court and its lawns – the ensemble shaped like a rectangle fastened to a semicircle, resembling an elongated, round-bottomed mediaeval shield – to form the centre of the Birmingham campus. All around was ornate redbrick architecture, including the Poynting Institute, home to the physics department. As for Old Joe, the technical term was *campanile*, in the Italian renaissance tradition: the world's tallest free-standing clock tower.

A more obvious place to resurrect Dr Gavriela Wolf would have been Manchester, home to the civilian world's first electronic computer, thanks to Alan – *damn you, Dmitri, if it was you who killed him* – but the problem was that AMT's colleagues knew her already, as Gabrielle Woods. Still, among physics departments, Birmingham was near the top of anybody's list.

Carl's headmaster had been reluctant to release him before the end of term, but changed his mind overnight after a phone call instigated by Rupert (its details unknown to Gavriela, but clearly effective), allowing Carl to trip off to Oxford on the train (though it seemed only yesterday he called them *choochoos*) where he would stay with Auntie Rosie and Uncle Jack. Or perhaps it was Anna, his own age and pretty, he looked forward to seeing.

From the long enclosed lounge of the Bridge – it spanned the road-like pathway separating Maths from Physics – she scanned the campus while listening to the students behind her: off-colour jokes regarding Poynting's Balls, referring to the apparatus Poynting had used to determine G (known as Big G), the universal gravitational constant.

A voice muttered: 'Blighters.'

She turned to see a red-bearded man watching the undergraduates depart. Blue-grey smoke rose from his pipe.

'Dr Anders,' said Gavriela. 'It's just end-of-term spirits, and I don't think they realised I was here.'

'Lewis, please. And you're right, they didn't see you, but I'm not sure that's the point.' Then he cracked a smile. 'Mind you, I finished delivering my end-of-year elec-and-mag lecture with the aphorism that every couple has a moment in a field.' And, with a tweed-shouldered shrug: 'I take it you understood the Poynting reference?'

'I knew about E-cross-H already' – Gavriela meant the Poynting vector that declared the energy propagation of an electromagnetic field – 'but the gravity apparatus, I only learned about yesterday, reading up on the place.'

'It's not the most significant work we've done here.' Anders looked from right to left, checking they were alone, then held his pipe to his chest and stoppered it with his palm, as if closing someone's ear to prevent them hearing. 'Radio cavity work and the magnetron, and I was here throughout the war.'

'Oh,' said Gavriela.

'I've said nothing to my colleagues, but you've appeared overnight, while the department listings and so on make it look as if you've been here for ever.' He put the pipe in his mouth and sucked hard three times, causing it to release a smoke-cloud. 'Brings back memories.'

Of war work and the need for secrecy. Understood.

The Soviets had detonated an H-bomb last year, but it was the American test four months ago that had fired up reporters everywhere. With its 14-megaton blast catching the crew of a vessel called the *Lucky Dragon*, nasty indeed, and how about that ship's name for irony? The Cold War, and the likelihood of its growing hot, was on everybody's mind.

Perhaps that was why Anders jumped now, seeing the stranger standing fifteen feet away, near the end of the Bridge.

'It's OK,' said Gavriela. 'He's friendly.'

'We keep an Alsatian, my wife and I,' said Anders. 'He slobbers over us, but if you're a stranger, he'll bite your hand off.'

Gavriela laughed.

'You're right. He's exactly that kind of friendly.'

Him and the other watchdogs.

'I hope he keeps you safe,' said Anders.

'Yes. So do I.'

'I'll leave you to it.'

Anders strode away, leaving her in the middle of the Bridge on her own, visible to anyone outside who cared to look up, which was of course the point.

A Judas goat.

Just like you on Molsin, Roger.

One of those strange thoughts that sometimes flitted into

her mind then evaporated, sublimating like dry ice to invisible gas. Yet somehow she felt better, despite her conviction that the darkness was somewhere beyond the edge of her ability to see it, like the tiger lurking before he bursts from cover to a sudden end.

His own, the goat's, or both.

THREE

Bullies arise everywhere, even in a city-world of infinite wonders: witness this small boy shivering with his back against a wall, confronted by bigger lads. Roger, coming on the group from behind, allowed his inductive energies to grow inside him, eyeballs growing sore with the need to release until the resonance caused the boys to flinch, sensing him at last, picking up the potential for destruction. Then he damped the energies back down as the boys – call them a gang – walked away, all apart from two, including the biggest, less attentive than the others, about to push his fist into the victim's face.

But his pal grabbed his sleeve, receiving a startled look; then they were summoning a shaky fastpath rotation. 'He's a peacekeeper, must be, you moronic—' The words disappeared as the rotation shut down.

Only the trembling boy, their victim, was left. Roger knelt down beside him.

'You'll be OK.'

But the expression in those wide obsidian eyes said that the problem went far beyond the incident Roger had interrupted. This was the boy's everyday world, not an isolated event.

'I remember when I was your age,' Roger continued, still kneeling. 'Adults seemed to have forgotten what the world was like when *they* were young. I could never understand that.'

The boy's eyes widened further.

Dad, I didn't think I'd use your gifts for this.

Espionageware in Roger's tu-ring slipped through the defences of the simpler tu-ring that the boy was wearing. The ware accessed everything, including where the boy lived, and his educational record. That history, lased directly onto Roger's retinas (and after he had waded through the bullshit wording), told of a youngster with quirky imagination, his intellectual potential unfulfilled due to lack of courage and self-discipline.

'I'm going to tell you something difficult,' Roger went on. 'You can deal with these bastards' – he used the term deliberately, calibrating his perceptions of the boy's reactive body language – 'but not straight away, by applying yourself in secret. I mean you practise every day, every single day, and meantime you observe what's around you, to avoid them, the bigger guys, all right?'

A nod.

The boy's tu-ring flared, acknowledging receipt of unasked-for ware.

'Exercise is part of it, stuff you can do in your room.' Thanks to his Fulgidus education, Roger was able to tailor the data via subliminal commands while continuing to speak. 'You will need to practise fighting techniques as well.'

Some of his words were pitched as covert commands. The ware, now loaded in the boy's tu-ring, would alter his bedroom at home, extruding partial fighting mannequins from the flowmetal walls, altering the timeflow and acoustic properties so that no one would know what he was up to. There was also the matter of inspiration – and Roger grinned as he discovered copies of *Fighting Shadows* episodes stored in his tu-ring's deep memory. He had thought his youthful self's favourite holodrama lost for ever, along with his world.

There was a storyline called *Ambush* that would save Roger having to tell the boy how this should play out. After months of training – preferably a standard year, mean-geodesic – it would be time to forestall a group ambush by taking them out, one by one, until the threat was done.

It was the kind of harsh truth people with no experience preferred to ignore.

'Which means you'll also have time to study and have fun,' Roger concluded, 'because there's more to life than combat, OK?'

A part of him thought *what if there isn't?* but that was for an adult in wartime. And even so, there had to be something worth fighting for.

The boy blinked at him.

'I'll do it.'

'You have my respect.' With solemnity, Roger extended his fist, and they bumped knuckles. 'Success.'

It was a benediction. He watched as the boy summoned a rotation – with more aplomb and accuracy than his attackers – and disappeared into it. Then a female voice came from behind Roger.

'Good for you.'

He whirled, taking in the lithe form.

'Rhianna? What are you doing here?'

'I thought I'd take my boy to school, what with it being his first day and all.'

'Your b—? Shit.'

She meant him, and Tangleknot.

'Now, now. No cursing, son.'

Rhianna Chiang was barely old enough to be his biological mother, but after their training on Molsin, you could say she had enabled the creation of Roger as he was now. He remembered their first sparring, when he had tapped out as she locked on an armbar – and Rhianna had ignored his signal of submission, continuing her leverage until the arm snapped through, because she was not teaching him a sport, or how to give up.

Because limits were there to be pushed through and destroyed.

'You don't want to be late,' she added. 'Not on your first day.'

'No, ma'am.' He smiled. 'I certainly don't.'

'So we'll go together.'

Rhianna raised her hands, summoning a fastpath to take them both.

To his new beginning. To Tangleknot.

Tangleknot disappointed, but only in a single regard: on his first day, Roger had hoped for advanced sabotage-and-silent-killing training. But after navigating through the twisted topological transformations that physical entry entailed, where the academy's defences could have destroyed them at any stage, he and Rhianna separated outside an interview room. His first mission was to get through a start-of-course interview, and he knew without being told that he could be kicked out at any time.

The welcoming committee comprised two men and a woman; they gave their worknames as Havelock, Deutsch and Palmer.

'Growing up on Fulgor,' said Deutsch, leading the questioning, 'how did that make you feel about the ordinary humans around you?'

'I needed to hold on to my, um, self-image in secret.' Roger wanted to explain his world to people who could have no conception of it. 'They're all impressive, especially the Luculenti and their ...' He noticed a twitching smile from Palmer. 'All right, I had an unconscious bias, a part of me that thought I was superior, but my point is that I learnt metacognition via the Fulgidus education system.'

'The people your father died attempting to save. By fetching a rescue fleet.'

'Yes.' Roger did not try to prevent his voice from thickening. 'And if I achieve a fraction of what Dad did, I'll be happy.'

'Fame and glory, then?' Palmer looked intense.

Mum and Dad's funeral had been a state occasion.

I'd rather you were still alive.

But they weren't, so he would have to carry on.

'It's the work that matters.' He stated it as an assumption: that he would be an intelligence officer. 'Seems to me, most of the time, my success will depend on people *not* knowing what I've done.'

'And what if we had moved against Fulgor, because we had to?'

'Like bombing the planet to pre-empt the Anomaly?' Roger remembered the first thought that had come into his mind on seeing Labyrinth: *I would die to keep you safe*. But his answer was more complicated than that. 'The person I am now is a hundred per cent loyal to Labyrinth. The events that ended Fulgor are part of the process that made me. For me, now, a conflict of interest is impossible. And' – he turned to stare at the wall on his left, at a surface that looked like pale-apricot marble – 'you obviously know I'm telling the truth.'

The other man, Havelock, gave a narrow-faced smile.

'Very astute,' he said. 'And besides the deepscan array, what else do you notice?'

In this place, it was impossible to lie. At least without a level of training Roger had yet to undergo.

'May I?' he raised a finger to create a holo sketch.

'Carry on,' said Havelock.

'You have weapons arrays here, here, here' – he drew the room as a blue frame outline, the weaponry in red – 'and here, not to mention whatever it is you're carrying, ma'am.'

The woman, Palmer, gave the tiniest of smiles.

'Do you see yourself as more of an intelligence analyst, Pilot Blackstone, or an agent in the field?'

'I hadn't thought it would be my decision,' said Roger. 'But fieldwork, definitely. I believe I can work effectively on real-space worlds for extended periods of time.'

Stating the obvious.

'Cut and thrust among the boardrooms of commerce,' said Deutsch. 'Is that the milieu you're aiming for?'

It was where Dad had spent much of his time on Fulgor, after all.

'I'll go where I'm needed.' Roger would rather fight the darkness, but how could a single person without resources do that? What would it even entail? Bombing the hellworld of Fulgor, if any dared approach that close? Wasting his entire life searching the other worlds for that bitch Helsen? 'I'm not old enough to be taken seriously in those circles. But later, when I have the experience, I can do it.'

He concluded by using the parasubjunctive definite future tense, simultaneously subtle and emphatic in a way no real-space language could emulate. And there was something else, an element of faith involved in submitting oneself to Tangleknot: they would not, could not, tell him about the work they intended he should do on graduating. His words implied awareness of the paradox.

'So you're ready for hard work and pain?' said Palmer.

'I am.'

'Then welcome to Tangleknot.'

Reality swirled, taking him to the heart of the academy, to the harsh magnificence that was Tangleknot Core: barracks and many-dimensioned landscapes and simulation halls where the threats were real enough that it was possible to die, and sometimes people did. It was a place of dog-eat-dog rivalry and also blood-brothers-until-death camaraderie; a torturous hell which could be the culmination of a driven person's dreams; where a strong student might, with sufficient drive, become more powerful than even the most imaginative neophyte thought possible.

A place where the price of success was everything.

FOUR

EARTH, 778 AD

The people in the village were targets, nothing else. The raid itself, however, was more than a day in the life of a reaver band: it was Fenrisulfr's first test as battle chief. The prior training, led by him, had been subtle: drilling the fighters in slipping techniques as well as sprinting onslaughts, using individual combat as a metaphor for manoeuvring the entire band. They had taken to it only because of Fenrisulfr's own ferocity, and the *berserkergangr* lying just beneath the surface of his every movement, every twitch.

They were no strangers to warrior madness, his reavers; but they had known no one who could enter and leave that raging state as a matter of conscious will. It was why they approached him always with respect and care, knowing that only his war-hound, the ever-faithful Brandr, was allowed close without qualification.

And so, the village.

Understand them as humans, so you know their weaknesses; and as they are distracted by the everyday concerns of work, acknowledge they are simply *things* with vulnerabilities and openings you have identified, because now is the time to act, so form the wolf's-head hand shape and make the cutting gesture – *now!* – as you pull your weapons free of the ragged cloak that hid them because this is it, the battle and frightening confusion, the stink and the rage, the slippery greyish guts sliding out of meat – *there* – the slickness and stickiness of blood, warm as it coats your skin, alters the way you grip your sword-hilt, as if that mattered when all around is chaos and red rage as your vision narrows, and the screams are distant whispers because that is what happens in battle – the howling world grows quiet – and the scheming part of you approves of the vanguard – *run, my fighters* – of the *berserker* fighters sprinting uphill, uncaring of the difficulty, using the effort to push their bodies further into warrior insanity; while the others take down the fighting villagers like two wedges inserted from the sides before all tactics are forgotten because you are in the midst of it yourself and there is only room for this:

The rage.

For Eira.

They took her, *it* took her, the deadly Norns or the Middle World itself, and this is your response: to kill them all.

And you're deep among them now, whirling and lunging, your victims' limbs and torsos slippery with the fluids of war, with blood and sweat and worse, but your hands are raging claws so you grab and twist, smash a hilt into that face, slam an elbow down – *got it* – to the back of a neck, tear them off balance by the nose and eyes, knee into liver, and a warhammer is yours for the grabbing and three skulls – four – are crushed beneath your blows before the weight of numbers tangles you up so you drive the handle into a larynx, use hooked thumbs to rip outwards from an enemy's nose – *lovely* – taking both eyes, then elbows and teeth are your weapons in a maelstrom of moving weight – *hit me harder* – of impact – *harder, you weaklings* – where vision counts for little and feeling is everything while the spirit drives the fight because you will never, ever give up until they're—

Breaking free, breathing hard.

—dead, because you've done it: see that, the slumped pile behind you, tangled corpses and the flailing of the dying; and their squeals grow louder as hearing returns because you are sloughing off *berserkergangr* as if it were a handy cloak to be donned and shed at will. Your own warriors are staring because they have seen the wolf and it is you.

Yes!

These are your reavers, these haters and lovers of the blade, and you snarl with salt blood in your mouth, because this is victory that burns, howling, inside you.

YES!

Now they will follow you for sure.

Across the sea, on an island linked by a causeway to the greater land, a different form of agony falls upon the pain-filled, one-eyed man called Stígr where he thrashes on a wooden cot, contained in a coating of sweat, scarcely aware of the tightness of bandages or the poultice-stink. Neither his wounds nor his memories of evil – of all the filth the darkness has caused him to perform since his limb-tearing crucifixion and the rape of his soul – torture him the most. Something far worse is hurting him now.

It is the gentleness of the monks' hands as they tend to him, and the peacefulness of their spirits, that make him weep and groan.

FIVE

It calmed every Pilot, this golden void of mu-space, or so the theory went. But Piet Gunnarsson, his mood matched by that of his ship, was restless in what should have been a sleep period, drifting near a crimson nebula whose thousand subtle hues were worthy of meditation and artistic awe in their own right. He had screwed up twice in a matter of subjective weeks, and it haunted him.

Most recently, as part of the squadron keeping distant watch on Fulgor, he had allowed a ship to slip past because it was heading *towards* the hellworld, not launching from it, and because its Pilot was Admiral Schenck. Call it respect for authority, from someone trying to make amends. Except, except...

It turned out that, if Piet had obeyed protocol and signalled his fellow Pilots to check the situation, instead of just accepting the admiral's genuine credentials, he would have found that Schenck was a creature of corruption – whose exact relationship to the Anomaly enveloping Fulgor was not clear to Piet – and capturing him would have been a triumph.

Several tendays before that, through simple self-absorption in his own troubles, Piet had ignored a distant fleet of Pilot vessels heading for Fulgor, thereby missing the opportunity to help rescue some of those poor people now merged into the Anomaly.

Two personal failures later, and here he was, still tasked with keeping a distant eye on Fulgor, remaining in position when the rest of the watch-squadron besides Alice, currently in command in realspace, had flown home to Labyrinth, and a fresh squadron – two wings, each fourteen strong – took their place. At any time, half were in realspace on watch, and half were in mu-space, as Piet was now, theoretically resting.

The other ships and Pilots appeared to have no difficulty with the concept, as they drifted here, quiescent. But Piet's thoughts roiled, imagining Alice – why exactly *had* she stayed? – and the others on watch in realspace, some hundred kilometres from the surface of the hellworld: far enough away to prevent the Anomaly from reaching through the realspace hyperdimensions to absorb them, or so the Admiralty analysts believed.

The watchers' brief was to destroy any small craft that lifted from the surface, or flee before a larger fleet, because no one knew how long the global mind would remain satisfied with living on a single planetary surface. Perhaps it would take a thousand or a million years for the urge to spread to manifest; or perhaps it was already preparing to launch.

Anyone else picking up movement?

The signal was from Jakob, on the other side of the nebula.

Not me.

Movement in mu-space? There was no reason for anyone else to be here.

Me neither.

Negative replies came from everyone but Piet, who was immersing himself in long-range sensitivity, listening, at one with his beautiful ship as he-and-she cranked up maximum gain, alert for the tiniest pulse of mu-space energies that had no realspace names; and after a moment they found something.

This is it.

With luck this could be salvation, a resurrection of pride, and – dare he think it? – perhaps a reason for Alice to take an interest in him the way he hoped.

Even as Piet-and-ship flew towards the disturbance, the nature of the approaching craft remained questionable, right up to the moment it came within viewing distance (via the tunnelling of impacted fractal-vector quasi-bosons through the ship's protective membrane, no photons involved). Then it was too late to call the others, because ship-and-Piet had insufficiently accurate bearings, in this choppy region, to send tightbeam signals.

We have to do something.

Ship-and-Piet could blast out a wider broadcast, but the approaching ship would sense the transmission, just as clearly as Piet's fellow Pilots would. If they remained quiescent, however, the newcomer might draw close without realising anyone was here.

Because this was a Zajinet vessel, no Pilot ship, and the aliens' major weapon systems appeared to be powered down – but that was no guarantee because some energies could be loosed with almost no warning. The one certain way to destroy the bastards was before they saw you.

Then a signal from Jakob sounded loud.

What is your purpose, Zajinets? Know that the realspace-tangential planet is maximally dangerous.

So Jakob was trying to warn them about Fulgor. All very well, if you assumed the Zajinets were not on the Anomaly's side; but after four centuries of contact, was there a single Pilot or ordinary human who could claim to truly understand even the simplest Zajinet communication? Never mind their hidden motives and political manoeuvring.

<<Cold-black is yes.>>
<<Safe is not here or there.>>
<<Black-cold a bad awakening.>>
<<Brace for reception.>>

With no change in trajectory, the Zajinet vessel continued to draw near. Piet-and-ship remained the closest among the Pilot squadron, which meant they would be first to die; and how else could you analyse the situation?

Stay back.

That was Jakob's command, having no effect on the approaching ship. The follow-up was to his fellow Pilots:

Make ready but do not power up your resonator cavities.

Piet-and-ship had already followed the first part of that

command, hearing but not processing the second, because –
look! – something was happening, and this was it – *now* – the
moment for proving courage.

<<**Cannot.**>>
<<**Receive/refuse not.**>>
<<**Your kind is reason.**>>
<<**Refuse not.**>>

The smooth Zajinet hull was cracking open, and no one but
Piet-and-ship had noticed.

It's firing!

I see it, my love.

Piet-and-ship kicked hard into a swooping geodesic that led
closer to the Zajinet ship and the risk was huge—

Hold back. Gunnarsson, hold back!

—with some kind of defensive sparkling around the target's hull as something launched but whatever was about
to happen the rest of the squadron had to live – *Alice, if
only* – and ship-and-Piet filled with massive build-up, acceleration bringing the enemy closer, close enough to be sure
– *aim now* – and then there was a mental shout of triumph
and release – *yes!* – as resonator cavities let loose and energy
burst out in one massive pulse with Piet-and-ship arcing sideways and hoping for escape while not betting on it since the
point was the Zajinets must die and here came the explosion
now.

Like a many-dimensioned snowflake formed of fire.

Beautiful flames, denoting death.

We did it, my love.

Yes, we did.

More vessels came out of nowhere, shimmering into existence, and for a moment Piet-and-ship panicked; but it
was Alice and the Pilots she commanded, come in response
presumably to a cross-continuum signal blasted through by
Jakob or one of the others.

What the bloody hell?

A long dark tube, glistening like a beetle's carapace, was

skimming through golden space towards Alice's ship. Piet felt terrified, enough to twitch right out of conjunction trance, just for a moment. He sent a desperate signal:

  It's a Zajinet torpedo!

Alice, in danger. He had killed the vessel but failed to stop the—

  Piet, stay back.

Ship-and-Piet, reintegrating, slowed to take a long, curving glide around the cloud of glowing debris, all that remained of the Zajinet vessel – *we got them!* – while desperately trying to scan the tube-like object that Alice was snagging, controlling, bringing alongside her ship.

  Oh, Piet, you fool. You bloody stupid fool.

  Alice! What are you doing?

It was slipping through her hull's event membrane – allowed inside! – through a dilated opening into a cargo bay, then hidden as everything closed up once more. Had Alice really just taken an alien bomb on board her ship?

Shining light accompanied her disappearance, as she transited back to realspace.

What's going on?

I don't know.

After a moment to prepare, ship-and-Piet did likewise, following Alice's insertion angle.

Black space and silver stars surrounded them.

Alice broadcast a realtime image of her cargo bay's interior, as ship's bulkheads extruded tendrils with fractal branching fingers to explore the torpedo-like object's hull. It did not take the tendrils long to crack the thing open, because that was what the tube was intended to do: split itself apart in order to deliver the contents.

Oh, no.

Which were not a detonating weapon, not at all.

Another screw-up.

Revealed was a dark-clothed man in a foetal position: a man

who began to tremble and shiver, eyelids flickering. Within a minute, he was mostly awake.

'H-hello?' he said in Spanalian.

'You're safe.' Alice appeared on the edge of the holo image, having left her control cabin to enter the cargo bay. 'You're safe, my friend.'

'Yes. Saved. Me.'

'Who saved you? And who are you?'

'T-Tannier. Peacekeeper. Molsin.'

A survivor of the catastrophic fighting among Molsin's sky-cities! That was incredible. But how could the man be inside a—?

'Zajinets. S-saved me.'

Piet Gunnarsson felt his personal universe collapse.

31

SIX

THE WORLD, 5570 AD

The desert excavation was huge, lit primarily by the silvery light of Magnus which, like the other two visible moons, was almost full. Only Magnus showed, as it always did, black filigree across its shining disc. Here, it was cool enough to work comfortably from a while before midnight until pre-dawn; but the teams were dedicated and the shifts were long, often starting when the night air retained its warm edge.

From time to time, Seeker had wondered about Starij and Kolarin, whether their leadership style was too harsh; but when he checked, no trace of disgruntled flux leaked from the working men and women. All two hundred were volunteers, everyone's skin showing as polished silver, a sign of health and tranquillity, not to mention excitement about their goal.

What lay beneath the heavy, compacted sands was a trove of Ideas whose trapped flux tantalised him even during the day while he slept, enthralling him in dreams as well as wakefulness. But this was not just whorls of flux, fragments of knowledge floating on the winds – these Ideas were trapped within a buried, ancient vessel capable of flying across the voids of space, out among the moons and stars; and that vessel's existence was a startling concept in its own right.

This night, Seeker had arisen early, and remembered staring at his hand for a disconcerting moment in the moonlight as he woke, seeing only living crystal before the tag-end of his daymare faded. By the time he sat down to breakfast, algal flakes and sweet pear milk as usual here in camp, all dreams were forgotten.

Now, as he watched the excavating teams at work – at the moment, they required no Seeker's guidance – he sensed an approaching female presence before she rounded a sandstone pillar and walked into view, pulling down the hood that had covered her head. Not one of the volunteers, then, for Seeker knew them all.

The work proceeds well, Seeker?

He did not know her, but a Seeker always dealt politely with strangers.

It seems that way. Does the project interest you?

It was a long trek from the nearest cavern town. Although supply caravans were a regular feature these nights, pure visitors to the project were rare. Not everyone shared a Seeker's need to pull Ideas into mind, to knit Ideas into Themes, to revel in knowledge.

You don't recognise me, do you, Harij?

Seeker had no good way to respond to that.

What do you mean?

We were in Mistress Ahn's class together. Or is that gone too?

For a frowning moment, it seemed Seeker might pull back something from the past, some trace remanence encoding a memory; then it slipped from him, was lost.

I'm sorry.

Ah, Harij ... I'm Zirkana.

Reflected moonlight flowed upon her flawless polished skin. She smiled, and Seeker could not help smiling back.

You never really noticed me back then, Harij. Do you mind if ... If I call you that? At least when others are not around.

The question shimmered with implications that Seeker did not want to examine too closely.

You can call me that, yes. Would you like to look around the project?

And to find a place on it. A way to help.

Perhaps her inner excitement, resonating to make him feel the same, was half-driven by the hunger for new Ideas; but there was more to it than that, undeniably, as mutual induction caused Seeker's and Zirkana's flux to mirror each other, no longer strangers, despite having just met.

This way.

As they walked, he held out his hand, and she took it, silver in silver; and they continued on, rendered by moonlight into a single shining form.

On the ninth night after Zirkana's arrival, Kolarin's team dug through to the long-buried hull: a huge success following sustained effort. In the meantime, Zirkana had found a job with the project manager, Starij, helping him with his massive workload. During the days she slept in the single women's cavern: like the other shelters, something of a trudge from the excavation site, but protected.

At night, before and after work, Seeker kept her company.

You always dreamed of Seeking, Harij. And now you do.

Her private cast possessed a melancholy tinge, but how could he regret forgotten desires? Especially when they were nevertheless fulfilled in present reality.

And then, the breakthrough.

Everyone back!

The warning cast, ferociously strong, came from Kolarin at the central dig: flux whirling through the air in response to collapsing ferrimagnetic sand, but instead of disaster, it brought the final uncovering of the hull, previously revealed trowel-stroke by careful trowel-stroke.

That ancient hull was a dull grey-green, marked with paler excrement-like streaks. Once, many generations ago, it had shone a lustrous dark green with glistening white bands, sailing the heaven-void; now it was a relic, its crew long dead, but perhaps their Ideas might still be unearthed.

Stolid Starij and lean Kolarin grinned and clapped each other's shoulders. The volunteer diggers were smiling and laughing, while trying not to cause too much disturbance, because this remained a fragile dig.

Triumph, right enough.

It's there. It's really there.

Zirkana and Seeker embraced each other, glad of the public excuse.

Overhead, the black-webbed disc of Magnus shone down upon metal that had known only darkness and extinction for so very long: longer than anyone here could calculate.

And yet, and yet ...

Every lifeless desert, given unexpected moisture, is capable of blossoming almost in an instant, as if ancient life can always find a way to remain dormant in shelter, waiting indefinitely for the environment to alter, at which point everything will change.

The next night, another Seeker joined them. This was the man whom Seeker-once-Harij had saved from alien corruption. Seeker-once-captive had been trapped by invaders, the crew from another spacegoing ship, destroyed in a vortex storm. They had been of two varieties, those demons: some looking very human, yet lacking silver skins – their softness repulsive – while others were metallic and winged, but refusing to venture far out of their ship, as if the world's air were toxic to them.

Most abominably, the creatures were conjoined as single mentality. A blue glow had accompanied their absorption of Seeker-once-captive; but when the flux-storm fell, Seeker-once-Harij harnessed its energy, desperately retaining inductive control, severing the captors' link. At the time, as the two Seekers crawled away beneath the storm, they scarcely perceived the captor-demons' fear and shock; but later, it seemed obvious that no one had ever before freed a trapped individual from their collective, composite self.

Their ship, already damaged, had crashed and exploded when trying to take off inside the storm. Such wreckage as remained was unapproachable, permeated with wild flux likely to wipe minds, much as had been done in the past to

Seeker-once-Harij, erasing his former identity: this he understood without remembering.

Now, the two Seekers clasped forearms in greeting. Then Seeker-once-Harij introduced Zirkana to Seeker-once-captive, who responded:

You resonate well together, you and this hero who rescued me.

Zirkana smiled, while Seeker-once-Harij grew mottled with embarrassment.

Kolarin came up, greeting Seeker-once-captive, who had visited before. Together, the four of them went to examine the unearthed section of ancient hull. Everyone kept their flux resonance tightly controlled, because the Ideas trapped deep inside the vessel might be fragile, prone to easy collapse.

Truly, it seemed impossible that so much remained intact. The ancients had possessed incredible engineering capability.

Now, someone spun the tocsin-coil to announce the end of shift. Time to get under shelter before the dawn. Back inside the main communal cavern, they sat together at one of the long tables, drinking mycomilk and discussing the unknown mysteries trapped within the ancients' ship.

Two nights earlier, at just such a time, Kolarin had reminisced about his dead wife Ilara; later, Zirkana had disturbed Seeker-once-Harij by asking whether he remembered his own Ilara, his sister. Of course he could not; he did not understand how Zirkana would ask such a question. But then they had embraced, and the past ceased to matter.

Now Seeker-once-captive shared a free-floating partial Idea he had captured nearby:

** ... flowmetal arrays governed by quantum resonance effects induced by successive 'sequential observation' manipulation by programmed smartatoms. Addressed femtatomic eigenvalue storage with cross-qutrit resonant entanglement is fashioned into memory and logic gates. Furthermore, any correctly aligned induction, any signal at all, can be used during emergency bootstrap procedures, since it is modality more than content that verifies the signal's provenance.**

Zirkana thought it was too complicated to understand

without some kind of context. But Seeker-once-Harij touched her shoulder – love-hysteresis swept through them both – and gave his suggestion.

It's an echo of something inside the old ship. Don't you sense the flavour?

All four looked at each other, then Kolarin cast:

Perhaps it defines an emergency procedure. Something that works without exact wording, for use by panicking passengers.

The Idea talked about modality being more important than content. But if it referred to a ship's operation—

Seeker-once-Harij swallowed, scarcely believing his own hopeful thought.

Something like opening a door?

Could the ancient vessel really be intact with regard to more than superstructure? Might it even respond to flux commands?

Zirkana took hold of his hand.

The sun is nearly up.

But if we hurry ...

It was dangerous, but none of them could hide their emotional intent. Just a quick look, to see if they might generate a response. Very quick, and then they could hurry back to shelter without getting burnt.

Come on, then.

Wrapped up and hooded, the four scurried back to the dig site, Seeker-once-Harij holding hands with Zirkana, while Kolarin and Seeker-once-captive forged ahead. Then, at the exposed hull, the two Seekers went forward together, knelt down, and placed their palms and foreheads against the metal.

There is something. Not a door mechanism, but ...

Yes, deep inside. I've got it.

Together, they caught a tumbling fragment of an Idea and hauled it out *through* the hull, allowing it to float between them:

** ... labelled Minissimus, Minor, Magnus – our destination which we will not reach – along with Major and Maximus. That last is the *only logical site for crash-landing given the state of our ...***

It was a shard, a tiny piece, but of such clarity!

The World. By Maximus it means the World.

That was Zirkana.

Yes, you're right.

But her silver skin was darkening, because the sun was almost up.

We need to get into shelter.

And quickly.

They rushed back towards the caverns, Seeker-once-Harij and Zirkana supporting each other, because the person you loved was and always would be precious, more precious by far than any ancient find, however culturally significant it might turn out to be.

Even a Seeker knew that life is defined by more than Ideas.

SEVEN

Rhianna would not hug Roger in case he misunderstood, but she was proud that he was now enrolled officially (though secretly) in Tangleknot. Her own days at the academy were strong in her memory, and always would be: the pain as much as elation; the endless training and striving; stoicism always, the Aeternal term derived from *shūgyo*, implying austere discipline, unflinching and with total focused effort.

They said farewell in a turquoise and silver hall used to impress security-cleared visitors without exposing them to the harsh realities of Tangleknot Core.

'I don't know how often we'll get breaks,' said Roger, 'or be allowed to exit the place.'

'Less than you'd like.'

'Probably, but it's where I want to be. And will you even be in Labyrinth?'

He was a trainee asking an established intelligence officer about the next step in her career; but they had survived Molsin together, and that made a difference.

'I'm full-time inside Admiralty premises for now. Short-term tasks to occupy me while I work out what to do next.' And because this was Roger, her only protégé: 'I'm meeting Max today.'

'The Commodore? That's impressive.'

Not many officers dealt directly with the director of the service. Even a neophyte knew that.

'Not really,' she said. 'Look, I'm not going to wish you luck, because you'll be great.'

'If I am, it's thanks to you.'

Roger had toughened up – more than that, had been transformed – but right now his emotions were open, on display. Reversing her previous decision, Rhianna hugged him hard.

'I'm proud of you,' she whispered.

Then she stepped back, summoning a rotation.

Roger nodded.

Everything revolved around a host of axes, and as Tangleknot and Roger disappeared from sight, Rhianna wondered for a moment whether she would ever see him again, because meetings with Uncle Max had a way of changing one's life, not always in expected ways.

You'll do fine, Pilot Blackstone.

They were *senpai* and *kohai*, he and her, as much as *sensei* and *deshi*, a bond inexplicable to one who had not experienced mentoring through harshness for mortal stakes. In teaching him, she had learnt much about herself; more importantly, she had bequeathed all she knew to someone worthy, someone who would fight for Labyrinth just as she would, willing to sacrifice the same.

Meaning everything.

She had not met Clayton before, but Roger had mentioned him during the long hypnosis session back on Molsin when she had uncovered all his memories, including the ones that he accessed only in dreams of the far future, the most disturbing of all. Other enquiries since returning to Labyrinth had unearthed only good reports about Clayton.

He was waiting, a large bearish man, in the director's antechamber. They shook hands as he introduced himself.

'The Commodore wondered if you knew this guy.' Clayton gestured a holo into existence. 'This was taken yesterday, mean-geodesic.'

It was a head-and-shoulders shot of a scar-faced, hard-looking man.

'So he survived.' Rhianna nodded, still looking at the image. 'His name's Tannier, and he's a peacekeeper – was – on Barbour. That's a Molsin sky-city. If you've access to Roger Blackstone's debriefing—'

'I was there when he delivered it.'

'Then you'll know Tannier's the man who helped him. And that's definitely Tannier in the holo. But how did he get away?'

When the sky-cities perished, she meant. Then she remembered their confrontation with Helsen and her assistant Ranulph, dead at Roger's hands.

'I'm guessing it was the Zajinets,' she added. 'Returning the favour, after Helsen tried to get at them, and Tannier, Roger and I stopped her.'

Clayton looked as if he were trying not to bite his lip.

'Thanks for the confirmation,' he said.

'You don't sound happy about—'

A ginger cat with white patches walked out of the wall from the direction of Max's office, stopped, and turned to look at them with unblinking obsidian eyes. Then he continued on, walked inside the opposite wall, and was gone.

Clayton sighed.

'Don't ask,' he said.

When they entered Max's office, there was a cream-coloured cat, too elegant to be male, sitting on Max's lap. She flowed onto the floor, turned in circles like a kitten chasing her tail, and fastpath-rotated out of sight. Had any Pilot besides Max attempted the same, here in the heart of his defences, they would have been obliterated.

He stood up with massive arms open wide.

'Rhianna. My favourite niece.'

'Uncle Max.'

They hugged strongly and kissed each other on the cheek, while Clayton stood with his mouth open, like a man whose heart has stopped.

'Er,' he said.

Clearly being assigned to assist the director of the intelligence service meant one surprise after another. Knowing Uncle Max, poor Clayton probably had not learnt the half of it, not yet.

The floor budded flowmetal chairs, and everyone sat.

'Pilot, um, Chiang,' said Clayton, 'confirms Tannier's identity in the file.'

'That's not good.' Max looked at Rhianna. 'His survival is good news, but not the circumstances by which he arrived in our hands.'

Together, the three of them went through the logs and reports from the watch-squadron placed on Fulgor surveillance, along with background on one Piet Gunnarsson, who seemed to have a knack for causing disaster, although Rhianna knew that careful, rigorous statistical analysis was always required to distinguish guilt from unlucky coincidence.

And then Max played a segment from Tannier's debriefing interview, held on board a Pilot's vessel in realspace, in which Tannier described his confrontation with Helsen, how she dropped through a cracked-open sky-city hull, in what looked like suicide at first, except that a silver-and-scarlet Pilot's ship had been hovering underneath, waiting to catch her.

'Schenck,' said Clayton, at the first mention of the ship's colours. 'Bound to be Schenck.'

'Shit,' muttered Rhianna. 'Too bad the bitch got to live.'

They replayed the footage of the Zajinet ship launching a torpedo-like tube, which of course contained a comatose Tannier, while Piet Gunnarsson interpreted the action as an attack and launched a strike that destroyed the Zajinets.

'That's a more immediate concern.' Max closed down the holo. 'If you were a Zajinet in authority, to whatever extent they have such a thing, how would you interpret Gunnarsson's actions?'

Only one answer came to Rhianna's mind.

'I'd call it an act of war.'

As if the Anomaly and Schenck's renegades were not trouble enough.

EIGHT

EARTH, 2033 AD

Lucas was not sure about the cyberphysics gathering in Denver. Was it the smallest important scientific conference he had ever attended? Or the minor conference with the highest opinion of itself? But Gus had wanted him to be here, and she was his new boss as well as friend.

Back at Imperial, his former colleague Fatima once said that Lucas clearly possessed an innate sense of entitlement. What she meant was, he would walk up to anyone he admired to tell them so – people that others would be scared to approach. Over the years, that had included two Nobel laureates and the Irish prime minister. Lucas disagreed: it was not entitlement, it was other people who were desperate for a celebrity's approval, even though fame was nonsense.

Whatever the reason, he found it easy to be friends with Augusta 'Gus' Calzonni, the rich and often feared scientist-turned-entrepreneuse (as the smarter zines had it) who had discovered mu-space. For some it remained a metaphor – a visualisation to aid understanding of the equations – while others believed she had uncovered something real: the actual ur-continuum, the ultimate context.

'Consider the universe as a net curtain, if you've ever seen such a thing,' Lucas said in the hotel's lounge to a handful of attendees, 'which is what you get if spacetime is quantised at the Planck length and time. Now drape it across a pointy landscape, so miniature mountain peaks insert through some of the holes, giving the curtain the possibility of shape. That's what *context* means, in this, er … context.'

One of the group – her fluorescing name-badge read *Jacqui*

Khan – stared at him with the deepest, most intelligent gaze he had ever experienced. She was a little overweight and not pretty, but as they abandoned the mu-space discussion, standing up in response to the next talk being announced, as everyone's qPads chimed in time, Lucas could not take his eyes off her.

Not pretty, but beautiful.

The next speaker was a computer scientist, a grey-haired fellow Brit with a background in cyber-forensics who might have been in his fifties, though he looked so fit it was hard to tell. His name was Gavin Case, and he surprised Lucas by referencing C.P. Snow, whose once-famous 1954 lecture Lucas knew of by chance and expected no one else to have heard of, not these days.

Snow had talked about two cultures, how people educated in the humanities were proud of their ignorance of, say, the second law of thermodynamics, which was the same as a scientist not knowing about Shakespeare. 'Although he later amended that,' said Case, 'to the equivalent of not being able to read.'

There were chuckles from his no-doubt biased audience, as he continued to criticise Britain's Ministry of Computation for its short-sighted views on commercial quantum crypto – and criminal cryptanalysis – before stepping everybody through mathematical formulations of the latest advances, together with a demo of working software.

Someone asked, when the time for questions came, why Case and his team had not used open-source technology; his reply mentioned client requirements, which seemed to satisfy. Lucas wondered if he was the only one to realise what that really meant: this was defence-funded work, with mathematical models – but not the working code – publicised here as part of a deliberate effort to spread anti-criminal techniques to the wider technical world.

The talk finished with another scathing anti-anti-science remark, about the famous quantum scenario that was the

Schrödinger's cat *paradox* – because a real cat is alive or dead, no middle ground, which is exactly the point – and how few people grasped the significance.

'Present company excepted, of course,' Case concluded. 'You understand that subatomic particles are weird, but the real mystery is how they behave in a *non*-quantum way in large numbers.' He held up his qPad. 'Except in these.'

For decades, researchers had been entangling larger and larger collections of particles, which meant that qPads and qPins were an advance that people should have seen coming, although investors had spectacularly failed to do so. It was a steady advance, unlike graphene, say, whose discovery – as far as Lucas knew – came from nowhere, luckily for him.

Or I couldn't have sent a message six centuries ahead.

Unless he and Gus had deluded themselves, and consigned a memory flake to simple destruction. That would be a shame, since it had contained perhaps the last uncorrupted copy of observational data from the gamma-ray burster event. All other copies around the globe had been subject to cyberattack – hence, presumably, Gus's newfound interest in crypto and leading-edge countermeasures.

But Lucas had just found his own reason for being here.

Jacqui Khan's applause, as the lecture ended, seemed half-hearted. Lucas wondered if commenting on this was the best way to begin a conversation; then he stopped second-guessing himself and allowed the words to flow.

'You don't look entirely happy with the talk.'

'There's a difference between assuming specialist knowledge and, well, not talking down to people. He didn't get it right for me, but then I'm no physicist. More computers-by-way-of-psychology.' She held out her hand. 'I'm Jacqui, by the way.'

'Lucas.'

When they shook, it was like completing a high-voltage circuit.

'I could tell you my opinions,' he finally went on, 'over coffee.'

He no longer cared about the conference, and was willing to bet that she didn't either.

'An excellent idea,' she said.

Because the real conversation was occurring far below the verbal level, and some important conclusions had already been reached. They were both smiling as they left the conference centre and came out onto the pavement – sidewalk – in downtown Denver.

'Have you been there yet?' She pointed to the Rockies, visible through a gap between buildings. 'Or are you local?'

Most conference attendees had flown in for the event.

'Not yet,' he said. 'And I'm definitely not local. You?'

'LA.'

'I live in Pasadena.' He was tempted to add something stupid about quantum entanglement and destiny, but instead gestured across the street. 'Coffee shops and civilisation are pretty much synonymous, I've always thought.'

Vehicles moved quietly past, flywheels humming. As Lucas and Jacqui headed for a crosswalk, she said: 'If you think it's hard to breathe here, try Pike's Peak.'

Lucas had noticed a shortness of breath during the past hour and particularly the last few minutes; he doubted the altitude had much to do with it.

'Up in places like Fairplay,' Jacqui added, 'they call Denver folk "flatlanders".'

'And what would they call people like me?'

'Oh' – smiling – 'a weird foreigner, I should think.'

Waiting at the crosswalk, he said, 'Where I come from, jay-walking is not a concept. Everyone has the freedom to cross where they like.'

'The freedom to get squished?'

'Our life in our hands. Germany's like this, though.' He pointed at the temporarily empty street, while fellow pedestrians waited on the other side. 'The concept is very, well, Teutonic.'

'Is that what you Brits call "taking the piss"?'

Lucas could not help his laughter.

'You're obviously a world traveller.'

A transcript of their conversation might contain apparent insults; but anyone observing their body language or hearing their tone of voice would conclude that something else entirely was going on: more dance than dialogue.

Over iced mochas, Lucas explained the cat paradox in greater detail, ending with, 'When Schrödinger and Heisenberg did their work, young people were dancing the Charleston and the Great Depression was years away from happening.'

Jacqui rubbed her forehead.

'Iced-coffee headache,' she said. 'Or maybe it's quantum.'

'My friend Arne, back in Imperial, who's a bloody great Viking and into martial arts, says that aikido and Japanese karate date from the 1920s also, and they're considered *traditional*. So why don't people realise that quantum physics is old?'

There was a distinction between Japanese and Okinawan disciplines, but that was not what Jacqui picked up on. 'Imperial? As in London's answer to MIT?'

'Or Caltech, right. I went there in—'

Sharing life history already, he outlined his modest upbringing, and she talked about growing up in Alaska where moose bolognese was part of the staple diet – that, or taking the piss was not a purely British art – and how she could shoot with either hand, but preferred not to.

'I'm more into reading, chatting and sunshine, thanks all the same. Why I moved to California.'

'That's good,' he told her. His own reasons for ending up there, involving a possibly imaginary conspiracy, a memory flake and breaking into Caltech at night to use Gus Calzonni's mu-space apparatus, could wait until another day. For now he just told her how much at home he felt on the Left Coast; and he meant it.

Exiting the coffee shop, his old feelings of paranoia and fantasies about quantum-entangled minds came tumbling back, but the apparition across the street was no coincidence: it was simply that Maria, bloody Maria, had finally taken it into her mind to track him down.

His name had been on the membership list for the conference – probably his first appearance in public cyberspace – as opposed to corporate and government systems – since he had scarpered from London.

'Shit-crap-bollocks,' he said.

'*Excuse* me?'

'That' – he pointed at Maria – 'is my very, *very* ex-girlfriend.'

Jacqui gave a start, and clutched Lucas's upper arm.

Balls. She's coming over.

Whether Brazil possessed the concept of jay-walking, Lucas had never learned; but what he did know was that Maria Higashionna belonged among São Paulo's upper classes, and she could blaze with full-on haughtiness when she chose – as she did now, crossing the street without regard to anything, including traffic, and dismissing Jacqui with a glance.

'Lucas, *meu amor*. You left the flat in a mess.'

Like the parquet flooring he had dug up. Understood.

'That's what first-month deposits were invented for.'

The natural thing would be to introduce Jacqui, but for some reason he wanted to keep her out of Maria's awareness. Luckily Maria's gaze was fastened on him. She had never seemed so reptilian.

'I always wondered what you dug up.'

'Everything I had was on a memory flake,' he told her. 'And it's gone. Doesn't exist, anywhere in the universe.'

Those chestnut brown eyes had always seemed so beguiling. Was this the first time he was actually seeing her for what she was?

'You're telling the truth.' She looked like someone at home

in the sun, but her voice was icy. 'And you've left everything behind.'

'Everything, Maria.'

So very cold: not just her voice, but her eyes, when she turned to Jacqui.

'All yours.'

Maria went back across the street, climbed into her shiny car, and hauled away from the kerb. At the end of the block she turned right, and that was that: Maria was gone from sight.

Gone from his life.

There was a delay that felt like hours and like nothing at all before the world re-engaged, and he realised that Jacqui was still holding his arm in a fashion that was exactly right, the way things were meant to be.

'I'm not into New Age schizotypal thinking.' She was staring down the street where Maria had driven. 'No one walks around with a glowing aura, not literally.'

'Er ...'

'But there's such a thing as synaesthesia, and when I see a strange sort of darkness surrounding your ex-girlfriend, I'm inclined to think I've picked up on something real.'

'You mean Maria?'

It seemed a convoluted way of calling his former lover an evil witch, but the oddest thing of all was how deeply he agreed with Jacqui. Like the quantum collapse of a wave function to a single eigenvalue – as though it had always been that way – history seemed to have changed in retrospect, as if Maria had all along been reptile-cold, a lizard sharing his life for her own logical ends.

Their qPads chimed.

'The conference,' said Jacqui. 'The next talk. Did you want to go back in?'

'Not really. I'm already where I'm meant to be,' he told her. 'Does that sound weird?'

'It sounds exactly right.'
'You want to walk around downtown?'
'That's exactly what I want.'
So arm in arm, they did.

NINE

After the first extended training exercise, four of Roger's class-mates were hospitalised because he had put them there. This was an environment designed to break people down before reconstructing them: a place where controlled sparring meant beating up anyone who tried to dominate you; where endur-ance runs through strange, shifting landscapes involved doing your best to leave your mates behind; and where games of deception in simulated social situations were always zero-sum – the only way to win was by ensuring the others lost.

None of this, presumably, was accidental.

Some of his classmates were highly talented in areas strange to him, and some possessed a great deal of experience in the soft skills arena of influencing new contacts, which would eventually involve recruiting assets, even running agents on hostile territory; but Roger was 'serious as a bastard', as he overheard in the dorm block, determined to be implacable, even when others took advantage of unobserved moments to slacken off.

He was making up lost ground, and more.

The history of espionage was one of their classroom sub-jects, and Roger chose to present a paper on the paramilitary aspects of intelligence organisations upon twentieth- century Earth. It was the variation that struck him, and became the paper's thesis: how some organisations relied on infiltrating diplomatic bureaucracy and mixing at the right parties, while others stood somewhere further along a sliding scale that, at the far end, featured the KGB (later the FSB) and GRU. Those two services maintained their own *spetsnasz* companies:

special forces trained beyond Spartan standards, every soldier a master of *rokupashniboi*, a combat discipline as close to Pilot fighting methods as realspace had ever seen.

Perhaps that was why, during the tracking exercise, when his classmates closed the trap in a deserted alley (role-playing an opposition cell who had seen past Roger's anti-surveillance tricks in a simulated cityscape), Roger responded in the all-out way he did. Or perhaps they simply misunderstood the consequences of not leaving an escape route for an ambushed rat.

There were eight of them in total, closing in, relying on hand-to-hand because his solitary smartmiasma was equal to all theirs combined, neutralising the femtoscopic threat. What remained was primitive, and his first whipping kick destroyed an attacker's knee joint, curving elbow fracturing the same poor bastard's jaw, dropping him in another's path; and a lunging strike came at Roger, a near-instantaneous closing of distance, but Roger entered the cyclone's heart, spinning the man – no, woman – face first into the wall and driving a horizontal elbow into her spine. The wall and two fallen enemies helped close off angles, but the danger was high regardless, and when a big guy grabbed two-handed, Roger dropped his weight to keep on balance, shovel-hooking hard, left-left-right in half a second, to the holy trinity of liver-bladder-spleen, which did it: third bastard down.

The maelstrom was upon him then, but he drove them back, strangling one cobra-like, his inner forearm striking the carotid so fast that unconsciousness was instantaneous, then a tangled mess of in-fighting until a gap appeared – *there* – so he broke clear with sweeping forearm blocks that shattered joints, thanks to old-school conditioning, then he drove palm heels into jaws and temples followed by long thrusting kicks to make distance and that was it: five opponents down, one limping away, the other two running.

Calm. Assess.

Before the training officers descended to sort things out

– everyone's tu-ring had received the *exercise suspended* signal – he reviewed the downed opposition and his own self, going through the protocol, putting his hands inside his clothes, rubbing his torso and groin and neck, and checking for blood on his palms, in case he had been stabbed and not felt it.

Nothing.

His ribs were broken on both sides and his nose was pointing off to his right, against the cheekbone. Trivial, and the only reason he noticed was that two of his attackers had fallen to similar blows, giving up the fight in psychosomatic surrender.

They had not been through the mill with Rhianna Chiang; that was the difference.

However, 'If you damage your classmates like that again, you're off the programme,' the lead instructor, Eira Magnusson (who according to Corinne should have been Magnusdóttir) told Roger during their one-to-one afterwards, her voice flat and hard in the conference chamber.

'Ma'am.'

He could have argued that the programme was designed to be harsh, to cause people to fail instead of incrementally building confidence; but she would know that. His response to the chewing-out was just one more test, stoicism the key as always.

'Redeploying drop-outs,' she said, 'is someone else's problem. I don't care who leaves the programme, or how. Except that' – with a hint of softening in her voice – 'when the most promising fighter I've seen in years comes along, I want him to succeed. We like strength, and so long as you can keep the aggression hidden in civilised surroundings, maintaining your cover, just keep on doing what you're doing, and ignore the complaints from your classmates, because there will be a shedload. Understood?'

'Er, yes, ma'am.'

Not strictly true, but he could dwell on her words later. Attitude in the moment was paramount: right now, she was looking for his determined obedience.

'Keep the wolf controlled inside you, Roger.' A momentary hint of a smile: 'Except when it's time to slip the leash.'

He nodded, knowing that she was right, that he *was* the wolf – *at ulfr ek em* – and control was entirely possible.

'Resolve the paradox of fighters not fighting,' she concluded, 'and you'll go far. Dismissed.'

'Ma'am.'

He fastpath-rotated out of there.

It could be argued that the only way to excel in the programme was to become monstrous, at least for the duration; but humanity was here as well, and of the few classmates who increasingly admired Roger, the one whose friendship-and-more he appreciated most was Corinne Delgasso. Roger knew from Jed, whom he had not seen in person since entering Tangleknot, that Leeja Rigelle, Roger's older lover from Molsin, was to be relocated to a realspace orbital, somewhere safe, while Alisha Spalding, his earlier almost-girlfriend from Fulgor, who had forgotten him following cognitive rollback therapy, was officially among the dead; but they belonged to a closed-off past.

Eating together in one corner of the refectory, after a chase-the-courier exercise through yet another simulated realspace city, he listened while Corinne criticised her own performance. 'It's all right for you,' she added, 'being a mudworlder and all, but I can't get used to the lack of reality-shifts.' In this morning's scenario, that problem had led her to run into a setup from which there was no escape. Only Roger drawing off the opposition had allowed her to get away.

'While a born Labyrinthian has the advantage,' he told her, 'that shifts and rotations are pure reflex. You never know where we might have to operate.'

That was true, particularly with the absence of Schenck and his renegade Pilots hanging over everything, forming a threat of unknown – therefore worrying – extent and capability. More than in previous training programmes, the classmates

– other than the three who were Shipless – worked hard away from Labyrinth in their ships, addressing ship-to-ship combat as well as the more traditional Tangleknot training in stealth flying and unusual navigation.

Corinne stared down at her food.

'I'd rather get back to my rack' – her gaze rose – 'to recover before the next session.'

'You want a hand to debrief further?'

'That's what I'm thinking of, Blackstone.'

'Come on, then, Delgasso. Let's get to it.'

They summoned a fastpath together, stepped in as one, and fell out of the rotation in Corinne's room with their garments already sloughing off, combat sensitivity serving another purpose as they wrestled each other, laughing, onto the bed.

And began the climb to temporary joy.

TEN

During her four weeks in Birmingham, the place had grown on Gavriela: the house in a leafy, genteel part of Edgbaston, and the redbrick campus court with the clock tower that would have looked at home in Florence. The buildings were different from the Munich of her childhood and the ETH in Zurich (always München and Zürich in her thoughts), yet inside, the labs brought back her youth: parquet floors, display cases filled with scientific instruments of brass and steel, textbooks old and new.

To celebrate the end of rationing, some of the faculty and postgraduate students travelled *en masse* to one of the new Berni Inns, where they tucked in to solid food that the *haute cuisine* critics disparaged but which, to poverty-stricken PhD students, was worth every penny of the seven-and-six they paid for it.

'Seven shillings and sixpence will hardly break the bank,' Anders had said, before raising an eyebrow as he realised his faux pas, because if you were counting the ha'pennies then any expenditure at all was significant.

Gavriela's enjoyment was spoilt only by the knowledge that her watch team were outside in the night, unable to eat, apart from the lucky team member who got to dine alone, behind a square-edged pillar, keeping her in view. But it was hard to keep her mind on Dmitri and the clandestine world, because something odd had been happening: at the age of forty-seven, she was falling in love – all over again – with physics.

The move of GCHQ from Eastcote to Cheltenham was pending, and if relocating to Gloucestershire was on the cards, then why not somewhere else? A theoretician over thirty was doomed, but age did not constrain experimentalists. Could she? What if she failed to make a change her metaphorical spirit needed?

'—in the City?' asked Patrick, a Jamaican post-doc with the most beautiful voice Gavriela had ever heard. 'The archaeologists, I mean.'

Only yesterday she had passed a boarding-house in Kings Heath bearing the far-too-common sign: *No Blacks, No Irish, No Dogs*.

'Which city? Birming-gum?' She tried for a Brummie accent, and failed.

'He means jolly old London,' said Anders. 'Threadneedle Street and bowler hats, don't you know.' Not that bowlers were unknown among the faculty. 'And now a Roman temple.'

Too busy with the contents of the departmental library, Gavriela had been ignoring the newspapers; the conversation was making little sense.

'The Temple of Mithras,' explained Patrick. 'Uncovered intact during building work.'

'Next to one of the so-called secret rivers, the underground Thames tributaries.' Anders nodded to Patrick. 'It *is* interesting.' He smiled. 'People are saying the place is haunted, a mysterious figure glimpsed at night, that kind of thing.'

But that was as far as the topic stretched among rational scientists, so Gavriela asked Patrick about his work with the new cryogenics equipment, investigating fluids that could flow by themselves unrestrained by viscosity, or conduct currents without experiencing resistance.

'Stuff that spontaneously creeps up inside a flask,' said Patrick. 'Spooky weirdness at a dimension you can see.'

There were understanding nods all around, because solving Schrödinger's wave equation was mechanical: as pragmatic practitioners, they ignored philosophical weirdness, and simply put the recipe to work, hoping that someday a new theory would bring forth a more reasonable metaphor. Counter-intuitive quantum phenomena, challenging concepts as basic as cause and effect, were unsettling in objects you could hold in your hand, although in this case you would need a massively insulated gauntlet.

After the meal, Anders gave Patrick and Gavriela a lift in his new Morris Minor – for propriety's sake, dropping Gavriela off first. But she paused in the redbrick porch with the stained-glass panel above the front door, waiting for the Morris to drive out of sight, and her escort team to pull up at the kerb.

Only then, with her protection, did she go inside.

An empty house reveals itself by lack of vibration, but there is such a thing as self-deception, not to mention bombs and timers, so they went through the place – tonight they had been too overstretched to leave a watcher on guard – and at first found nothing. But during the second pass—

Oh, no. Don't bring children into this.

In the bedside drawer – how had Dmitri, if it was Dmitri, known she would check there first? – she found a glossy monochrome photograph featuring a youngster and two adults, and she might have ignored it except that the schoolgirl, some eleven or twelve years old – around Carl's age – was like her brother brought back to life: Erik's features in feminine form.

With Ilse, Erik's wife – widow, and it was a surprise that she had survived – standing alongside a smiling Dmitri Shtemenko, they looked like a family group. Gavriela wished she could believe it to be technical trickery on the KGB's behalf, instead of what it seemed: Dmitri, so monstrous, in her dead brother's place.

And Gavriela had a new family member: for niece, read hostage.

So when are you going to make your move?

But if Dmitri were intending to exert pressure on Gavriela, recruiting her for his Soviet masters, there was a way to neutralise the threat: render herself unsuitable. In operant conditioning terms she now had both positive and negative rewards awaiting, should she choose to resign: returning to her first love, and avoiding the betrayal of her adopted country.

Assuming that was Dmitri's intent.

Term-time came and with it the end of the operation, without results, since Gavriela had said nothing of the photograph she finally burnt, an action she regretted afterwards. Back home with Carl, and with moving house inevitable even if she stayed in her current job – because of the organisation's westward relocation – she made her decision, and went to talk to Russell Sheffield, the head of section to whom she reported.

From behind his desk, he listened to her explanation as he whittled through his unlit meerschaum with a flexible pipe-cleaner. In the past, he had often given her unused pipe-cleaners to take home for Carl: they were excellent for creating geometric framework shapes, though her attempt to explain a hypercube had been premature. Perhaps when Carl was older.

'I found an old acquaintance working at Imperial,' she said, 'who'll put in a good word for me. And they're actively looking for researchers.'

Lucas Krause, last seen heading off to the States with his new wife during the war, was back in London and settled down. It would be strange to have a link to her student days, all the way back to attending her first lecture and Professor Möller with the flowing white hair and the spectacular demonstration with the tall wire basket.

'I rather considered that kind of thing myself, returning to the halls of academe' – Sheffield looked up from his pipe-cleaning operation – 'when I was younger.'

'Point taken, sir.'

At least he had not insulted her by dragging out the matter of her pension, and the extent to which it might be reduced by her departing now. But she was not the only one making big decisions: the atmosphere around the place, as work-in-progress files went into archive cases for transportation to the new site, was very odd, with choppy conversations and unsettled expressions everywhere.

'If you're truly certain' – he put down his pipe, stood up, and reached out across the desktop – 'then I'll shake your hand and wish you the best of luck, old girl.'

She stood up, and they shook.

'You know I—' But there was no way to complete the sentence.

'After they kick me out of this place, I'll be tending roses,' said Sheffield, 'or pushing up daisies. Certainly not good for anything else. I do believe I'm rather envious.'

Gavriela gave a sad laugh.

This was a lot like leaving home.

On her first day at Imperial, walking beneath an open window of the Royal College of Music, she heard a breath-catching rendition of a Mozart piece for string quartet. Across the road reared the dome of the Royal Albert Hall, where perhaps the students would play one day, if they hadn't already. As for her, this was like the first day of term, a new beginning – like Carl off to school in his cap and gaberdine raincoat, satchel and plimsole bag slung from one shoulder – except that she had an old friend waiting for her in the Huxley building reception: Lucas, his once-curly hair now receded and merely wavy, controlled by hair-tonic. She could smell the Silvikrin.

'Gabrielle.' It was a good start, remembering not to call her Gavriela. 'I'll show you to your office.'

They shook hands while the porter watched, though Gavriela would rather have hugged him.

'How's your wife, er—?'

'Enjoying Nebraska,' he said. 'Come on, we'll drop off your coat and you can meet everyone.'

Upstairs, she found that her room was pokey, featuring a scarred desk maybe half the size of the one she had used in Eastcote, with cardboard folded beneath one leg for stability.

'It's wonderful,' she said.

A stack of loose-leaf pages bore columns of figures with headings like Declination, Azimuth and Peak, along with pencil-drawn graphs.

'Readings from the old instrumentation,' said Lucas. 'You'll have plenty of your own soon enough.'

'I'm sure.'

'Most of us really aren't that good at stats.' Lucas meant statistical analysis 'Good luck on plucking meaning out of that lot, but the rest of us can't.'

He was not really talking about the data; it was more an oblique acknowledgment of her time spent on work she could never discuss, for most of the eight years since the war, a gap she would have to fill with fiction as far as her other colleagues were concerned.

The strange thing was, as she fell asleep that night, she half-dreamed of deciphering a pattern in just such data, though not now, not yet: something do with meson detection and an equilateral triangle that could not be explained, yet neither could it be ignored. An insight she would keep to herself … A comforting thought, as she drifted further into sleep.

Secrecy kept her safe.

ELEVEN

Crystalline and serene, Roger and Gavriela held hands as they stared up at the crimson-banded disc of Earth. To him it was the species' birthplace, an ancestral home, but she had been born and lived her organic life there, half a million years ago.

—*What do you think is going to happen, Roger?*

—*I've long given up trying to read Kenna's mind.*

Kenna had told them, pleased that they were here at this time together, that something interesting was about to occur, and they might like to view it from one of the many balconies. And so they had come outside, watching from mid-way up the titanic, complex palace that their headquarters had become over hundreds of millennia. In the beginning, electromagnetic distortion fields had hidden the place, but for a long time, according to Kenna, there had been no need to hide.

No explanation embellished that item of information, and Roger and Gavriela knew better than to ask, because there were severe limits on such knowledge as could be taken into the past to their original minds, despite such thoughts being buried beneath layers of amnesia and misdirection, unavailable to their long-dead conscious selves.

They both remembered what Kenna had told Roger a century earlier.

—*This is not the first Ragnarok Council.*

—*If we're the second, what happened to the others?*

—*They perished in paradox. I will not allow you to fall that way.*

Silver discs were growing on the planet's surface, thirteen of them fully or partly visible, covering land or sea without distinction, then stabilising as unmoving dots.

Kenna stepped onto the balcony.

—*The Diaspora has been a long time coming. Its execution is fast.*

Gavriela asked:

—*Humanity's leaving Earth?*

—*You could say that.*

Whatever craft they used would be invisible from here.

—*And do Pilots like Roger still exist?*

—*I dare not learn the answer to that myself.*

Roger was about to ask a question concerning the future, but Kenna forestalled him.

—*We should wait a century for things to settle. Perhaps two centuries.*

—*Before doing what?*

Starlight reflections painted Kenna's crystal smile.

—*Making Earth ready for the warriors to come. Our very own Einherjar.*

They were perfectly adapted to vacuum; yet Roger and Gavriela shivered.

Perhaps a part of them had hoped that Ragnarökkr could yet be avoided.

TWELVE

Since its construction in the decades following first contact with the Haxigoji, the orbital called Vachss Station had become a floating city, kept in geosynch orbit above Mintberg (once Mint City, its renaming a xenosemantic subtlety), one of the hubs of global Haxigoji culture. Up here in orbit, the architecture was a complex embellishment of the station's original cage-like design, with polyhedral nodes, some the size of a single cabin, others the size of a thousand-room hotel, linked by giant spars, some of which were important thoroughfares, their corridors busy. Much of it glittered gold, due to the use of an exotic 2-D sulphur allotrope in its construction.

Everyone said the Haxigoji were a fine species, which was an anthropomorphic slant on things: their behaviour paralleled the best of human virtues, even the self-sacrificing pain involved in child-rearing, in the passing-on of knowledge. Only the manner of that sharing disconcerted human observers.

'I find cannibalism hard to swallow,' Jed said in Spanalian.

He was in his control cabin, on slow approach to the orbital, its image rendered in sharp-contrast chiaroscuro in the holoramic display. A secondary volume showed Clara's face, her expression neutral. She was on board the orbital, having made things ready. Waiting for him.

'Spanalian is not the only human language that talks about digesting knowledge,' she said. 'And while Faraday used the concept of "field" as a metaphor to help understand electromagnetic phenomena, Einstein said that physicists of *his* day "imbibed the concept with their mother's milk", considering fields as real things.'

'You're saying Einstein was one of the Haxigoji? Never saw antlers in any of the old holos.'

'Food absorption, potentiation at the molecular level, and neural connection formation: it's all biochemistry, and languages reflect that. Metaphor from intuition. The human brain is basically a structured lump of fat.' Still no trace of a smile. 'Some more so than others, wouldn't you say?'

'I have no idea why I put up with this,' said Jed.

'Because you love me.'

He looked at her lean, endurance-athlete features in the holo. Now she was smiling.

'That must be it, then,' he said.

'Good.' For a second, they stared at each other. 'All right, we're ready to receive them both. Check their autodoc status?'

Still lightly conjoined with his ship, Jed knew the answer without checking the tertiary holo floating beside him: like bodily sensations, he *felt* the signals inside the passenger hold.

'Check,' he said. 'Both passengers fine and healthy, the autodocs say.'

'Healthy.'

'Yeah, until they wake up and remember everything.'

'Shit,' said Clara.

Never mind all that stuff about fields and metaphors and cannibals, keeping them occupied while the on-station facilities made themselves ready. This was the Clara that Jed had fallen in love with: hard-edged, with the kind of practical compassion only a tough person can possess.

Station management gave Pilots a great deal of leeway – the orbital's total dependence made that a given – which they usually made little use of; but today, several tunnels were closed 'for maintenance' to allow Jed and the two autodocs to pass unhindered, all the way to the on-station Pilots Sanctuary. In comparison to the set-up he had enjoyed on Fulgor, the elegant walled enclosure on the edge of Lucis City, this Sanctuary would be utilitarian, but never mind: this was no holiday.

Jed, along with his colleagues Angus and Al, had destroyed that other Sanctuary's systems before getting clear of the place when the planet fell, but the superstructure would have remained intact. Now any humans on Fulgor were components of the global gestalt Anomaly. He wondered if they used the buildings, or stood about outdoors in herds, uncaring of physical comfort.

Ants in a group mind. Cells in a body.

The Vachss Station Sanctuary entrance folded inwards, and the two autodocs slid inside, Jed following. As things sealed up behind him, the welcoming committee came forward: Clara, not huggable while working, with her boss Pavel Karelin, plus a hatchet-faced woman unknown to Jed.

'Dr Sapherson will be on hand as we wake them up,' said Pavel. 'Tannier has already been conscious for a period after leaving Molsin, so we'll do him first.'

'And the other?' Jed placed a hand on the autodoc.

'You talked to Leeja Rigelle, not to mention rescuing her. Perhaps yours should be the first face she sees.'

'I'd only just said hello when everything went to hell. There's no actual, er, relationship. Although she was more than friendly with Roger.'

'Friendliness is good.' The tiny muscles of Clara's face moved when she smiled.

'This Roger—' began Sapherson.

'Not available,' said Pavel.

Clara looked satisfied at the way he cut Sapherson off. No love lost, then.

'We'll tell Leeja Rigelle, when she wakes up,' said Clara, 'that Roger sent his love. Wishes he could be here, sort of thing.'

Sapherson said, 'Why reassure her? The more off-balance she is, the easier she'll be to question.'

'She's not a prisoner,' said Pavel.

Clara stared at Sapherson with loathing.

'I'll make myself scarce,' said Jed. 'Just in case some of that classified stuff comes up, things I'm not meant to know.'

'Yeah,' said Clara, still focused on Sapherson. 'That might be best. When people learn a little too much, it doesn't always turn out well.'

Sapherson looked away.

I am so not going to ask.

Jed headed for an inner doorway, hoping that the on-board systems could produce a decent cup of daistral.

'Leeja thought Tannier was a bad influence,' said Clara later, when she and Jed were sitting up in bed together, drinking daistral. 'When they met first, that is. Tough cop, getting Roger into trouble. But she's beginning to mellow towards him. To Tannier.'

'And her world being destroyed? How did she cope with that?'

'Ah, not well,' said Clara. 'Not well at all.'

They hugged, side by side, careful with the daistral, thinking of all the ways the universe could rip people apart from each other.

'I'm glad I found you.' Jed kissed her ear.

'That's just what I was going to say.'

'You want to know how glad?'

She smiled, putting down her drink.

'Show me, show me.'

Pavel and Sapherson departed the next day, leaving Jed and Clara with the opportunity to spend delightful time together – 'They owe me leave, but this counts as work, which is even better,' she told him – but after three more nights, it was time for her to go as well.

'Just a few more days here for me,' said Jed. 'I'll be back in Labyrinth in no time.'

'You'd better be.'

The Sanctuary resident was a Pilot called Draper, one of the Shipless and an expert in xenoanthropology, busy turning his study of Haxigoji culture into his life's work. Draper's girl-friend was a non-Pilot, an Earth-born bioengineer, pleasant enough company when they dined together, the four of them, before Clara left: Jed and Clara, Declan Draper and Emma Mbaka. Several hundred tonnes of export goods were due, later than scheduled, to be shuttle-lifted up to Vachss Station over the next few days. With the original Pilot pick-up cancelled, Draper was arranging for Jed to get the business, taking these and other products to Finbra V, Yukitran and Earth.

'They'll expect a discount, what with you being here already,' Draper had said.

'Perfectly reasonable,' Jed had answered.

'And you'll deliver my report to Far Reach?'

'Of course I will.'

Perhaps, as a Pilot without a ship of his own, Draper's anxiety to have full disclosure on any commercial deal, to show he was not receiving kickbacks, came from his dependence on others and his position in Sanctuary. But Pilots living in realspace were generally nervous. Schenck and his mu-space renegades were gone from Labyrinth, but no one knew how many Pilots still working among ordinary humans, whether undercover or openly like Draper, had been part of the conspiracy.

Everyone was under scrutiny, and Admiralty observers were everywhere, deconstructing history, reading between the lines. Every now and then, it was whispered, people disappeared for questioning, and did not necessarily return.

A few hours after Clara's departure, Jed was in a diamond-windowed lounge watching space tumble past. Different portions of Vachss Station rotated in different ways – spars along longitudinal axes, larger sub-assemblies of nodes and arcs around their individual centres – forming a kaleidoscopic mandala, something to watch while he thought about Clara.

His tu-ring beeped, and he acknowledged the request.

'Got an arrival,' Draper said in a virtual holo. 'Dropping off refugees from Fulgor. An *unscheduled* arrival.'

'Sounds unusual.'

'Says he picked them up while making a delivery on Berkivan-deux. They wanted to come here. Weren't being treated well where they were.'

'Poor bastards.'

All Fulgor survivors had been double-checked by Admiralty teams for trace of Anomalous influence, but paranoia was understandable.

In the holo, Draper shrugged. 'Holland didn't go into detail.'

'Holland? That's the Pilot?'

'Guy Holland, Labyrinth-based.'

'Don't know him, but never mind,' said Jed. 'I'll pop over and say hello.'

He considered taking Tannier and Leeja along: survivors of Molsin having something in common with refugees from Fulgor. It seemed a good idea, so he made the call, arranging to meet them in Receiving Lounge 17A. They must have been keen enough, because by the time Jed reached the lounge, Tannier and Leeja were already there, standing next to each other with shoulders almost touching.

Survivors together.

It seemed Tannier had already got to know some of the long-term station residents. He introduced a tall slim man called Vilok, who greeted Jed by pressing palms in the manner of someone from Hargdenia Polity.

'We're not the only ones interested,' said Vilok, 'in an unexpected arrival. See there.'

Through the far entrance, several Haxigoji were entering: six or seven antler-racked males, eight or ten females (or perhaps some young males), all in a group. Their fur ranged from cream to dark chocolate beneath their ornate, brocaded tunics and trews. Half again as tall as humans, with double-thumbed hands and amber, horizontally slitted eyes.

By the standards of xeno evolution, they were practically identical to humanity.

In fact Clara, before leaving, had shown him holos of Vijayan embryos, so like their Terran counterparts, clumps of cells that twisted early on into a topological cylinder. She had shown off by quoting a centuries-old Earth scholar: '"It is not birth, marriage or death but gastrulation that is truly the most important event in your life."'

Thinking about her, Jed took several moments to process Vilok's tension as he focused on a virtual holo emitted from his tu-ring. 'Is something wrong?'

'Pilot Holland is being ... prevented from leaving his ship.'

He shared the holo: Haxigoji were crowding a flexible corridor whose far end was a smartmembrane placed against a visiting ship's hull.

'And the refugees?' Jed glanced at the Haxigoji here in the lounge. 'They're still on board the ship?'

'They're almost here. Came directly from the hold via another—'

Jed ignored the holos, because the Haxigoji were moving towards an entrance from which a confused-looking group of people were emerging. No ... They were converging on a single member of the group, a dark-skinned young man with an odd expression and disjointed gait, who stopped and said to the xenos: 'My name. Is. Rick. Mbuli from. Ful-gor.'

Jed's skin crawled.

I've heard that name before.

The Haxigoji were shuffling from left foot to right foot and back, over and over, in a form of agitation that appeared to surprise Vilok as much as Jed. But the name ... And there was holo footage Jed had watched, he and Roger mulling over all that had happened.

Vilok said: 'Why have they switched off their torcs?'

He meant the Haxigoji; Jed understood.

No.

It came to Jed that the Haxigoji were psyching themselves up to attack a human for the first time ever, but if they were right then the danger was immense.

Not here.

Clara was away and safe, but there were others here, hundreds on board and an entire inviting world below, and that could *not* be allowed to happen, not another Anomaly, not again.

Now.

Fire exploded from Jed's tu-ring – not a feature of normal rings, not at all – and Mbuli's head detonated into strawberry spray, spattering everywhere; but that was not enough, so with tightened fist Jed kept the beam directed, playing up and down along the corpse, obliterating it, while sending a coded signal for Draper to get here now, and be ready with a smart-miasma capable of spreading through a room and hunting down every human cell with a given DNA sequence, because nothing of Mbuli could be allowed to persist.

Automated beam weapons, designed to be highly visible threats, swung down from the ceiling, while security personnel were already entering the lounge; but as Jed powered off his tu-ring's weapons, his viewpoint was blocked: over a dozen Haxigoji were moving between him and the security team, forming an arc with their backs towards Jed.

Protecting him.

Their torcs were still switched off, but a soft scent of triumphal rose petals rose from their bodies: a vote of thanks and approval for what he had done, whatever the legal consequences.

He hoped that Clara would not be disappointed.

THIRTEEN

EARTH, 2034 AD

Lucas and Jacqui trailed Gus and her friend Ives into the Mexican restaurant. At a table just inside the door, a stocky, grizzled, bearded man was telling his grey-haired female companion: 'A galaxy is like an M&M. The sugary coating is a dark matter halo.'

'And the central black hole,' the woman asked, 'is the chocolate centre?'

Jacqui looked at Lucas and winked.

'No, see, there's a hundred billion stars, order-of-magnitude approximation' – the man might look like a lumberjack, but he answered much as Lucas might have – 'making up the whole of the visible galaxy. All of that is your chocolate centre.'

'But I thought there was a—'

'You've then got ten per cent of the stars comprising the bright bit in the middle, your actual galactic core. That would be like a tiny lump inside the M&M, at the centre of the chocolate. And the black hole would be microscopic. Smaller, in fact.'

Only in Pasadena.

Actually, come to think of it, any university town.

As the four of them were shown to their table, Jacqui said, 'Seems like your kind of place, Lucas,' and Ives smiled at them both. He was very tall, elegant in a tweed jacket with an honest-to-goodness bow tie whose spots were tiny spiral galaxies. He was also Gus's oldest, closest friend.

Once they were seated, the waiter came over for their drinks order. Ives stared up into the young man's eyes while

73

discussing his choice in soft Spanish. After the waiter had left, Gus said: 'He's too young for you, darling,' prompting Ives to answer that he knew as much, darling Augusta, but the truth was that she was jealous.

'I hate it when you're right,' she told him.

Ives was a mathematician, a topologist with a sideline in topoi logics, a very different field, whose work on knots had once threatened to revolutionise both string theory and M-theory, by taking a traditional approach to analysing knots – focusing on their context, known as not-knots, and who says mathematicians have no sense of humour? – and applying it to the hyperdimensional twists known as Calabi-Yau manifolds. As a visiting lecturer in Oxford, during a sabbatical from MIT, he had befriended a precocious young student called Augusta 'Gus' Calzonni, and their collaboration produced both the computer game that kick-started Gus's fortune – Fractal of the Beast – and her mu-space theory which, if mu-space turned out to be physically real instead of purely mathematical, might some day revolutionise humanity's place in the universe.

Waving fingers, before his eyes, jolted Lucas back to Earth.

'—images in your head,' Gus was saying.

Holy crap.

His stomach rocked as his eyes refocused.

'Eyeballs triangulate on a point in space,' explained Ives, 'when you're strongly visualising. It's a shock when some bad person' – he patted Gus's hand – 'breaks up the virtual image like that.'

Gus smiled. 'Sorry, Lucas. You were miles away, and I couldn't resist.'

'It's because of the entorhinal cortex,' said Ives, 'And the neurons forming the spatiotemporal array inside it, which are geometrically quite fascinating.'

'Feynman visualised colour-coded equations floating in front of a fuzzy picture of the phenomenon,' said Lucas, referring to his science hero. 'Like, I asked one of my PhD students to imagine electrons in a wire, and she saw a glowing white necklace moving along it. They wouldn't really form an exact loop, but it highlights the mutual repulsion, right?'

'Right, but no one teaches physics' – Gus pointed an emphatic finger – 'by teaching students to make visual hallucinations.'

'Exactly,' said Lucas.

'Exactly,' said Gus.

Ives looked at Jacqui.

'Hobby horses,' he told her.

'And soap boxes.'

'They really can't help it.'

And that would have been that, a friendly meal spiced up with badinage and banter, a touch pretentious but balanced by self-mockery, had not a stranger approached their table: the grey-haired woman who had been sitting near the door. The stocky bearded man, still seated, looked furious.

'Dr Woods?' She addressed Lucas directly. 'My name's Amy, and I'm a medical researcher, and I'd really like to talk to you. Just for a moment.'

If her lumberjack friend caused trouble, Lucas hoped that Gus would deal with it – of everyone at the table, she was the one who knew how to fight. The lumberjack looked to be in his late fifties, one of those guys who got tougher as they aged.

'This thing' – the woman, Amy, held up a small silver device – 'is a DNA sampler, online to a wide-array sequencer in the Cloud. It only takes seconds.' She looked at the others, then back at Lucas. 'I guarantee to destroy the results afterwards. Delete the data.'

The logical response was refusal, but the bearded man was approaching, looking about to intervene, and some devilry made Lucas hold out his hand and say, 'What the hell. Why not?'

'Lucas—' began Jacqui.

There was a pinprick, and Amy nodded. 'Thank you.'

'Oh, for fuck's sake,' said the lumberjack.

He had been talking about dark matter and galaxies, hadn't he?

'If I left it up to you, Brody, we'd never find out.' Amy held up the analyser. 'Five more seconds, and we'll know for sure.'

As if they had agreed to a countdown, everyone waited until Amy nodded, told this Brody that it was true, and turned the device so Lucas could see its small display. Two strips, labelled *alleles #1* and *alleles #2*, contained clusters of dots. 'The lower one is yours,' she told him. 'And look how similar they are.'

'Very nice,' said Lucas. 'What the hell are you showing me?'

But Ives had slipped a qPad out of his jacket, and finger-gestured to transfer data from the analyser to his own device. He tapped away, and touched his collar to enable a throat mike, allowing subvocal commands.

'Amy, grow up.' The lumberjack was practically growling. 'This is unnecessary. We gotta go.'

'Maybe,' said Amy, 'you should introduce yourself.'

'Sod off.'

You could hear it now: the man was English, underneath the Americanised accent.

'Perhaps' – Ives pushed his chair back, allowing him space to cross his legs – 'I might be allowed to summarise the results. I'd like to introduce,' he went on, gesturing toward the lumberjack, 'Dr Brody Gould. And over here, Dr Lucas Woods.'

This Brody was frowning, and Lucas felt himself do likewise.

'Bloody hell,' said Gus, craning to see the qPad. 'Lucas, you won't—'

'What is this?' asked Brody. 'A sodding soap opera?'

'Your brother,' Ives told Lucas.

My—?

He felt Jacqui take his hand, heard her telling him to breathe.

'Half brother, to be precise.' Ives directed his attention to Amy. 'You've livened up everyone's day, as I'm sure you've noticed.'

Then Gus took command, as was her privilege and habit.

'Waiter? Two more chairs, please. Brody and Amy, you'll join us.'

And so they did.

An hour later, Brody and Lucas had yet to shake hands. A big mitt like that could crush Lucas's fingers. But it seemed Brody would never use his strength against Amy, which was how she had been able to go against his wishes. 'High school sweethearts, is what we are,' she told everyone at the table. 'Met in London, when my Dad was working there. Brody got stuck with me then.'

Lucas rubbed his face.

'Tell me again,' he said to Brody. 'How come you knew, and I didn't.'

'My dad – our dad – never married my mum. Sort of childhood sweethearts that *didn't* work out, eventually. He was well out of the picture, as far as Mum was concerned, *my* mother, when he hitched up with yours.'

Brody was in his late fifties, older than Lucas by over two decades, old enough to be an uncle rather than a brother. Half-brother. *But Dad was in his forties*, thought Lucas, *when he met Mum*. She was a grad student at the time.

'Plus there was Granny Woods's war work,' Brody went on. 'All that sneaky-beaky stuff, as Mum used to call it. And *her* mother, Granny Gould, worked there too. They were best friends, but our father didn't know anything about it, because of the secrecy regs.'

Lucas was going to need diagrams and notes. He ordered a second cappuccino – they were still at the same table, meal and coffee over, while most of the other tables had emptied.

'What secrecy regulations are we talking about?'

'The thirty-year rule and all that. Bletchley Park. Until the 1970s, no one knew what went on there. Our father, Carl, was totally ignorant about it. Granny Woods told *me* back in, what, 1989?'

'Yes, because that was the year we met,' said Amy.

'Forty-four years ago. And I remember your Granny Woods. She was wonderful.'

Yet again, Lucas felt Jacqui squeeze his hand. So much was changing: his father was not his alone, while even Brody's partner knew the grandmother who – presumably, if none of this was a hoax – had sent a message from the past. If it *was* her.

'She was Gabrielle Woods,' said Amy. 'Lovely place in Chelsea. Previously known as Gabby. Your gran, I mean. Not the house.'

How had the mysterious letter been signed? Oh, yes.

> *Love,*
> *Gavi (your grandmother!)*
> *X X X*

So here was the first inconsistency in—

'Except,' said Brody, 'she was really Fräulein Doktor Gavriela Wolf, and I think she escaped from Germany, but I never quite got that part of the story.'

'Oh,' said Lucas.

There had been intermittent periods of silence, and another descended now. Finally, Gus announced that she had a breakfast meeting at her Seattle plant in the morning, and preferred to travel today in good time. As disappointed blinks appeared around the table, she added: 'So I'd take it as an honour if you could all travel with me, and keep the family atmosphere going. The Lear's at the airfield, and the limo's big enough for all of us.'

'Bloody hell,' said Brody.

Lucas knew the feeling. He too thought of Gus as a scientist, rather than a businessperson with astounding wealth.

'One grows used to it,' drawled Ives. 'All this tedious luxury.'

Everyone laughed. As they stood up to leave, Ives looked from Lucas to Brody and back.

'You know,' he began, 'I always like to judge a man by his eyes ...'

'Er,' said Lucas.

'Um,' said Brody.

'… And *your* eyes are identical, the two of you. Or am I the only to notice?'

'He's right,' said Jacqui, and Amy nodded.

'He's always right.' Gus slipped her arm inside Ives's. 'But I forgive him anyway.'

They ambled out to her limousine.

FOURTEEN

Rhianna moved with the ferocity of a fighter, not the elegance of the dancer her mother once wanted her to be (as daily recreation, at best an avocation – Rhianna's future as a 'proper' working Pilot was always the main goal). There was a difference: in most aggressive moves the power starts from the big toe and whips wave-like through the body, raw and violent.

Today she punished the flowmetal mannequins with elbow strikes and knees, with whirling kicks and punches both long and close-in, smashing the figures into the ground with fast-flowing throws: beating them over and over again until the rage came under control; and then she stopped, commanded the mannequins into immobility, and walked back and forth inside the shining hall currently configured as her dojo.

Within fifty seconds her breathing and heart-rate had slowed almost to normal.

I should've killed that fucking Gunnarsson.

Following up the reports, she had finally interviewed the idiot in person, working alongside Clayton who *was* professional – no wonder Max had come to trust him – and all they had learnt from Gunnarsson was that civilisation would be safer if some people were killed at birth. Not only had he allowed Schenck's ship to fly to Fulgor and leave unchallenged – and what the hell was Schenck doing there? – but Gunnarsson had subsequently fired on and killed the Zajinets who rescued Tannier from Molsin.

Shit shit shit.

Helsen free, Schenck free, renegade Pilots en masse, Fulgor

a hellworld and new data coming in from Molsin that had Uncle Max worried. Everything she had learned from Roger Blackstone's subconscious mind, all the far-future dreams he had no conscious memory of, was coming dangerously true. One dead world at least, and probably a second, formed compelling evidence.

After the Gunnarsson interview, having relocated to an officers' mess within the Admiralty's Orange Zone – where classified matters could be discussed, up to a point – she listened as Clayton told her about the white-and-red memory flake sent through from the past, from half a millennium ago, identifying the galactic anti-centre as the direction from which the darkness was advancing. Strange evidence, but consistent again with Roger Blackstone's dreams.

'And Max is happy with you telling me this?'

'If he weren't, I wouldn't be telling you.'

'Fair enough.'

At the back of her mind was a humbling thought: the galaxy was vast, as was its (literally infinite) corresponding volume in mu-space; yet both were lost in the greater immensity of their respective continua. Even in realspace, galactic clusters and superclusters were separated by cosmic voids, and the timescales on which the darkness operated went far beyond the limits of human intuition: hundreds of millions of years at the barest minimum. If it operated according to some hyper-intelligent purpose, how much further could that intellect – or myriad intellects – develop over the aeons?

She wished she could dismiss these notions as delusion.

'And the Zajinets.' While Clayton was here, it was worth picking his brains. 'You think they'll retaliate?'

'What, you think they won't?' he said. 'If they'd hit us sooner, I'd have been less worried. If they're massing for an all-out strike, I hope Max knows about it, because the rest of us don't.'

From the open area of the mess, a murmuring grew. Rhianna and Clayton looked at each other, then popped up urgent-bulletin holos and saw what was causing a stir: the reappearance of a big name from the past, Admiral Dirk Mc-Namara, back into mean-geodesic timeflow after another relativistic flight. He had been missing for decades, had aged perhaps minutes.

Rhianna knew that young Roger Blackstone was one of the few Pilots to have talked with the famous Dirk's mother, the reclusive Ro, who used slowtime layers of reality to likewise absent herself from normal timeflow. Some people, Rhianna thought, just had to discover how the future played out: given the capability, they could not resist the urge. Or perhaps these two simply hoped someday to find out what had happened to the mysterious Kian, Dirk's disfigured twin, long lost but rumoured to appear from time to time, guiding Pilotkind to peace.

Some hope, these days.

'The First Admiral's son,' said Clayton. 'Back from the dead yet again.'

'He killed the first Admiral Schenck, remember.' Rhianna clicked her fingers to dismiss the holo. 'Be nice if he could manage the same for the grandson.'

It was of course a landmark on Borges Boulevard: the volume of spacetime asymptotically approaching eternal stasis, inside which Schenck, loser of the duel against Dirk, was torn apart in the moment of death for ever.

'I read once,' said Clayton, 'that the tragedy of Dirk McNa-mara was the continuing absence of war. Maybe he's about to come into his own.'

Pilotkind had never produced a great military leader – had never needed one. Most would say that was a good thing.

'No realspace culture has managed to stay peaceful throughout its existence,' said Rhianna. 'Why should we be any different?'

Away from the Admiralty, this might have been idle conversation; but in these surroundings, it carried import. The idea of Labyrinth going to war was frightening; the idea of

Labyrinth losing was pure abomination.

Fighting is bad, but when it becomes inevitable, one thing is necessary above all else.

Winning.

There was no such thing as telepathy, not as portrayed in weak-minded realspace holodramas, but Uncle Max on occasion came frighteningly close. For a time they sat on low, soft chairs at an oblique angle to each other, the cream cat on Rhianna's lap and the ginger-and-white on Max's, and it was pleasant even though it felt like play-acting, because they were not a normal family – to the extent the concept made sense in Labyrinth – and as an agent, the only extra privilege she might expect was this: if he were going to throw her to the wolves, he would tell her in advance.

But the hint of mind-reading occurred when he asked, with one hand on the tomcat's back, whether Rhianna spent much time dwelling on the nature of past, present and future, a mystery that was never resolved, merely recast as ever more intriguing questions as scientific knowledge progressed.

'Like destiny and predestination?' she said. 'Why ever do you ask?'

Alert for minutiae of expression that might indicate Max knew all about Roger's dreams – that there had been surveillance in place when she worked with Roger on Deltaville – she detected no particular subterfuge when Max answered: 'Just natural thoughts, because of a new world that's opening up. A very philosophical culture, although *philosophy* is not quite the right word. They have some interesting linguistic terms for knowledge, epistemology and research.'

'How very ... academic, Uncle Max.'

'All right.' He smiled, gently stroking the cat with one huge hand, his forearm muscles like load-bearing cables. 'I've a strong strategic interest in Nulapeiron, but there's something else I want to talk through first.'

Holos blossomed in a semi-circle in front of Rhianna. On

her lap, the cream-coloured cat twitched her ears. The central holo caught Rhianna's attention: Haxigoji shuffling into place, as if to protect a Pilot from human security personnel. Other holovolumes showed the event triggering the security reaction: using tu-ring weaponry to blast a young man into oblivion. But there was no mystery in that – not to Rhianna, who had spent a long time on Molsin poring over footage from Fulgor, analysing the appearance of the Anomaly.

'The Pilot showed initiative,' she said. 'By the time that bugger's eyes started glowing blue, it would have been too late.'

'Very astute of you. The on-board personnel took a lot longer to convince, and there are still some legal hoops to jump through before Pilot Goran gets free.'

'Jed Goran? Roger's friend?'

'The very one,' said Max. 'Which is part of how he reacted so fast: he'd seen footage of the young man before. Someone Roger knew.'

'A coincidence, that he should happen to be there?'

'More like causal linkages we don't know, but can guess. Perhaps there was even some buried fragment of awareness in Rick Mbuli's mind – that's the dead man – that made him volunteer to be one of the Anomalous components that travelled on Schenck's ship.'

'That's two nasty thoughts right there,' said Rhianna. 'That the poor bastards have some human feeling left, and that Schenck transported a bunch of them from Fulgor.'

'We know his ship went there and left again, and if Mbuli was on board, why not others?'

Rhianna did not say *so you're tightening up patrols around the realspace worlds, and infiltrating their immigration agencies and the like*. Commenting on the obvious wasn't her style; nor was it Uncle Max's.

Speaking of which, what exactly was she missing?

'Oh, bollocks.' She had never needed to watch her language

in front of him. 'Now I remember why you're the boss. People here are frightened of you because they don't know you, Uncle Max.'

'Really?'

'Yeah, because if they understood how sharp you really are, they'd be too shit-scared to work for you at all. That footage is ambiguous, but this one off to the side is significant.'

Max smiled at her.

'I guess I remember why you're my favourite niece.'

The holo footage she pointed out was of Haxigoji crowding a flexible tunnel leading to a mu-space ship's control cabin. The field of view was skewed but the Haxigoji's purpose was clear: to prevent one Pilot Guy Holland from leaving his vessel and coming on board Vachss Station. The question was, were the Haxigoji in contact with their colleagues in the lounge where the refugees had arrived?

Or were they simply able to sense that there was something wrong about Holland?

'Send Roger,' she said. 'He can check it out.'

Max looked surprised.

'I genuinely hadn't thought of that. Out of sight in Tangle-knot, and quite out of mind.'

'He's close to graduating from Phase One. I'd be surprised if he's not acing the course.'

Not guesswork: she had contacts among the staff.

'It's early to put him in the field, even if he is your protégé.'

'Go on, Uncle Max. You know you want to.'

They laughed hard then, enough for the cats to look up disgusted, and disappear into simultaneous fastpath rotations. But Max's mood changed again, as he pointed out another option.

'We could let the word spread, about Haxigoji possibly being able to sense the darkness. Let Schenck get wind of it, and we'll be waiting when the renegades turn up in strength to bomb the planet.'

'Or keep quiet, and with luck gain a huge advantage, an

entire species with Roger's ability. Instead of relying on a guess about Schenck's strategic thinking.'

It had come to this: discussing the fate of a human-equivalent species in terms of military advantage, and no hint of ethical considerations. They talked over the implications for a while, then Max turned back to his main objective here, the new world – and experiment in deliberate social engineering – called Nulapeiron.

He came at the subject in a roundabout linguistic way, via the historic distinction between *if* and *when* – in Neudeutsch, significantly, *wenn* and *wann* – and Novanglic's semantic colouring of conditional logic in the sentence construction of *if* <condition> *then* <do calculation>. It was not the first time Rhianna had thought that a marginally happier upbringing might have produced Max the schoolteacher, a more contented man.

'The point,' said Max in Novanglic, 'is the extent to which *then* is temporal. To which logic implies computation. The statement *if it rains, then put on a coat*, implies the ability to test whether it is raining, and afterwards – in chronological sequence – to put on a coat, because otherwise the logic is semantically ill-formed. Or is it?'

Rhianna stayed with Aeternum when she answered. 'Which means computation implies timeflow, and we could spin out nuances for ever in realspace languages.'

'On Nulapeiron, that's exactly the kind of game that the aristocracy like to play. They're creating a very intellectual élite, or so the reports imply.'

'And you want me to be an agent-in-place among people like that?' But Max's argument had been subtle, because the point had been to demonstrate to Rhianna that she was capable of following such thoughts, and so suited to the mission. 'Haven't you got some would-be intellectual who'd feel right at home there?'

'I don't want someone who'll kick back and enjoy themselves,' said Max. 'There's a rumour that a certain Count

Avernon – they've already started using such titles – has an interest in some weird and speculative research, and if it were any other world I'd probably ignore it.'

'And you want someone who can kick ass to get hold of what they need.' Deliberately, she left out reference to herself. 'Is that the implication?'

'I want *you* on the mission, because' – with a smile – 'it's the kind of job you were destined to do.'

Rhianna rubbed her head. Uncle Max could play these games better than anyone. She should have conceded defeat a lot earlier; but of course, he would have been disappointed.

'What kind of speculative research?' Her question was almost a sigh.

'Reading the future,' said Max.

Which made it clear: this really was the job she was destined for, that had to be hers alone.

The rest of the conversation involved her trying not to appear too determined to accept the mission, because Max would wonder why, and she really could not explain her thinking, not this time. But in the end, he assigned her officially, and all that remained were the details of briefing and logistics, because she *was* going to fly to Nulapeiron.

It was inevitable.

FIFTEEN

A dozen years had passed since the death of Jarl at Fenrisul-fr's hand, in the days when he was simply Ulfr. The five most recent years were the emptiest, since courageous Brandr died in battle, the war-hound licking his master's face even as the blood pumped through Fenrisulfr's fingers, desperate to hold closed the wound while the heartless trio that was the Norns, in their desolate other-world, cackled and wove the threads of Fate so that dark-brown, loving eyes grew clouded with the opacity of death. The best of all creatures to walk the Middle World was gone.

Were it possible to go back and avoid that day, to let the rich travellers pass by unmolested, he would do it without hesitation. But the Norns set the rules, and the only way to dim the memory was with unremitting violence, to force his pain back upon everybody else.

Ah, the screams and blood he had waded in since then.

Twice in that time, lieutenants in his reaver band had left to form groups of their own, needing independence and far too wise to fight Fenrisulfr for leadership. It was a form of success and maturity that sometimes caused Fenrisulfr to think he might be a good man; but as he nodded now, signalling Brökkr the Cloven to commence the attack, the imminence of violence revealed the lie.

We fight because we can.

It was a shingle beach they streamed onto, his fighters, his lovely warriors; and then they were into the mêlée, cut and smash and rip amid the spurting blood, the confused stumbling of victims who could not summon their warrior's spirit in time; then the reavers' stomach-dropping disappointment that it was over too soon, the opposition too shallow; and the need to rein in the madness because the fight was done.

The surviving travellers were on their knees, some with arms behind them already lashed in place, heads bowed, awaiting whatever Fenrisulfr's band decided: fast death or playful torture. The reavers took whatever pleasure they desired, made sweeter by struggles and screams, later selling their victims into thraldom, or – if they could not be bothered – perhaps letting the survivors go free, more than likely hobbled by tendon-cuts.

'What of the boat, Chief?' Brökkr gestured with his axe towards their victims' beached vessel. 'Burn it?'

After stripping it of valuables, that was understood. Then they turned, hearing an angry voice.

'Enough of the evil eye, woman.' One of their warriors, dread Ivarr, was pulling out his dagger. 'In fact, I think I'll have that eyeball.'

Lithe and unflinching, she stared up at him from her kneeling position, a woman of Fenrisulfr's age, showing no fear.

Not you. Not here.

Memories tumbled. 'Stop, good Ivarr. Not this one.'

'Chief.'

Fenrisulfr went down on one knee before the woman.

'Heithrún,' he muttered. 'No *volva* should suffer this.'

So many years.

'They call you Fenrisulfr as well as Chief. I heard them.' Her features were older, strong more than pretty. 'You are ill-named, my lover, but it suits you.'

He called young Thollákr to fetch the crystal-headed spear.

'I still bear your gift to me,' said Fenrisulfr. 'It served me a second time against troll-spirits. I've wondered, from time to time, how you might have possessed such a thing.'

The rest of the Middle World faded, the prisoners and his reavers, the beached boat and inland hills and the grey, cold waters: it was just him and Heithrún, seeress and priestess and so very briefly his lover. She was dangerous – any *volva* was – but by clasping his cloak's brooch-pin, feeling its sharpness, Fenrisulfr believed he might prevent her from leading his spirit into dreamworld.

'It came from the eastern ice wastes,' said Heithrún, meaning the crystal that had once adorned her walking-staff. 'Chief Gulbrandr journeyed far when he was young, and that was one of many gifts he brought back. They say it came from a sky-ship that was crushed by Thórr's hammer, for thunder filled the air. Or perhaps by trolls, for they were around the smashed ship. So they told Gulbrandr, and he told Eydís.'

Her mentor, he remembered now.

'And how did you know it would hurt that troll?'

So long ago, the day the two travelling parties met, hers and his, and it seemed that a troll reared from the earth to attack them, though later he would wonder whether its target had been the dark poet Stígr, journeying with Chief Gulbrandr's party, his nature not yet obvious even to a *volva* like Heithrún.

'Because of the rune that glowed within,' she said. 'Or you could say I guessed.'

'And Chief Gulbrandr gave it to you as a gift?'

'To Eydís, when she saved his wife's life during labour, and delivered the child.'

Thollákr was keeping his distance, looking fascinated. Beyond him, stocky Ivarr was making a better pretence of disinterest, but listening anyway. None of the band knew much about Fenrisulfr's life before he became their chief, rearing out of nowhere to slay Magnús.

'As for your old clan,' said Heithrún, 'I have visited from time to time, and Folkvar still rules. These days it is Vermundr and Steinn who are his strength, along with ... Ormr, is it?'

'Ormr or Kormr?'

Faces and names came tumbling back across the years.

'I'm not sure, Ulfr. I'm sorry.'

Of course she would call him by his old name.

So what will I do about her?

He looked out across the waves, at the greyness of dusk descending, then stood up, centring as if preparing to fight.

'Guard them all,' he commanded Ivarr and Thollákr. 'In the morning I will decide.'

'Chief.'

Pulling his cloak around him, he walked away alone.

So many years.

Such oceans of blood.

During his mist-cloaked sleep in the damp, uncomforting night, he conversed with crystalline figures who called him brother and begged him to return, to fight on their side in the twilight days to come, when the armies of dread would hear the call to *Ragnarökkr* and fall upon the Middle World, destroying everything unless they could – at some awful cost – be driven back. Of course he refused yet again.

That night he dreamed of making love to Heithrún as he had long ago. It seemed so very real, though it happened in dreamworld and he did not waken.

My wolf, she said as he slipped out of her, and then she was gone and simple restfulness remained.

In the morning, Njörthr was humping a dead woman in the bushes – Fenrisulfr pretended not to see – while down at the beach, beside the abandoned boat, Ivarr and Thollákr stood with hands on weapon-hilts as though alert, in contrast to their unfocused eyes. There was bare shingle next to the wooden hull where there should have been a group of prisoners, tied up and waiting to learn what Fenrisulfr had decided to do with them.

She did not ensorcel me.

He was sure of that, convincing himself that he had known before he slept how this would turn out.

Should have cut her tongue out.

To push away that thought, he slapped both Ivarr and Thollákr. They staggered, then cried out, panicking.

'I can't see!'

'Blinded, I'm blinded ...'

Fenrisulfr thumped them and told them to shut up. 'It'll wear off,' he promised. 'Before night falls again.'

At least that was likely: he did not know Heithrún's abilities for sure, but he remembered how his beloved Eira had been, the punishments she had wrought within the clan, and the harsher spells that Eira's teacher Nessa cast in her time.

Brökkr came forward, leading a big man bound with leather ropes. 'I had this one prisoner at the forest's edge, where the witch didn't see him.' Behind the prisoner walked Ári and Davith with swords unsheathed. 'A real fighter, and I didn't let him get away.'

Brökkr was called Brökkr the Cloven, although not to his wounded face, because of the old purple-and-white axe-wound that rippled down his features. It had cut into cheek-bone and forehead, and distorted the shape of his lips so that it was not always possible to tell when he was being sarcastic.

Or challenging.

You want to fight me, is that it?

So much for the nurturing of his lieutenants. The previous two, forming their own bands, remained potential allies should there ever be advantage in combining into a larger fighting force; but while Brökkr had many of the same attributes, he liked taking shortcuts. Perhaps he thought that taking over a ready-formed reaver band would be easier than creating his own.

It's what I did.

But that was irrelevant. Fenrisulfr pushed aside Ári and Davith's blades, and used his own dagger to cut through the prisoner's bonds. Then he waited while the big man's blood slowly returned to his hands and feet. The man stamped with the pain but made no other sound, then loosened his shoulders and jogged on the spot, getting ready to accept the invitation which must be showing in Fenrisulfr's eyes. No one had spoken, but everyone knew what was happening.

The prisoner was a fighter, knocked out by chance during

the confrontation – everyone knew that skill and ferocity could still be overcome by the Norns' contingencies – needing this to redeem himself.

When he was ready, he grunted and nodded, too far into warrior-state for ordinary speech, and he snarled as Fenrisulfr laid his own dagger and sword on the shingles, then walked backwards, nine short paces.

'Let him walk free if he beats me,' Fenrisulfr commanded.

'We'll do that,' said Brökkr, his cloven lips curling. 'By Freya's perfect buttocks, not to mention the sweetness of her golden cup, I swear it.'

There were smiles and frowns as the other reavers drew near enough to watch – first Sveinn and Nörthr, then Logmar followed by Torleik and the rest – but not too close, because anyone could get hurt when violence exploded.

Like now.

Stones flew at Fenrisulfr's face as the fighter used the environment, kicking shingle as weapon and distraction, but his objective was obvious – sword and dagger – so Fenrisulfr whipped forwards, two long thrusting paces to cover the distance of nine short ones, hand and forearm deflecting the stones and then he was slamming the man's left wrist across the body – *knife* – and the heel of Fenrisulfr's right hand smashed the jaw around, then he clawed back, trying for the eyes, while his left arm wrapped the bastard's knife hand close, and he pumped his knee twice into the spleen – *again* – then lower ribs, and spun him – knee deep into kidney – then slammed his right elbow into the back of the man's neck – *good* – and ripped the dagger free from the weakened left hand before slamming it point-first with a crunch exactly where the elbow-strike had hit, severing the spine at the base of the brain.

It dropped, the dead thing.

The body lay atop Fenrisulfr's sword, which the dead man had picked up but never had the opportunity to use, because Fenrisulfr had not let him.

Fuck you, Urd, Skuld and Verthandi!

His men gasped, some raising a fist in the shape of Thórr's hammer or thumb-and-finger as the All-Father's eye, several stepping back, and he realised he must have uttered the curse aloud. His reavers would face vicious, bloody enemies as a matter of course; but to curse the Norns by name was a dangerous thing: they would not dream of it.

Brökkr the Cloven looked away, understanding the lesson here.

Good.

Fenrisulfr would not have to kill his lieutenant.

Not today.

SIXTEEN

After a long sleep, Roger felt full of energy and cheerful optimism, bouncing right back from the surveillance-and-tracking exercise whose main difficulty had been the prior seventy standard hours of wakefulness, sleep deprivation forming the backbone of the test. He and Corinne, too tired to debrief in their favourite fashion, had gone to their separate rooms.

=The Logos Library.=

He nearly lost bladder control as Labyrinth's words resonated in his brain.

'What about it?'

But no elaboration followed, no indication that he had not just imagined the message – which here in Tangleknot Core was the only way of delivering information that could not be eavesdropped on and recorded.

A tiny non-urgent holo, hovering by his bedside, unfurled at his gesture. He had been assigned a free day – today – with leave to exit Tangleknot and go anywhere he liked within Labyrinth. As he used the ablution facilities, he wondered if this was another exercise or test, or whether it was a day off that he could spend with Corinne, in which case going to a library, even one that perhaps possessed an infinite knowledge-store, was a long way down his list of possible activities.

But there was no reply from his attempted signal, and when he went along the dorm corridor to check first Corinne's room and then his other classmates', everyone had gone.

'Rotation,' said the first instructor he found, a hard-faced woman called Medina. 'Only one or two people out of the group get R & R at any one time. Today, it's you.'

If there was subterfuge, Medina's skills were too advanced for him to read it.

Alone, Roger tuned his clothing to dark colours and went out to explore Cantor Circus and Hamilton Helix, where myriad Pilots went about their busy lives, here in the heart of Labyrinth. He poked around, found a café near the most elegant stretch of Legendre Level, and went inside.

Over daistral, he caught up on the news – in Tangleknot they were isolated – and saw that the legendary Dirk McNamara had been sighted once more in Labyrinth. Commentators made bets they would never pay out on regarding the duration of McNamara's stay.

It would have been an interesting oddity and no more, had Roger not twice met Dirk McNamara's mother, an even more shadowy figure from the past, among the study-carrels in the Logos Library. At the time, he had not appreciated just how unusual and striking those fleeting meetings were.

And how likely was it that the city-world's mention of the Logos Library, the instant he woke up, had been a coincidence?

He finished his daistral, placed the empty goblet on the tabletop before him, and watched the goblet dissolve. When he stood, chair and table melted into the floor, and he spent a moment visualising coordinates and least-action geodesics before summoning a fastpath rotation.

It deposited him in the Logos Library.

There was no sign of Ro McNamara as Roger walked the infinite balconies and halls. Crystals were racked everywhere, indexed contents searchable via search engines not subject to Gödel's Incompleteness Theorem or Turing undecidability. A primitive human might have thought that Labyrinth and the Logos Library were in themselves gods.

There were Pilots here, many Pilots, but in the vastness they seemed few. Roger enjoyed his long stroll and occasional topological shortcuts within the endless structure and all its beautiful decorations. But finally he had seen enough, and summoned a study-carrel into existence from one of the microscopic spacetime knots floating ready.

A random choice. It was impossible – or should have been – that she could be waiting inside this particular carrel.

'Hello, Roger,' said Ro, mischief on her triangular features. She was cross-legged on a high-backed chair.

'Ma'am.'

'Oh, please. That was my mother. Sit down, won't you?'

Another chair was extruded, and he sat.

'You're not unique,' she added. 'You'll be glad to know.'

'Excuse me?'

'No one's going to tell you, but there's a possible source of other individuals – many, many individuals, not human – who can sense the same thing you do. And there's something else: every renegade was turned while spending time in realspace. The investigators are close to one hundred per cent certain.'

Tangleknot training made Roger fast on the uptake.

'You mean it can't reach into mu-space, the darkness.'

Plus there might be an entire species that could sense what he could: no need for the Admiralty to take his word for it.

'Some of its subjects, like Schenck, show exceptional charisma. But of course, they're not the only ones. My son Dirk, for instance, would make an equally fine figurehead for a radical political movement.'

'Er …'

Max Gould and Pavel Karelin had spent years building up a counter-conspiracy against Schenck's thousand-strong group of committed supporters, and that was just one hidden aspect within the immensities of Labyrinthine politics that Roger knew so little of. Isolationist versus pro-humanity was just one among a multitude of political axes whose combination produced the background for the so-called Stochastic Schism, the widening separation of views that had been temporarily halted by the revelation of Schenck's true nature.

Within that, there was clearly room for using an historical, romantic figure like the dashing Dirk McNamara as a popular icon; but exactly which movement or individuals, Roger did not know.

'It would be nice,' Ro went on, 'if Dirk had a friend without an agenda. At least someone who knew what really happened in the past.' Ro gestured toward the carrel walls. 'Infinite knowledge all around is very nice, but getting it inside your head is the real trick, isn't it?' She stood up. 'You are interested in history, aren't you, Roger?'

'Yes, but—'

He was talking to an empty carrel.

That's one hundred per cent impossible.

With no hint of summoning a rotation – which you could not do inside an unfolded carrel anyway – she was gone. But she had been real, not holo: both his tu-ring and his own senses could detect the difference.

Where she had been sitting, a small infocrystal sparkled.

'History,' he muttered. 'What if I said it bored me rigid?'

But the past could fascinate as much as the future; and how could he refuse an invitation from Ro McNamara, the first of all true Pilots?

Much of the content was episodic, rendered with unexpected impact and detail as he immersed himself in scene after scene, checking metadata when required, following a theme.

Explosions cause the building to shudder. Sirens vibrate the air. In a large room furnished with archaic laboratory devices, a Zajinet lattice-form, glowing softly, is curled in upon itself.

'Sir?' shouts a capable-looking woman.

[metatext person.id = 'Zoë Gould, UNSA intelligence officer'; context.desc = 'XenoMir facility, Moscow (*mask-VAH*), Earth, 11/10/2143']

She's addressing a glowing Zajinet, and not getting the reply she needs. 'It's your former colleague, isn't it? We need your advice.'

The Zajinet pulls itself tighter, and responds:

<< *...danger ...*>>

<< *...yes ...*>>

<< *...yes ...*>>

<< *...it comes ...*>>

A metal door crumples, torn down by a blocky, three-fingered hand. A slender female Pilot draws back – a young-looking Ro McNamara, cursing: 'Jesus.'

The other woman, Zoë, draws a handheld weapon [metatext weapon.desc = 'pocket lineac derringer'; narrative.significance = 'abandoning pretence of being a civilian'] *and snaps on its laser-sight, aiming at the squat, brown, cuboid invader tearing its way inside: one of the Veralik delegation.*

'THE FEMALE,' emanates from a device on the Veralik's chest as it waves a stubby pseudoarm in Ro's direction: 'HOLD HER.'

Zoë says, 'Why are you—?'

A man's voice sounds from the corridor outside.

[metatext person.id = 'Piotr Yavorski, senior xenobiologist']

'The centrifuge hab ... fail ... Energy drain ...'

'HOLD THE FEMALE,' says the Veralik. 'IT WILL ATTEMPT TO TAKE HER.'

Ro circles away from the Veralik [metatext biography.threads.concepts = 'aikido footwork; tai sabaki; mind-body integration; combat skills'], *avoiding it.*

'ZAJINET, THE RENEGADE. IT STOPPED ROTATION. ENERGY—'

Ro swivels away once more, then halts. Strange energies whirl and flicker, an electric sapphire blue predominating, surrounding her.

'STOP HER.'

'Ro!' shouts Zoë, her friend. 'What's happening?'

The air is curling, twisting, folding up around Ro McNamara, enveloping her. Zoë, hand covering her eyes for protection, tries to reach inside the disturbance.

'Ro, take my hand!'

But Ro is no longer there.

*

It was a very different kind of unexpected disappearance. Roger had read about Ro being kidnapped by Zajinets from a xeno facility on twenty-second-century Earth; but most of this was new to him.

He resumed the narrative.

When Ro wakes up, her disorientation is immediate and obvious. She is in a tubular, bluish glass-like corridor, and a woman with cropped blue hair [metatext person.id = 'Lila O'Brien, assigned to Beta Draconis III research station'] *is kneeling beside her. A man stands behind Lila.*

'You're awake,' says Lila. 'Jared, call Lee. Our visitor's waking up.'

'Ugh—' Ro's face clenches with pain as she sits up.

'You'll be all right, I think.'

'Where—?'

From around a bend, two men hurry into view.

'She needs the doc.'

'No way, Lila.' One of the men stops. 'Not till we— Just where the devil have you been hiding, young woman?'

'I don't—'

'For God's sake, Josef. Look at the state of her.'

'Until we find out what's going—'

A large hand grabs her wrist, and Ro reacts: rising to her knees and twisting, as the big man whips head over heels, smacking heavily onto the floor.

Then Ro is on her feet and backing away.

'Who the hell are you people? How did I get here?'

Roger paused the narrative once more. The metatext had already revealed that Ro was on Beta Draconis III: a strange planet with a tiny human settlement, half diplomatic consulate, half xenoanthropological research station, initially considered the Zajinet homeworld, but actually no more than a colony that was later evacuated, leaving humanity ignorant of the Zajinets' origins.

He skipped to the next chapter.

After trekking beneath purple-with-turquoise skies, twenty-two humans find themselves at a Zajinet event that might be a criminal trial, a political debate, or some form of interaction without a human analogue. Flickering, overlapping occurrences of glowing Zajinets fill the dome-shaped hall.

Watching from a stable dais where reality is not shifting, the humans witness two Zajinets (one scarlet, one blue) in their fiery trace form, while the audience/witnesses/congregation are clothed in sculpture forms, using everything from naked rock to decorated ceramic spheres.

<< ...preserve ...>>

<< ...in finding, hold onto ...>>

<< ...converse manifests ...>>

<< ...obliterate ...>>

<< ...a focus ...>>

The first Zajinet's legal adversary – or whatever it is – blasts a reply:

<< ...single thread! ...>>

<< ...single thread! ...>>

<< ...saved softly in confusing dark ...>>

<< ...their only hope ...>>

Lila, her hair a shining violet today, examines a small disc embedded in her glove.

'One of them' – Lila points – 'we've dealt with before. The other Zajinet's a stranger.'

A wave pattern shimmers in the air between the Zajinets, linking the scarlet and the blue; then it fades. Each Zajinet twists, shrinks to a point, and is gone.

As the other Zajinets flicker out, the humans wonder what the hell they have just witnessed.

Aware that he had to return to Tangleknot, Roger transferred to the narrative outline level and jumped far ahead, to an UNSA base in Arizona, Earth, on the day that Ro's twin sons,

Dirk and Kian, were to attempt their first flights into mu-space, knowing nothing of the bombs planted in their ships.

Three viewpoints were tagged with high priorities. Roger opened them all.

Up in the control tower, Deirdre Dullaghan, the twins' closest friend, stands next to Chief Controller Bratko. From here, through blue-tinted windows, the poised ship appears to be dark metal banded with black, though her true colours are bronze and dark turquoise.

'—clearing you to go,' says one of the controllers.

Pale flames expand into brightness at the rear. The vessel rocks, straining against the brakes.

'My God,' says Deirdre. 'Will you look at that.'

'Makes my heart thud,' says Bratko. 'Every single time.'

Then he is leaning forward. Two of the controllers rise from their seats.

A lone man is sprinting towards the runway.

'Who the hell is—?'

'Dirk.' Deirdre is unnaturally calm. 'Something's wrong.'

'Shut down,' commands Bratko. 'Immediate shut down.'

The controllers work the system, their movements frantic.

'No response. Main thruster's still burning.'

'Shit.'

In the Pilot's control couch, Kian closes his eyes.

'Pulse engines are go.'

Here the engine roar is muted. Status displays brighten. His ship is straining against the leash. But even with all that happening, his inductive senses can reach beyond the hull, because he is a twin, and he knows when his brother is near.

Dirk is running hard and scared.

'Control? Come in, control,' says Kian, then switches his focus to the ship. 'On-board command: shutdown-shutdown-shutdown.'

Nothing. No comms response, no reaction from his ship.

Some processes, once started, cannot be stopped.

*

Dirk's legs are pumping as he runs, filled with adrenaline, red-lining the anaerobic systems of his body because the bomb is concealed within the starboard delta-wing, and there can be only seconds left before – no! – a percussive blast slams him to the ground – Kian! – but it is the engines, kicking up to a new level of thrust, and the bastard thing has not exploded yet. He is on hands and knees, blood dripping everywhere, and whatever he does he will have to do from here.

It begins as a pulse inside his head, the build-up of energy from the satanin-satanase reaction. An onlooker would see glimmering sparks of gold inside his obsidian eyes, brightening further, vision inoperative as both eyes shine, yellow and lupine; and then he lets rip – careful – but keeping control as he senses the device's countermeasures – there – and fights them down because detonation is the last thing he wants – got it – and the detonator circuits die, but the bastard thing is dangerous still. The next priority is to get it off the ship.

A dorsal hatch opens, and Kian looks out, sees Dirk and senses the situation, and uses his inductive senses to work the ship's systems directly, causing an access hatch to pop open beneath the starboard wing. Working with him, Dirk disables the bomb's electromagnets as he runs forward once more, and is in time to catch the deadly white box as it drops from its hiding place.

Heavy as a bastard.

Up in the control tower, they must have seen something was wrong, because emergency TDVs are hurtling across the runway, strobing orange. Within seconds, the lead vehicle has screeched to a halt.

'Hey pal, you OK?'

'Get away!' Dirk swings the heavy bomb – and himself – on board the vehicle's flat bed. 'Get us the hell away from here!'

'Bozhe moi, you got it!'

The driver spins his TDV on the spot, then accelerates away from the runway, heading for the airbase boundary and the red Mars-like desert beyond.

*

But this was no single-pronged attack. Up in the sky, two shapes are growing larger; and everyone knows that the airspace should be clear when there are UNSA launches scheduled.

Kian slides back into the control seat.

'Oh, God.'

The brakes come free and his ship begins to roll.

At the boundary the TDV brakes, its thermoacoustic motor whining. The driver calls: 'You all right up there, pal? If you want, I could—'

But Dirk has already flung the bomb away.

'Take us back,' he yells. 'Don't hang around.'

'Bozhe moi!'

After the explosion, a black twisting column of smoke crawls up into the sky ... where two vessels are growing much larger, their target clear.

Kian's ship is still on the runway, accelerating.

The first intruder ship lets rip with an energy beam, missing Kian's ship but ploughing a trench in the runway before it, causing Kian to brake. His ship howls as it pulls off to the side, coming to a halt.

As the enemy ship banks, ready to curve back on a strafing run, the second intruder flies diagonally behind it: two sets of weapon systems on the brink of cutting loose.

Seconds remain, no more.

Then a new vessel bursts out of the sun, shining silver and delta-winged, its graser-gatlings splitting the air, and the paired intruders have no chance.

Both Zajinet ships explode.

Standing beside the TDV, the driver wipes grease from his forehead.

'And what the Devil was that silver ship?'

Dirk's laugh is shaky but proud.

'That was my mother.'

Roger switched back to overview. The main narrative thread proceeded with the twins' friend Deirdre delivering a massive kick in the groin to one of the controllers, Solly, who had planted bombs in both ships. A military team disarmed the second bomb. Roger really had to go, but he could not take this crystal with him – no personal possessions were allowed in Tangleknot, plus any item was subject to long examination before being brought inside. He tried to work out the minimum he must experience in order to understand the point.

The theme strongly pointed to one more scene in which a disaffected UNSA intelligence officer called Paula – soon to become Deirdre's long-term lover – related what happened to the captive Solly during interrogation.

Roger jumped into the middle of the scene.

'They pushed the questioning further than the usual "What's your contact's name?", "How do you meet up?", that sort of thing,' Paula tells Deirdre.

The setting is an airfield beneath a grey German sky, and they are standing outside in the rain, having attended a memorial service officially for Ro McNamara, unofficially for her missing son Dirk as well.

Roger paused, realising he had gone too fast. The scene needed background to make sense.

He checked the context summary. Dirk, Kian and Deirdre, some time after the Zajinet attack on the first day of flight, were attacked during an anti-xeno demonstration in Arizona. The mob had thrown petrol-bombs, burning Kian badly, leaving him disfigured and initially close to death. A raging Dirk had let rip with a single, coherent biolaser pulse from both eyes, burning out the eyeballs of the mob, killing dozens, blinding the rest.

Under arrest, he had escaped and fled to mu-space in his ship, exiting directly from inside a hangar: a feat hard enough for modern, latest-generation vessels.

As for Ro, she was missing, last seen departing an orbital

called Vachss Station, thought to have flown into a Zajinet ambush.

He resumed the scene featuring the soon-to-be lovers, Paula and Deirdre, mourning for Dirk and Ro, and discussing the interrogation of Solly, the Zajinet agent who had planted bombs aboard the twins' ships.

'They asked the question' – Paula means the interrogators – *'that no one's been able to answer: Why do the Zajinets hate humans? Why have they targeted Pilots, specific Pilots?'*

'So why? What's the answer?'

'Solly said: "They'll allow the darkness to be born. It will spread across the galaxy, and they won't fight back until billions have perished. I've seen it." *That's what he said.* "The Zajinets showed me the future, and I've seen it." *It may sound insane, but Solly believed.'* Paula looked bleak. *'He was in no fit state for joking by that time.'*

'You're using the past tense,' said Deirdre.

'He did not survive the interrogation. A pre-existing medical condition, they said.'

And that, of course, was the section Ro McNamara had wanted Roger to know about.

They'll allow the darkness to be born.

It provided one hell of a motivation for Zajinets to prevent human expansion into space. Whether it also implied a basis for negotiation, or simply made them enemies for ever, he could not tell.

Why show me this?

You might say that he was the first Pilot who could appreciate the Zajinets' viewpoint. But he thought it might be a little late for such understanding.

En route back to Tangleknot, he stole time for one more cup of daistral, and found that Dirk McNamara no longer occupied top position in the news. Settlements on Deighton,

Berkivan-deux and Göthewelt were burning after Zajinet raids, in each case centred on a Sanctuary location.

Whatever Roger's future turned out to be, peacemaker was no longer an option.

SEVENTEEN

EARTH, 1956 AD

Walking back from lunch along Kensington Gore, with Hyde Park stretching away to their right on the other side of the road, the three of them slowed down for a minute – Gavriela and her friends Jane and Keith from Imperial – so that Keith could break off pieces of a Bournville bar. He handed them round, still a treat, two years after rationing had ended.

In the park, mounted officers of the Household Cavalry were taking their horses through drills. The three scientists watched, then walked on.

'Add this' – Jane waved her chocolate – 'to travelling by bus instead of walking, and people are going to start getting fat.'

'Chance would be a fine thing,' said Keith. 'Do you still feed sugar sandwiches to your son, Gabby?'

'Not any more.'

'See?' said Jane. 'It's starting already.'

'And smallpox will disappear,' said Keith, 'communism will fall apart *sua sponte*, and look, is that a pig flying among the clouds?'

Jane touched Gavriela's sleeve.

'Gabrielle? It looks as if he knows you. That chap on the corner.'

Pinstripe suit and spotlessly brushed black bowler: it was Rupert Forrester, his hair showing grey, his taut patrician face lined like porcelain.

'I'll see you two later,' Gavriela told her colleagues.

Rupert looked grave as she crossed the street.

'Gabrielle, how lovely.' He might call her Gavriela at times, but never outdoors or in unsecured premises. 'Shall we walk? And perhaps a spot of tea. Or coffee, if we're being cosmopolitan.'

'Why not?' she said.

They found a milk bar close to South Kensington Tube, and took a seat inside near the back. It was mostly empty, and from the way the man behind the counter ignored them after fetching coffee, he was an SIS asset, and never mind that domestic operations were the province of Five. Every service needs local safe houses.

When no other customers remained, Rupert picked up his cup and Gavriela's – 'This way, old girl' – and led the way out back, up creaking stairs (good for warning of night-time intruders) to a musty-smelling room overlooking an unkempt yard.

She sat on an overstuffed couch, while he took one of the mismatched armchairs.

'What's happening, Rupert?'

'The world's falling apart, didn't you know? Ten years ago, we knew who the enemy was. Now there's civil unrest right here.'

'You mean Teddy Boys ripping up cinema seats.' Showings of *Rock Around the Clock* had erupted in trouble all over the country, causing Gavriela to forbid Carl from going to see the film. 'I should have thought the real threat to Empire was the state of the pound.'

'The PM received a confidential briefing from Macmillan,' said Rupert, 'concluding that there are two root causes to inflation: the commitment to full employment, and our massive defence spending. While Europe's in a golden age.'

'I took Carl to Paris last year.'

'So you did.' That was Rupert letting her know that leaving the service did not mean dropping out of sight. 'And you'll have seen it, Continental cities booming while we have bomb craters still, and prefab houses for the squalid classes.'

'Oh, Rupert.'

'French success stemming partly, I should say, from creating technical institutions along the lines of Imperial.'

'How remarkably enlightened for a classicist.'

'I didn't say I *approve* of the necessity.' Rupert crossed his elegant legs. 'Nor the extinction of Empire, but it's a fact, even if to the PM we're still a great power.'

If Eden continued to commit the country's budget to defence against world communism, then SIS must benefit. For Rupert to argue against it spoke of serious misgivings.

'And Nasser has kicked us out of Egypt' – Gavriela wanted to show she kept in touch – 'which Mr Eden thinks is about to become a Soviet dominion.'

'Not if he reads his JIC reports.' Rupert meant the Joint Intelligence Committee.

For three months, the British army had been massing in Cyprus, getting ready – alongside French regiments – to invade Egypt and retake the Suez Canal Zone.

'When the Wehrmacht invaded Poland and Belgium,' said Gavriela, 'it was pretty clear where the morality lay. If *we* invade another country, what does that make us?'

Rupert shook his head. 'It's a moot point, because Eisenhower won't allow us to invade. That's classified, by the way.'

'Won't *allow* us?' said Gavriela.

'The American Sixth Fleet is massing in the Mediterranean. If our ships set sail from Cyprus, the Yanks will move to stop it.' None of this was in the newspapers. 'On the other hand, in a few weeks' time,' Rupert went on, 'French envoys will call in to Chequers, to see the Chancellor and request that Anglo-French combined forces make a move. We have this from the Deuxième Bureau.'

Gavriela nodded. The information might have come via semi-official channels or from eavesdropping on French intelligence: both were par for the course.

'But this is in fact an Anglo-French-*Israeli* initiative,' continued Rupert. 'And you and I will have our ears nailed to the wall if we give a hint of knowing that.' He related the details, and they were explosive: Israel to invade Egypt under secret agreement with Britain and France, after which the combined Anglo-French forces would 'liberate' the place while the Israelis withdrew.

'Do the Cousins know this?' asked Gavriela, meaning the CIA.

'Maybe I should ring the Kremlin and ask.'

It was a year since Burgess and Maclean had surfaced at a Soviet press conference. Since then Kim Philby, SIS's liaison to Washington and tipped to be a future head of service, had denied being the third man; but dirt tended to stick. Internal investigators, Rupert added, were right now tearing the Recruitment Office apart.

'I'm glad I'm out of it,' said Gavriela. 'All that makes the news is defection and failure. The Crabbe thing was a disaster.'

In April, Premier Kruschev and Prime Minister Bulganin had sailed into Portsmouth Harbour aboard the *Ordzhonikidze*, a Soviet cruiser which had been too tempting a target: the famous wartime diver, Commander Crabbe, had been despatched to fix bugging devices to the hull. When his torn-up body eventually washed ashore, the UK government owned up to the operation.

The official story involved his being caught up in propellers. Not likely.

'Berlin and the Stopwatch débâcle,' said Rupert, 'are more to the point.'

'In what way? What point exactly?'

Portrait of a spy grandmaster sitting in a dusty room moving pieces across the board, but she was no longer in the game.

'I mean, dear Gavi, your popping over to Berlin. Let me ask Alfredo to fetch up more coffee, and perhaps a plate of biscuits, before we discuss the details.'

'No,' said Gavriela. 'No coffee, no biscuits, and definitely no Berlin.'

Rupert's voice went as mild as she had ever heard it.

'And no curiosity,' he asked, 'about the niece you have yet to meet?'

And that was it: game, set and match to the master.

She might have known.

Intercepts from Berlin, earlier in the year, had begun to reveal uranium shipment details – East Germany being currently the largest Soviet provider, while Prime Minister Bulganin's public announcements had hinted at nuclear tests under way in Siberia. It was all part of Red paranoia regarding Western intent, said Rupert, and Eden's intransigence over Suez was likely to trigger World War III.

'We desperately need more info,' he told Gavriela, 'but with Stopwatch/Gold all over the papers, our chaps are having to lie low.'

And this, he went on, was where it fitted Gavriela's personal interest. Normally, a schoolgirl civilian wanting to defect meant nothing to UK interests; but the dissatisfied daughter of a senior KGB officer with responsibility for the security of East Germany's uranium mines, that was something else.

'Her name is Ursula,' he said. 'Ursula Shtemenko, and at this stage we don't know if she's aware her birth certificate reads Ursula Wolf.'

Up until April, Operation Stopwatch, an SIS brainchild but funded by the CIA who called it Operation Gold, had delivered priceless intelligence. But four days after the Crabbe operation – and before his body appeared – somehow the Soviets had found the secret tunnel between Schönefelder Chaussee and Rudow, filled with telephonic equipment for eavesdropping on KGB signals; and the world's press went crazy: a propaganda coup for Moscow.

Gavriela wondered if Philby had had anything to do with the tunnel, but knew better than to ask.

'I've photographs of the girl.' Rupert drew an envelope from inside his jacket, and passed it over. 'Taken since she made her first enquiry.'

Exactly where that was, Gavriela would find out when she agreed to the operation; but they both knew she was unlikely to back out, having learnt this much. None of the pictures were posed. Clandestine surveillance, then.

'Identical to my brother Erik, near enough,' she said. 'And Ilse?'

There was no need to explain who she meant: Rupert would have briefed himself beforehand on her family, on her brother Erik and on Ilse, the wife whom Erik adored.

'Passed away six months ago, I'm afraid. Another trigger for Ursula's current crisis.'

Gavriela leant back against the couch, resting her head on the antimacassar.

'One more factor for us to take advantage of, is that, Rupert?'

But of course, he had a counter-argument ready, probably cooked up days ago.

'You think she's better off with Dmitri Shtemenko as her stepfather?'

Gavriela let out a sigh, and asked him to brief her on the details.

Two hours later she was walking home through a damp grey pea-souper fog, inured by frequent exposure to the airborne tang of sulphur dioxide, wondering why she had agreed to help, while knowing there was no other choice. There was evidence she had worked hard to confirm that Erik had been a slave at Peenemünde, almost certainly starved and worked to death on one of the projects headed by Werner von Braun, now sunning himself in Florida and raking in the big bucks from NASA, never mentioning the doodlebugs and V2 rockets that had devastated British cities, bringing fear and death to civilian adults, children and their pets.

So now there was Ursula Wolf, who called herself Ursula Shtemenko, asking someone on the British Council, at an artists' event in East Berlin, for help in defecting. Did she really have access to her stepfather's information? Or did Dmitri plan on using Ursula as leverage against one Gavriela Wolf? He might believe that Gavriela-turned-Gabrielle was an intelligence officer still; and even if he knew she was retired, there were secrets worth pulling from her brain.

What if the real game were Dmitri versus Rupert, while everything else was context?

Berlin beckoned, regardless.

EIGHTEEN

Realspace, where every one of the countless points of light-against-darkness may be a distant star, an even more distant galaxy, a cluster or an ancient supercluster beyond a cosmic void. The photons that convey this information have travelled for up to thirteen point seven billion years without experiencing the passing of a moment – it is only those photons that reach non-vacuum media, such as human-built windows, that slow down and experience the march of time.

Here floats an Earth-like world, large for its type, its purple-grey continents strewn with clouds, showing no sign – save for some near-deserted orbitals – of the humans carving out a new society in strata below the cheerless surface. They call it Nulapeiron, the name implying boundlessness, with a paradoxical irony typical of the human culture's designers, for the dwellings are subterranean.

And now a golden ship appears, banded with cobalt blue, polished and magnificent.

We're here.

Another new world, my love.

Yes.

Rhianna Chiang disengages from her ship, wanting to review her briefing material before descending to the surface; and it is that decision which will account for the deciseconds-long delay reacting to movement on the periphery of her ship's senses.

In a tenth of a second, everything can change.

Shortly, she will discover that.

Before the disaster occurs, she will have time to display only a first-facet projection of her briefing material:

LANGUAGES: Plentiful.

In the four centuries that Nulapeiron has been inhabited, deliberate design has prevented single-language monopolies (cf. Whorf-Sapir hypothesis and the Web Mand'rin Catastrophe) from jeopardising cognitive-*Weltanschauung* diversity. Only one of the major language groups is fully artificial, the others deriving from recognised Terran antecedents.

ECOSYSTEM: Constrained.

In the lower strata, light and oxygen are provided by force-evolved fluorofungus, which is plentiful. The foundation of habitable-area ecology is imported autotrophic bacteria; in a real sense, the planet's native lifeforms exist outside the human demesnes and realms, especially upon the surface.

ARCHITECTURE: Deliberate.

The aristocracy's subterranean palaces in the upper strata are a far cry from the habitation tunnels of the lower strata. Note that various leitmotifs are global, cf. the use of simple hangings to form walls and doorways in dormitory tunnels, contrasted with the wall membranes of well-to-do dwellings; likewise the use of fluorofungus compared to soft-luminescence smartmarble.

EDUCATION: Encouraged.

Despite the deliberate creation of an aristocracy (justified by the Founding Lords with reference to the controversial emergent élites doctrine as being inevitable therefore requiring optimisation), education is available in the poorer (lower) strata, while educational content is monitored and censored. The use of logotropes as femtoscopic drug-like treatments form an approach in contrast to that of the Fulgor education system designed by LuxPrime, and may (among the aristocracy at least) surpass it.

ARISTOCRACY: Powerful.

While the power structures are amenable to normal sociological deconstruction, note that the *soi-disant* Logic Lords and Ladies almost invariably possess superior intellects by virtue of their intensive training in the all-purpose academic discipline of <u>logosophy</u>.

Ethico-cognitive modelling by Admiralty analysts notes that the presence of repressive social elements, including <u>slavery</u>, occasional employment of <u>cyborgs</u> and a pitiless <u>legal system</u>, may be overlooked by future historians if the integration of all academic disciplines (including philosophy-as-science) in <u>logosophy</u> matures as promised.

There are three points of movement. The moment is now.

Ships.

What—?

Zajinet ships.

All briefing notes are forgotten as Rhianna slams downward into emergency trance, the kind that produces physical after-effects due to shocking suddenness, irrelevant unless the Pilot survives; but these vessels are closing fast, and ship-and-Rhianna experience a hull-tingling resonance of powered-up weapon systems: the attack is imminent and movement is necessary *now*.

They corkscrew away but something tears into their left wing – *bastards!* – as their own weapons come online, pulsing with build-up – *there* – and they cut loose with their beams, Rhianna-and-ship; and the first of the attackers explodes – *die, you fucker* – but the others are swerving and two more beams lance towards them, and the second hits – *damn damn damn* – as ship-and-Rhianna fling themselves through another evasion, firing at another of the Zajinets and hitting it – *good* – and then the last – *all dead* – but not before more pain blossoms in their hull and then they are—

I love you.

I've always loved you.

—falling.

Rhianna has killed the Zajinets, and they have killed her. She screams as reality explodes and a fragment is flung away – the fragment that is her – tearing her mind so that the smartgel and extruding stubby wings mean nothing, because everything is over.

It happened so very, very fast ...

Dying now.

But that is not the tragedy.

'—be all right if we—'

Fragments impinge on the awareness that was human, that was Pilot once.

Man, bearded.

Images like shards.

Hurts ...

Pain. Oceanic pain.

Beads of computation in sequences, in threads, in damaged processes.

Diagnostic: *livelock-free – achieved.*

Such agony, the negentropy of working things out, of logic activated.

Diagnostic: *deadlock-free – achieved.*

Reality flickers.

'Activating you now.'

Steadies.

'I am Duke Avernon.' The bearded man produces acoustic vibration to be parsed and rendered into semantic-analytic components for matching. 'You're alive again.'

Tonal analysis estimates likelihood of irony at 27 per cent.

'It's been a standard year since the crash, Pilot.'

Self-model indicates send-signal capacity is 30:70 vision:speech.

Ambulatory capacity equals zero.

Tracking facial analytic vectors now. Mood-model reference Avernon constructed.

Smile arc $\Delta\theta \approx 11.7°$

Intent.Interpretation = tactic::rapport-attempt.

'I don't know your name, Pilot,' Duke Avernon continues. 'What is it? You can speak, by the way.'

OutstreamConnection.status = 100 per cent confirmed

Internal.Ident.Label = Rhianna_Chiang

Internal.Ident.Label.status = unsatisfactory

'I've had to reconstruct … Well, everything, Pilot. But this is life, trust me. Now tell me your name.'

The thing that was Rhianna Chiang tests its output channel.

'Nnnname …'

'All right, if you need time. Let me show you what you look like. Here's a mirror holo.'

ImageField.hasAttribute(contains face) = true

Eye-like mouth-like components present OK.

Remainder is [Adjectival.Query(Topology.Similar) = *splayed*]; attitude is vertical.

'Ah, so I won't need to reinitialise you this time. Very good.'

It is no longer Rhianna; no longer Pilot; no longer human, the construct embedded in the wall.

Self.Status =

Self.Status =

Self.Status =

timeouttimeouttimeouttimeou—

ThreadEndInterrupt

Self.Status = pending

'My.'

Let n:Name = Concept.heuristicMatch('one who knows')

'Name.'

Result n = null

Retry n = Concept.heuristicMatch('one who knows', RadixContext.ancestor_languages)

'Is …'

Internal.Ident.setLabel(n)

Self.Status = activated

'…Kenna.'

Two thousand eight hundred milliseconds pass.

'Repeat that, please.'
SpeechBuffer.replay( )
'My. Name. Is. Kenna.'

NINETEEN

LUNA, 601000 AD

Kenna sat between the empty high-backed seat reserved for Ulfr – unoccupied these past hundred millennia – and the one occupied by Sharp, his crystalline antlers shimmering with reflected light. Before them hung a many-dimensioned strategy model, which from time to time they altered, and returned to meditating on. Meanwhile, at the far end of the hall, Roger and Gavriela were wielding refined crystal blades, testing new designs, their cuts leaving glimmers of gamma radiation in the vacuum.

Only zero-point energy could affect the darkness directly, but there were many aspects to warfare, and more than one kind of enemy.

It was an ordinary lunar day, until the moment a sapphire blue glow began to manifest near the geometric centre of the hall. Kenna dismissed the model and strode forward, while Roger and Gavriela stood with blades ready. Sharp remained where he was.

A crystal humanoid stepped out of the light.

No one moved.

The newcomer's face rippled in something like a smile.

—*Fascinating. I'm so glad I returned to the old solar system. Nearly passed right by, you know.*

Once upon a time, this base had been hidden. Now its great buttresses and many balconies glinted against the lunar landscape. Being open necessarily meant being defensible, and so their fortress was; but Kenna believed the stranger was no enemy.

—*Greetings, sir. My name is Kenna.*

121

—And greetings to yourself. How very interesting. You have modern forms, not too different from my own, yet you are individually very old, every one of you. Archaic, even.

Call it a form of first contact.

For so long, they had cast their plans and made their preparations without dealing with wider humanity and their descendants. Ragnarökkr could, if necessary, be fought in the future using only resources from the past and the things that Kenna and the others constructed; but what if they could find allies among the newer peoples?

She was about to say as much when the newcomer added:

—Ancestral humans and Haxigoji. Brachiating primates. And you still use names?

Kenna felt something akin to a stab of rage, immediately deconstructed and brought under control. This New Man sneered out of fear, his superiority an illusion. The blades, she thought, made him uneasy.

—If you had a name, sir, what would it be?

The man stared at the shields and weapons decorating the hall, then back at her.

—Why, then. Call me Magni.

Kenna bowed her head. He had processed the linguistic/cultural history implied by her name very fast indeed, given how ancient that knowledge was: the tongue known as *Norræna* was over half a million years dead.

—Welcome, good Magni. You understand why we prepare to fight?

To his pacifist eyes, she suspected, these were disturbingly martial surroundings. Surely, though, Magni and his contemporaries knew what was coming eventually.

—I understand why, Lady Kenna, in half a million years, it would be a good idea to have fled this galaxy. You've achieved modern bodies. Why not travel, and see the cosmos?

—You know why. If people always flee, eventually every galaxy will fall.

Magni shrugged in a very human way.

122

—Everything dies finally. We've already left the homeworld behind.

—Yes, you have.

Magni looked surprised, correctly reading the undertones in her words.

—And you're making use of it?

—Did you think an army could consist of four individuals? Kenna smiled. *We will be billions when the time is right. And welcoming to our allies.*

For nearly six hundred millennia, she had been refining logosophical models, and there were some she could have deployed now as a form of persuasive rhetoric: those that showed how evolutionary strategies based on fleeing invariably led to an impoverished state, and finally extinction. But Magni would dismiss them as relevant only to others, not to his refined self.

—I really don't think so.

Magni raised his hand, a languid salute to Roger, Gavriela and Sharp, then spun on one heel, turning the gesture into a geometric rotation cloaked with sapphire light. For a second it glowed; then the light and Magni were gone.

Roger was the first to comment.

—If that's how the children turned out, I'm not impressed.

—They've tried communicating with the darkness. Gavriela was looking where Magni had stood. *You can tell they've tried and failed.*

Sharp's antlers swung as he shook his head: once a purely human gesture, now natural for him as well.

—Tried and died, I think.

It confirmed what they had predicted. But there was more to think about: the advances of contemporary humanity, apparently negated by fatalism, to judge by Magni's rejection of fighting at Ragnarökkr. After a moment, Gavriela gestured towards Ulfr's empty seat.

—Being civilised is not what's going to save us. The further back you go, the truer the warrior.

—We can't force his return. Kenna raised her palms. *You know that.*

Roger and Sharp commented together, a form of resonance occurring ever more frequently as the millennia passed:

—Our preparations are the same, regardless.

—They are indeed. Kenna inclined her head.

—So I'll check the body-halls. Roger's face looked like diamond. *It's time to speed up the growth.*

—It is that, agreed Kenna.

Roger teleported out of the hall.

TWENTY

Christmas was coming and the weather was hot. It might be the northern hemisphere, but this was California, which made its own rules. Lucas was bemused because the only snow in sight was polystyrene in window displays. Thanksgiving (which he mockingly celebrated as Bloody Ungrateful Day) had been spent at Brody's place. Amy had cooked and Jacqui had helped, because one of the things the half-brothers had in common was culinary ineptitude.

'I know two full sisters with thirty years difference between their birth dates,' Amy had said, 'so I suppose it's not that weird for you guys. With different mothers and all.'

It was not so much the age gap as the fact of Brody's existence that still astounded Lucas. And the way that Brody had known their grandmother in her later years, while all Lucas had experienced was strange letters from the past, from before he was born.

'We should have a cousin, at least one,' Brody had said. 'But something happened, something Gran didn't want to discuss. I'm not sure what it was.'

With three weeks to go before Christmas, Lucas had invited Brody and Amy to spend the weekend with him and Jacqui. They would go out for dinner later – the table at Laughing Benny's was booked – while for now they loafed on soft couches in the lounge, with dishes of pretzels, nuts and chips on the coffee table, and beers in progress all round.

Half asleep, Amy called up a display on her qPad.

'A cousin called what, surname-wise?' she said. 'Wolf, Woods or Gould?'

125

'No,' said Brody. 'It was Russian, or do I mean Ukrainian? Shimenko.'

A list of results came up, and Amy shook her head. 'Too much, too vague.'

'Yeah.' Lucas pointed his qPad at the big wallscreen, popping up a games menu. 'What do you fancy, guys?'

'Narrow it down by cross-links,' Jacqui told Amy. 'Related to Woods, then whatever else you can think of.'

A new list came up and Amy shrugged.

'Still a bit too much. I'll try again later, maybe.'

'3-D go, Viking Rampage or CyberTrivia,' prompted Lucas. 'What do you think?'

'Shtemenko,' said Brody, sitting upright.

'Do what?'

'That was the name.' Brody grinned at Amy. 'I remember.'

'There's still quite a few—Oh, wait.'

Lucas stopped on the verge of selecting Viking Rampage. 'What have you found?'

'Something right up your alley.' Amy gestured at the wallscreen. 'Can I?'

'Er, sure.'

What appeared on the screen was the beginning of a scientific paper, the body of its content available for a reasonable price.

AN ANALYSIS OF LEAKED GAMMA-RAY BURSTER EVENT DATA: PROVENANCE AND INTERPRETATION

Barabanshchikova, I.V., Rukovskaya, A.V., Shtemenko, L.A., Fedotova, L.L., Khudorzkina, M.G., Putyatin, A.S., Luzhkov, V.I., Wang, J., and Yagudin, I.G.

Abstract: Following the release of cosmological event observations into the public domain in Arxiv-compliant format, we present a forensic analysis of the data provenance that suggests a high probability ($\approx$97%) of authenticity. In addition, we present Fourier analysis and distance-estimating results based on known type-luminosity correlations to give a best estimate of the event's origin, assuming the authenticity of the data. We conclude that the origin lies at a distance of 420 **MLY** from Earth, beyond a cosmic void located in the direction of the galactic anti-centre. The authors are aware of the importance of further verifying the observational data.

'Holy shit,' said Lucas.

The others looked at him. He had shared something of the events that led to his meeting Gus in the lab at night and sending a graphene memory flake into mu-space, but not everything.

'The gamma-ray burster event.' Brody tapped his qPad. 'If this is our cousin, he's got similar interests to you, Lucas.'

Amy had searched for intersections between Lucas's work and the unknown Shtemenko's.

'And there *she* is,' Brody added, causing a secondary window to pop up on the wallscreen. 'How do you pronounce that?'

Lucas was about to attempt sounding out the Cyrillic – it read **Людмила Артуровна Штеменко** – though his Russian vocabulary was zero, but Brody tapped again, replacing the words with **Ludmila Arturovna Shtemenko.**

'Moscow University,' said Jacqui. 'How about that? Another physicist in the family.'

Amy pulled up her knees and leant sideways on the couch towards Jacqui. 'You've not been on vacation with Lucas yet, have you? Since moving in, I mean.'

Lucas blinked.

'Why, no,' said Jacqui. 'Do you think Moscow is pretty this time of year?'

'It's December,' said Brody. 'Are you kidding? It's bloody freezing.'

'Er ...' Lucas gestured at Brody and Amy. 'I thought we'd spend Christmas hanging with these guys.'

Jacqui nodded, solemnity in everything but her eyes, which danced. 'So we'd better fly back before then.'

Lucas looked at Brody, who laughed.

'*Touché*, Lucas, *mon frère*.'

'Bring us back some of those dolls,' said Amy.

'And vodka.' Brody waved his beer. 'Definitely vodka.'

Lucas rubbed his eyes.

Their hotel was not what they had expected: heavy on the dark wooden furnishings, including thick doors that slid open rather than swung, and the twin beds were laid end-to-end along one wall, like bunks in a submarine, instead of side by side. In the hotel coffee shop – something familiar, they thought – when Lucas bit into his jam-and-cream scone, he nearly spat it onto Jacqui in reaction to the shock of salt and fish.

'What the—?'

'Oh,' said Jacqui. 'It's red caviar, not strawberries.'

'Holy bleeding crap.'

He wiped his mouth with a paper serviette, and pushed the plate aside.

'It's fun, Lucas. New culture. Exotic details you'd never learn by staying at home and reading.'

'Ugh, right.' He swigged coffee to get rid of the taste. 'Are you sure you're American?'

Jacqui kicked his shin under the table, but gently.

'You are a bad person, Lucas Woods.'

'Yes, ma'am.'

The wide, traffic-choked boulevards were Paris writ large. Lucas and Jacqui wandered the city, used the famous Metro with the palatial marble-lined stations, saw Red Square and St Basil's Cathedral, found nothing much to look at in the Cultural Park that was also Gorky Park – Lucas had thought they were different places – and had dinner at the hotel, took NoLag tablets and went to sleep.

Next day, feeling odd from the travellers' medication, they took a taxi to the Sparrow Hills north of the city proper. Their appointment was at ten, and without the meds they would not have been awake at that time; but Lucas regretted taking the stuff until they were standing in clean cold air at the campus: suddenly he felt great.

Moscow University looked the way it should: neo-Baroque and magnificent, rearing above a snow-covered plaza that overlooked the curving river and the spreading city beyond.

'I'm glad I thought of coming here,' said Lucas.

'Yes, dear,' said Jacqui.

Their qPads worked with the campus systems, directing them to Astrophysics, along a corridor that led to a small office with one of those heavy doors on runners. As they approached, it slid open and a black-haired woman looked out.

'Ludmila Shtemenko,' she said. 'How do you do.'

'Lucas Woods, and this is Jacqui Khan.'

They shook hands and went inside, where his putative cousin poured them tea from a pot – Lucas was disappointed by the absence of a samovar – and handed over the steaming glasses.

'Please call me Ludmila Arturovna.' She smiled. 'Is what colleagues do.'

'Your father Artur,' said Jacqui, 'was Lucas's uncle, though they never met. Sorry I don't know your father's patronymic.'

Lucas shrugged, not knowing how to cope with this cross-cultural minefield. From his cousin's frown, they might have offended her – or she might just be concentrating on the English words. He was a monoglot, and embarrassed by it.

'Perhaps,' said Ludmila Arturovna, 'you should call me Luda. And I call you Luke and Jacqui, OK? If we are family.'

No one had ever addressed Lucas as Luke.

'OK,' he said.

Before coming, they had chatted online about the possible family connection, and a bit about their respective jobs. Now they went over the same ground in person, as a form of reassurance, growing used to each other.

'Have you finished tea?' asked Luda finally. 'I show you laboratories.'

They poked around offices and cluttered labs with wire tangles everywhere, including the industrial-looking cryogenics area devoted to solid state research.

'I was with Professor Zbruev' – Luda dropped her voice as they neared one of the cryo chambers – 'when gamma-ray burster event occurred. Interesting to see if you—Ah, there he is.'

Zbruev was an ordinary shaven-headed man in rumpled clothes – but Jacqui clutched Lucas's arm and muttered: 'Let's go past.'

'So,' said Luda.

They ignored the remaining labs, and used a fire exit to walk outside into the snow.

'Luke is my cousin,' Luda went on. 'But *you* saw it, Jacqui, no?'

Jacqui reached down, scooped up a little fresh snow, and rubbed her face with it.

'Lucas had a girlfriend once,' she told Luda, 'who was just like Zbruev. Nasty bitch.'

'Nasty ...? Ah, I understand.' Luda looked at Lucas. 'You did not see lovely darkness?'

'Lovely?' said Jacqui.

'Is ... strong attractive, you understand?'

'Alluring,' said Jacqui. 'You have to fight it.'

'Yes.'

Lucas shivered, disoriented and wondering how much the meds had to do with this conversation. On the rare occasion Jacqui had raised the subject of dark auras, she said they repelled her. Luda's reaction was different.

'But you *do* fight it,' said Jacqui. 'That's the main thing.'

Tears sprang out in Luda's eyes. 'I am so glad you are here.'

'Me too.' Jacqui touched her arm. 'We know we're not alone. What we see is real.'

'Oh, I know is real. Always.'

Something in her voice broke Lucas's heart.

Darkness fell, and they were still talking, but indoors. From the students' union – if Lucas understood Luda's description correctly – they moved to a faculty common room, and stayed until seven p.m. Now, besides night workers like cleaners, there was still a small number of people around, some carrying out research that for one reason or another was best done at night.

But Lucas, Jacqui and Luda were able to move around the corridors in the main physics block without seeing anyone. The room they ended up in was cluttered with SQUID scanners and atomic magnetometers; and to one side stood a glass-fronted cabinet, locked for the night, with shelves of items waiting to be analysed.

'From archaeology.' Luda pointed into the cabinet. 'Found in grandfather's, um, belongings when he died. FSB gave to Professor Zbruev's department. Mother knew about crystal, but story was bitter. I don't know details. Is very old,' she added. 'Centuries. Looks new.'

The object was crystalline but shaped like a spearhead.

'Belongs in a museum,' said Jacqui.

But Luda was lost in thought.

'Grandfather told Mother, crystal was best thing to come from London, apart from Mother. Made Mother angry. I do not know why.' Then she shrugged. 'Had something else, FSB not know. Stayed in family. Also old, from Siberia. My grandfather found old site, kept piece no one knew about.'

Luda dug inside her pocket, and pulled out a metal shard. Then she held it close to the glass.

'Holy crap,' said Lucas.

Red fluorescence brightened inside the spearhead: sharp lines forming what looked a symbol:

ᛏ

Then Luda tugged at his arm, pulling him 90 degrees to one side. The upper 'branch' was hidden by the change in angle, while orthogonal lower 'branches' were revealed:

ᛉ

'That's not natural,' said Lucas. 'Really not natural.'

'Pattern in crystal. Like two *futhark*s superimposed.' Luda gestured with the metal shard, and the red lines grew brighter. 'Runes, you understand?'

Jacqui pulled out her qPad and searched.

'Alternate runic alphabets,' she said. 'They sort of coexisted, and mingled.'

'Coincidence.' Lucas could not believe how far they were pushing this. 'Fracture lines of some kind.'

'Energy comes from where?' Luda stepped back, taking the metal shard with her, and the red fluorescence dimmed to almost nothing. 'See?'

She pushed the metal inside her pocket.

'One hour, we meet my friend,' she added. 'Important. All of us, OK?'

Lucas looked at Jacqui. On one level, they were here on holiday, long-lost family members a side issue, and never mind dark auras. But this ...

It seemed like fantasy, but last year's cyberattack that took out the gamma-ray burster data around the globe, that had been real and had originated from somewhere. Perhaps from the country that pioneered clandestine cyberwarfare, while allowing everyone else to think China went first.

He wondered how many of the academics here were sponsored by the FSB.

They trudged along paths in the snow to a tram platform,

and rode the thing into the city. There they changed twice and ended up in a wide dark street, where a blank door led downwards into a cellar-level nightclub with primary-colour spotlights whirling and music throbbing. They found seats in a darkened booth. Lucas fetched four vodkas from the bar, because of the friend they were due to meet, and when he returned to the table, the guy was already there.

He was overweight and heavily bearded, and placing a small wrapped package on the tabletop.

What the hell are we mixed up in?

Conspiracies abroad. FSB. Dark auras and museum trinkets. Anti-jetlag meds that messed with your head.

Some holiday.

Unwrapped, the package contained a crystal spearhead, its dimensions the same as the sample back at the university. The nameless friend rewrapped it and slid it to Luda, who tapped her qPad – she had already logged in to her bank account – and thanked him.

They exchanged farewells in Russian, and the guy left.

'We leave something behind,' said Luda, raising her vodka, 'when we steal original. Is *duplicate*, right? Ordinary quartz.'

'When we—?'

'And you smuggle out of country, dear cousin.'

'That's insane,' said Lucas.

'You can count on us,' said Jacqui.

Truly insane, except that he had known, from the moment he saw the red fluorescence, that he was meant to safeguard the crystal, for some purpose he might never know, besides keeping the woman he loved happy, not to mention his new-found cousin and their shared synaesthetic ... experiences. Whatever. Right now, he planned to keep on drinking vodka until things made sense or he stopped caring; but when it came to paranoid-schizophrenic conspiracies, one thing was already clear.

He would have to stop blaming the meds.

*

They flew back next to a couple called Gerald and Virginia (call me Ginny) Hawke, two aerospace engineers in the process of moving from Seattle to Los Angeles, Gerald to take up a teaching position at UCLA and Ginny – 'for the time being' – to be a mother: the swelling of her abdomen was scarcely visible.

The meds or forgetfulness must have affected birth-control measures as well as rational thought, because the following autumn, Jacqui would produce a daughter just two months after the Hawkes produced their son. They would become friends, and their children would go to school together; and there would often be joint celebrations at Brody and Amy's place, Thanksgiving included.

From time to time across the years, Lucas would experience an unfocused feeling, a notion that he was obliged to send the crystal spearhead into the future, just as he had the graphene flake. It was not until the birth of his and Jacqui's first grandchild, when he decided it was time finally to write a will and work out who should own the crystal when he was gone, that he realised he *was* carrying the thing forward, at the same rate that everyone else in the world was engaged in time travel.

One minute per minute, one day at a time.

TWENTY-ONE

Labyrinth was the link, Roger realised, as he and his wonderful ship burst into realspace in the vicinity of his destination, Vachss Station. He had time to spare before contacting the orbital became mandatory. At this distance, it would not challenge him for ten minutes: that was protocol, though one in need of revision, given the existence and unknown intentions of Schenck and his renegade Pilot fleet.

Roger allowed himself to drift in a disjunctive trance, having released conjunction with his beloved ship, needing to think by himself.

It has to be Labyrinth.

The city-world itself, when he had been granted a day's leave from Tangleknot, had prompted him to visit the Logos Library, where Ro McNamara had granted him insight into past events unknown to all but the most dedicated history scholars. And his beautiful ship was grown parthenogenetically with Labyrinth's connivance, heir to his father's ship but not identical to it, with latent memories only just becoming accessible to Roger now that he-and-ship were far from home, on their first operational mission.

He had access to knowledge that no one would expect him to have, giving him a different perspective on the events he was caught up in – a perspective predisposing him to take action, he assumed, in ways that Labyrinth itself would approve of.

Perhaps it was the clearly benign nature of the city-world that made questioning its purpose seem pointless; or perhaps even Pilotkind possessed mental blindspots.

135

Whether this trip had hidden objectives or was simply the jaunt it appeared to be – Jed was clearly not guilty of the original charges, and the Vachss Station authorities just needed to complete the formalities and release him into another Pilot's temporary, nominal care – he would try to work out later. For now, it was the newly uncovered secret memories that occupied his attention.

The first sequence of Dad's memory had come to Roger shortly after leaving Labyrinth, as he-and-ship entered the violet-edged vastness that was Spiderblood Drift.

sequence [[[
Fear and hysteria, laughing and crying as he drifts in blazing space amid a billion suns, a thin quickglass suit protecting him from vacuum, while he is overwhelmed by the beauty of the galactic core.

Oh, my love. I've missed you.

She is coming, he knows.

My name is Carl Blackstone, and I'm alive!

It is the desperate presumption of a mote, the ego struggling to maintain existence within transcendent immensity, as he revolves and the thousand-lightyear needle comes into view, the jet spurting from the galaxy's heart, the first time any Pilot or human has seen the thing with a chance of reporting back on its existence.

Everyone else witnessing the jet has been suborned by the darkness.

Or they have died.
]]]

It had been a disconcerting memory-flash, a prelude to a detailed remembrance of events happening to his father ten subjective days before he was set adrift to die.

sequence [[[
Fairwell Rotunda, one of the lobbies within the thirteen-deck

structure: that is the rendezvous point. Carl Blackstone watches several tourists admire the deep-orange quickglass opulence, but by the standards of Pneumos City this is something of a dive: the visitors just aren't used to Molsin's superior standards.

He likes this world.

Churchgoers are celebrating a quiet ceremony – most likely praying for a safe voyage – in a small group in the corner. Their foreheads are tattooed with three glistening dots that form an equilateral triangle enclosing a golden symbol: γ. This is the five hundred and seventh anniversary, according to his tu-ring, of the mythical event that eventually produced the Church of Equilateral Redemption, a cult so small that Carl is surprised to find the knowledge-base entry.

A woman walks over, presumably Xala, his contact. Her head is shaven, sporting motile tattoos.

'Devlin Cantrelle?' she asks.

'That's, er, me.' Carl allows nerves to surface in his voice. 'Looking to buy—'

'Passage to Nerokal Tertius.' Smart-ink unicorns slide across her scalp. 'The xeno ruins. And you're a teacher with Gregor TechNet.'

'How—? Yes.'

Xala's smartlenses grow opaque, then clear.

'Orbital ascent in fifty minutes.'

'You're travelling too?' asks Carl.

The others are a family with defeated-looking eyes, a group of dark-suited, hard-faced men playing virtual cards around a table, and a seventh man, scar-heavy, with callused knuckles.

'Along with them.' She gestures towards the hard men. 'The priests.'

'Priests,' says Carl.

'We don't pry into reasons. Not even yours, Mr Cantrelle.'

'Um, right. Yes.'

He has already paid for the trip by clandestine transfer. There was always a chance she would simply not turn up; but it looks as though the offer might be real, at least up to a point.

The Admiralty Council has, for good security reasons, placed a strict embargo on Nerokal Tertius. So a black-market outfit offering trips to that location implies one of several possibilities, none of which can be legitimate.

Hence his presence here.

The people in the lobby stir as a presence enters, and the shock makes Carl want to throw up, because she can *not* be here: it is not possible. Not her.

Lianna Kaufmann was the person he loved, or possibly just worshipped when he was a neophyte, a Pilot Candidate who ostensibly became one of the Shipless during Graduation, while secretly gaining a red-trimmed black vessel with more power and manoeuvrability than he had thought possible. He had been recruited by Max Gould himself while still at the Academy, well in advance of that shaming public ceremony when Lianna saw Carl Blackstone apparently failing to gain any ship at all.

She is wearing a black, gold-edged cape with her black jump-suit. Old school and formal. But there is no time to wonder what she is doing here, because if she sees him the operation is blown. He gestures to the quickglass with the gotta-pee sign (as it's usually known), and as the chamber opens, he tumbles inside. It seals up fast.

Before she glimpsed him, he thinks.

His tu-ring hides him from internal surveillance – unless Lianna's tu-ring has similar capabilities, he is now hidden from her. It also renders a section of the wall transparent, one-way, so he can see what Lianna does next.

Which is to point at a nervous-looking man and say: 'That's the one,' as proctors enter the room, raising weaponised gauntlets. The man tumbles to the floor unconscious. Lianna crouches down, running her hand along the suspect's clothing. 'There. And there, woven into the material.'

A smuggler.

When the proctors have bound him with glistening membrane, they place the prisoner on a frictionless slide-sheet and drag him away with ease, while their officer ceremonially thanks Lianna, who says: 'My pleasure, and I was happy to illustrate the point. So if we can return to the talks?'

'This way, Pilot.'

There is much conversation when they have left – not many people get to see a real Pilot, never mind like this – while blood begins to return to certain faces, including Xala's.

Lianna. Oh, Lianna.

Their friend Soo Lin used to say that strength means swallowing bitterness.

Concentrate.

'Five minutes to detachment, everyone,' announces Xala.

The fake priest with the scarred features and hardened knuckles approaches the small family group. 'Hey, kids. You looking forward to this?' And, as they shrink back: 'What are you looking at? Are you trying to insult me?'

It is a good time to slip out of a hiding-place, while no one is looking this way. Carl does so, then walks openly towards the man – mental label Scarface; unkind but that is not the point – to get his attention.

'You got a problem, my son?' asks Scarface.

'Er ... No.'

Then the cold, psychopath laugh.

'Three minutes,' says Xala in a low voice.

Soon enough – as seen through a holoview opened by Xala – the Rotunda they are in has detached from Pneumos City and is rising through gold-and-orange clouds, leaving the sky-city shrinking below. Among the family, the baby is crying and the parents look worried.

'Um, Miss ...' The father approaches Xala. 'We were wondering. I mean, about the Pilot for the journey. How does—?'

'Don't,' says Xala.

'I beg your pardon?'

'Don't wonder. Go back to your wife and children.'

'Oh,' says the man. 'Oh.'

Scarface calls over: 'Pretty daughters you have, old man.'

It is enough to drain the blood from the father's face and send him to his family, who shrink together as if for protection, really just for comfort. False comfort, tactically speaking.

For Carl to break cover might ruin the operation. If there really is an illegal mu-space voyage taking place, he needs to discover the same thing the father wanted to know: who or what will be flying the vessel. But there comes a point when mission integrity becomes secondary.

He will not allow Scarface to touch the children.

And there is the danger of mono-focus, because if he deals with Scarface then the six other hard men are likely to react. One of them, mental label Greybeard, has a carry-case at his feet that might contain anything, weaponry included. He will need to take them all down as well, while remaining alert to the third danger: that there is someone or something else here, a threat he has not identified. If that threat is automated, it might react in femtoseconds.

Blinking, he cranks up his tu-ring's weapon displays.

Hoping they will remain unused.

]]]

Roger checked: Vachss Station was still waiting for him to initiate approach procedures. He ought to do just that. But one more segment first, just one ...

sequence [[[

When the chamber reaches the edge of space beneath its vast extended balloon, impellers kick in and it rises higher, to Congregation Orbital where other ellipsoids like this one, balloons reabsorbed into their quickglass hulls, form a huge shoal, many linked by tendril-like tunnels, while others drift around the periphery, and a small number move alone, approaching or leaving the rest.

Off to one side floats a magnificent, unusual silver vessel, largely teardrop-shaped. Even if he had not seen it before, Carl would have known it for Lianna's ship, as distinctive as her personality. In the Academy she was consistently top of the class yet remained an individualist.

'Is that our ship, Daddy?'

'Shh. Maybe.'

No, child. Not for a flight to an embargoed world.

'Delta-bands all round.' Xala is handing out the strips. To the father: 'Children first, and then your own.'

'Shouldn't we wait until we're—?'

'Delta-bands now. It's a condition of travelling.'

Scarface calls over: 'No one's making us miss this flight.' He waits for the father to gulp before adding, 'See? Blessed are the fucking peacemakers, right?'

None of the hard-faced men disguised as priests show a reaction, not even a smirk. As potential threats, Carl scales them upwards once more. Amateurs use intimidation as a social game, professionals as a tool.

Then he has a delta-band in hand, given to him by Xala, while all around his fellow would-be passengers are settling on couches newly extruded from the quickglass deck. As they put their delta-bands on their foreheads and press the tiny studs, their eyelids flutter and they fall into deep, protective coma.

Lying there helpless against anyone left awake.

Time to choose.

He did not expect this, and it's another form of cut-off: to go along with the risk or blow the whole thing open, when he has not even seen the rogue mu-space vessel – assuming one exists.

Luckily, autohypnosis is a basic part of Labyrinthine education.

'Thank you,' he says to Xala, as if grateful. 'Press here?'

'That's right.'

He takes his time lying back on the couch and getting comfortable, while his internal voice talks his divided self through progressive relaxation with definite commands – *move your hand* – designed to kick in if he senses danger or ambient mu-space – *remember to move your hand* – before pressing the stud and falling backwards into sleep.

]]]

Roger shivered at the memory of risk, although it predated his own birth by more than a standard decade, therefore his father had clearly survived whatever followed. Only selective mindwipe had rendered those memories inaccessible to Carl, even when conjoined with his beloved ship, who retained these fragments in her own deep unconscious.

It was strange to immerse himself in his father's memories of Molsin, after his own experiences there last year.

sequence [[[

Golden sleep, and his hand is rising, reaching for the delta-band—

Coldness.

—and falls, as they drop straight away into realspace once more. Perhaps they were in mu-space for longer than it seems: perhaps it took time for the suggestion to kick in, to remove the band and come awake while the others slept.

He feels a hand on his forehead, and the delta-band comes off.

'—are we?' someone was saying.

It is the father of the family, Carl realises, squinting his way to wakefulness. They are in a cabin formed of something akin to flowmetal, but not a material used by Pilots.

A Zajinet ship. It was always a possibility.

But he had not intended to sleep in coma while surrounded

by wakened human criminals, never mind the Zajinet crew, and even the ship itself: Zajinet vessels are mystery.

'What kind of a ship is this?' asks someone.

'Ain't no kind of ship at all,' says one of the pseudo-priests. 'It's a robbery.'

Someone has already pocketed the funds paid in advance. Do the passengers really have anything worth stealing? Worth setting up a real voyage with Zajinets?

'No robbery,' says Xala. 'That's not it at all.'

Carl misinterpreted the hard man: it was not a threat but an assessment.

'We have a little problem,' Xala continues. 'Someone isn't who they claim to be.'

Oh, shit.

He feels the pulse behind his eyes, energy building up. His tu-ring is ready to cut loose.

'Someone's not quite human.' Xala nods to the nearest bulkhead. 'So they tell me.'

Zajinets could sense Pilots. Of course they could.

Ready.

But the chances of being able to fly a Zajinet vessel, even if he can take out the crew without causing damage to the ship, are minimal. And then there is the family, with children he will not allow to be harmed.

The fake priests are sitting up but saying nothing, analysing the situation.

All except one.

No!

Carl sees it now, the thing that the Zajinets must already have sensed: the shards of darkness, twisting. The sense of something deep and awful controlling what might once have been a normal man; or perhaps there had to be something odd about a person to render them vulnerable to such manipulation.

Greybeard.

It is stronger now, the darkness, as Greybeard stands amid

glimmering smartmist, ready to destroy everyone. For the sake of visible persuasion, he grabs Xala by the throat one-handed, while keeping hold of the carry-case he has had all along; but the smartmist is the deadly threat.

Carl should have seen this coming.

But the darkness …

It's a weird, faint phenomenon – and for now, irrelevant.

Everyone is holding still, Scarface included. Even Xala is not struggling, for the one-handed pinch-hold around her throat is to intimidate, not kill. Not yet.

'No need to speak, sweetheart,' Greybeard tells her. 'It's your weird-minded masters I'm talking to. You hear me, Zajinets?' Then, to Scarface and the other hard men: 'Change of plans. We're going to drop off the case all right' – he hefts it briefly, his other hand still firm against Xala's throat, fingers and thumb ready to pinch the larynx fatally shut – 'but not on Nerokal Tertius. And you bastards are not coming with me.'

As their faces tighten, Greybeard adds: 'You've already been paid, so nothing else matters. Check it now.'

There are glances exchanged and holovolumes opened, and nods among the hard men.

'I don't like threats,' says Scarface.

'Me neither,' answers Greybeard. 'But that doesn't— Oh, look. One of the xeno bastards is here.'

A section of wall is flowing open, revealing a shining scarlet lattice-form. On the deck lies a pile of what looks like blue sand. Zajinets clothe themselves in solid material, but perhaps they act more freely in their natural form.

Pretty much everything Carl knows about Zajinets is conjecture.

<<Darkness will not flee.>>
<<Weak agents so we do not care.>>
<<Strength in coherence.>>
<<Beware the light.>>

As a Zajinet communication it is typical, perhaps clearer than the average, but useless to Carl.

'I think you're bluffing.' Greybeard squeezes Xala. 'I think you care what happens to her.' He speaks as if he understands the Zajinet.

You know the lightning.

The words are a splinter of memory, from one of his Tangleknot instructors.

You know how fast it moves.

So often there have been misunderstandings and violence between Pilots and Zajinets, though it has never spilled over into protracted military engagements. Can they be allies here?

Xala's scalp tattoos are writhing in response to her agitation.

Become the lightning.

Then Greybeard's tu-ring shines, and the Zajinet's lattice-form jumps in the air and pulses – as if receiving a shock – before returning to its normal steady shine.

>> **<<Entanglement is mutual.>>**
>> **<<Beware beware beware.>>**
>> **<<Agree to projection.>>**
>> **<<Severance or mutual death.>>**

Carl holds back, tensing with the effort. The Zajinet is somehow entangled now with Greybeard's tu-ring. Any attack on Greybeard will injure the Zajinet also.

'Drop me off where I tell you,' says Greybeard. 'And I'll release the link and you go on your way, everyone safe and sound.'

He releases Xala. She slumps to the deck.

'Do the honours, will you?' Greybeard adds to Scarface. 'Delta-bands for everyone. We're flying onwards now.'

The Zajinet drifts out, ignoring the pile of blue sand on the deck.

'You don't look very scared.'

Shit.

Greybeard is addressing him.

'I-I'm scared.' The shake in his voice is easy to produce. 'Believe me.'

'Good.'

All around, Scarface is pressing people's delta-bands, sending them back into sleep. When everyone but he, Carl and Greybeard are under, Scarface says: 'You'll be last to activate the band, is that it? While we're helpless.'

'You've been paid and you're safe. If I needed to kill you, I could do it now.'

Scarface nods. 'All right.'

Greybeard and Scarface turn to look at Carl. He has no choice but to lie back, check the delta-band is snug on his forehead, and put his finger on the activation stud; but he does not press down. He hears the two men lie down, and senses the activation of their delta-bands; then he opens his eyes.

Transition.

It is like liquid amber filling the air: spacetime as it is meant to be, the fractal freedom that exhilarates. Carl swings himself off the couch and onto his feet.

He is in his element, but so is the Zajinet crew. Through the still-open doorway he finds a short corridor and follows it, entering a round windowless chamber where three Zajinets are floating. One is blue tinged with green; another is green tinged with blue.

The last Zajinet, a deep scarlet, shifts towards Carl.

<<Greetings, Pilot.>>
<<Greetings, Pilot.>>
<<Greetings, Pilot.>>
<<Greetings, Pilot.>>

'So you did recognise me.'

<<When you awoke, we knew.>>
<<When you awoke, we knew.>>
<<When you awoke, we knew.>>
<<When you awoke, we knew.>>

Carl has never heard of such clear unambiguous communication from a Zajinet. Most people would say it is impossible.

146

<<The darkness must not spread.>>
<<The darkness must not spread.>>
<<The darkness must not spread.>>
<<The darkness must not spread.>>

He has no idea how to assess the situation. The humans, Greybeard included, are helplessly asleep back in the hold; but this Zajinet is in some sense a prisoner, entangled with Greybeard's tu-ring.

<<Wake Xala.>>
<<Wake Xala.>>
<<Wake Xala.>>
<<Wake Xala.>>

The vessel shivers into realspace. In seconds, the delta-bands will power down automatically.

'Shit.'

Carl sprints back to the hold, leaps towards the unconscious Xala and tears the delta-band from her forehead. Kaleidoscopic colours swirl across her bare scalp before coalescing into maroon-and-silver dragons, scaled and fierce as they coil and slither.

'Ah, my head,' she moans. 'The case.'

'What?'

'Open his—'

'Got it.'

His tu-ring is working furiously, and the case pops open as his spyware succeeds in defeating its locks. Inside is a small, complex device about the size of Carl's fist. He has no idea what it might be. But Greybeard's closed eyes are shifting from side to side, moments from waking, so Carl abandons caution to reach inside, closes one hand around the device and—

What the hell?

—totally fails in his attempt to tug it upwards. It feels massive.

'—interacting with the darkness,' Xala is saying. 'They told me, the Zajinets.'

'What was that?'

He tugs, and perhaps it shifts slightly.

'We're just shadows. Ghosts,' says Xala. 'I mean because we're baryonic matter.'

'Yes, but that doesn't—'

Greybeard turns his head, eyes opening. 'Well, how about that?'

Too late.

'Where did this come from?' It is the most important thing for Carl to ask. 'Who made it?'

'No one alive,' says Greybeard. 'No one who's left any trace of their work.'

'Fuck you,' says Carl.

Because the implication is right there: no trace means zero survivors.

'Open up.' Greybeard swings his feet to the deck, takes the case one-handed – at his touch, it closes up around the device – and lifts it without effort. 'I mean the hull.'

His tu-ring sparks, and Carl senses a wild pulse of energy – the Zajinet equivalent of howling in pain – from the control cabin. After a moment, a large section of inner hull grows transparent, and Xala sucks in a breath; perhaps Carl does likewise.

It is a magnificence of stars, an incandescence of a billion suns.

'Where is this?' whispers Xala.

'Galactic core,' says Carl. 'The only place it can be.'

Greybeard's smartmiasma glitters deliberately, reminding them of the threat. Then he looks at the inner bulkhead to address the Zajinets, and raises his fist, emphasising the tu-ring.

'Detonation in thirty seconds.'

'No!' shouts Carl.

Greybeard turns and runs at the transparent hull which, liquefying, allows him to pass through and tumble into space. There is only one chance for Carl and that is to follow, sprinting hard before the hull can harden, throwing himself through – wetness sliding across his skin – and then stars are whirling as he tumbles over and over, trying to sight Greybeard – *there* – but the bastard is out of sight again because Carl's tumbling is chaotic, so hard to orient himself to—

A blaze of light marks the Zajinets' exit from realspace. The ship is gone.

Oh, you stupid bastards.

Thinking they could break the quantum entanglement by entering mu-space while Greybeard's tu-ring remains in this continuum.

Haven't you heard of a deadman switch?

Whatever Greybeard rigged up, it will have detonated the instant the Zajinet vessel entered mu-space.

Issue the command.

It is the voice of panic inside his head.

No. Too soon.

Panic because he cannot breathe and soon his blood will boil. His eyes are already bleeding, hence his stinging vision while the most magnificent sight of his life in realspace shies everywhere: the centre of the galaxy, where a billion suns are gathered.

There it is, the thing that had to be here: some kind of craft taking the figure of Greybeard aboard.

Wait.

Such an ache in his desperate lungs.

Can't—

Just wait.

Tumbling still.

Going?

It is hard to tell, with his smeared vision, whether the vessel is moving away.

Yes.

A flare and a spurt of motion, and it accelerates away, leaving him.

In the void, tumbling and dying.

Now?

It is a vast relief.

Yes, now.

He presses his tu-ring and it commands the quickglass, in emergency mode, to spread fast across his body. From the band around his waist, inside his clothes, it extends across everything, including his eyes – he has to fight against reflex to keep them open – and into his open mouth, forcing its way down into his lungs, painful and hard, or at least it feels that way – *shit* – and the pain increases – *shit shit shit* – before something wonderful happens and suddenly he feels euphoric.

Oxygen entering his bloodstream.

Fantastic.

Soon the hypoxia fades, but the euphoria remains, because he is floating in magnificence.

How many have seen what I'm seeing?

Well, more than one might expect, given that Greybeard had allies here: allies possessed of at least one ship and probably more, perhaps even permanent stations, and you had to wonder how they got here without assistance from Pilots. Were Zajinets involved?

Given their reaction to Greybeard, maybe not.

Pilots, then.

Helping ... whatever it was that manipulated Greybeard.

Tumbling still, but breathing and surviving.

Help me.

He understood the artificial link that Greybeard formed between his tu-ring and the Zajinet: that understanding had been immediate because of that other link, the one that Pilots did not talk about (other than perhaps the Shipless, who knew only theory, never the reality), the bond between Pilot and ship. They never discussed it because they did not need to. They knew how beautifully lucky they were.

Come now.

Knowing she has heard him.

Come to me, my love.

And is even now, black and scarlet-edged and powerful, soaring through golden space to reach him.

I love you.

Twenty-five thousand lightyears and transition between universes are not enough to keep them apart, and never will be.

Oh, my love.

Soon enough, she will come for him.

And they will be together, as they are meant to be.

As they will always be.

]]]

When Roger disengaged from the memory sequence, his face was chill, with cold tracks down his cheekbones left by evaporating tears.

I'll do my best, Dad.

To be half the man his father was: still his only real ambition, more than enough for a lifetime's work. Now, though, he was in realspace, with more immediate tasks to attend to.

'Vachss Station Control to Pilot. Are you status green?'

He wiped the back of his hand across his face.

'Pilot to Vachss Station Control. Status green, and commencing approach now, if you're willing.'

'Approach approved. We'll pour some daistral ready, Pilot.'

Roger smiled.

'I'll hold you to that.'

He immersed himself back in wonderful conjunction with his ship, and together, slowly, they moved towards the orbital, concentrating on the work, fulfilled by it. Worrying about Jed Goran and the legal niceties could wait: just manoeuvring to a docking-port was enough to occupy ship-and-Roger.

Call it Zen and the art of Piloting.

'Contact made, Pilot. Welcome to Vachss Station.'

'Thank you, Control.'

He sighed as he slipped out of conjunction trance.

Time to deal with people.

TWENTY-TWO

EARTH, 1956 AD

His daughter's outburst kept coming back to him: 'You're a monster.'

Not yet seventeen, yet so sure of herself, so willing to judge him.

Though she barely suspected the things he had done.

'*Du bist ein Ungeheuer*,' had been Ursula's exact words, and while she was in fact his stepdaughter and he was in truth a psychopath, according to the diagnostics described in KGB-approved psychology texts, Dmitri Shtemenko was hurt by her accusation. At least to the extent that he understood how words might wound an ordinary person.

'I haven't killed anyone for years,' he had told her.

It had been the wrong thing to say, but he had been distracted by the details of Ilse's funeral, the senior colleagues he would have to talk to and the opportunities that might be presented. Such tactical thinking separated him from the weak-minded, and he was normally efficient in hiding it; at the same time, he did have regret at Ilse's passing.

There would be a certain emptiness in his life, at least until he filled it.

It was in going through her mother's things, poking around the old shambling house they lived in – surrounded by fields, far from the tenements of the proles – that Ursula had stumbled upon the trail to the garden shed, the boxes buried beneath unused spades and forks, and sprung open the box containing finger bones. Another girl – he still could not think of her as a woman – might not have recognised the withered human digits, but Ursula was interested in both painting and biology, anatomy the intersection of the disciplines, and knew exactly what they were.

He should have denied ownership, of course.

Once before, during the Great Patriotic War, he had thrown away his little souvenirs before setting sail for Japan. For a long time he had felt little need to indulge himself, forcing himself to leave all evidence behind on those occasions when he gave in to overwhelming urge. Eventually, though, he had felt settled enough to return occasionally to his old ways.

'Give the box to me,' he had commanded. 'And say nothing of this. Do you understand, Ursula?'

Trembling, so that the box rattled as if containing dice, she handed it over.

'I understand.'

Cold loathing, so very adult, coated her voice. She was mature enough to understand what happened to anyone who crossed a KGB colonel; and a colonel with his proven homicidal background was even more dangerous than the rest. He felt a hint of paternal pride in her ability to assess risk during fraught times.

Alone now in his bare study, he opened another box on his desktop. Ursula had seen inside this one also, but had failed to sense anything special about the metal shard. As for Dmitri, he felt the stuff was strange, but possessed no means to analyse it further.

There had been other remnants for the research team to keep, and make sense of if they could. Somehow he thought they would fail.

For Dmitri, it was victory enough that he had brought it back from Siberia without his superiors' knowledge. Metallurgical analysis did not excite him. The only person he had showed it to was young Daniela at work: she was twenty-one years old, lean and angular with a cruel face that excited him to look at. He had not yet taken her as a lover, Lieutenant Daniela Weissmann, but he thought it would happen soon.

But his third and real treasure ... That was in the loft, and he was never sure what had called him to it, two years ago. People had been excited about the archaeological find in London, yet no else had sensed the presence of the buried crystal inside damp clay. Call it a gift of the darkness – except that no stirrings in his head accompanied his digging the thing out.

No commands from the darkness at all.

Perhaps his sensitivity to the crystal had simply been a side effect, nothing intentional or useful, of the dark power that corrupted him.

He remembered the thrill of sneaking past the guards, going down into the dig beneath the City, wondering what he was doing there. With his shielded torch, he had his own private viewing of a stone mask dating back to Londinium; but it was a blank wall of wet clay, the edge of one of the excavation pits, that had drawn him. Then the digging with fingers by torchlight, the slick-yet-sticky feel of the stuff, and the glint of crystal when he found it.

Crystal, shaped like a spearhead, and buried for centuries in London mud.

So precious, and yet he would never sell it.

Nor tell his KGB masters what he had found.

Of course, he had been in London for operational reasons. Going across to the West had kept him on edge; perhaps stealing an unsuspected archaeological find had been less dangerous than giving in to his other desires. A police manhunt might have made things awkward.

And what about Ursula?

He really did not want to think of her as a woman.

She is a problem, though, is she not?

Not as another potential victim.

Or would her screams be all the sweeter for their overtones of innocence betrayed?

Berlin, at least the Allied sectors, formed an island of western freedom in a Communist sea. But once there, for all the dangers if discovered and the recent tightening of access controls, it was relatively easy for Gavriela, with all the assets available to SIS, to slip into the Russian Sector.

Living in London, so different from the rest of Britain, made it natural to adopt the tough-humoured Berlinerisch attitude, and lose the hard *g* in words like Inge. Coats were even drabber than in England (Paris, on her holiday, had been a revelation), so she had dressed for the part, as had the two men forming her protective escort.

It was the 23rd of November, and freezing fog was everywhere.

The contact who met them at the safe house in Treptow, inside the Russian Sector and close to the black-looking waters of the Spree, was a grey-haired dour man who said: 'She's a schoolgirl, didn't you know? Not exactly prime defector material.'

'So what?' said Gavriela, a hard-edged *Ja, und?* 'It's not her we're interested in.'

'Got it.' His expression was one of grim camaraderie. 'She does a good job of hiding how scared she is.'

'Good.' Meaning both things: the fear and not showing it.

Likewise Gavriela's own fear, that things would go to hell and Carl would end up living with Rosie and Jack in Abingdon. But she pushed those thoughts aside as she climbed the bare wooden stairs, and entered a room whose floor was covered in cracked green lino, older but not so different from her kitchen back home.

Ursula was sitting on a plain wooden chair at a card table, wearing a grey cardigan and skirt, looking pale. The resemblance to Erik at that age sent a dagger into Gavriela.

'Who are you, please?' asked Ursula formally: *Wer sind Sie, bitte?*

Gavriela was not a field agent. If she had been, her answer would have been a conscious choice. 'I'm your aunt,' she said in German. 'Gavriela Wolf. I loved your mother Ilse like a sister.'

'You died—' Ursula stopped.

'So you do know that Erik was your father,' said Gavriela. 'Your real father.'

'Mother told me' – with a dry-eyed blink – 'to stop me cutting myself. Knowing I'm not doomed to inherit his ... obsessions. There's a reason I wear long sleeves.'

Gavriela wanted to reach out and hug her, but it was too soon, far too soon.

'It must have been hard, given your stepfather's profession.'

Caution now, sounding out the girl's political worldview.

My niece!

'It's not his job that's the problem,' said Ursula. 'The things he's— Never mind.'

Gavriela swallowed. 'He ... hurt you?'

'Oh, no! Not the way you ... No.'

So Dmitri's victims remained outside the family at least. Plus, Ursula separated her stepfather's actions from his job, implying violence that even the KGB would not sanction. But this would be guesswork on the girl's part, nothing more.

Still, it was dangerous ground to cover so soon, so Gavriela broke the conversation, taking a chair and placing it opposite Ursula. She sat down, neither too far back – which might convey coldness – nor close enough to intimidate.

Being careful.

'The war ruined everything,' said Gavriela. 'I believe Erik died, but I lost all traces of Ilse. And you ... I didn't know you existed.'

'I contacted the British. I don't understand why you are here.'

The thing was not to think of this as conducting an interrogation, although there were dangers in two-way information exchange – Gavriela felt exposed enough just being on the wrong side of the Curtain. The intent was for Ursula to help them willingly.

'In 1940 I reached England,' said Gavriela. 'I've lived there ever since. Because of my war work, the Secret Intelligence

Service knew how to contact me.' She switched to English: 'I'm really British these days. And I use a different name, but let's stick to Gavriela for now.'

That was a little colloquial, but Ursula seemed to understand.

'Do you know how many people died in Hungary?' she asked, also in English. 'Forty thousand.'

'I know,' said Gavriela.

'But my stepfather says' – in German once more – 'that if it weren't for Britain throwing its weight around over Suez, the Kremlin would not have had to react so hard. They have to show strength, he says.'

All Gavriela knew was that the PM was in Jamaica to 'rest', his health shattered by the crisis, having backed down following explicit threats from Washington and Moscow, including a Soviet promise of nuclear missiles destroying London if the British army, currently twenty-three miles from Suez, did not depart. Meanwhile, in the Commons, Macmillan had told backbenchers of Britain's new place in the world: Greece to the United States' Rome.

'And what do you think, Ursula?'

The girl – *my niece* – clasped her hands over her belly.

'I don't know any more.' She sounded old. 'But I can't help you kill him'

So she understood that she was of interest to British intelligence only as a way of getting to Colonel Dmitri Shtemenko

'We don't want him dead, Ursula.'

It seemed safe to promise that much.

Five days after the extraction of Ursula from the East, Gavriela faced the real challenge.

Getting Ursula into the British Sector had been only stage one, but after that she wore an RAF uniform and carried official documentation, journeying aboard a military lorry on one of the three authorised roads to West Germany. Still, Gavriela had been nervous. When the *package received* signal finally came in, Gavriela had gone for a walk around the Kleine

Tiergarten in falling snow, where wind and cold were sufficient explanation for the tears in her eyes.

Now Gavriela was making the journey from Ku-Damm to
Alt-Moabit on foot, while two armed officers in heavy over-
coats trailed her, and four more were already in place around
the café where Dmitri was due to appear. In one sense, it was
a show of strength on both their parts: Dmitri had chosen the
area, demonstrating that he, too, could cross between sectors
via clandestine means.

Gavriela was not party to the operational details, but somehow messages had moved both ways between her and Dmitri,
requesting and agreeing to a rendezvous.

Much of the cityscape she walked through was ruins. The
major difference between now and a decade ago was that the
rubble had been stacked and sorted, even cleaned, to produce
an urban paradox: a tidy catastrophe. Cities like Frankfurt and
Munich were revitalised, but sad old Berlin had only one thing
to show for the new freedom in the western sectors: rich department stores amid the ruins, especially on the Kurfürsten-
Damm, with a dazzling array of goods on offer in their bright
interiors. *See what you'll get,* they whispered to East Berliners,
if you overthrow your Communist masters.

In the café, a large radio was playing 'Hound Dog', and
Dmitri was sitting behind a table at the rear with his legs
crossed – a posture that reminded her of Rupert – and a cup
of thick Turkish coffee in front of him. There were no genuine customers, and according to the sign on the door she had
entered through, the place was closed.

The bulky owner fetched a coffee for Gavriela and placed
it on the table, then moved back behind the counter where
his weapons would be at hand. An SIS man stood with coat
unbuttoned, watching. One of his colleagues would be upstairs, two more outside at the rear. The pair who had followed Gavriela remained on the street.

'I'm very impressed,' said Dmitri, giving no sign that almost
three decades separated today from their only other meeting,

hiding in the loft above a school assembly hall. Afterwards, he had saved them both from SA attackers in a churchyard, then escorted her home.

Where he first saw Ilse, at that time engaged to Erik.

'Precautions seemed in order,' said Gavriela. 'Danger seems to follow you around.'

'Oh, no. I mean I'm impressed with your callous manipulation of a vulnerable schoolgirl, your own niece, in order to serve your political masters.'

Gavriela controlled her breathing.

Keep balanced.

'Don't think I'm impressed with you, Colonel.'

Surrounding Dmitri, flickers of darkness, like licking tongues, came into existence and disappeared like short-lived particle-antiparticle pairs.

'May I?' He pointed at a cloth-wrapped bundle. 'Your people have already checked it.'

She looked at the man behind the counter, then said: 'OK.'

What Dmitri unwrapped was a shard of metal, nothing more. 'I was stationed in Siberia after the war, until I proved myself.'

Because initially he had remained in hiding, here in Berlin. SIS found out because he had been forced to use an old cover identity, which rang alarm bells during routine denazification procedures. Returning to Moscow, he must have faced some difficult times before his rehabilitation and reinstatement within the KGB.

Gavriela smiled.

'Don't tell me,' she said. 'Tunguska event, 1920s. Cataclysmic meteor strike, but you're going to tell me – what, exactly? A crashed UFO?'

There were rumours that the USSR was planning to get devices into orbit, followed by actual people. Some kind of KGB-designed disinformation was consistent with this, enemy confusion being the goal.

'I didn't say the material was extraterrestrial, Dr Wolf. You did.'

A wide area of tingling curled around her back.

Something very strange about it . . .

Dmitri wrapped the metal once more.

'My archaeologist friends were puzzled, because this was *beneath* ice-preserved fossilised wood that was carved with runes. If the Tunguska event was anything, it was a successful take-off performed by a similar vessel, while this is a fragment of one that blew up centuries before. Maybe it was searching for the first one, the one we found. Assuming you believe any of that, of course.'

The word *Russia* derived from the Rus, the red-headed Vikings who headed east to explore and trade, and settled there, producing descendants. While Gavriela's father, who claimed Viking descent, had never been further eastward than Berlin, she remembered Ilse's words from the night that Dmitri had met her and the Wolf family.

'Never mind Erik,' Ilse had told Dmitri. '*You* and Gavriela could be brother and sister.'

That intense stare, Dmitri's stare, was not too different from the gaze that Gavriela encountered daily in the mirror.

'I find it curious,' she said, 'that a repressive Communist state where religion is outlawed is nevertheless rife with superstition. Or maybe it's because of that repression that people believe in such nutty things.'

'As you say.' Dmitri pushed the bundle aside. 'That's a more likely explanation, isn't it?'

'If you were thinking of offering that to the British Museum, Colonel . . . Well, it's not much of an offer.'

'So what did you have in mind? Details of uranium shipments?'

They were getting to the heart of it.

'Possibly,' said Gavriela. 'What would you want in return?'

'My daughter back, of course.' Dmitri's eyes shone hard. 'What did you expect me to demand?'

161

'She's safe in the West. Why would she want to come back?'

'Why would her wishes matter to your government? Ursula is a schoolgirl. A *German* schoolgirl.'

'Not Dutch?' said Gavriela.

Ilse and Erik had been living in Amsterdam when the Wehrmacht invaded.

'You want to turn me,' said Dmitri. 'So I can feed you classified information, now your famous tunnel has been blown. Very well, I agree. Provided you send her back to me.'

If it had not been for the flickering darkness, Gavriela might have agreed.

'No,' she said. 'That's not acceptable.'

Rupert might have made a different decision, but he wasn't here. In such matters as recruiting agents and turning the opposition, nuance and context – and the case officer's interpretation – were everything. She could justify refusing Dmitri's demands simply by stating that she did not believe they were genuine.

The last thing London wanted, particularly after Burgess and Maclean, was to be played like fools, fed titbits of truth along with massive lies, manipulated from Moscow.

But they should also realise – Rupert certainly must – that she would have no intention of handing Ursula back to her monstrous stepfather. A new thought: Gavriela wondered if Rupert was in fact counting on that, because he believed in the darkness but could not share that belief with his fellow officers.

Perhaps Rupert, unlike his colleagues and superiors, *wanted* her to sabotage any attempt by Dmitri to work for SIS.

'If I were to live in England,' said Dmitri, 'would I have access to Ursula? Controlled occasional access with your people watching – that would be acceptable.'

'Who said anything about England?'

Dmitri's gaze flicked towards the counter, and the SIS man standing ready.

What are you capable of, Dmitri?

If he could call on pseudo-mesmeric powers the way she had seen others of his kind utilise before, only violence on her part would stop him. This meeting could yet become catastrophe.

'Surely, Colonel,' she went on, 'you're not content with working for a single master?'

Unspoken: they both knew he already served two powers, and could not always work for the benefit of one without betraying the other – and that if anything he revelled in the ambiguity.

'Ah, dear Gavi,' he said. 'You think you know me, don't you?'

The use of the familiar form – *du denkst dass du kennst mich* – caused her to freeze.

'Ma'am?' The outer door had opened without her noticing. 'We have company.'

A military staff-car had pulled up outside, its red pennant showing the yellow hammer and sickle. The driver and two officers inside did nothing for a moment; then a door opened. Nobody got out.

'You'll excuse me,' said Dmitri, rising.

He took the cloth-wrapped metal and pushed it into his pocket.

'Nice catching up with you,' he added.

Then he walked out of the café, nodding to the SIS man who stepped aside for him, and slid into the staff-car. For a second, he looked back at Gavriela; then he pulled the door shut. It was a signal for the driver to drop in the clutch and power away from the kerb.

'What just happened?' asked the man who had been standing guard.

He tried to find out where Ursula is.

That would be the other reason for Rupert's using Gavriela: besides the relationship with Ursula, there was her immunity to any psychological influence Dmitri might employ. Meanwhile, Dmitri, for safety and as a fallback plan, had informed his people that the British had approached him. It allowed him

163

to turn the play in either direction, unless Gavriela blocked the game totally.

She answered, 'I have absolutely no idea.'

What she knew for certain was that her first loyalty was to Carl, her son. Going home to be his mother again was her main objective. If she could keep her newfound niece safe as well, that was an added benefit; but Gavriela no longer wanted to work for Rupert, and had no interest in Dmitri Shtemenko's future, so long as he stayed a long way away from her, preferably on the other side of the Iron Curtain.

Not that such parochial, ephemeral divisions meant anything to the darkness.

TWENTY-THREE

VACHSS STATION, VIJAYA ORBITAL, 2604 AD

The judicial hearing was held *in camera*, with two non-Pilot humans on the panel, matching the two Pilot representatives and the two Haxigoji. Roger had not expected an even-numbered group, and was curious about the possibility of deadlock in deciding a verdict; then he pushed extraneous thoughts behind him. His primary goal was to make sure Jed was freed.

'Keep your eyes open,' had been his briefing officer's final comment, a throwaway remark that was really something else. So far Roger had not worked out what he was meant to be alert to.

Jed's incarceration meant confinement to the Sanctuary section of the orbital, no prison cells involved. If he and his fellow Pilots wanted to make an illegal getaway, they had the resources. This was a matter for diplomacy, not military tactics.

The panel was chaired by a soulful-looking Pilot called Ibrahim al-Khalid, who early in the proceedings announced: 'Vachss Station authorities have agreed to treat certain security matters, to be touched upon in this hearing, as classified material. As one of two Sanctuary representatives here, let me add an official statement of gratitude for that wise decision.'

Beside al-Khalid sat the long-term 'permanent' Sanctuary resident, name of Declan Draper. The two humans on the panel were Emma Mbaka, who just happened to be Draper's partner, and Vilok Khan, who had witnessed Jed killing Rick Mbuli – or the thing that once been Rick – which

165

Roger would have thought disqualified him as an objective judge.

The Haxigoji pair were a female called Nectarblossom and an antler-bearing male called Acid Tang, whose arrival by shuttle from the surface had been marked by a great deal of ceremony, almost reverence, among the station-resident Haxigoji. Since the Haxigoji who witnessed the killing had protected Jed and appeared to approve of his actions – Roger had seen the holo footage as part of his briefing – there should be no problem here.

Not that he was complacent about any aspect of this mission, though it appeared to have little in common with the scenarios he had drilled in so hard in Tangleknot.

'We look forward to exploring the implications of the defendant's actions,' said Nectarblossom through her translation-torc, 'as a matter of the greatest importance.'

Jed was sitting to one side, wearing old-fashioned mag-bracelets and anklets that could be commanded to snap together, immobilising him. It was a matter of form and outmoded legislation, Roger had been told. Jed had given his usual muscular grin on seeing Roger – they had not been allowed to meet beforehand – then put all his attention on the panel.

'First I would like to show on-board recordings of the event in question. Mr Khan?'

'As a witness myself' – Vilok Khan had raised a finger to speak – 'I will be interested in confirming my subjective memory. If Nectarblossom and Acid Tang agree?'

There was the faintest of perfumes in the air – the Haxigoji conferring with translators turned off – before Nectarblossom said: 'We too are interested.'

When the holo played through, the Haxigoji pair watched via smartmiasma-distorted air, acting as a dynamically configurable lens, as they sniffed the poorly reproduced scents from the surveillance fragrance-recorders at the original scene. Roger turned away, wincing, but too late: he had already seen

Rick's head being blown apart, and it was as awful now as it had been during the briefing.

He was a witness giving evidence, but there was more than that. The Haxigoji had known that something was wrong about Rick Mbuli – and they had prevented Pilot Holland from coming on board Vachss Station.

Suddenly, Roger understood the unspoken elements of his briefing, the reason for their choosing him specifically, what Ro McNamara had hinted at – and why this really was an intelligence operation. As far as the Admiralty was concerned, Jed's freedom was secondary; what they wanted to know was simple: could the Haxigoji sense the darkness?

'We have a question,' came from Nectarblossom's torc, 'regarding the defendant's targeting the abomination. How did he determine its nature?'

Everyone looked at Jed. He took control of the holo, and replayed an audio portion at high volume: *'My name. Is. Rick. Mbuli from. Ful-gor.'*

'I remembered my friend Roger' – Jed gestured – 'telling me about his time on Fulgor, and that name, Mbuli, rang a bell. And I knew Roger had searched the refugee lists: he wasn't a known survivor.'

Acid Tang's nostrils widened then closed almost fully. It was a reaction that Roger did not know how to read. Then his attention was drawn by Khan, who asked him to confirm Jed's statement, which he did. Everything proceeded step by step, until Khan finally declared: 'I believe Pilot Goran's actions to be neither homicide nor manslaughter, given that the deceased was not a coherent entity, but a tiny component of the Anomaly engaged in a terrorist action against the station. Dr Mbaka, do you agree?'

It sounded like a memorised speech.

'I do.' She looked at Jed. 'And I would like to thank Pilot Goran for his heroism. His fast thinking and swift action saved not just this orbital, but the entire planet of Vijaya from total catastrophe.' Then, dropping her formal tone, she added: 'You were fantastic. Thank you so much.'

Jed grinned, muscles playing in his face.

Roger felt himself relax.

Good. It's over.

The Haxigoji leaned close to each other, Nectarblossom angling her head to avoid Acid Tang's dipping antler, then straightened up.

'We would like to call one more witness,' said Nectarblossom, 'before concluding this examination.'

Al-Khalid looked surprised but said: 'Of course. Please do.'

Everything changed in an instant.

A bulkhead pulled open. Four huge Haxigoji dragged a bound human into the chamber—

No!

—and Roger was on his feet because the darkness was swirling around the man, in fact a Pilot. But it was the darkness itself that Roger had reacted to.

The Pilot hung, semi-conscious, from the grip of massive double-thumbed hands.

'This,' announced Nectarblossom via her torc, 'is Pilot Holland.'

So they had not prevented him leaving his ship: they had caught him in the corridor. Which meant his ship must be waiting nearby in congruent mu-space, waiting for the chance to free Holland without risking his life.

Kill him …

Roger's tu-ring was blazing with scarlet fire, though he could not remember arming it.

Control.

He looked into Nectarblossom's amber, horizontally slitted eyes.

'The darkness,' he said. 'It's strong. This man is fully corrupted.'

'Yes.'

Acid Tang said: 'So there *are* humans who are not blind. This is powerful news.'

'An heroic day.' Nectarblossom rose to her feet, taller than any human, her presence magnificent. 'We will share the message.'

The implications and the mutual recognition rebounded in Roger's mind, distracting him and the Haxigoji alike, but he was supposed to be a professional and you had to remain alert when—

Yellow fire exploded.

Amid deadly danger, an element of slapstick intruded: Jed leapt at Holland – like Roger, he was unaffected by the blaze of energy – but his electromag bracelets and anklets snapped together, immobilising him and dropping him in Roger's path, which gave Holland the second he needed.

The Haxigoji guards had staggered back, blinded, as Holland took the opportunity to stumble back through the hatch he had entered by, and cause it to slam shut.

From the floor, Jed said: 'They'll be OK. The bastard's weak.' But his voice was slurred, and blood was pouring from his forehead. 'Go get him.'

'Wait.' Roger went to Vilok Khan, who appeared to be panicking the least, and used a gentle thumb to draw up an eyelid. 'Jed's right,' he told everyone. 'The flash wasn't full strength. You'll recover.'

Nectarblossom appeared to have closed her eyes in time, because she looked at Roger now, and said: 'You do not need to stay and bear witness. We will spread the word.'

So she understood: their new mutual understanding was the most important outcome.

'You're sure?'

'Yes. Good luck, Pilot.'

Jed was out of it, and Draper was Shipless, but Ibrahim al-Khalid was a Pilot too. Roger turned to him, expecting an offer of help, but saw only an expression of devastated emptiness, tears running down al-Khalid's face.

Find out later.

It was time to give chase.

No place in Vachss Station was far from an outer hull, and emergency evacuation points abounded. By the time Roger obliterated the hatch that Holland had escaped through, turning it into powder, an exterior-view holo was showing a teardrop shape, originating here, in the act of making rendezvous with a dark-green and purple ship that had, just seconds ago, blazed into realspace.

Well, good.

A strong enemy meant a decent challenge, and while Holland might still be weak, his ship was anything but. Quickglass was already spreading across Roger's skin as he commanded an exit to become permeable; then he took a moment to judge the trajectory – there, a spar was rotating past, and he would have to be careful to miss it – before launching himself through the liquefied wall and popping out into vacuum.

Come to me.

His own beauty, black and powerful, webbed with scarlet and gold, crashed into realspace existence, so very close to Vachss Station. Proximity alarms would be sounding aboard the orbital, but there was no risk because she was a genius, taking him into her control cabin—

We hunt?

Oh, yes, my love.

Good.

—and diving sideways, away from everything, getting a clear angle on Holland's ship except it was too late because white light accompanied a skilful transition into muspace—

On home ground, then.

Exactly.

—which would not be enough to save them because Roger-and-ship were equally adept, probably more, and within a subjective second, golden splendour was shining all around them.

Mu-space, and a quarry to kill.

Call it their life purpose.

It was a long and tricky chase, following the faintest of spoors through mu-space void, close to black fractal stars and through the heart of a scale-free fern-like nebula; but just as ship-and-Roger were about to open fire, Holland-and-ship shone white and disappeared, transiting back to realspace.

Ambush?

Conscious that the insertion point was far from the galactic core and therefore the renegade base, they took the risk and followed, bursting through into realspace at maximum speed – *planet!* – and tumbling into orbit of a greenish, cloudy world – *I see it* – but the dark-green and purple ship was already a tiny dot diving deep into atmosphere.

Where are we?

Must be Siganth.

It was not a human world. Various indigenous species, if that was the correct term for classifying entities that seemed scarcely organic, were both sentient and vicious, metallic and ferocious. Neither Pilots nor the human xeno-contact teams they brought here had achieved much by way of communication.

And we follow?

Yes.

There was no way to tell whether they were under observation as they descended through a sequence of cloud layers and came out over a sharp-edged mountain range, following the fugitive's trace.

There.

It led into a vast cavernous opening. Ship-and-Roger descended to the ground outside the entrance, every weapon filled with energy, standing waves building up in resonance cavities, aching to be cut loose. After a few seconds, great

171

bronze-and-black metallic forms clanked their way out into the open: native Siganthians, whose carapaces concealed intricate body-mechanisms, cables and pumps for sinews and muscles, some with heavy metal wings, looking incapable of flight, launching themselves nevertheless into the air.

Sparks of sapphire light shone among their multitudinous eye-sockets – *Anomaly!* – and ship-and-Roger let loose a single burst of weapons-fire – *we need to bug out* – then ploughed all energy into thrusting flight, hauling upwards at maximum acceleration – *we won't make orbit* – ignoring the heat – *I know* – before embracing the moment of risk.

Transit now.

They burst through.

Yes.

Golden void, scarlet nebulae in the distance, and the knowledge that they had achieved transition under the most dangerous of circumstances. They scanned for renegades, but the region was clear, and Holland was no doubt among his own kind on the realspace planet, among the inhumans.

So Siganth is a hellworld.

And collaborating with renegades, although Holland must be desperate to take the chance.

Looks that way.

This was news that had to reach the Admiralty.

So much for his planned journey of victory, flying home from Vachss Station with Jed's ship alongside, taking their time. When Roger reached Labyrinth, he left his beloved ship in one of the clandestine docking hangars – having entered unobserved as always – and requested immediate debriefing. One of the two officers who responded was a familiar face: Havelock, who had interviewed him on his first day in Tangleknot. The other Pilot was also someone he recognised, though it had taken a few seconds to work out, and the conclusion was a shock.

Dad. Did you really want me to know this?

Her name was Lianna Kaufmann, and he remembered being smitten with her at the Academy ... except that he, Roger Blackstone, had never attended the Academy. Those were Dad's memories.

In his mind Lianna was the same age that he was now; but in reality, the woman sitting across from him in the interview chamber had greying hair, and her face showed the lines of hard decisions made. It made him think of Leeja, now living on Vachss Station: he had not even tried to contact her. But events had moved quickly.

'This is important news,' said Lianna as Roger concluded his report. 'You've done well.'

'Thank you.'

He was careful not to use her first name, this being their first meeting in reality.

Havelock seemed thoughtful. 'I agree, it was good work. You understand why it was decided to send you in particular.'

'Yes, sir,' said Roger, wondering what the issue was.

'The Vachss Station judicial hearing was not public.' Lianna was frowning. 'But some important events took place there. Even if the recordings don't go public – I'm afraid your name is destined to become well known on Vijaya.'

'Crap,' said Roger.

'Well, precisely,' said Havelock. 'You said previously your success would depend on remaining unknown, but this time it's worked out differently. Not an entirely secret victory.'

So much for subterfuge and infiltration.

'Since the Göthewelt raid,' Havelock went on, 'there have been seven more Zajinet attacks in realspace. With Labyrinth on a war footing, you and your classmates are likely to be operational immediately on completion of training. The nature of those operations is ... malleable.'

Meaning not what they had been trained for.

'Understood, sir.'

But it was Lianna's words, at the conclusion of the meeting, that would stay with him.

'Your father would be proud,' she told him. 'Very proud.'

In return, he could have told her how much Dad had been in love with her when they were young, and how hurt he had been by her dismissal when she believed him to be Shipless; but some thoughts are best kept hidden for ever.

'Thank you, ma'am,' he said.

TWENTY-FOUR

THE WORLD, 5575 AD

When the potential for flight among the worlds was discovered, the possibility of sailing the heaven-void, they cast for more Seekers to join them, and seven came. Alongside Seeker-once-Harij and Seeker-once-captive, they should be enough to respond to flux-queries from within the vessel – or so they believed.

Zirkana's thoughts were entirely different.

It cannot fly.

The excavation had completely uncovered the ancient vessel, which looked ... younger. Newer. Vast and lustrous, dark-green banded with white. It seemed capable of holding hundreds, perhaps a thousand sleeping people stacked in bunks, as the ancient legend said.

In dreams through golden space they fled/Till xeno demons cut them dead.

There was more to the old verse but, even among Seekers, few bothered with it; for it was clearly allegory and filled with indecipherable allusion: for one thing, space was most obviously black. In the absence of other Ideas from that period, the references made little sense today.

What had surprised the two hundred workers as they dug sand, brushed hardened clumps from the uncovered ship, and polished every part, was that the underlying metal – if it was metal: its properties were odd – had failed to deteriorate despite being buried for so long, a great many generations.

And after a time, as they had approached the end of the cleaning, the ship had begun to hum, a soft low flux-cast that lightened every heart, made every person smile and wonder.

That included Zirkana; but unlike the others, she broke away to spend time worrying, because the intent had arisen among the group without discussion: if the ship could fly, the Seekers wanted to try her out. They thought of the ship as female, for no reason they could decipher.

Zirkana was afraid for Seeker-once-Harij.

Let the others try it, if they must.

In their alcove within the dormitory caverns, when day was beginning outside and everyone else was asleep, she would hold him very tight. But they both knew that the urge to Seek was as strong as love and that to set them in opposition could only bring pain.

On the final night before the attempt, travellers arrived, twenty in number, from a settlement within a distant mountain. What they brought was a gift, a chunk of virgin dreamlode, its crystal free of contained flux. It was both a celebration of the project's triumph and a potential tool for the Seekers intending to fly the vessel.

Then the night came when all was ready, and there was no reason to delay, except perhaps for the breaking of one woman's heart. With over two hundred people gathered for a noble purpose and sharing a dream, an individual's fears were irrelevant. Zirkana kept her thoughts wrapped tightly in herself.

No one could know.

Seeker-once-Harij lost sight of Zirkana during the speeches by Starij and Kolarin, the leaders of the dig, when the combined flux of two hundred volunteer workers heterodyned into a blazing cheer. They were standing close together and the effect was awe-inspiring, so that the nine assembled Seekers could only stand at the base of the newly constructed ramp, letting the flux sink in.

Then it was time to climb to the opening that had appeared in the hull five nights before, revealing a chamber in which decay had not occurred. Emotions whirling, the Seekers entered and waited. After a moment, as they had known it would, the opening flowed shut.

Amazing! They were aboard a sky-vessel on the verge of—

Zirkana? How are you here?

She rose from the floor where she had been curled up, holding her flux inside herself.

The ship allowed me in.

There was no time for Seeker-once-Harij to remonstrate with or hug her, because the other Seekers were focused on the dreamlode crystal – Seeker-once-captive was holding it against his chest – combining their thoughts to create a clean command.

Except that it would be request more than order, to such a wondrous ship as this.

Rise, good vessel. Please rise.

The floor and walls shivered as the air grew warm. It came to the conjoined Seekers that the ship was very old, and they were asking a great deal. People grow feeble, so it stood to reason that a living ship would—

A massive force slammed into them.

There was time to deal with bleeding noses while the ordeal lasted, time for their skins to lose the mottling of emotion and return to polished silver equilibrium. Finally, the ship's trembling lessened, and they felt themselves sinking.

Surely descending to the dig. There had been time for nothing more.

Finally, they felt the sensation of slowing descent, of settling in place; and everybody smiled.

The wall flowed open as before, and a strong draught swept through the chamber.

The air feels oddly—

Suddenly all communication with the other Seekers was gone. Only Zirkana's and Seeker-once-Harij's thoughts whirled together, pulsing and urgent.

Physical contact. Keep hold. It's as if the air is dead to flux.

Yes. You're right.

Maintaining his grasp on Zirkana's hand, Seeker-once-Harij clasped the nearest Seeker's shoulder; and after a momentary disorientation, that Seeker in turn grabbed two others. Soon they were communicating, panic over.

We can breathe the air.

It sustains life, but not flux. How can that be?

But of course, the answer was right outside. They just did not want to look, to process the sight of what was there.

There are old Ideas treating those concepts as separate, but this is not the time to—

Stop. Just perceive.

Together, they looked out of the vessel.

Silver sands stretched far to black mountains that were webbed with silver streams, rendering them visible against black sky.

No place in the World has a desert like—

We're not on the World.

That's hardly—

This is Magnus.

A landscape of silver and black.

They had seen it all their lives: on the face of the largest moon floating overhead. And now they were upon it, and it was vast, as big as the World.

Slowly, slowly, the ship extruded a tongue-like ramp of its own. She had not communicated with them in coherent flux, but this message was clear. Or was this whole flight a senile interpretation of everyone's wishes back at the dig site? She was so very old.

What do we do?

Old Ideas told of distant worlds that were airless, but this was different, and disconcerting: they could breathe, yet flux did not tumble through the air; it was attenuated to a faint echo of normality. There might be danger, but their course of action was obvious.

We Seek.

In a human chain, they walked down the ramp.

A new world!

Then the Seekers disengaged physical contact, leaving only Seeker-once-Harij and Zirkana holding hands. The flux-silence was eerie.

When they looked back, the ship was unmoving. It seemed a promise that she would wait for them, though of course they might be wrong. But something winked on the distant mountainside, and a few heartbeats later, it did so again.

Nine Seekers and Zirkana felt the lure of new knowledge upon them.

It was time to Seek.

The passing of time was hard to reckon, but it took longer than a normal night to reach the black mountain. There was nothing to eat and nothing to drink as they trekked across silver sand, but Seekers were used to privation, and Zirkana was determined to match them. The closer they drew to the mountain, the more certain they were that buildings of some kind awaited them.

And so they did. Huge and ancient. Tall and shining, formed of obsidian and silver, all clean lines and cold beauty. Also empty, as if they had never been lived in.

Zirkana cast her opinion:

There were never inhabitants.

All ten were holding hands at that point, considering what to do next.

Never? Then who built them?

In a polished, bare hall, they turned in circles, overwhelmed by the structure.

A ship, or something like it. Something that went ahead.
Seeker-once-Harij stared up at a high arch, considering this.

Why would it build them, my love?

For us to live in.

Surely that's not—

179

I mean our ancestors. The ship was supposed to carry them here, to Magnus.

The Seekers were unsure.

You really think it's the Ark?

You really think it isn't?

But as they searched amid the polished magnificence, it was the absence of food and drink that was growing in their minds: so mundane a detail, but without supplies there could be no exploration. Zirkana would not let them set off early because of her; but soon enough, the Seekers, experienced wanderers all, were in agreement. They had reached the cut-off point, beyond which returning to the ship was dangerous.

We'll come back with supplies. Plenty of them.

You think the ship will carry us back and forth from the World?

What else does it have to do?

Perhaps it was true – perhaps even a ship needed a purpose in life. The thought made it easier to abandon the empty, unexplored buildings and begin the reverse trek, steadily moving across glistening sand, plodding anti-parallel to their own footprints. There was always the possibility that the ship would have decided not to wait; but they had trusted her, and she remained in view as they approached.

Finally, on board, they sank down on the metallic deck, hamstrings aching, ankles sore, and waited for something to happen. But nothing did.

Ship. Take us home.

The opening did not seal up. There was no thrum of power to whatever mechanisms allowed the ship to fly; only her steady background hum remained, as if she were waiting for something. But whatever it was, they could not give it to her.

Desperately, the Seekers tried geometrically intricate flux-patterns and every trick of rhetoric they knew, but nothing produced a response from the ancient vessel. Perhaps she really was senile; perhaps she had finally completed her original mission – as she saw it – and was resting here until she died.

No one railed at her for long. Fatigue and hunger were metamorphosing into lethargy, and soon enough they would be unable to do anything as their bodies shut down and that was that: the end of them. But they were Seekers, and one Seeker's wife, and they could summon composure if nothing else.

Eight Seekers sat cross-legged in a circle, hands joined as they entered flux-trance, chins on chests and drooping forwards as their strength failed, sinking fast inside themselves, preparing. Lying apart from them, Seeker-once-Harij and Zirkana clasped each other, merging their thoughts.

I love you.

But death would soon be here.

Whether Seeking carried with it a sense of fatalism, Zirkana could not quite say, but she alone roused herself at the tiniest pinprick of distant energies, of disturbance propagated only faintly through the insulating medium of air, this strange dead air that Magnus possessed. She squeezed Seeker-once-Harij, who roused himself – it would be so easy to slip back into sleep – and forced himself to move, to shake the other Seekers into wakefulness.

And slowly, painfully, to shuffle to the exit and down the ramp.

Standing on the silver sand, they watched a huge vessel – or was it a creature? – move slowly in the night sky. Then, with twin bursts of pure white light, two more craft burst into being. All three bore some kind of resemblance to the ancient ship that brought them here; but they were different also, slowly morphing in shape, uncurling external tendrils, billowing gently.

From them, streams of bubbles began to descend.

What are they, Harij?

I don't know, my love.

But each bubble, as it approached the ground, clearly

contained a person. Or rather, a near-human lacking silver skin. Seeker-once-Harij felt none of the panic that he experienced with the other soft-skinned beings – no sense of abomination, of that inhuman group mind – and Seeker-once-captive looked equally calm. That was good, because it took the last of their energy simply to stand here and wait.

For whatever was about to happen.

Each bubble, as it touched the sand, dissolved. Its former occupant walked clear. When there were some thirty folk gathered, they walked slowly forward, approaching the Seekers and Zirkana; and then they halted.

Seeker-once-Harij cast a greeting.

Two of the strangers moved their mouths in an odd fashion. One had ordinary human eyes (perhaps lacking protective membrane) despite the soft skin; the other's eyes were pure black: polished obsidian.

Communication.

That was the oldest Seeker, searching his memory for Ideas, then touching each of his fellows in turn with his fingertips, sharing his thinking: words without flux, nevertheless cast upon the air. But the two newcomers looked to be thinking equally hard, blinking as if at sights only they could see – and suddenly the black-eyed stranger, surely a woman, raised her hand and a silvery mist spread outwards – from her ring, Seeker-once-Harij thought – and spanned the gap between her and the nine Seekers plus Zirkana.

This time, when her mouth moved, the mist came alive with blazing flux.

GREETINGS!

The Seekers staggered, and Seeker-once-Harij tripped and fell backwards, thumping into the ground. Zirkana went down on one knee beside him, but he was laughing; and after a moment, she was laughing too.

Seeker-once-captive managed to keep composure and reply.

Greetings.

But they were all smiling, even the soft-skinned beings, even the ones standing well back. This was a strange world and they did not know each other, but there was a sense only of warmth, of the possibility of friendship; and so long as no one did anything stupid, that was how things would proceed. Seeker-once-Harij was sure of it.

The World was going to be different now.

TWENTY-FIVE

NULAPEIRON, 2604-2657 AD

For fifty-three years, the system self-identified as Kenna was immobile. It existed as a network of components embedded in a wall deep inside Palace Avernon, itself located in the Primum Stratum of Demesne Avernon, some hundred metres below ground. Then, towards the end of that fifty-third year, Kenna decided that it was female once more.

Her internal computation had upgraded with the addition of neuropeptide-analogues, so that she manifested emotional cognition, the gut-think which comprises a huge portion of human neural processing; and that meant it was time to begin reconfiguring herself into a human personality. Choosing a gender was a major step, so she searched the standard human classification that reduced the choice to only thirty-five options; from among them she picked a feminine-tough trope-complex not dissimilar to the former Rhianna Chiang.

The old Duke Avernon, the first and best of them, would have approved of her choice.

'Fear is *literally* felt in the stomach,' he had told her once, 'and heartache in the heart. Peptide flow in organs forms the third nervous system. Descartes would have got it right,' he had added, 'if he'd said *cogito capioque, ergo sum*. From *capere*, meaning to feel, experience, charm and suffer. A fetching semantic spectrum, don't you think?'

She missed the Duke, such a contrast to the grandson ruling now. Lord Dalgen Avernon (his father had relinquished duchy status, to reduce the demesne's tax liability) of the flighty mind and political ambition, saw himself as worldly-wise, rather than simply worldly.

Or so she thought until she watched him poring over the spacedrone experiment results, the laboratory chambers filled with holo diagrams, with billowing phase-spaces and five-dimensional lattices of linked, glowing equations. Her pseudo-face was embedded in the wall of the largest chamber, but over the years, this Avernon had grown to think of her as a decorative mounted sculpture rather than a cognitively functional, though immobile, cyborg.

She encouraged that notion by remaining silent during his devious political planning sessions.

This new experimental work, however, was based on logosophical research initiated by Avernon's forebears and continued by current members of l'Academia Ultima, which sometimes lived up to its name. The investigation harked back to the old mystery of time's arrow, to the time symmetry of 'fundamental' equations describing the natural universe, and their failure to identify the three aspects of timeflow: the moving reality of past, present and future. But the work was not just theory and laboratory experiments.

Something odd was happening in the vicinity of Nulapeiron.

The initial results had come from experiments on board drones placed in orbits of different radii around Nulapeiron, orbits chosen almost at random. Some of the results matched predictions, but others showed strange yet consistent deviations. To investigate, the researchers had commissioned more spacedrones – something most people in Nulapeiron would not dream of, given their mental blindspots regarding the uninhabitable surface, never mind what laid beyond – until there were shoals of the things, orbiting at all sorts of distances from the surface, allowing a clear mapping of the phenomenon.

Producing unambiguous readings, but not understanding.

The heart of it was a set of reactions in the spacedrones' cores, which produced the usual spray of short-lived particles and resonances – so far, so good. But in some locations, there were too many kaons extant. Unexciting to the average person, deeply troubling to the researchers.

An imbalance occurred strongly within a kilometre-wide shell some hundred thousand kilometres from the centre of Nulapeiron; outside of that shell, subatomic reality behaved as normal. But for seven hundred years, that normality had been known to possess an inexplicable feature.

'Take an electron moving forward in time,' Kenna remembered one of Rhianna Chiang's childhood teachers saying, 'and try to distinguish it from the behaviour of a positron moving backwards in time – and you'll find there is no difference, so how can you decide which it really is? It follows logically – and is actually true – that subatomic reactions are reversible in time.'

The teacher had shown footage of a smashed egg leaping up into someone's hand and spontaneously reforming.

'You know I'm showing this in reverse. But only vast collections of particles, like the number of atoms required to make up an egg, show timeflow in their larger structure. At the atomic or subatomic level, footage going forwards or backwards is equally likely.'

At an early age, Pilots were expected to understand timeflow as an emergent property. But there was a twist in the tail regarding realspace, and if an equivalent was unknown in mu-space, that might be only because Labyrinth's researchers had not found it yet.

Because of the startling exception to the rule: neutral kaons and their opposite-spin antiparticles appear to know the difference between past and future. Seven centuries of data backed up that observation.

Now the present Lord Avernon was looking at readings that appeared to show a K^0 imbalance in the wrong direction, as though time itself were wobbling, as if the present were threatening to flow from the future into the past.

And if he were the one to monopolise the technology accruing from this phenomenon, not only would Demesne

Avernon be a duchy once more, he would become a Lord Primus and probably—

'Father! My Lord!'

—have better servitors, ones who would know to bar his over-energetic son from his private laboratory chambers, even if he had not issued instructions to that effect.

'What is it?' He gestured the holos into non-existence, because the boy was bright and you never knew what he might notice. 'Tell me there's a good reason for this outburst.'

'More an inburst, surely,' said young Alvin. 'But we've a visitor and you'll never guess what he is.'

'You're right, I won't guess. Just tell me.'

Alvin looked disappointed for a moment; then he gushed: 'His name is Caleb de Vries and Mother's talking to him in the Great Hall and he's a *Pilot*, Father. A Pilot!'

If people, deep in their underground strata, rarely thought about the planet's surface, then they had almost forgotten about mu-space and the Pilots who had brought their forebears here. Nor was this a culture that had come about by accident; deliberate design ran through customs, politics and language. But of course the Lords and Ladies still, on occasion, dealt with Pilots as required.

So long as the others, the servitors and commonfolk, forgot about the rest of inhabited space, that was good enough. Isolationism was a tool for social engineering, not an end in itself.

Today was nevertheless doubly unusual. Kenna, observing, felt an unexpected excitement.

It had been so *very* long since she had seen a Pilot.

Pilot deVries stood in formal jumpsuit, black edged with gold, with a knee-length black cape that was more than a simple garment: it could if necessary become shield or weapon. For an offworlder, he made a decent job of the nuances in bowing to the correct angle, with leg turned correctly, as Lord Avernon entered the Great Hall. The Lady, from her ornate chair, smiled approval.

'My Lord,' said deVries. 'Lady Suzanne was just pointing out your grandfather's work.' He gestured at the holoscape showing in an alcove. 'A deliberate unbalancing of the golden ratio to produce a visual momentum, combined with a fractal dimension of 1.66 throughout.'

'Indeed, sir,' answered Avernon. 'My Lady is privy to more than art appreciation.'

It was an indirect way of indicating he could discuss business.

'Pardon my intrusion,' said deVries. 'I gather that you lodged interest in commissioning a voyage, before the Lords Major at the Regional Convocation.'

The high point of that Convocation, some fifty days past, had been the upraise of a servitrix to noble status, by virtue of her enormous self-discipline in using every educational opportunity available, and her superlative work. Now she ruled her own demesne in Penrhyl Provincia: a shining example for every commoner, except that upraise occurred maybe twice a century, no more.

But most of the actual work done during Convocation had been the usual – trade negotiations, strengthening or reshaping political alliances – during which Avernon had indeed lodged a discreet request.

'Not exactly a mercantile voyage.' Avernon's tone lightened. 'More along the lines of logosophical investigation.'

'My Lord?'

'I'm looking for a sequence of short flights in ever-wider orbits of Nulapeiron. Additional data to build on spacedrone investigations we've already carried out.'

(In Kenna's judgement, the *we* in that sentence was unjustified.)

'The details are in here,' added Avernon, holding out an infocrystal. 'Will you be able to carry out the work?'

Pilot deVries took the crystal and scanned it with his turing. 'Absolutely, my Lord.'

'Then we're done here.'

'My Lord.'

As deVries bowed out, his obsidian eyes turned to an ordinary-looking patch of wall that formed one of Kenna's thousands of covert optical sensors, and then he winked. Inside herself, Kenna laughed: Pilots were as sharp as ever.

In contrast, Avernon had forgotten or never bothered to realise that Kenna's distributed presence reached this far.

'Pilots.' Lady Suzanne continued to stare at the grand doorway after deVries had exited. 'Are we still so dependent on them?'

'Not so much,' said Avernon. 'But what would it be like, my Lady, if you could perceive events that were to come? How much power would accrue from such an ability?'

'None at all, my Lord, if what you saw was your own ruin.'

Avernon blinked several times.

(And again, Kenna was amused.)

'I'd be interested,' Lady Suzanne added, 'in how one might engineer such a thing.'

'It's, um, early stages yet.'

'And when do you *foresee* those ideas maturing?' Then she laughed and placed her palm on Avernon's arm. 'Forgive me, love. I'm only teasing.'

'Yes, well. Of course you are.'

Then Lady Suzanne signalled for the palace steward to attend, and summoned up holo lattices of accounting data – Palace Avernon's upkeep was a complex matter. As her steward stood before her in his white-and-platinum livery, cane of office in hand, he responded to his Lady's questions and gave occasional recommendations, which she accepted. Lord Avernon gave the occasional nod, his attention elsewhere.

(Kenna followed his example, searching the Palace systems for deVries.)

In realtime she saw this: Pilot deVries stopping in a deserted corridor, kneeling on the floor, and keeping that pose as the quickstone whirled and he sank downwards, and out of sight.

*

The person that deVries met four levels down – still within the Primum Stratum, a lower level of the Palace complex – was a thin, hard-faced woman in the clothing of a drudge: an epsilon-level servitrix at best. Except that to Kenna's perceptions, the smartlenses were obvious, and so was the conclusion: the woman was a Pilot living in deep cover.

'I'm Linda Gunnarrson,' said the servitrix.

'Caleb deVries.'

'Let's get my standard report out of the way.'

There was a flash of light from deVries's tu-ring.

'Got that,' he said. 'You're doing a good job, clearly. Any concerns?'

'I don't need the case officer pep-talk, deVries. All I want is—'

'Working off the sins of the father?'

Gunnarsson flinched. 'So you did your homework. But my father wasn't— You think I'm after redemption?'

'I've done the time-distorting hellflight bit myself. But look ... My sister died on Göthewelt. I don't blame your father for the Zajinet raid, and I sure as hell don't blame you.'

'Damn you.' Smartlenses do not prevent tears. 'All right.' She blew out a breath. 'Perhaps I needed that.'

'And perhaps I can't imagine the stress you live under, in this place.'

Gunnarsson reached inside her plain garments and extracted a cloth-wrapped bundle. She folded back one corner, revealing a crystalline object. It looked like a spearhead. 'It came from an archive chamber,' she said. 'Part of the Palace museum. The stores are filled with old stuff.'

'Surely they check inventory.'

'I replaced it with a quartz replica. Here.'

As he took it from her, deVries's eyes widened.

'Right,' said Gunnarsson. 'Hard not to feel it.'

'But it's a forgotten relic? Where the hell could it have come from?'

'That's going to take Labyrinth's finest to work out. *If* they manage it.'

(Kenna cursed. Whatever she might have been once, her sensors picked up nothing untoward now.)

Then deVries switched his attention back to Gunnarsson's welfare, and she unburdened herself by sharing stressful details of her life, but refusing deVries's offer, clearly genuine, to extract her from Nulapeiron. 'There's opposition to the status quo,' she said. 'I've gathered some of them together and the group has a name, Grey Shadows, with an elected leader. Not me.'

Recruiting assets, running networks. Kenna remembered how that went.

Meeting over, deVries ascended to the part of the Palace he was staying in for the duration of his contract. The start date was immediate. Looking exhausted, his sleep-wake cycle clearly out of synch with this place, deVries performed a light stretching routine, ate a frugal meal delivered by a servitor, and went to bed, leaving his cloth-wrapped bundle on the bedside table.

His tu-ring nicely subverted the bedchamber's inbuilt security system, so that it kept watch *over* him more than *on* him. But his espionageware remained unaware of Kenna's system intrusion, subtle and deep: she had had five decades to work on it.

Motile fibres extruded from the wall.

For seconds, they sniffed the air for smartmiasmas, sensing nothing. Then they stretched out, growing microscopically fine as they extended all the way to the bedside table, to the cloth-wrapped package on it, and finally through the fabric.

It took an hour, while deVries slept but could have awoken at any time, to determine the shearing angle and the force required, and projection angles for collimated anti-sound to counter the tiny *snap* accompanying the act itself: the cutting-off of a tiny sample.

Slowly, slowly, the motile fibres drew the minute crystal

splinter back to the ornate wall; then the splinter was inside the quickstone, and the first stage of the operation was complete.

By capillary action, the crystal splinter moved within the Palace walls, with speed no longer an issue, only the need to keep it undetected as it travelled to the laboratory chambers, close to Kenna's main components that remained, static as ever, in place.

There was no hurry now.

TWENTY-SIX

Jared Schenck was orphaned two days before his seventh birthday. The call came for Rekka at 7:32 in the morning, while Jared was asleep in her guest room, no doubt with his chocolate-brown teddy-bear in his arms. She was already up, even though it was Sunday, her limbering-up *asana*s complete, and about to drink her one and only espresso of the day.

'No,' Rekka told her wallscreen. 'They can't be dead. Not Randolf. Not Angela.'

She put down the tiny cup.

'I'm so very, very sorry.' Google Li, on screen, looked shocked herself. 'It was only a short passenger hop, but they're saying everyone on board was killed.'

Rekka stared at the door to Jared's room.

'Oh no.'

'Do you want me to come over?'

In the seven years that Rekka had worked in Singapore, Google Li had not become a friend, but there was no real enmity. Google Li cared only what UNSA management thought of her; and provided you took that into account, you could at least deal with her as a colleague.

Jared's door clicked open.

'Auntie Rekka?'

He was holding the teddy bear.

'Oh, honey.' She turned to Google Li. 'I'll call you later.'

'Do it any time. I mean *any* time.'

And then there was the stomach-wrenching task of telling a young boy that his parents were gone. It was one of those things you see on holodramas and hope never to have to do yourself; one of those dealing-with-tragedy procedures you don't get to rehearse in advance, and wouldn't want to.

'They're gone away,' she told him. 'Gone to ...' But she did not believe in heaven, because a single copy of software does not survive the immolation of the hardware it resides on; and she had a deep distrust of education founded on the concept of lies-to-children. 'They don't exist, Jared. Dead means gone for ever, and there's never any way to—'

But then the sobbing took hold of her, and she crushed Jared to her, as he in turn hugged the bear, and he cried because she did, for he surely could not understand what she was telling him, not yet.

It would be Randolf and Angela's continuing absence over the years and decades to come that would render meaning to untimely death.

Of course Jared's biological parents were Amber and Mary. Amber was committed to her life as a Pilot, and deeply unhappy during her times on Earth, for her eye sockets were metallic I/O interfaces linking her to her ship, her occipital lobes and visual cortex having been nanovirally rewired for that purpose during the procedures that turned her into a Pilot.

Mary, absent from Jared's life since before his first birthday, had contributed the rest of the DNA; and she had also stolen fractolon infusions from the long-preserved Ro McNamara cultures, so that Jared might be a true Pilot. That had still required Amber, who carried Jared inside her, to spend the final months secretly in mu-space, there to give birth to her beautiful, wonderful obsidian-eyed boy.

Jared's legacy would be a golden universe unimaginable to ordinary humans, and yet he would be fully functional on Earth: a child of two continua.

Rekka was technically, legally, a friend of the family, still seeing Amber and shunning Mary, who had eloped with Rekka's partner Simon. Randolf and Angela had been Rekka's friends, and Rekka had introduced them to Amber and facilitated their adoption of Jared.

Until now, it had worked out perfectly.

As the month progressed, legal processes crept into action.

Given that Rekka had exactly zero rights where Jared was concerned, you could say that UNSA did everything right. The shocking thing was her own ambivalence: love and obligation on the one hand, against a deep conviction that she would be an awful stand-in mother. After all, had Rekka's own mother not tried to kill Rekka along with herself? Was she not an accidental survivor of a Suttee Pavilion? And what kind of legacy was that? But she needed to know that Jared would be safe; and perhaps the UNSA welfare psychologists who talked to her picked up on that: Rekka left those meetings feeling reassured, without ever understanding what had been accomplished.

Perhaps, in retrospect, the same psych specialists were equally adept at manipulating Amber and Mary. Legally, it was the biological parents whose wishes counted now.

'Zurich is supposed to be the best,' said Amber, sitting in the tropical garden at the back of Rekka's apartment block. 'With Karyn McNamara in charge.'

It would be a long way for Rekka to visit; but the point of a residential school was that you saw children only on holidays, wasn't it? She had no right to tell Amber what to choose.

It was now three weeks since the memorial service.

'But I told the welfare people,' Amber continued, 'that Switzerland was too far for Auntie Rekka to travel to, and Sue, that's Dr Chiang, told me that Kyoto is excellent. Better in some ways than Zurich.'

'Oh.'

'And you can come with me to check the school out. I mean without causing problems work-wise.'

It was the UNSA culture: if they decreed that an employee was to spend time on some UNSA-approved human welfare task, that employee's line managers had better show enthusiasm, or *they* were in trouble. Often Rekka thought that the organisation was too involved with people's private lives, though her own solitary existence was unaffected; but at times like these you could take advantage of the corporate parental attitude.

'Of course I'll come with you,' she said.

'Good.' Amber picked up her iced lemon tea, then put it back down. 'Am I a terrible person, Rekka?'

'No.' Rekka took hold of her hand. 'You are the very best, and Jared is proud of you.'

'He's my son, and so very young.'

On Earth, Amber saw herself as a cripple in several ways – those metal eye sockets were incapable of shedding tears – while in mu-space she soared, like a ballerina or gymnast or perhaps a dolphin in her natural element. However much Rekka thought secretly that Jared needed a full-time parent, she could never even hint that Amber might wrench herself from life as a Pilot. A bitter, half-insane mother would be worse than none at all.

'The only family I've got is an aunt in Oregon.' Amber sounded miserable. 'But a stranger, you know? Wouldn't even know Jared's name.'

She sounded so *empty*.

Rekka squeezed Amber's hand and said, 'You will make the best choice for your son, and I'll be there to help.'

'I love you, Rekka. You know that, don't you?'

Rekka was straight and Amber wasn't, yet there was nothing awkward in the moment.

'*We're* family,' said Rekka.

The family that you choose, you make, which need not be the one you were born with.

'Yes, we are.'

But all families have the power to screw up children's lives, and their decisions over the coming weeks would affect Jared for ever.

Zen gardens in the heart of the city, silence punctuated by children's laughter during the breaks, gleaming polished halls and classrooms, laboratories and gymnasia. Rekka, her hand on Amber's arm to guide her, walked through the school premises, increasingly impressed.

'We are teaching freedom and self-discipline, respectful of but not constrained by the local culture,' said a recorded holographic Frau Doktor Ilse Schwenger at the start of the tour. 'While much of the teaching is in English and Nihongo, we also deliver lessons using Puhongua, and the advantages of that are obvious.'

One of those advantages was that knowing Puhongua – still 'Mandarin' to the uneducated – made it easier to use Web Mand'rin online.

'Excuse me, ma'am. Pilot,' said a young boy with black-on-black eyes. 'I'm Carlos Delgasso and I'm nine years old. Would you like to see an aikido class?'

'We would, thank you.'

Rekka's sole physical discipline was yoga, and other stuff bored her; but aikido and Feldenkrais body-awareness training had been part of Amber's initiation into Pilothood. Any mugger who laid a hand upon a Pilot, including those who were blind in realspace, was likely to find their face smashed into concrete, and their shoulder dislocated, or worse.

The class was impressive. A slight grey-haired man, in white gi jacket and black floor-length hakama split skirt, moved with magical ease while bodies flew everywhere. His demonstration was against adult black belts; when he took his younger charges through training drills, they seemed to spend most of their time rolling without hurting themselves.

Rekka said nothing of what she glimpsed, or thought she had, from the corridor that led here: a soundproof glass panel on a dojo door that revealed a mêlée of lean figures in black jumpsuits in swarming, robust combat, with throws and kicks and punches, almost too fast to see.

'You like living here?' Amber asked young Carlos, back outside in the corridor.

'It's the best,' he said.

'Some Pilot children live in ordinary homes,' said Rekka. 'With families.'

Carlos looked solemn as he nodded.

'We're very sorry for them.'

Perhaps that was the moment that clinched their decision. Before Rekka and Amber left, Jared was officially enrolled, and all that remained was the logistical task of getting him to Kyoto with his belongings.

And saying farewell, of course.

The only surprise, when Rekka returned to work, was that Google Li had handed in her notice and already left. No one seemed to have any idea of her plans, or even whether she remained in Singapore.

It would be many years before Rekka bumped into Google Li by chance at a conference in Frankfurt, where they did something very rare for both of them: got tremendously drunk on schnapps, Cointreau and tequila, and woke up the next morning on separate twin beds in Rekka's hotel room.

That morning, Google Li would share the suspicions that caused her to question her career aspirations and leave UNSA without a word; but by then, Rekka had been asking herself similar questions for years, regarding the likelihood that Randolf and Angela's death had really been an accident, instead of orchestrated murder in which their fellow passengers and flight crew were collateral damage within acceptable parameters, by the standards of an organisation grown too big and remorseless to own a conscience.

Or in which schemers like the two UN senators, Luisa and Robert Higashionna, wielded such unquestioned influence, pursuing goals that no ordinary people could guess at, moving like sharks through a sea of political and corporate power that minnow-like citizens would never understand.

Rekka and Google Li would share tears and hugs that morning, and never see each other again.

TWENTY-SEVEN

Call him a fuck-up seeking atonement. As far as Piet Gunnarsson was concerned, the first part – without the atonement-seeking – was what everyone did already.

Self-loathing and desperation do not lend attractiveness to any business proposition, but somehow he persuaded the Far Reach Centre logistics people – he talked to someone called Rowena James – to let him make a rescheduled cargo delivery to Vachss Station, in orbit around Vijaya, along with a personal package for one Jed Goran, Pilot. It was urgently required, the main cargo load, because some sort of onboard crisis had caused the original delivery to be cancelled.

The schedule was almost impossible, unless Piet followed something close to a hellflight trajectory. A whole bunch of other Pilots, he was sure, had already turned down the job.

'This is important, then?' he asked.

'Lives aren't at stake, but' – Rowena touched the personal package – 'you know what people are like.'

'Whatever. I'll take the job.'

'Thank you, Pilot Gunnarsson.'

Her straightforward politeness was very different from the glances he received afterwards, walking along the Poincaré Promenade, heading for the great docking bay where his ship was waiting for him, filled with unconditional, understanding love.

You're OK, my love.

I'll try to be, for your sake.

For his sake, she acquiesced in the choice of geodesic; and as they flew the almost-hellflight, their conjoined selves filled with pain as well as the exhilaration of effort. Their suffering brought them closer than ever, offering the possibility of healing and redemption in a way that Piet did not feel he deserved.

Tearing through an unusual spiralling trajectory, Piet-and-ship burst out of a blood-coloured nebula close to their destination, finding themselves behind three Zajinet ships whose weapon systems were in the process of powering up.

So. Zajinets.

Whatever Piet's role in causing hostilities, there had been open attacks on seven worlds that he knew of: it wasn't just about him. If this was another such raid then he could *not* allow it to happen.

We fight, my love?

Oh, yes. We fight.

Only soft people who have never experienced conflict believe in the concept of a fair fight. There has never been such a thing. When the objective is to take out the enemy, an attack without warning is the surest strategy. Ship-and-Piet followed the three Zajinet vessels through a realspace insertion and cut loose immediately, taking out the centremost vessel and arcing right, away from the explosion, aware that violet beams of not-quite-analysable energy split vacuum only metres away from Piet-and-ship's wing. The surviving Zajinets were zig-zagging to set up a pincer attack on ship-and-Piet, whose weapons-fire sprayed past them, finding them hard to target—

They're so fast.

And used to working together.

—and glimpsing the complex orbital that was Vachss Station, so vulnerable to such a sudden attack from nowhere—

Look out!

—as the trailing edge of their left wing burned with pain, but they tumbled into a desperate escape trajectory, firing bursts designed to make the bastards think and hesitate, and Piet-and-ship were scared that this was the end and not for themselves alone—

There.

Yes. Got it.

—but they screamed through a hard turn, letting loose with everything they had and causing no damage but getting the effect they wanted, both Zajinets coming round to deliver the final weapons burst, but they were not going to succeed because the bronze-and-silver ship streaking this way was moving very fast indeed and its weapons were—

Got one.

—powerful, tearing one of the Zajinets apart in a tenth of a second, and clipping the other as it turned away and white light blazed—

Give chase?

No, we can't.

All right.

—and the Pilot ship hung there as if hesitating, deciding whether to follow the survivor into mu-space, then gliding around to come close to Piet-and-ship.

You're wounded.

Yes, but treatable.

Agreed, and you should be in Labyrinth.

Vachss Station, their destination, lay before Piet-and-ship.

We have cargo to deliver.

All right, give me one moment.

After a few seconds, as Piet partially disengaged from his ship, an ordinary realspace comms holo appeared in the control cabin.

'I'm Ibrahim al-Khalid, in Vachss Station Control,' said the morose-looking Pilot in the image. 'You have our gratitude, Pilot. Jed Goran tells me you want to deliver cargo.'

'Jed Goran? He's in the other ship?'

Something very sad and proud was involved in al-Khalid's expression. 'That's him.'

'Then I've something for him, too.'

'He's heading back to Labyrinth. Fly together, and you can give it to him there. If you like, to save time, you can eject the rest of the cargo from your hold, and I'll come out with a shuttle team to pick the stuff up. The containers are tagged with long-wave markers?'

'Standard encoding.'

'Good enough. And ... That was well fought. Thanks again, Pilot.'

Piet blew out a long breath.

'Any time,' he said, and closed the comm session.

I told you that you're all right.

Only because of you.

Closing his eyes, Piet re-entered conjunction trance, as he-and-ship opened their dorsal surface and let go of their cargo. As the containers tumbled free, ship-and-Piet dropped away and sealed up their hull once more.

Ready, Pilot Goran.

With me then, Pilot Gunnarsson.

They performed the mu-space transition quickly, just in case, but no Zajinets were lying in wait: the golden void was clear. So they chose an easy geodesic, and both Pilots-and-ships turned in synchrony, matching trajectory.

We'll be OK.

Yes, we will.

Flying easily together, heading for Labyrinth.

Inside the great docking bay, small self-guided tenders clustered around Piet Gunnarsson's wounded ship while he disembarked. Before stepping onto the dock's walkway, he went down on one knee atop his ship's wing and pressed his palm against her warm soft surface, while his other arm clasped a package against his torso.

They'll look after you. Heal up.

Yes. Come soon.

Of course I will.

From the walkway, he watched as the tenders gently shepherded his wonderful ship into a wide white tunnel leading deep into Ascension Annexe, where Labyrinth could bring all her healing powers to bear. She would be all right, his ship.

'You saved Vachss Station.' Pilot Goran, from the bronze-and-silver ship, had a muscular face and an easy grin. 'Well done, Pilot Gunnarrsson.'

'Call me Piet.'

'And I'm Jed.'

The two Pilots shook hands. Then Piet held out the package. 'I was supposed to give this to you on the orbital.'

'Well ... A personal delivery?' Jed pressed the outer wrapping to display the manifest data. 'Ah.'

It read *Sender: Clara James.*

Piet said, 'Shall I leave you to—?'

'No, let me unwrap this, and then we'll go for a drink.'

'If you like.'

The wrapping unfolded at Jed's command. Inside was a box containing a small medal, shaped like a knot formed of Möbius strips, on a chain. And a holo note that read: *If you're going to dash around saving worlds, you'd better marry me. –C*

Jed looked as if someone had just dug him in the solar plexus.

'Er ...' he said.

'Wow,' said Piet. 'Are you going to say yes?'

'Oh. Yeah. Hell, yeah.'

'I'd better you leave you to it, then.'

'No ...' Jed stopped with the medal and chain in his fist. 'I was going to buy you a drink and tell everyone what a hero you are.'

'There's no need.'

'But people think—'

'It doesn't matter what they think,' said Piet quietly, 'so long as they're wrong.'

Jed stared at him, then activated his tu-ring. It swapped ident-codes with Piet's tu-ring.

'Let's meet up later,' said Jed. 'For a private celebration. Good enough?'

'More than.' Piet pointed at the medal and holo. 'Good luck.'

'Yeah. Thank you.'

They nodded at each other then turned away, each summoning a fastpath rotation.

The Admiralty debriefing report was copied to Clara, and displayed as a her-eyes-only virtual holo while Max and the others continued the conference. Anything tagged *Jed Goran* was for her immediate attention, and she grinned as she realised he was back. Then her lean, endurance-athlete's face and body tightened as she read through the annotations and watched holo footage of ship-to-ship combat against Zajinets.

'Clara?' said Max. 'Are you with us?'

'Sorry, sir.' She gestured, and the virtual holo became a real image above the conference table. 'Just in from Vachss Station. Seems Piet Gunnarsson has redeemed himself.'

They watched, the seven people in the room, and nodded at the destruction of two Zajinet vessels.

'There was only one Pilot at the orbital?' asked Bob Weng, one of Admiral Asai's strategy aides. 'Doesn't it have a Sanctuary?'

'With one permanent resident and one semi-permanent,' said Clara. 'But they're Shipless, Draper for the usual reason, and al-Khalid because his ship died. Some of you might remember the incident.'

People shivered. For a Pilot to live on past the death of their ship—

'Poor bastard,' said Clayton.

'I can't imagine it,' said Weng. 'How can he face waking up in the mornings?'

'Or going to sleep and dreaming.'

'Hell.'

There was a silence which took a few moments to shake off.

'We need to spread out a protective net,' said Copeland, who was Weng's opposite number on Admiral Zajac's staff.

'The question is, can we assume that they'll continue to attack in small numbers, two or three vessels at a time?'

Max flattened his big hands against the tabletop.

'The longer we're occupied with Zajinets,' he said, 'the less we know about Schenck and what he's up to.'

Everyone in the room was cleared for knowledge of the renegade base near the realspace galactic centre. Also for intelligence regarding the darkness, to the extent they knew anything at all, and of the strategists' best guesses as to its intentions.

'You think the renegades will mount an attack fleet?' said Clayton. 'On what target?'

'I don't know,' answered Max. 'And my ignorance is what scares me.'

He gestured, and Clara's holo report disappeared, replaced by the familiar view of the galactic core and the shining needle, a thousand lightyears long, emanating from the centre.

'I'm guessing—' He started, then coughed wetly.

'Max?' Clara was out of her seat.

Clayton was already sending an emergency signal.

'Medics,' he said. 'We need medics.'

Bending forward, Max's fists were in his lap, fighting the pain. *Black. Stone.*

'Don't talk,' said Clara. 'Medics are— Here.'

The air rippled apart, and three uniformed medics stepped into the conference room. The rotation held open for an auto-doc to slide out, its carapace already opening.

'Positive ... Vetting,' said Max.

'Using Haxigoji.' Clayton took hold of Max's shoulder. 'Get Roger to train them up, right?'

'Right ...'

'Everyone, we need room.' The lead medic moved Clayton aside. 'All right, Commodore. We're with you.'

Golden sparks blossomed all around Max, interacting with his normal medical femtocytes that should have sent warning signals of any impending medical catastrophe. Perhaps he had spent too long working inside security-sealed rooms from which all comms were blocked; perhaps it was that simple.

Pavel Karelin rotated into the room, his face pale. 'Commodore ...'

The medics were bundling Max into the autodoc, which after a few moments sealed up.

'Casevac now,' said the lead medic. 'Back off, everyone.'

'I'll handle security,' said Clayton. 'A watch team at all times.'

To guard Max, he meant.

'Do it,' said Pavel.

Clayton disappeared a second before the medics, and the autodoc that looked so like a coffin, rotated out to a secure layer of the Med Centre. After the rush, everything transitioned to stillness; then everybody moved and talked at once.

'All right, listen up,' said Pavel. 'I'm Deputy Director *pro tem*, so let's settle down and keep things running. And don't worry, I want Max back in charge as soon as possible. I'm sure you do, too.'

But Clara thought of all the massive strain Max had been under for so long: it wasn't just the torture he underwent while a prisoner; it was the years of being the only one who understood the threat the darkness represented inside Labyrinth, of identifying first Schenck and then the most powerful of his co-conspirators, slowly and secretly working without ever knowing whether he had just confided in an agent of the darkness few people could sense at all, and then only dimly.

Apart from Roger ... and possibly every native inhabitant of Vijaya.

It took hours to get things organised, to respond to the shock of Max's collapse. When Clara finally fastpath-rotated back to her apartment and Jed was standing there grinning, saying, 'The answer is yes, my love. Definitely yes,' there was a long, dislocated pause during which she did not know what he was talking about. Then it came to her, and for the first time in years she came close to crying as she kissed the man she loved.

'Bloody right it is,' she told him. 'There's no escape for you.'

They clasped each other hard.

TWENTY-EIGHT

EARTH, 793 AD

Chill wolf of the willow was the storm-wind's name, and Fenrisulfr snarled in the face of it from his place on the prow-beast: the longboat which was leading the raiding squadron across the grey, chopping seas; and it had not escaped the grim-humoured warriors on board that their leader's name meant he was a hell-wolf. His lieutenant, Brökkr, rode the second longboat, and that was good. For a while after Byzantium, Brökkr had commanded his own fighters; now he had rejoined Fenrisulfr along with his men, on the promise of blood and gold and danger.

Sometimes Fenrisulfr wished he could employ rhetoric and magic as that bastard poet Stígr had so long ago, using words to control men's minds. But Fenrisulfr's actions and decisions, and his ability to control *berserkergangr*, would have to suffice, as they had since he slew the reaver chief Magnús, fifteen summers before.

'Do they have good warriors over there?' Thollákr shouted against the wind.

'There are people who can fight. There always are.'

'Good, then.'

Fenrisulfr half-smiled against hard wind and spume. 'You know why we have so many water kennings for blood? Battle sea, sea of spears, current of the sword? Spears' torrent?'

Thóllakr's hair whipped in the wind as he shook his head.

'No, Chief.'

'Because we swim in it or drown!'

A grin was Thóllakr's answer, along with: 'And it makes you puke if you drink it.'

Fenrisulfr laughed, sea air deep in his lungs.

It was a heady pleasure to be alive and the bringer of death, never the recipient – until the Norns betrayed you, as they would in the end.

Finally, the shadow of land grew amid the grey blend of sea and sky, a promontory atop which stood a stone fort-like structure; except that if they had been told the truth, it was occupied by holy men, not warriors. Something other than the icy wind caused Fenrisulfr's innards to chill, and by the time they beached the prow-beast on shingle, the recognition was strong, despite the gloom enveloping the world.

I was here before.

That other day, long past, when he had been transported by troll magic: bright sky and summer sun had shone as he slew the imprisoned troll-spirit. It had glowed blue, and was comrade to the red spirit that had carried Fenrisulfr – then simply Ulfr – across a great distance in the space between heartbeats. Somehow Stígr had been making use of the imprisoned troll's magic, using it to transport himself at will.

Ulfr had removed that power by killing the captive, using the crystal-headed spear; but had failed to destroy his real enemy, that bastard Stígr, before the 'good' troll-spirit snatched Ulfr home.

'They call it Holy Island,' Thóllakr told Ivarr.

'I know.'

'Ári says they pray to a trinity, meaning Óthinn, Baldr and Loki, except they use different names.'

'They'll be praying while they shit themselves, soon as they catch sight of us.'

Several warriors walked downwind to piss, or squat down shielded by their cloaks, while they waited for the other long-boats to beach. Finally, when the whole band was gathered,

Egil Blood-Sword and Bjartr Red-Tooth called them to order.

The two chiefs were more important than Fenrisulfr, if not as feared.

'We take only tribute here, remember,' said Egil. 'And a small one at that. Keep your weapons sheathed, men. And not inside the local maidens, Davith.'

'Or the sheep,' said someone. 'Or pigs.'

'Why, did your mother sail with us?'

Chuckles and jeers were almost drowned by storm-wind.

'The nicer we are to the locals,' said Bjartr, 'the fewer fighters need to remain here on guard, while we make a little incursion on foot.'

Later they would hug the coast until they found a suitable river inlet, and make use of the prow-beasts' shallow draughts. Riverside settlements were rarely prepared for the sight of sea-going vessels suddenly appearing beside them: normal ships would smash their keels if they attempted to sail inland; but when raiders went a-Viking, they slipped deep into the country at will.

'Don't worry,' added Bjartr. 'We'll all see Axe-Time soon enough.'

'And Shrieking when Davith gets his cock out.'

There was laughter at the punning, for Axe-Time and Shrieking were two of the All-Father's Death Choosers who might swoop down to take their spirits back to Valhöll, where they would train and fight among the Einherjar, and never die again before the final battle that was Ragnarökkr.

Orange flame-light showed at the holy men's tower.

'They've seen us,' said Fenrisulfr.

'I thought I smelled someone shitting themselves,' said Ivarr.

'That was me,' Fenrisulfr told him. 'Thinking about Davith getting his weapon ready.'

Chuckles accompanied the loosening of blades, the hitching of hammers and axes, the hefting of spears by their balance points, the rolling of shoulders and jogging on the spot, shingles crunching, to get ready.

The way to negotiate was to be ready for slaughter.

*

There was a tonsured holy man – chief of the holy men – and a village leader who began by saying they wanted peace, and were prepared to pay tribute to such mighty men of the sword. Ivarr and Thóllakr looked at Davith and smirked, while others tried to keep a straight face. Chief Egil and Bjartr glanced at each other and nodded, then turned to Fenrisulfr who did likewise.

'Your terms are well offered,' he said to the holy man, who spoke the Tongue. 'We accept them warmly.'

Many of the raiders possessed a smattering of languages, but in matters like this it was best for someone fluent to translate. Fenrisulfr knew enough of the local tongue to understand that the holy man translated correctly, while the relief on the village leader's face was answer enough.

As the tribute arrived, Egil directed some of his men to take it to the longboats, rather than make the locals carry it all the way. Fenrisulfr understood the reasoning: allowing the locals to see the vessels up close would lessen their fear; best that the prow-beasts remain like waiting dragons, redolent with danger.

All went well until Thóllakr cut himself on an unsheathed blade: a gift, part of the tribute that he should have known how to handle properly. Fenrisulfr felt like killing him on the spot, for showing such ineptitude; but dissent within a force is also a sign of weakness. Fenrisulfr forced his fury down.

'We have healers,' said the holy man. 'Let us help.'

'I should hamstring the whelp,' muttered Brökkr, behind Fenrisulfr's shoulder. But for the locals, those words were drowned out by Bjartr's loud acknowledgement of their kindness.

Fenrisulfr hoped that the healers' ministrations, whatever

they were, would burn like the flames of Surt, the Fire Giant who ruled hot Múspellheim.

Ivarr and Knótr helped Thóllakr – at least he had the sense not to whimper – follow the holy man back to the village by the sacred tower, or whatever it was.

In broken Tongue, the villager said: 'We feast. Now. You join?'

They would need to keep watchful and go easy on the mead or ale, but eating well would be a good thing after the voyage.

'We will feast with you,' said Bjartr Red-Tooth.

And so they did.

When he had eaten enough of the local fowl, and drunk a horn of watery mead, Fenrisulfr clapped several of his men on the shoulder, then went outside. In the wake of the storm, the night smelled fresh beneath a white full moon, strong enough to cast shadows.

He felt good, and knew there was a small task left undone: telling Thóllakr what an idiot he was. Fenrisulfr grinned, since the young warrior's clumsiness seemed to have done no harm; but he would use harsh words nonetheless.

Someone was throwing up in the stinking middens. On the way back, he would check that it was not one of his own band, whom he expected to maintain discipline. The locals seemed cowed, but there was always an element of doubt in an unknown country, the possibility of allies secretly summoned and moving through the night – it was bright enough to travel by – for a dawn attack.

Possible, not likely.

And then he heard it.

Dah, dah-dum, dah-dah-dah-dum, dah-dah.

The nine-note sequence was faint, not as if the darkness were distant, but as if it had grown weak. And what of that? A weakened enemy was easier to kill, that was all.

It's been fifteen years.

So it was possible the tainted spirit belonged to someone

other than Stígr; but as the *berserkergangr* roiled within Fenrisulfr, begging to take over, he knew it did not matter: whoever this was, they were going to die.

He hefted his twin war-axes, lately his weapons of choice – he wore his sword as status symbol and back-up weapon, along with a dagger, while the crystal-tipped spear remained at the longboat, guarded – and set off at a jog, following a flattened path through moonlit silver grass, towards a large roundhouse inside which an orange fire burned. If his quarry was warm and relaxed, so much the better, for cold wind and chaos would enter along with him, the hell-wolf, and destruction would follow.

Ready.

His foot smashed the door in, and he was inside.

Stígr!

The one-eyed man was there, mouth opening—

NOW!

—as twin axe-blades cut down through his collar bones and into his chest, cutting his heart so that unconsciousness came instantly, but that was not enough because the spirit might yet feel agony before it left the body, and this one deserved to suffer, so in his *berserkr* rage Fenrisulfr continued to cut and smash, to kick and hew, smashing the dead thing into butchered parts, over and over—

Done.

—and then it clicked off, the *berserkergangr*, as only he could manage, and Fenrisulfr was a man once more, only a man.

The inside of the roundhouse was wet, all dripping red, painted by Stígr's blood. A warrior knew, as a non-warrior could not, just how much blood might spray and gush from a human body; but even so, it was spectacular, the scarlet decoration of the interior: ceiling, curved walls, the table and cots, and the spattered clothing and faces of the people staring at him, shocked.

Thóllakr, his wound bandaged and wrapped with a poultice, was the first to speak.

'Chief? Why, uh ...?'

Fenrisulfr answered: 'He was possessed of the darkness.'

A holy man was there, not their chief but a relative youth, along with a young woman who looked to have been holding Thóllakr's hand: under other circumstances, Fenrisulfr would have thought *Good for you*. But there was the aftermath of destroying his enemy to deal with.

'He prayed,' said the young holy man in passable Tongue. 'For many years, he prayed to weaken the demons that tortured his spirit. And the darkness is weak, he said. It can only touch men's spirits, and that barely, and makes do with that because it cannot move worldly objects directly, so it really is not mighty but very, very weak ...'

He seemed to realise he was babbling, but could not help spilling more words: 'Stígr said the dark powers needed a bridge that was not Bifröst. That everyone forgets Múspellheim in their schemes. And he said only you would understand that.'

'You've never seen me before.' Fenrisulfr shrugged, spilling blood from his axe-heads. 'You cannot know me.'

The holy man wiped his face, then looked startled at the sight of his hand, as if he had thought he was wiping off sweat instead of dead man's blood.

'Stígr said a wolf from hell would come for him.'

There was more the young holy man wanted to say, but though his mouth worked, his throat seized up; and then he turned away, making a mystic gesture – hand to forehead, stomach, then either side of his chest. Fenrisulfr had seen it before, as far east as Byzantium, and now here in the west.

The scrape of blades withdrawing from scabbards came from outside.

Fenrisulfr crouched and growled, ready to strike. Then he heard: 'Chief? Fenrisulfr?'

'Come inside, good Brökkr.'

Behind Brökkr came Egil Blood-Sword, then his warrior

215

Davith, and Ári from Fenrisulfr's band, along with the chief holy man, whose face was pale.

'Y-you killed Stígr. He was under our protection.'

Fenrisulfr felt himself tremble.

'Don't think much of your protection,' said Davith, while Egil frowned.

'This was a creature of darkness,' said Fenrisulfr. 'A *seithr* adept. An abomination, holy man, that *you* sheltered.'

'You had no—'

But the holy man reached out to grab Fenrisulfr, and that was a mistake.

'*Agh!*'

Blood gushed again as Fenrisulfr's axe severed the arm.

'Shit,' said Egil.

He punched the howling holy man in the back of the neck, and the holy man dropped face-first and silent, blood spurting from the glistening stump.

Then Egil looked at Fenrisulfr and grinned.

'Guess we just changed our plans.'

Behind Fenrisulfr, Thóllakr groaned as he swung himself up from the cot, and put one arm around the young woman, who had not spoken and who looked in shock. It was a wordless claim of ownership or at least protection, which his fellow warriors would not break. The remaining young holy man shrank back, as if hoping no one would notice him.

'Blood and death,' said Fenrisulfr quietly.

'Blood and death,' agreed Egil Blood-Sword.

And Brökkr laughed.

'The Hell-Wolf is with us again.'

Fenrisulfr growled once more as *berserkergangr* came upon him. Egil dropped to one side and Brökkr to the other, understanding the danger, and allowed Fenrisulfr to rush outside first, before following with weapons ready. Fenrisulfr, sprinting hard, gave vent to his wolf-warrior's roar, and everywhere the raiders responded, heartbeat-fast, drawing and swinging weapons, instantly transformed in a way soft villagers and holy men could never understand or cope with.

And the slaughter began, as the Middle World reduced to two things only, for in warrior rage it is hard to hear the screaming.

Blood and death were all.

TWENTY-NINE

Every war needs a name, though its survivors normally term it just that: The War. In human history there had never been a war across the stars, never mind spanning continua; but as the hunt for revenge against the Zajinets intensified, the massively non-linear dynamics of mu-space engagements, not to mention the indecipherable thought processes of the enemy, meant that for Pilots, only one name sufficed for the struggle thrust upon them.

They called it the Chaos Conflict.

And while human warfare requires dehumanising the enemy – because over ninety per cent of men and women possess strong inhibitions against killing their own species – the Zajinets were clearly alien already. The difficulty for strategic planners was in understanding them enough to predict their actions and reactions.

Roger Blackstone knew of the Zajinets' fears, thanks to Ro McNamara, and he had shared what he knew with his superior officers. The key quotation was this: '*They* [meaning humanity] *will allow the darkness to be born. It will spread across the galaxy, and they won't fight back until billions have perished.*'

The numbers of Pilots training for combat and adopting full-time military roles continued to increase, to perhaps two per cent of Pilots possessing ships, but that figure was a guess. Roger did not have clearance for accurate numbers. Conversely, details of his ability remained classified, because there was only one of him, along with a tiny number of Pilots with a weak sensitivity to the darkness.

Hence the importance of allies who might share Roger's

ability, even though they were confined to realspace.

On first arrival at Vachss Station, Roger had checked the residents' list and failed to find the name he was looking for. But al-Khalid had given him access to the arrivals/departures data, and it seemed that he was four standard tendays (or a Vijayan month) too late: Leeja Rigelle had departed for Earth, no return journey booked; and a certain Tannier had flown with her.

There were things to distract Roger. His work meant spending half of his time on Vijaya's surface, based in a luxurious building in Mintberg that would have done justice to Imperial Rome or Byzantium, with some high-tech embellishments. It was in many ways a Renaissance or neo-classical culture, and he came to enjoy being among the Haxigoji.

Whenever possible, he flew, coursing mu-space and filling himself-and-ship with energised elation; and when Corinne, also graduated from Tangleknot, had leave from her classified Admiralty work, she would fly to Vachss Station where they would book a suite together and not venture outside until it was time for her to leave.

Their future was a subject they avoided.

Local Haxigoji, when Roger was in Mintberg, were used to seeing him pound the streets early in their twenty-eight hour day (he had adjusted his circadian rhythms to suit), running and returning to his quarters for strength and combat training. On occasion, to their mutual benefit, he sparred with Haxigoji bannermen from the City Guard.

Working alongside Nectarblossom, he embarked on creating a training programme for Haxigoji recruits: learning how to move among humanity, deciphering their cultures, and the clues that might lead them to a darkness-corrupted human, and how to deal with the authorities when they detected such a person. Combat skills were a part of it, and Roger drilled them hard because it was more than their own lives at stake; but he also emphasised the extent to which this was a last resort.

Then there were anti-surveillance skills and the like, because once Haxigoji started living among humans, and the darkness-corrupted individuals among them understood the threat, all Haxigoji would be at risk of assassination. It should not be a high risk, since any act of violence brought attention, but it was a factor.

It took time to get the programme up and running, but by the end of two standard years, the third batch of trainees was getting ready for their final test. Partly for psychological reasons, to seal in the previous training, every intense programme needs a rite of passage on completion.

And that, for these very special recruits, was where the human prisoners came in.

On several occasions, Nectarblossom told him, 'You should not feel sorry for them, Roger. They're not really human. Their infection makes them something else.'

'We can cure infections,' he had answered the first time.

'Not this one.'

Initially, for safety, Roger preferred to use non-Pilot agents of the darkness, captured on sweeps through realspace cities or orbitals. At first, those sweeps had been carried out by other Pilots on Max Gould's books, recorded as possessing a tiny portion of Roger's ability. Some of the current batch of prisoners had been detected by Haxigoji graduates of the training programme.

They normally resided, the non-Pilot prisoners, in ultra-secure facilities on one of three isolated realspace worlds; but for the test, Roger had commandeered a long-disused deep-space research station. He had wanted a place where he and Nectarblossom had total control, and got it.

Roger had not been party to the Admiralty discussion regarding renegade Pilots, but it had been decided on high that certain trusted Haxigoji would be told of the renegades' existence – to the best of Roger's knowledge, Nectarblossom was the first to learn of it – on the basis that the programme's graduates needed to be prepared for anything, including the detection of renegade Pilots operating among ordinary humans on realspace worlds.

It was not a secret to be shared with humanity at large. The Chaos Conflict, war against the Zajinets, was open knowledge; the notion that Pilot might fight Pilot in all-out warfare, that was something to keep quiet for as long as possible.

Realspace populations needed to feel safe, and they could only continue to do so if they did not realise the extent to which Pilots felt fear, like anybody else.

And so, the prisoners.

This time around, there were in fact three Pilots, all caught while operating on realspace worlds undercover, all equipped with countersurveillance measures. Their captured tu-rings had been of great interest to Admiralty scientists. Two were caught simply because of superior concentrations of surveillance tech. The third had been recognised by a Pilot delivering goods to Göthewelt; after the prisoner was taken and fifty unconscious passers-by were revived from the smartmiasma-induced coma used in the arrest, local Sanctuary representatives had spun a story about a new Anomaly seed, rather than a darkness-corrupted Pilot. The local authorities were satisfied, and awarded a civic medal to the Pilot who had recognised the threat.

If renegade Pilots were beginning to operate undercover in greater numbers, Roger's Haxigoji trainees had better know for sure they could spot them. So this time around, Pilots would be part of the final test.

Which the trainees had better, after all of his and Nectarblossom's efforts, pass with ease.

When Roger had first boarded Metronome Station, protected by a quickglass suit, he had watched while engineers brought the lonely facility back to life, installing modern technology, bringing the station up to a stable spin and restoring warmth and breathable air, section by section, until the whole thing might have been in its heyday, had it not been for the lack of crew.

Because of his meetings with Ro McNamara, Roger had become something of a history buff where Pilots were concerned; and so he made a private pilgrimage to the long-abandoned control room where long ago a scientist on duty, one Dorothy Verzhinski, had picked up a wordless distress call whose audio signal contained only one thing: the sound of a baby crying.

The drifting mu-space ship contained an unconscious and fading Pilot, along with the baby she had given birth to before transiting into realspace: a breach birth delivered by performing a Caesarean upon herself, using her inboard robotic tool-arms. The Pilot, saved by shuttles despatched from Metronome Station, had been Karyn McNamara; and the baby grew up to be Dorothy McNamara, named after Verzhinski, except that she hated her first name and shortened it to Ro.

By mean-geodesic time, that had occurred four hundred and eighty-three years ago. No wonder Ro remained hidden from the rest of humanity: how could anyone cope with a society that had advanced by nearly half a millennium from the one they had grown up in?

Today, on the occasion of the final test for the third run of the six-month training programme, Metronome Station was once again warm and comfortable. Roger wore only a normal jumpsuit, though a nodule of quickglass fastened against his skin would spread to cover him should it be necessary, while Nectarblossom wore a heavy white tabard, decorated with gold brocade, over a pale-blue silk-like tunic and trews: her formal best, designed to intimidate the candidates beforehand, and increase the sense of ceremony afterwards, when they were told they had passed.

Assuming they did pass.

Roger and Nectarblossom walked along a grey-carpeted central corridor, wide and tastefully lit and scented, trailed by twenty-four hopeful Haxigoji of both sexes, dressed in the dark sleeveless jackets and breeches that served as tac uniforms, giving off a faint odour of excitement that even Roger had learned to recognise. To Nectarblossom, the scent would be anything but faint, he guessed. Then he stopped, and the recruits did likewise as Nectarblossom walked on to check the testing area.

'All right.' He turned to face them. 'Good luck, everyone. We'll call you in one by one. The exit from the testing-area is on the other side, where you'll meet up afterwards. You can do it.'

Amber eyes with horizontal slits were fastened on him. Several Haxigoji nodded: a learned human gesture.

'Crisp,' he added, 'you'll be first. Two minutes, and we start.'

Then he strode ahead, passed through unfolding security doors, nodded to the two heavily armed Pilots on guard – there were half a dozen others stationed at sensible locations – and passed through to what had been a viewing gallery. The entire wall to his right formed a window on space, opposite a relaxation area on the left, now transformed into a series of seven open-fronted cells. Each cell's opening glowed dull orange: inbuilt weaponry ready to blast any person or thing that tried to pass through.

Inside each cell was a single captive; and the central cell was occupied by a Pilot called Morik, the one captured on Göthewelt. He sat pale and glowering, darkness lapping strongly around him. A smartmiasma guarded him, sensitive to his biochemistry, ready to respond to a build-up of adrenaline, satanin or other precursor to physical action.

The teams of guards were highly trained, with careful procedures ensuring only one prisoner was on the move at a time. With Roger and Nectarblossom present, there was the added advantage that any change in the quality of darkness would be apparent to them. And also to the recruits they were about to test, they hoped.

Cells two and five contained guards who had been

'volunteered' to act as prisoners; the recruits were expected to detect their freedom from dark influence.

'Time to start,' said Nectarblossom, and summoned Crisp.

Crisp was tall even among Haxigoji, straight-shouldered as he walked to the first cell, stopped and considered the enemy for a few moments, moved to the second – this time a twitch of those shoulders indicated his amusement at the deception – and on to the next cell and the next. The prisoners this time were well-behaved, or rather subdued – during the two earlier tests, some had become aggressive – and when Crisp stopped before the cell containing Morik, he seemed rapt in concentration due to Morik being a darkness-controlled Pilot rather than ordinary human.

It took Roger over five seconds to realise that something was going wrong.

Shit!

Crisp shuddered as the darkness entered him.

'Shut him down!' Roger shouted. 'Shut Morik down!'

One of the guards gestured, and in his cell, Morik collapsed. But that did nothing to stop Crisp falling back onto the deck, where a tremendous shaking took hold of him, limbs thumping in some awful response to the twists of darkness around his head, and how could anyone prevent such an infiltration? If Crisp became a creature of the darkness then what did that mean for—?

Stillness.

The change had happened so fast.

'We will honour him,' came softly from Nectarblossom's torc.

'What?' said Roger.

Those amber eyes were matt-looking, no longer lustrous. Medical scanners opened up holo phase spaces all around, with textual annotations explaining the readings' significance, summed up by three words: Crisp was dead.

When Roger looked up, he realised that all of the cells' occupants were unconscious, including the two unfortunate volunteers. Guards swarmed, taking up new positions. Total lockdown.

'I'm sorry, Nectarblossom.' Roger did not know what else to say.

Morik had been careful, setting up whatever process he had used – perhaps it was similar to the way the Anomaly spread, perhaps it was something else: Admiralty analysts would be poring over data from the smartmiasma and other devices here – and aiming to influence one of the Haxigoji rather than a human, either because he thought the guards would be less likely to suspect what was happening, or because for the process to work, the intended target had to be an individual naturally sensitive to the darkness.

That latter seemed more likely to Roger. He was trained to continue thinking while danger or potential danger threatened, but all the while, sour regret and mourning swirled through him. He had been with these recruits for half a standard year, and liked them all no matter how tough he was with them, and Crisp had been one of the best.

Nectarblossom's huge double-thumbed hand clasped Roger's shoulder.

'I'll tell the others the test is cancelled,' she said. 'And explain why.'

She went off, ceremonial tabard rustling against the silk garments beneath, dressed for a different kind of eventuality to this tragedy, poor Crisp's body lying sightless on the deck.

There's always another way to look at things.

Dad had drilled that dictum into him. When you had good reason to mourn, you must mourn: using cognitive techniques to bypass such a process would make one inhuman. But in perspective shifts lie the possibility of future resolution: as a heuristic, there are always three ways (or more) to view a situation.

Crisp was dead, and Roger would mourn him.

You were a good person.

And if Roger could find a way to kill Morik undetected, he would do that too.

You were—

He realised what his subconscious had already noticed, the reason he had remembered Dad's words about perspective shifts: because Crisp's death had another implication.

The Haxigoji could not be suborned by the darkness.

Better than human.

If they could not fight it off, they reacted at a deep cellular level – the evidence was in the shifting, coloured holo images surrounding Crisp's body – shutting down all the way into death.

Roger would have to fly to Labyrinth.

But first he summoned the most experienced of the team leaders, explained his thinking about Crisp, and told her to pass the word on to the others, because if something happened to him, this news needed to reach the Admiralty.

Then he braced himself for the painful part: rejoining Nectarblossom and the remaining recruits. For even with the strategic importance of what he had learned, these were his people and he had to mourn with them.

THIRTY

Gavriela punished Rupert by insisting they meet at Imperial, where they sat in a lecture theatre in the Huxley building listening to her friend Jane talk about warfare among ants, Jane's words being illustrated with bizarre and gruesome colour slides. The point was that Rupert wanted Gavriela to debrief while she wanted to go to Oxford to pick up Carl – she had flown into Heathrow from Tempelhof late last night – so she compromised by agreeing to talk but refusing to go to Headquarters on Broadway.

Rupert sat with elegant legs crossed, his trousers steam-pressed with knife-edge creases, and gave every sign of enjoying Jane's lecture, which had not been Gavriela's intention.

Several slides showed African termites, *globitermes sulfureus*, squirting sticky yellow fluid from their mouths. 'They eject the nasty stuff,' Jane told the audience, 'pumped from two dorsal glands, and it snags up enemy soldier termites. The termites doing the ejecting are tangled up with the enemy. Guess what they do then?'

A few grins showed among the biologists, while most of those from other disciplines looked intrigued, then half-amused, half-horrified when Jane pushed the next slide into projector. The camera had caught the termites in mid-explosion, fluid and guts everywhere.

'They entangle themselves with the enemy, and blow themselves up,' Jane went on. 'Or to put it another way, there's nothing unnatural about kamikaze behaviour. Here' – she changed slides once more – 'we have *campanotus* ants. I took this picture in Malaysia. Liquid explosive in their mandibles, and again they blow themselves up, usually taking out multiple enemy ants from other colonies. Everyone here knows that war is terrible, but compared to these chaps, human beings are amateurs.'

Then she sidetracked, perhaps to give temporary relief from pictures of insectile gore.

'One of the interesting theoretical questions,' she continued, 'is whether the behaviour of an individual ant or termite can be viewed as altruism, in the same sense in which a mother bird will die to defend her chicks, or a chimpanzee will fight to defend youngsters in the same group who are not her offspring. Does self-sacrifice in war spring from the same Darwinian imperative that gives rise to family love?'

Everyone in the audience grew still, because no one had been untouched by the war that ended a decade before. For a few, it had been the making of them as determined and courageous adults; for all, the experience had involved tragedy.

And Gavriela knew better than most how war results in scientific and medical advances, because nothing concentrates the mind better than an enemy determined to kill you; although without the subsequent peace, there would be no way to capitalise on new understanding.

Jane finished with some cheerful thoughts and slides.

'Here we see various weaver ants, genus *oecophylla*, who are nearly all female. Sorry chaps, but they only need a few males for the purpose of impregnating the queens. And when it's time to go to war, they turn mature workers, not youths, into soldiers. In other words,' she added, 'it's their old women they send to fight, so you young gentlemen, consider yourselves warned.'

Then she grinned at the audience, who laughed and gave louder applause than most lectures received. The subsequent questions were good-natured, and the answers informative, and Rupert paid attention until the end. Finally Gavriela and

Rupert donned coats and left the building, because they could talk while walking.

Yesterday she had still been in Berlin, and Rupert needed her considered opinion on what had happened during the meeting at the café on Alt-Moabit.

'Colonel Dmitri bloody Shtemenko,' she told him, 'had no intention of coming over to us, in my considered opinion. He was trying to find out where Ursula is, so to that extent she's a leverage point. But it's as if ...' She considered her words. 'As if we've stolen one of his possessions, not a person who's precious to him. *Campanotus* might blow themselves up out of love for their fellow termites, but Shtemenko is a bit further down the evolutionary ladder.'

Rupert gave a twist of the mouth at the comparison, and tapped the pavement with the tip of his brolly as they continued to walk, heading towards Hyde Park. A Vespa scooter burbled past, producing a farting noise from its exhaust, and Rupert surprised Gavriela with a passable Goons imitation: 'Damn those curried eggs!'

Then he added, 'What about the factor we can't write in the reports?'

Gavriela knew what Rupert meant. 'The darkness seems weaker in him, I think. But he's as devious as ever. We should keep Ursula away from him.'

'Do you want to look after her, your niece?'

That surprised Gavriela enough for her to stop walking.

'I would,' she said after a moment, 'except that would make it easier for Shtemenko to find her. An evil stepfather isn't funny, not when he's a KGB colonel, and never mind the darkness.'

'You're right,' said Rupert. 'But I'll keep you informed of her situation, perhaps minus the specifics.'

'That might be best.'

They walked on, and Rupert asked, 'Do you think Carl would like to be a spy when he grows up?'

'I bloody well hope not,' said Gavriela.

They smiled together, old frictions seeming irrelevant.

'Fancy a spot of tea?' asked Rupert.

'Yes, I think I do.'

Paddington Station was a cavern of steam, the engines black and powerful-looking; and once the journey was under way, Gavriela was content to let the rattle of the carriage lull her into a doze all the way to Oxford, where the chill evening air brought her awake as she waited for a taxi that would take her to Abingdon. It took her along the old streets, among sandstone buildings she knew well, and finally out to Rose and Jack's house, where the new gas fire was hissing, warm and orange and friendly. Rose poured tea from a pot encased in a knitted cosy, and the three adults caught up on gossip while waiting for Carl to appear.

Before the war's end, Rosie Hammond, who had been such a good friend to Gavriela at Bletchley Park, had finally married her 'Jaunty Jack', who had survived the torpedoing of HMS *Royal Oak* unlike so many of his friends and comrades, helped take revenge in the strike against Narvik harbour that took out German destroyers and cargo vessels, not to mention Rear Admiral Bonte himself, and escaped the German reinforcements that sailed out of neighbouring fjords like longboats of old, but after a millennium of progress, with so many better ways to kill.

And as Mrs Rosie Gould, a little heavier but happy-looking, she was proud of her daughter Anna, and happy when Carl came to visit, and the two went off to somewhere like the theatre, as they had tonight.

'Bloomin' *Macbeth*,' Jack said. 'Poncey thing you'd know about, Gabs.'

'It's got sword fights.' Gavriela grinned at him. 'Plus the king of Scotland gets murdered. I thought you'd approve.'

'And do they install a fair and classless society afterwards? Do they buggery.'

'Jack . . .' said Rosie. 'So, Gabby, how was your conference?'

Everyone else but Rupert called her Gabrielle these days.

'As boring as I thought it would be.'

It was easy to sound cynical. The reality was as unsuccessful as the imaginary conference, with Dmitri back in East Berlin and nothing different, except that Gavriela's newfound niece was the right side of the Iron Curtain, and maybe some day they would get to know each other.

'Anna's school report was all As,' said Rosie. 'Trying to keep up with Carl.'

'Except for a C-minus in R.E.' Jack looked proud. 'For proving God doesn't exist, on the basis of Russell's bleeding Teapot.'

'Good for her,' said Gavriela. 'Did she mention Occam's bloody Razor, and dispose of Pascal's blooming Wager?'

'I wouldn't be bloomin' surprised.' Then, as if conversational momentum had allowed him to jump an obstacle, he added, 'I've left the CP, you know. Bloody Hungary.'

Gavriela put down her teacup.

'I'm sorry,' she said, meaning it. 'The Reds could never live up to your ideals.'

Forty thousand dead Hungarians had caused a flood of exits from the British Communist Party.

'He'll join Labour,' said Rosie, 'and everything will be fine. You'll stay the night, of course.'

'Course she will,' said Jack.

Gavriela relaxed into her chair. 'Can't bloomin' argue with that.'

Next morning, after Jack had left for the factory but before Anna or Carl had risen, Gavriela told Rosie she needed to go for a walk.

'Not a headache, is it?'

'The start of one,' said Gavriela. 'But a brisk walk and it'll disappear. Anything I can get you from the newsagent's?'

'Not for me. Maybe some Spangles for the kids.'

'They're getting too old for sweets.'

'Probably,' said Rosie.

Outside, Gavriela walked the quiet streets until she came to a corner telephone box, and went inside. She extracted pennies and a brass-coloured thrupenny bit from her purse, thought about what she needed to say, then lifted the receiver, shoved the coins in, and dialled. Wrapping the braided brown cord around her forefinger – a nervous tic – she listened to the ring, and stood straighter when a voice answered: 'Goodridge Haberdashery, Peterson speaking.'

'I'm checking on order number ZK927. This is Mrs Woods.'

'One moment, Mrs Woods.' There was a heavy click, silence, then a second click. 'Duty officer.'

'Reporting on a BCP affiliation. Jack Gould, G-O-U-L-D, resident Abingdon, resigned membership. Reason is disaffection over Hungary action. Gould is working-class, and continues to have no contact, that is zero contact, with CP-oriented intellectuals in Oxford.'

'All right, I've got that.'

'End of report.'

'Acknowledged, and thank you.'

She pressed Button B for the change, and went out into the morning air, feeling lighter than before. Of the CP's forty-three thousand members – the number before the recent haemorrhage – three thousand were named on a special list maintained by Five and Special Branch. On receipt of codeword HILLARY, police across the country would swoop, and if Jack were on the list – and living near Oxford intellectuals and attending Oxford meetings was a risk factor – he would end up with his fellow British internees in Epsom, the race course commandeered and transformed into a prison camp, while foreign-born Communists were imprisoned in Ascot, and those captured further north would end up in Rhyl.

Spying on her friends was the only way to remain in contact with them: the alternative was to exclude them from her life; and she did not want that.

Yet she wondered, as she walked past new council houses,

heading for Rosie's place, whether ants or termites, in their implacable aggression, ever spied on each other or caused an enemy to turn, to begin working for the other side; or whether it took sentience and civilisation to develop the concept of betrayal.

THIRTY-ONE

Fenrisulfr woke from the dream of life, and stared down at his crystalline hands. It had been so long since he had voyaged in the spirit world this way, but there was a strange ease in the way he stood, accepted that breathing was unnecessary here amid these shining halls, and set off to find the war queen Kenna, assuming she still ruled.

—*You answered the call, brave Ulfr.*

She was in the war-chamber he remembered, where she and her fellow warrior-leaders planned the final battles. Now, though, she was alone.

—*You know better than to call me that.*

—*But something has changed, has it not?*

He shrugged.

—*I slew Stígr.*

—*And has killing him helped you?*

—*Yes, it has.*

Kenna's crystalline face shimmered. Perhaps he had not told her what she was expecting to hear. He added:

—*He might have welcomed death. I do not know.*

Had Stígr failed to fight back because of Fenrisulfr's speed, coming out of nowhere? Or had the dark poet been slowed down by fatalism or the need to end his pain?

—*Where are the others, War Queen?*

She beckoned with one transparent hand.

—*Come and see.*

They walked through gleaming arched thoroughfares among giant halls, for this place had grown vast, until they finally came out on something like the balcony he had seen before. It overlooked the grey-black plain beneath the night sky, while the shining white disc, banded with scarlet, was the Middle World seen from this other realm ... except that 'realms' meant something different here, and he would need to give himself fully to Kenna's cause in order to understand.

Silver specks moved against the night.

—*Those are our friends, good Ulfr. Flying vessels to the Middle World.*

Fenrisulfr shook his head, for it seemed to him that such vessels were unnecessary, though he had no idea how he could know such a thing. Kenna forestalled his question by adding:

—*For the armies we raise there. For the billions who will fight against the darkness.*

Such numbers could not be imagined.

—*Then you do not need me, War Queen.*

—*Every individual can help, and you are a leader.*

Even without air, it was possible to laugh, or something like it. Fenrisulfr shook his head and spread his crystal arms.

—*Some leader. Is there room for butchers in this realm of yours?*

Again Kenna surprised him.

—*I think perhaps there might be. I wish it were not so.*

Fenrisulfr expanded his chest, then compressed it, though there was nothing to exhale in this strange place.

—*I name the nine realms on the three levels, War Queen. They are first, Ásgarth, Alfheim and Vanaheim. Then Mithgarth hangs there in front of us, level with Utgarth, Jötunheim, Svartalfheim and Nithavellir. And finally, below or beyond, lies cold Niflheim, where Hel rules over the dead who will wage war on us, come Ragnarökkr.*

Kenna answered him this way.

—*All is as you say, brave Ulfr. Our fellow Council members use different words, and think of realms differently, as you suggest. Mithgarth, the Middle World, stands for more than just that disc where men and women first lived. The five middle realms are those formed of 'baryonic matter', but these are just words.*

She seemed so implacably sure of herself.

*—You see the same realms, then, War Queen? The same as poets
and sorcerers and volvas from my time, just with different names?*

—Indeed so.

*—Then I pass onto you the words of a dead poet. People drop
Múspellheim from their schemes.*

Kenna's transparent eyes widened, at the mention of a
realm which was known and yet did not fit into the cosmic
scheme.

—I don't ... know how to think about that.

—And it needs a bridge that is not Bifröst.

She shook her head, no longer looking certain.

*—That I understand. The darkness needs its own Trembling Way,
along which it will advance, and destroy us if we do not fight.*

—Then I have helped you, as you asked.

Kenna reached out, starlight twinkling through her.

—Stay with ...

But the dream was over, the spirit world fading into nothingness as profound and empty as Ginnungagap, the Great
Void, the Abyss of Emptiness.

Nothing.

THIRTY-TWO

From her distributed surveillance motes throughout Palace Avernon, Kenna watched most of the preparations, while her own hidden programme continued slowly: that work was not to be rushed. The Pilot, Caleb deVries, used a lev-platform several times to return to his ship on the surface, via a giant vertical shaft on the edge of the demesne. The first time, he had taken the crystal spearhead stolen from Avernon's collection. Had Kenna wanted to blackmail deVries, the opportunity was gone, at least without betraying the undercover Pilot, Linda Gunnarsson, living the life of an epsilon-class servitrix in the lowest level of the Palace.

From a balcony protected by membrane, as well as the sharpest members of his personal guard, Lord Avernon watched a sequence of nine master-drones, each ten metres long, float one by one into the centre of the shaft, and then begin a slow vertical ascent to the surface a hundred metres above, there to gently glide into the cargo hold of deVries's ship.

Kenna noted that Avernon had not proposed going into space himself. He was content for deVries, or rather the drones that deVries was due to deploy, to carry out the experiments, while he, Avernon, would wait to collect, collate and analyse the subsequent results. Realtime images and readings would be tightbeamed down to a receiver near the shaft opening on the planet's surface. The chances of a neighbouring Lord eavesdropping on the signals were minimal; to involve oneself in tasks up above, even when others did the hard work, was scarcely thinkable, a blindspot in thinking that in the lower strata was taken to the extreme. Many were inhibited

237

against – not to mention prohibited from – ascending to the next stratum. Such concepts as ground and sky were as little thought of as, say, a mythical hell, and exactly as frightening to someone who seriously imagined it.

Had it not been for the theoretical work performed by Avernon's grandfather, the current Lord would scarcely have thought of this. But the earlier results were intriguing, with the kaon-antikaon decay rates indicating the potential for reversing time's arrow.

Finally, deVries flew.

Kenna's airborne surveillance motes showed her: from barely a metre above the surface, deVries's bronze ship disappeared in a white flash that Kenna knew to be as risky as it was flamboyant. There was no realtime signal relaying the ship's reappearance in distant orbit; neither the deployment of the first master-drone, nor the subsequent hops as it deployed the other eight, were tightcast to the ground. It was only when the master-drones themselves completed initialisation procedures that the signals began.

First, readings established that each drone was in clear space, with no hindrances to letting loose the cargo, comprising thousands of fist-sized mini-drones.

The last of the master-drones also sent holovideo footage of deVries's vessel, until it transited out of realspace, leaving nothing to see. If the experimental programme worked, any or all of the master-drones would commence a slow descent back to the shaft on Nulapeiron's surface that led down to Demesne Avernon, where the ruling Lord and his logosophical research team would commence work on whatever came back.

Soon clouds of mini-drones were spraying out into space.

I wonder what they'll find.

Kenna already possessed dangerous knowledge of the future, assuming that everything she had learned as Rhianna Chiang from placing Roger Blackstone into deepest trance so long ago was true, and not a delusion formed during her reconstruction and resurrection as a static cyborg formed of distributed components.

A few mini-drones performed initial checks on kaon-antikaon decay rates, finding them skewed further from previous readings by 0.06 per cent. There were no other unusual phenomena. This was a research programme whose payoff might come in days (as the current Lord Avernon hoped) or decades or never.

While deep inside the Palace walls, where no surveillance system beyond Kenna's own could see, her own programme of experiments was well under way, although she had to be careful because of one severely limited resource.

The splinter of crystal, removed from the spearhead now in mu-space, was so very, very small. She had to plan hard and ration carefully at every stage: that was obvious from the start.

But the energy spectrum ...

Whatever Kenna was, she was no longer a Pilot, no longer able to perceive mu-space or to work directly with Labyrinthine technologies; but she remembered things, and the results of her every analysis implied a strange construction pathway – transitions to impossible minima – to produce that splinter of crystal taken originally from the spearhead. It did not match any physical process in mu-space that she could remember or imagine.

Which was strange, because the crystal sure as hell did not originate in realspace either.

It doesn't matter.

Practicality overrode theory every time.

I only have to work the stuff.

In the event, it took fifty-one more years to achieve a breakthrough.

To the continuing sequence of Lords Avernon, Kenna made herself indispensable, because she could not count on them all ignoring her like Lord Dalgen Avernon. Ironically, he, short-sighted and machiavellian, had commissioned one of the most far-sighted experiments to be carried out by Nula-peiron's logosophers. But he lost interest during the years that followed, as the tiny anomalous results produced zero payoff.

People got on with the march of their lives, and in due course died, while Kenna remained immobile, her pseudo-face embedded in the wall of a laboratory chamber deep inside Palace Avernon. Her larger components were splayed across that same wall, while many more components, far smaller, were distributed throughout the Palace.

Lord Alvix, who had dropped the Avernon suffix though it remained the legal name of his line, was the fifth Lord chronologically, and the nearest so far to recreating the intellectual daring and humour of the old Duke.

But the demesne he had inherited was not financially stable, and so he was forced consciously to use his brilliance and expertise in areas he would rather have avoided – or so Kenna read the situation, on the basis of both passive observation and their personal chats, when Alvix felt there was no one he could talk to besides his immobile cyborg adviser.

What Kenna had kept to herself for decades was the truth about Dalgen Avernon's death, for the causes were not natural, as everyone in the demesne had believed: not unless you counted an assassin's work paid for by Lord Vikal, a scheming Lord Minor from Realm Grisengahl, as a natural occurrence.

'Bloody hell,' said Lord Alvix now. 'Kenna, will you look at this?'

He was in the centre of the lab chamber, surrounded by a plethora of holovolumes: sheaves of numbers; intricate, shifting phase spaces rendered in a thousand hues where every nuance of colour held meaning; and many-dimensioned emergenic maps, which tracked the generation of properties emergent from complex substrates, always checking and attempting to predict the emergence of order from chaos.

Alvix's self-mending tunic had failed to do so: his faded

once-black-now-grey garment looked as if a rat had been chewing at the sleeves. In public he knew how to dress with propriety, but when he withdrew himself from matters political, he became the distracted scholar he was meant to be.

'Not that old thing,' said Kenna.

Lord Alvix laughed.

'My grandfather's great disappointment,' he said. 'But look at these gamma-rays.'

'Holy shit.' Kenna absorbed the readings, allowing herself to feel surprised. 'You've found a *second* temporal phenomenon.'

Was this the beginning of a successful logosophical attempt to read the future? It was over a century ago that Max Gould, dear Uncle Max, director of Labyrinth's intelligence service, had despatched her here – or rather, despatched Rhianna Chiang – to investigate the rumour.

'I always thought,' Kenna added, 'that only the kaon-antikaon thing was sensitive to the direction of time. But this one was always there, waiting to be seen.'

'Yes,' said Alvix. 'Except that I never thought I would see it.'

He dimmed the holovolumes, except for one that he shifted to the centre, and caused to magnify and brighten. Inside, successive layers of spherical waves, with a common centre, shrank inwards to that central point and were absorbed.

Over and over, wavefronts diminished to nothing.

In terms of subatomic process, the kaon reaction stands alone; but there is one other phenomenon not seen in nature, because it would be the equivalent of a smashed egg reforming. Emissions of radiation outwards from a point are common; what is rarely seen is the reverse: spherical waveforms shrinking inwards – except that was what the data was showing Alvix now.

'I'm going to call them spinpoints,' he said. 'Singularities being born. They're appearing in the regions around Nulapeiron where the kaon-antikaon decay was most strongly affected before. Just *look* how they behave.' He could not stop smiling. 'Time to contact l'Academia. This is going to cause such a stir.'

'Or you could call on your friends' – Kenna meant his allies – 'to fund a private research effort.'

Alvix paused, then: 'Practicalities. That's why I like you hanging around, Kenna. Unless you've reconsidered my offer.'

'Of a drone body? I thank you again, my Lord,' she answered. 'And decline once more, with gratitude.'

'We're alone. You don't need the polite rigmarole.' He grinned. 'And point taken. You'll help me work through the details?'

'Of course I will,' she said.

But either because of coincidence or the subtle psychological effects of Alvix's breakthrough – the realisation that decades-long effort could provide sudden insight – Kenna's attention would become distracted in a matter of days, as she broke through her own private research barrier. In her case, there was no one at all with whom to share the news.

A microscopic fragment of crystal suddenly *wriggled* under gamma-ray bombardment.

The manner in which that tiny sample had become not just liquid – though highly viscous – but actually motile ... that might not have seemed like much, any more than spherical absorption rather than emission of radiation might be radically significant.

It might take decades more, even a century, to grow enough of the crystal to work with, and then to learn the ins and outs of engineering with the stuff; but it was a start.

Roger Blackstone's dreams might come true.

Such a strange reason for the feeling of triumph that spread throughout Kenna's dispersed, distributed self.

Five years later, the prototype Oraculum was ready, and a more hardened-looking Lord Alvix was getting ready to receive his noble visitors, the Lords and Ladies who had sunk finances into his project and were intrigued at the notion they might get a return sooner than expected.

Whether that was true, Kenna was less sure than Alvix. Lately the practicalities she had been dealing with had been those of engineering, helping develop new manipulation techniques that might some day help her directly, but for now were key to the manipulation of harvested spinpoints.

Those spinpoints were gathered by mini-drones in far orbit, and brought down to Nulapeiron by one of the master-drones that deVries had deployed fifty-six years ago.

Each spinpoint was a tiny seed, wrapped in magnetic fields and glowing in visible wavelengths once stabilised, and in the more energetic end of the spectrum before capture. A hall had been refashioned to hold them, with massive coils embedded in its walls, located close to the vertical shaft down which the master-drone descended, bearing its strange cargo.

In that hall, magnetic fields guided spinpoints into new carry-drones fashioned for the purpose, the lower surface of their carapaces formed of flowskin, so that they could move snail-like along the Palace corridors, bearing their magnetically trapped spinpoints, one per carry-drone.

Perhaps if it were not for the state in which Kenna herself existed, she would have felt more ethical concern at the treatment of the young people whom Alvix's research team were hoping to turn into Oracles. The notion of perceiving the future, as described in primitive folklore, was ill-defined, akin to seeing distant events without technological intervention. But practical precognition was 'simply' one of future memory: of 'remembering' thoughts and perceptions from one's own future mind.

'It's cosmology and the subatomic realm,' Alvix had said at the start of the project, 'going hand in hand yet again. That resonance between the cosmically large and attoscopically small has been fascinating scientists and now logosophers for hundreds of years.'

When Alvix had first sought investors, seven of the currently visiting Lords and Ladies had come to Palace Avernon, and attended a presentation in the Great Hall. There Alvix had projected a huge holo, of a globe filled with filaments and membranes of light surrounding empty spaces that looked like biological cells.

Each cell interior was in fact a cosmic void, and the tiniest points of light constituting those filaments and membranes represented galactic superclusters; because this was the entire realspace universe.

And of course, he caused it to shrink back to the tiny point that was the Big Bang, before expanding it to the fill the hall once more.

'When I shrank the cosmos, as it were' – Alvix had smiled at his audience – 'was I predicting a Big Crunch, or showing expansion from the Big Bang in reverse?'

His point was that a universe as viewed from outside might be seen to shrink, but the cosmological arrow of time seemed predicated on the future always being the direction in which the universe was bigger. It indicated that timeflow might flip into reverse, should a Crunch occur.

And that meant you could never know whether you were in a universe that an outsider would say was expanding or collapsing.

'Whether the whole of realspace will ever contract,' he told them, 'is irrelevant. We aim to create tiny regions of spacetime that shrink inwards to produce negentropic timeflow, and by stabilising them within normal reality, we have conduits via which to "remember" the future.'

Those regions, naturally enough, would need to be inside a human brain: a human whose normal brain could interact with the world, while selected neural cliques and groups experienced timeflow emanating from the future, allowing memories of future perceptions to be remembered in the present.

All you needed was a temporary abeyance of humanist ethics.

And children on whose brains you could operate.

244

Now, five years later, it boiled down to this: thirteen members of the nobility standing on an internal balcony halfway up the wall of a lab chamber, twenty or so research assistants moving around, and eight drooling youngsters: the proto-Oracles.

These were aged between seven and seventeen standard years, some with left and right eyes that moved independently, all largely confined to couches from which they observed ceaseless holo footage. Three of them could speak with some coherence.

'Steam. Pudding. Good to ...day ...' came from a ten-year-old girl.

'Timeline is thirteen days in the future.' An assistant checked displays. 'Location is right here.'

A sarcastic laugh sounded from the rear of the visiting group. At the forefront, Lord Welkin, oldest of the investors, was frowning. 'With respect, sir,' he told Lord Alvix, 'this is pitiful. The paltriness of your servitors' menu is hardly a worthy—'

But Alvix stopped the complaint confidently.

'It would have been too much coincidence, sir,' he said, 'had one of them just happened to deliver useful information as you stood here.'

'And when, my Lord, do you actually *foresee* gaining useful information?'

At the rear of the group, another laugh: it was Archduke Colwyn.

But Alvix had a reply ready, though it might cost him Welkin's support.

'We learned something a tenday ago,' he said to Welkin. 'Seven years and twenty-three days from now, my Lord, which is to say Dvaday the thirty-seventh of Jyu, a Convocation in Shantzu Province will rule on the dissolution of your cousin Lord Cheung's demesne. By the end of Jyu-ni, his neighbours will have divided up his realm among themselves.'

Welkin went pale, at least in part (Kenna was almost sure,

to a probability of 96.3 per cent) because he was party to the conspiracy that would in due course break up his cousin's realm. But the other Lords and Ladies, to judge by their microexpressions and skin lividity, were rationally assessing the situation, and revealing a tentative approval.

In some metatemporal sense, the future has already happened; and that being so, they wanted to know about it, whatever details they could pick up.

But Kenna knew something else that Lord Alvix was aware of yet had not divulged. One of the more coherent proto-Oracles, the girl called Mandia, had spoken of the Collegium Delphinorum, a place that did not yet exist, and which (from interpreting Mandia's fragments of information) seemed to be some future facility – or group of facilities – for creating and managing better Oracles in the future.

In one sense, it implied success for this venture, but those scraps of report made no mention of Demesne Avernon.

Perhaps this was knowledge that Kenna herself should be acting on.

Isn't foreknowledge the reason I'm here?

Perhaps it was time she made plans to leave Demesne Avernon, and found a place for herself in one of the deep interstitial regions of Nulapeiron, far from other realms and their ambitious schemes.

Time to change herself once more.

THIRTY-THREE

MAGNUS & THE WORLD, 5575 AD

Seeker learned that the obsidian-eyed woman had a name, which he rendered as Maree Delgasso in flux-speech. She was a Pilot, one able to voyage among the stars (though Ideas regarding golden space were not yet decipherable), descendant of a line of Pilots that stretched back some one hundred and twenty generations.

Pilots had existed for longer than there had been people on the World; and yet it seemed they had common ancestry, soft-fleshed people like the folk whom the Pilots bore as passengers in their magnificent living vessels.

The Pilots lived according to a code called the Tri-Fold Way, and were amused, as they explored the World, at the three sexes and three-way symmetry of 'native' species, such as flying tri-blades ... and at the failure of silver-skinned people, including Seekers, to deduce that their own ancestry was different, that the legend of the Ark had necessarily contained some truth.

But the Pilots' philosophy, which impelled them towards peacefulness, apparently had a tragic origin.

It came from healing, from the aftermath of war. Of so much death.

The flux, though representing Maree's words, emanated from the ring on her finger, mediated by a near-invisible mist. She was fascinated by the Ideas that Seeker-once-Harij captured, snagging them from the air. It made her eager to leave Magnus, and return the nine Seekers and Zirkana to the World.

Not just to get you home, but to investigate this wonderful air.

*Some kind of airborne ferrimagnetic colloid, perhaps ...**

Her musings had the flavour of some of those old Ideas, captured by wandering Seekers.

Other Pilots descended in bubbles to enter and commune with the old vessel that had taken the Seekers and Zirkana here. Finally, a pair of huge ships moved in overhead – Seeker was fascinated at their living forms, the way they could stretch and twist – and reached down with gentle tendrils to embrace the older vessel.

Gently, gently they lifted her from the sands, carried her up into the black star-powdered sky, and disappeared as Seeker-once-Harij watched.

What happened to them?

They entered the golden ocean, my friend. A void where we can fly fast, and take her to a city where she can heal, that old ship.

And fly her again?

Something shifted in Maree's black-on-black eyes.

**Her Pilot is long dead. When she is well, she will simply slip away, as all ships do when they are bereft. Where they go, we do not know, and must never ask. **

Your people are so strange.

Maree reached out and touched the back of his hand.

Your silver skin is strange also. That old ship transformed you, your ancestors, when she crashed upon the World.

She crashed?

And was broken, but healed as best she could. Your world was not hospitable.

So much to combine with other Ideas, so much for the Seekers to share with the World.

But for now, Seeker, it is time for us to take you home. Do you trust us?

Zirkana came walking, her skin shining purest silver, absolutely radiant.

This is so wonderful. Wait until Starij and the rest get to meet them!

Seeker took Zirkana's hands in his, and turned back to Maree.

We trust you. Can you find the way?

The old ship gave us the location

They called everyone together, getting ready for the return. Before they rose to her ship, Maree had a question for Seeker-once-Harij:

You're known as Seekers. Does it ever stop? Will returning like this mean the end of your careers?

But Seeker-once-Harij had his arm around Zirkana, and his smile was serene as he cast his reply.

I have already found what I Sought.

Maree looked at them both, and smiled.

Then she summoned transport bubbles to carry them aloft to her waiting ship.

249

THIRTY-FOUR

MU-SPACE, 2606 AD (REALSPACE-EQUIVALENT)

Commodore Max Gould was not a well man, in Pavel's estimation. Ever since the attack or breakdown or whatever it was – no one was forthcoming with the medical history of the intelligence service's director – Max had spent fewer hours in the Admiralty and more time by himself. The Admiralty Council had surprised Pavel by making his own position permanent, so that he was officially the deputy director; and Max had compounded that by handing over much of the running of the service, including some of the most strategically important and sensitive operations.

Now, in a gold-appointed lounge in Max's apartments, they lounged back on flowcouches, Pavel and Max, sipping daistral and looking physically relaxed. The operations they discussed were serious, however.

'Shireen Singh worked well on her last two assignments,' Pavel told Max, 'so I made her team leader on Coolth. There's no news on tracking down the leak, though.'

Someone had betrayed shipping routes and times to the Zajinets – two Pilots had died – and analysis suggested that one or other of their common destinations was likely to be the location of the leak, most likely Coolth, a world of ice and oceans, with only a few town-sized research stations inhabited by humans.

'I'm sure you'll sort it out.' Max's tone suggested this was trivia, beneath his notice.

'So I'm considering a decoy op,' said Pavel. 'With Jed Goran as the decoy, which is why I mentioned it.'

Jed was now Clara's husband, security-vetted but not

trained, increasingly involved in Admiralty work.

'Clara's a great asset.'

And never mind Jed's safety, Pavel noted.

'Agreed, Max. I won't do anything to jeopardise her ... well-being. Her concentration.'

'Tell me more about the last Council session. I mean their attitudes and so on, not the specifics.'

'Zajac and Whitwell' – in private with Max, Pavel did not use the men's ranks – 'are behaving in character. Bluster and belligerence from one, cool logic from the other.'

'No need to ask which is which.' Max gestured, ordering a fresh daistral, which his couch extruded. He broke the cup off the narrow tendril, and took a sip. 'Not bad. And the split among the others?'

'Fifty-fifty, if we're talking Zajac versus Whitwell. Get them to agree on a given matter, and you'll have unanimous support around the table.'

'And have they seen this?' Max gestured a holovolume into view. 'A sighting from mu-space, close to a sheaf of insertion points suitable for transit to Molsin.'

Pavel examined the ambiguous readings: a fast-moving ship, corkscrewing through an extreme geodesic, blurring surveillance either through desperate urgency or considered daring.

'It's not a Zajinet.'

That was the primary purpose of such set-ups: looking for Zajinet ships approaching realspace worlds from mu-space.

'The analysts think,' said Max, 'that the Pilot might be Holland. Guy Holland.'

It took Pavel a second to recall the name.

'Shit.'

'Agreed.'

Holland was the Pilot who had carried Rick Mbuli, once Roger Blackstone's college friend and more latterly an Anomalous component, to Vachss Station in orbit around Vijaya. And had subsequently escaped to Siganth, followed by Roger, who came back reporting that Siganth was now a hellworld with an Anomaly of its own – or an extended part of the same Anomaly as Fulgor: no one had yet decided for sure.

'If he's doing the same on Molsin as he intended on Vachss Station—'

'An SRS squadron is already en route,' said Max. 'There's no time for undercover trickiness, nor an all-out invasion fleet.'

A full attack fleet would take a handful of tendays to organise at best, even with planners using time distortion layers within Labyrinth, and ships using odd geodesics to make the initial rendezvous.

'But deploying special forces—'

'Is under way, Colonel.'

'Yes, sir.' After a moment, Pavel added, 'Zajac will love it, the old gung-ho romantic. Probably tell the Council how much he wishes he were going with them.'

'And Whitwell may well disagree,' said Max. 'Unlike Zajac, Whitwell actually *was* special forces, back in the day. Saw hard action, too.'

'He was? Not on his public record … Besides, I didn't think we had much for them to do before now, apart from play hard in their training.'

'Not since you became a department chief. But you'd be surprised how often in the past a swift covert action, military action, was the only way to avoid long-term misery.'

Pavel nodded. Seven standard years at his current level of security clearance, and there were still things to learn.

'You know Roger Blackstone passed selection, Max.' Aeternum allowed the explicit construction of sentences that were simultaneously question and statement. 'His posting on Vijaya was overt, or reasonably so, compromising his ability to operate covertly. And in any case he did not want a long-term undercover realspace assignment. So he asked for the transfer.'

The selection process spanned half a subjective year, some of it spent in quicktime layers of Labyrinthine reality, for those who made it all the way to the final trials.

'He's turning out to be different from his father,' said Max. 'Carl would have shunned special forces, or anything resembling their work. Young Roger's not on the Molsin mission, is he?'

Either Max was not keeping special track of the lad, or he was but did not want Pavel to know it.

'No,' said Pavel. 'But last time I checked, they were considering him for the other deployment.'

'The reconnaissance op?'

This time Pavel thought he detected a hint of false surprise. Max did know what Roger Blackstone was up to, Pavel was almost sure of it.

'That op, yes. I don't like it, Max. I hope they all come back from it alive.'

Max closed his eyes, thoughts hidden, then opened them.

'It would make a nice change,' he said.

Twelve silver-bodied attackers lay on the floor, terminated. Roger had put them down fast, and without emotion, largely thanks to the integration of his higher cognitive self – recognising the moistness of the corridor walls for what they were, areas of permeability behind which the enemy waited to burst through – with his reptilian core, the heart of every human brain that people disconnect from at their peril. The in-between portion of his mind, the mammalian, emotional part, had not been required; later he might process his feelings, but in the moment they would only have slowed him down.

Like any well-trained attack team, they had come from simultaneous angles. And so he had responded by spinning and manoeuvring, geometry the medium of his artistry, so that only one could reach him at a time, and he prevented those single attacks by pre-emptively shutting them down: defeating a tackle by combining a half-sprawl with a driving elbow to the spine; collapsing a knee with a thrust kick, a fatal neck-crank from behind to follow; another knee destroyed with a whipping circular kick, a thumb ripping an eyeball, spinning the attacker into one of its comrades; then a blizzard of crunching, whirling, thrusting and smashing them, taking them out. Then it was done, and he could disengage.

Isolation period: 2:17:00 hrs

It was regulations: the holo indicated the length of time he was confined to barracks, prevented from mixing with other people – particularly civilians – before he could release his killing rage and act like a civilised person. But telemetric scans were clearly updating the system, because a second later the display read:

Isolation period complete

The safety precautions were standard for all personnel, but special forces were required to recover faster than that. In Roger's case – he had a brief mental image of a snarling, long-haired warrior with axes in hand, then it was gone – he could snap the rage off when he needed to, or simply experience no rage at all, as in this ambush.

His attackers' silver bodies melted into the floor.

'Not as sloppy as I expected.' A woman's voice. 'You've got better, darling. I mean, even better than before.'

Corinne, his on-off lover since Tangleknot days, entered the corridor.

'Hello, sweetheart,' said Roger. 'That lot was a present from you, was it?'

'Sort of a welcome-on-board present, dear Roger.'

He had been heading for his quarters, with studying on his mind, when he had noticed the glistening walls and the attack erupted into whirling violence.

'Is there something you've not been telling me?' he asked.

Corinne was supposed to be Logistics Liaison, part of the support channel between the Admiralty Quartermaster Division and the civilian Far Reach Centre. Doing genuine work while spying on her fellow Pilots, a counterespionage role designed to detect attempted infiltration by any of Schenck's renegades or – worse, because harder to detect – dupes recruited by renegade sympathisers and controlled via cut-outs. It had been a convincing story.

Lying bitch, he thought, and laughed.

'I'm strategy and planning,' she said. 'Not combat.'

'I ran twenty kilometres in training this morning,' he told her, gesturing at the now-bare floor. 'And did more push-ups than I can remember. I didn't really need another workout.'

'That's too bad.' She made the raised-eyebrow, dipped-chin invitation he knew so well. 'Because I had another endurance test in mind.'

'Oh, did you?'

'Mmm.'

'Well,' he said. 'You know the Service motto: *Always up for it.*'

'That's not the motto, Roger.'

'It isn't? Then it should be.'

She took hold of his hand.

'Come and show me,' she said.

Nine 'wings' of five ships each played combat hunt-and-tag against each other during the tenday-long pre-deployment countdown, while in the barracks, the forty-five men and women spent their non-training hours clowning around, conducting ambushes with foam weapons and playing practical jokes.

Onlookers from other arms of the fleet were clearly disconcerted by the lack of serious demeanour from these legendary élite warriors, wondering just how the myths could have so distorted the embarrassing reality.

That puzzled dismay continued until an Admiral's team of aides unwittingly brought live weapons into the visitors' area: within three seconds, every one of them was face down, stripped of weaponry and petrified of the men and women kneeling on them and yelling. Several lost bladder control, which would have been hidden by modern garments, but this was a formal visit and they were wearing traditional jumpsuit uniforms, made of simple dumb fabric.

There was ironic humour but zero clowning on the final day, when the entire squadron slipped out of Labyrinth: the commencement of Operation Periscope, commanded by Ingrid Rhames, who chose to fly near the rear of the formation. The role of squadron leader was taken by Lee Nakamura, Rhames' second-in-command; the others with experience approved of both officers, while the three newbies, Roger included, took their word for it.

It was a long and difficult geodesic, impossible for pursuers to follow and, with luck, impossible to effectively surveil as well. More direct routes were available, but none offered the chance of sneaking all the way to their destination and, if they were really lucky, making their escape the same way, with no one the wiser.

Only a tiny minority of Pilots and ships had the stamina, expertise and will to fly a trajectory like this; but no one in the squadron allowed their ego to surface. This was, in a very real sense, just another day at work. And that attitude was the reason they would win.

Though winning without losses was not guaranteed.

A femtosecond-duration blip was the only transmission as they neared the transit zone.

This is it, my love.

You're beautiful, you know that?

Roger smiled as the transition occurred, golden void replaced by realspace slamming into existence all around; except it was not blackness dotted with stars in the way one normally experienced. Everything shone, and it would have been disconcerting but they had practised, so they kept their formation and slipped into a hidden zone behind a blazing sun, just one more star amid a magnificent profusion, a billion stars pouring out their energy, as if in simple joy at their existence.

From here, Schenck's renegade base could not be seen. For the moment, that was good, because it worked both ways:

they double- and triple-checked, and confirmed the absence of lookouts or surveillance drones. So far they were unobserved.

Nakamura sent a signal blip, and the squadron moved out. Slipped back into mu-space for the final approach.

THIRTY-FIVE

'They hate me,' Jared told her, 'because I smell funny. Please help me, Aunt Rekka.'

Yoga be damned: a migraine was pulsing over Rekka's right eye, refusing to diminish no matter how calmly she breathed. This trip was going dreadfully wrong.

The new orbital station, which would eventually be in geosynch above Mint City, where Sharp had died – had sacrificed himself – was filled with a mixture of Haxigoji and humans. This was to have been a happy reunion, Rekka's first meeting for nearly twenty years with Bittersweet, whom she had not seen since Singapore, and her first return to Vijaya itself. The world whose name she had chosen – first contact privilege, a practice since revoked by UNSA. It had been fully twenty years since her time with dear, courageous Sharp.

Instead, here was Jared nearly grown up – aged nineteen – and in trouble for flaring up literally, as only a Pilot could: using a bioluminescent flash to blind four Haxigoji who had grown perturbed by Jared's presence for reasons no one had explained, not to any human's satisfaction.

'That's what I've been trying to do,' said Rekka. 'I *am* helping you, Jared.'

Her protests to the on-board staff, that Jared had been frightened, a young Pilot away from Earth on a study trip, had caused massive debate among the Haxigoji – which they carried out with translator torcs turned off, so no humans could understand. Meantime, the senior human officials were furious with Rekka for the upset she had caused; she in turn raged back at them, because she had known Jared since he was a baby, *and* she was the person who had made first contact with the Haxigoji – didn't they *know?* – so why the *hell* was tension ramping up on both sides over an incident that could only be due to cross-cultural misunderstanding, and what kind of trained personnel were they if they could not sort out such a mishap, and prevent it from escalating to anywhere near the stage it had reached ...

Except that later, with time to herself, and now face to face with Jared in the cabin he had been confined to, it grew on her that she had known Jared *when* he was a baby, not *since* he was a baby. The young Pilot in front of her was a stranger.

Of course he had lived in the Kyoto school since Rudolf and Angela had died, and his visits home to Singapore had grown ever less frequent over the years. When he made the move to ShaanxiThree, Rekka found out only by administrative accident: she was copied in on the full itinerary for the two Senators Highashionna as they made another tour of UNSA sites in Asia, and it turned out that they were spending time with select young Pilots in China – not quite protégés, but youngsters they had mentored from time to time – one of whom was listed as Jared Schenck, in training at the biggest base in Shaanxi Province. Rekka had thought he was still living in Japan.

'I can't believe that *they* think *I* smell,' said Jared now.

His tone implied that the Haxigoji were beasts and he was slumming it by being here.

I really don't know you, do I?

Rekka's infostrand, worn as a bracelet, vibrated against her wrist. She tapped it, and a tiny holosigil representing Bittersweet was projected in the air.

'I'll try to sort something out,' Rekka told Jared, not answering the call yet. 'All right? So you can get off this station without fuss.'

'Well, good.' He made no move to step forward and hug her. 'Good.'

She nodded, slid the door open, and stepped out into the

259

corridor. Several male Haxigoji, bulky with muscle, guarded each end. She looked at them, then locked the door behind her.

'Sorry.' She opened the call from Bittersweet. 'I'm glad you're here.'

'I've just arrived on board.'

The words sounded flat, though the comms net was capable of transmitting the full emotional range of scent-speech as translated by the Haxigoji torcs.

'Our shuttle had to wait,' Bittersweet added, 'because of the passenger container.'

'What container?'

'It has humans aboard, including a senator. They are waking up very angry.'

This did not make sense, apart from the obvious part about waking up: passengers coming out of delta-coma, after a Pilot had dropped them off.

'Not a Senator Higashionna,' said Rekka. 'Not one of them.'

For a moment, she thought she was being stupid, expecting Bittersweet to know people's names. But Bittersweet answered: 'No, a Senator Margolis. Is this important, Rekka?'

'I don't ... It would have been a strange coincidence, that's all.'

'Then please come to the docking lounge.'

'Yes, I will.'

The comm session ended.

I've never been so confused.

But her questions about the Higashionnas derived from a hot Arizona day, back when Sharp was still on Earth, and they had watched Simon's brother Gwillem doing his aikido demonstration. Senators Robert and Luisa Higashionna had been there as VIPs. Afterwards, watching them depart in a TDV, Sharp had seemed puzzled by Rekka's lack of reaction towards them.

'Do you not taste their evil?' he had asked her.

'Evil?'

'Can you not smell dark nothing?'

She had been puzzled at the time, but had never forgotten his words.

Do you not taste their evil?

Another vessel hung near Vachss Station, maintaining a watch on the docked shuttle and eavesdropping on the in-station comms net. This vessel was shining and fast-looking, her central body pure silver, her delta wings copper and crossed with silver. Her Pilot had obsidian eyes, black-on-black, while another sat in the control cabin alongside her: an older Pilot, grey-haired, with metal sockets where his eyes had been before the surgery.

The latter was humming to himself as he listened in on the signals. Finally, he stopped and turned to the younger Pilot, Ro McNamara, who was sitting there and trying to remain calm. These were interesting days, because as the first natural-born Pilot she had not needed UNSA surgeons and bio-technicians to make her what she was; but without UNSA she would have had no ship, no way to fulfil her purpose in life.

What she could not abide was the notion that all the younger Pilots living now, and generations still unborn, would face a stark binary choice between effective slavery or an unfulfilled and hollow life.

And her friend here, Claude Chalou, though he had non-Pilot family on Earth, and worked as an academic – he had been Dirk's tutor at Oxford – missed mu-space dreadfully; but he was too old to fly, as decreed by the UNSA powers-that-be, and that was it. Career over.

No one in UNSA considered mu-space as anything other than a milieu for sailing-routes along which vessels moved at their direction, for the sole purpose of shifting goods and people among the realspace colonies, research stations and Earth. The idea that mu-space was an entire universe in which Pilots might want to live ... that had never, it seemed, occurred to them.

Until now, of course, there had been no place *for* a Pilot to live, no habitable location, except in realspace. But that was changing, and the stolen matter-compiler that Ro was transporting in her hold right now (and whose theft, or at least illegal export, Claude had assisted with) would be one more component in making this so.

But in order to carry out that mission – when everything she did was monitored by UNSA flight controllers, with no reason to go into mu-space except on a designated flight – she had temporarily abandoned a pod containing her VIP passengers, all deep in delta-coma, leaving them to float safely in deep space. Then she had picked them up once more, and delivered them here to their destination; but they were late, and the effects of such a long time in coma, with two insertions into mu-space, were unpredictable: severe headaches at best.

'Look ...' Claude's gravelly Gallic voice took her out of her thoughts. 'This explorer, Mam'selle Chandri, who has caused so much trouble ... If you slip away quietly, there will be little fuss. She's all they're interested in.'

He was right, but as yet, Ro did not know whether her passengers were OK.

'What if one of the passengers fails to wake up?'

'And what if station personnel demand to scan the holds?' Claude asked. 'Standard procedure in an accident.'

'They won't find any malfunction.'

'But' – Claude raised a bushy eyebrow above one metallic eye-socket – 'they might find the matter compiler which Mac-Lean and I stole for you.'

'Goddamn it, Claude.' She pronounced his name correctly, Claude-rhymes-with-ode, courtesy of her Zurich upbringing. 'The passengers are my responsibility.'

He considered this, then nodded. '*C'est ça. C'est exact, bien sûr.*'

So they were in agreement. But as soon as Ro learned that the passengers had woken without medical emergencies, she was taking herself and Claude out of here. It was not just that the matter compiler in her ship's hold was needed in mu-space – she had also made a binding promise to Claude that he would finally see, after years of blindness on Earth, the secret project-in-progress that select Pilots knew about. No one else in UNSA suspected that such a thing might be possible, never mind that such construction was already being carried out in a clandestine fashion, with volunteers working hard for the sake of the future.

Claude deserved to see the first huge constructions, the oddly growing halls and bays and courts that were already forming in ways that went beyond design parameters, with inherent systems evincing properties that excited the Pilots working there, for they exceeded anything that had been deliberately planned.

Labyrinth was going to be magnificent.

Bittersweet's eyes changed colour from amber to honey as the light shifted. Her tabard and trews were grey, edged with silver, and there were flecks of grey in her fur. She was accompanied by a broad-antlered male who bowed deeply when Rekka said: 'Redolent Mint. How are you doing, old friend?'

'Well, thank you, Rekka.'

It had been a long time since Singapore, when Redolent Mint had been foremost among the bodyguards accompanying Bittersweet; except he had always been more than that, and was now clearly of senior rank.

He withdrew now, leaving Bittersweet and Rekka to talk in private, in a screened-off area of the arrivals/departures lounge. No one else was around: the centre of attention was currently the medical bay, where human passengers were being examined and awakened from delta-coma.

'We always meet,' said Bittersweet through her torc, 'in surroundings your people have built.'

Rekka nodded, knowing Bittersweet understood the gesture.

'And yet you are family to this Jared Schenck,' Bittersweet continued. 'Is that not true?'

'Friend of the family.'

'Perhaps, in any case, it is not hereditary.'

'Excuse me?' Rekka tried to work this out. 'Are we talking about Jared?'

But Bittersweet was gesturing around the meeting area.

'This is official, Rekka. We wish to constrain the relationships between your people and ours.'

Rekka was not here as a UN ambassador: her objective had been to sort out the mess that Jared had caused, nothing more.

'Your people that Jared attacked' – Rekka knew that *attack* might imply some legal liability, but no longer cared – 'have refused medical treatment. They insisted, or their friends insisted for them, on returning to the surface.'

'To where they felt safe,' said Bittersweet.

More turmoil in Rekka's head: she had come to rescue Jared only to find him unlikeable at best; and now it seemed the Haxigoji were scared, of Jared or something more.

'I don't understand, Bittersweet.'

The reply stopped Rekka's heart for a moment.

'Do you not smell the darkness, Rekka Chandri?'

They finally said farewell in a calm, regretful fashion, after Bittersweet had detailed terms which Rekka knew that UNSA would have to agree with: Vachss Station alone to be where humans were based, with no more of the constant traffic between surface and orbital. Human individuals were to be allowed down to the surface only on occasion, after they had been vetted in advance, right here, by Haxigoji officials. The numbers of Haxigoji living on Vachss Station would diminish; and while they were here, they would live in separate quarters, capable of being isolated from the rest of the station, and equipped with drop-bugs that would allow them to evacuate and descend safely to Vijaya's surface in case of emergency.

No definition of a likely emergency was ever spelt out.

As for Jared Schenck, the Haxigoji wanted him off the station as soon as possible, with no word said about punishment. Rekka felt they needed him to be far away, and that was enough; of course she agreed.

Finally Bittersweet's double-thumbed hand grasped Rekka's shoulder.

'We will not meet again, I think.'

'No ...' Rekka blinked. 'I need to say ... about Sharp.'

The grip, which could have crushed her shoulder, tightened just a fraction.

'What about my brother?'

Rekka sniffed.

'I loved him,' she said. 'I've never met anyone as brave.'

'Neither have I, dear Rekka.' Bittersweet's alien eyes softened. 'Neither have I.'

She bowed and walked away.

THIRTY-SIX

NULAPEIRON, 2713-2721 AD

At one point early in the extended process of self-transformation, something happened to give Kenna pause. Inside the Oraculum, where Lord Alvix's proto-Oracles, still children, lay dreamily on couches and occasionally muttered fragments relating to future perceptions, the one called Mandia turned her head to stare at the wall – right where Kenna's main sensors were hidden – and focused her eyes to an unusual extent.

'Liquid. Crystal. *Moving*,' she said, then turned her head away.

Her shoulders slumped into normal listlessness.

No. This tells me nothing new.

In particular, it did not guarantee Kenna's success.

As for the alpha-class servitors who tended the poor, damaged children, they were unlikely to make anything of those words, for Kenna had hidden her project nicely. And of course the original crystal spearhead was long gone, no doubt in Labyrinth now. She wondered what the Admiralty analysts were making of it; but she had her own concerns, and in truth, she was neither Pilot nor ordinary human these days. She was a cyborg on the threshold of becoming something else.

Except that the transition took another eight years of preparation, by which time Mandia had become a young woman, or nearly so, and her Oracular perceptions had diminished as the rest of her brain rewired itself defensively: a process the researchers had allowed to continue, because it allowed them to analyse the warning signs of such reversal, and the complex neurochemical changes they would need to prevent in order to create true Oracles.

To Kenna, it implied that Mandia, unlike her fellow pro-to-Oracles whose health was dreadful and worsening, might some day be able to take care of herself, living a reasonably independent life, provided her environment was not overly challenging.

Kenna's timetable matched the weightiness of her intent: to get everything right, she expected another five years of work, and would be happy if it was longer. No sense of hurry infected her work, until one Shyedemday in the month of Jyu-eech, when her most distant sensors perceived alarm signals at the Palace perimeter, along with the tang of burnt flesh, before coherent graser beams tore through her furthest components and all sensation there was lost.

Palace Avernon was under attack.

My fault, Alvix.

Her Liege Lord – except that she had never sworn legal fealty, neither to him nor his forebears, not even the Duke – had made enemies, by virtue of his experimental Oraculum, and the potential wealth and political threat it represented. She should have been more forceful in telling him to form strong alliances, or else in strengthening his demesne's defences. Even now she could sense Palace guards, attempting to rush to the attack location, being blocked by quickstone walls flowing across corridors and hardening in place, resistant even to grasers: the result of sophisticated sabotage, subverting the Palace itself.

She had done the same, of course, for very different purposes.

I'm years from being ready.

But she was even less prepared to die, and if the Palace was being attacked with subversive femtovectors, she had to trigger the transfer now, before her distributed self could be caught up in the sabotageware attack, and her mind was rewritten. That could not be allowed.

So it happens today.

Quickstone under her control melted away, forming access

tunnels to a hidden chamber where her masterpiece lay on a couch formed of steel and platinum: a body of living crystal, grown and adapted from a tiny fragment of that ancient crystal spearhead, linked by a thousand crystal fibres to her cyborg nervous system, embedded in the Palace walls.

Some fibres ran all the way to her pseudo-face and other components splayed against the side of Alvix's main laboratory chamber, where he had been working but had now vacated – her optical surveillance sensors told her in the seconds before she shut them down for ever – and was now running towards the Great Hall, calling for Lady Suzanne.

Conscious of her face on that laboratory wall, she closed her eyes for the final time, and felt her sensations withdraw as she triggered the process now.

System.getController( ).getTransform(Project.Metamorph).initialize( )

Every part of her seemed to shudder, though she had no proprioceptive or autokinetic senses in her current form, the distributed body she was about to leave.

And she wanted to scream but her output channels were already disconnected; and then it began.

Transfer.

Afterwards, it was like remembering dying – again – with every separate thread and shard of cognition accompanied by howling, burning pain. Cascades of processes split apart, rushed headlong to their new receptacles, and came crashing together in a torrent of new computation, far closer to death than birth because a baby during expulsion from the womb is yet to have a mind, while she destroyed – had to destroy – every part of her complex, long-lived self in order to survive.

The ceiling was above/before her when she opened her eyes.

I will have to move.

This was supposed to have been years in duration, the process of learning to move once more, the gradual sharing of thoughts between her Palace-embedded self and this new – glorious! – form. But her old self was gone.

Really move, because they can kill me now.

She looked like nothing anyone would recognise. Any Palace guard or member of the attacking forces would trigger their weapons at the sight of her, and at this stage she was not even sure that she could walk, let alone run or fight.

The transformation, performed this way instead of to plan, had left her vulnerable. A baby without care will not survive; but she *had* to survive, because she was needed, and if she could not get through one armed attack, what use would she be in the great confrontation to come?

She wondered if Alvix was calling her, if he had time to be shocked or feel regret at her old self's death, or whether he was wrapped up in thoughts of his own and Lady Suzanne's survival. That probably depended on the attack force's orders: if their objective was to steal the contents of the Oraculum and get away, that would bode better than if they intended to secure the Palace while an occupation force made its way here, and then took over.

Strange sensations washed through her as she sat up – for the first time in over a century – and looked down at her new body. Everything was immediate and odd and beautiful in its intensity, and the danger lay in her growing enraptured at her own existence and failing to take action right now because this was mortal danger unless she got her act together and actually bloody *moved*.

Fibres withdrew into her, disconnecting her from the old, dead Kenna-system, and then she did something simple, ordinary and yet entirely miraculous: she swung her legs to one side of the couch, leant forward …

Amazing.

… and stood.

On actual feet.

With legs.

A body.

Arms and hands ...

Focus.

Everything so wonderful.

Focus now.

She swayed, balance tipping. Corrected herself.

Got it.

Took a step.

A second step.

Definitely got it now.

Third step, and it was almost automatic, in time with a distant bang followed by screams.

Time to really move.

She was most of the way to one of her primary escape routes, feeling guilty yet desperate because of her selfish focus on survival of self – and hang the rest – when she saw in her mind's eye a helpless, addled girl-woman, the victim of worldly ambition more than logosophical exploration, and then there was a feeling of relief that it was necessary to go back and confront the danger. There are times when you want to do something and are scared to, have found excuses to avoid it; and then some factor forces you to do it anyway, and all you can feel is thankful that you've been forced to do the right thing, to confront the fear: that was how Kenna felt now.

Mandia had foreseen liquid crystal moving, but to Kenna's knowledge the poor girl had never had an opportunity to see such a thing; yet every prediction was a verbal description of something she was to see in the future. For her prediction to be true, she must survive the armed assault in order to see ... well, Kenna as she was now. So for all her vulnerability in her stumbling new body, Kenna could not abandon Mandia, not if there was a risk of Mandia's dying.

The alternative was ... what? Death by paradox? The self-immolation of a closed time-like curve of events? Of people that had existed and events that had occurred but would turn out never to have been?

Once upon a time I was a fighter.

Never mind her notions of becoming a general, a chief of staff, a war leader in ages to come: this was immediate, raw, physical danger and she had to face it or the rest was nonsense. She gestured to the nearest wall, and waited for the Palace to recognise the codes she broadcast by microwave from her hand. It took a full half-second for the Palace to make the adjustment to her new form; then the wall liquefied and melted open, revealing one of the hidden servitor tunnels (it would not do for the nobility to be distracted by the sight of menial workers engaged on mundane tasks) and stepped inside.

Leaning forward slightly, she forced herself into a shuffling jog, a shamble compared to her mental image of running freely, but as she followed the tunnel her gait became smoother, then smoother again, through an incremental sequence of improvements; and by the time she drew near to the Oraculum, she was running faster than any but the fittest of endurance athletes.

Armed attackers were entering the tunnel up ahead, but she gestured and the quickstone wall slammed down on them, burying them. Then she was running past and a new opening was growing in front of her, and when she leapt through she was in the Oraculum, where the proto-Oracles were thrashing on their couches – only Mandia was upright, struggling to stand – and the staff were gone, either fled or helping the fighters outside: graser fire caused the air to crackle in the surrounding corridors.

Kenna grabbed Mandia.

The others were helpless, but Kenna had to accept her current limitations, and save the one she could. She hauled Mandia into another, newly opened servitor tunnel, commanded the entrance to flow shut, and pulled Mandia into a staggering run. When they had made enough distance horizontally, Kenna stopped, holding Mandia upright – the girl was wheezing, wet with sweat and trembling – and commanded the floor to melt.

At this point the Palace was five levels deep, but where they stood was above internal walls, five metres thick or more, in the lower levels. They sank downwards – in a bubble of air for Mandia's sake – until they were all the way through and below the Palace, coming into a corridor in the Secundum Stratum.

By chance it was deserted for the moment: a polished marble-like corridor with clean lines, not too different from the style of the Primum Stratum where the Palace was situated, except that here the surroundings were solid, not quickstone, with little in the way of inbuilt systems.

I'll need disguise.

So much for planning in advance. Leaving Mandia slumped against the wall, Kenna jogged along the corridor, knowing she had to do something fast: she was a woman formed entirely of crystal and there was no way she could blend in while looking like this.

Here.

It was a store fronted by vitreous membrane that was currently hard and opaque, not open for business, and it came to Kenna that this must be one of those areas where everything was brightly lit all the time, and people chose sleep-wake cycles to suit themselves individually, unlike the communal-consent approach which was the most common alternative.

The membrane liquefied and Kenna stepped through, leaving it softened because she was going to exit through it very shortly. There were clothing racks – the store was dark but she could see well enough – and she found leggings, pulled them on, then smart-boots that wrapped around her feet and calves, tightening themselves in place. Then a dark tunic with long sleeves, and when she pulled it on, the sleeves lengthened to cover her transparent hands all the way to the fingertips, and morphed to form integral gloves. Finally a full-length hooded cloak.

A small payment pad rested on a shelf, requesting recompense for the garments that the customer was purchasing.

Kenna had no time to decipher its protocols – there had been nothing like this in the Palace – so she reached out and crushed it into powder instead.

No alarms followed.

Good enough.

When she went back out, there was still no one in sight, but voices drifted from around a long curve in the corridor: easy conversation, a light laugh, and total ignorance of the violence taking place in the Primum Stratum above. Kenna slipped away in the opposite direction, pulling her hood low, and returned to Mandia, who was now sitting on the floor, back against the wall, staring blankly.

Once more Kenna pulled Mandia upright, and supported her as they walked, coming out into a larger thoroughfare where people did not quite stare at them – this was a polite place – as they headed for a large, platinum-inlaid disc on the floor. Ruby lights winked at their approach, and Kenna pressed Mandia's palm against a horizontal pad atop a waist-high stalk, a metre from the disc – which began to rotate and separate into a complex affair of blade-like segments that clacked and clattered, then dropped to form a helical staircase. The rotation stopped as the treads snapped into place.

Kenna kept one arm around Mandia's waist as they descended. Once down and clear of the treads, the whole assemblage reversed procedure, pulling upwards and turning as the disc reformed and locked into place – except that Kenna and Mandia were now below it: a circle on the ceiling of the Tertium Stratum, and one that would not grant access without specific authorisation.

Descent was straightforward; only upward movement required authorisation.

Fifteen more descents, and they were in a region of raw tunnels lit – and given habitable atmosphere – by ceiling fluorofungus, where dwelling-tunnels featured rows of hollowed-out alcoves that served as homes, and dumb-fabric hangings served as doors and interior walls, and the people were on the whole kind to each other, because this was a community strong in the face of poverty, where working together meant survival.

It was a good place to find a hospice, run by older folk with steady eyes and plain speech, who would not turn away the young girl-woman left at their door by a silent, hooded figure – her clothes far too rich for this stratum – who slipped away without greeting anyone. They helped Mandia inside with kindness.

Kenna moved on.

Other people were beginning to follow her, made suspicious by her clothing and lack of speech, so when the tunnel curved and her pursuers were out of sight, she broke into a run, moving fast and easily now, until she came to a high chamber formed of natural, raw rock in which a lava pool glowed and bubbled.

Dead end.

I will not fight them.

Let them wonder at her disappearance. She stared at the lava pool.

This will be fine.

With a neat motion, she dived into the molten lava and swam downwards through the hot, viscous liquid rock, not caring as her garments burnt away and the heat grew stronger, because this was freedom and wonderful. Something brushed against her – she felt angular flukes – and knew it for the one of the little-studied native forms that lived inside the magma, and drew inspiration from the ease with which it moved here.

This world will be good enough.

Give it a millennium or two, she thought as she swam, and then she would move on. There was no hurry.

It would take time to become the person she needed to be.

THIRTY-SEVEN

EARTH, 1972 AD

Alone in her flat, Gavriela lay one slightly arthritic hand upon a project notebook and said to no one at all: 'I always thought it would be the death of me.' But here she was, sixty-four years old and mostly healthy, mostly retired, mostly enjoying life. A label on the notebook's front cover explained the project's name:

High
Energy
Interstellar
Meson
Detection,
Amplification &
Lensing
Lattice

It rarely spooked her these days, the thought that she had written out an identical description during wartime Oxford, scribbling in her personal notebook *while asleep*, something she had never done before or since. When Charles, her department head at Imperial, had first suggested she take over the meson research team and showed her the name of a project that Lucas Krause had proposed, he had actually been concerned for her health because of the blood draining from her face. But she had recovered and accepted the job, and nothing had come of it save for a wealth of readings concerning the behaviour of mesons from cosmic rays.

Their decay-time was affected by relativistic distortion, because their velocities were so high, providing one more validation of Einstein's work: her hero, who had once played her nine discordant notes upon his violin, as an indication that they had more in common than a love of physics.

And Lucas Krause, whose team she had taken over when he left, was the same Lucas she had known as a student at the Erdgenössische Technische Hochschule, where Einstein had previously studied and even taught a little. There had been a brief period when she had taken to spending the occasional night at Lucas's house – romance and physical love were never frequent features in her life – but he had finally returned to his estranged wife in Nebraska, on hearing that she was diagnosed with cancer.

That was five years ago, and Mary Krause was still alive and doing well, which Gavriela was glad of.

Inside the notebook was tucked a typewritten note from one of her Caltech acquaintances, someone she had met at several conferences and was a good contact, because he worked with Gell-Mann frequently. He said that a few people were talking about renaming the meson family members – K-mesons, μ-mesons and π-mesons would now be known as kaons, muons and pions respectively – and asking what Gavriela thought of the notion.

She had not yet replied, uncertain whether her natural response would be perceived as European snobbery: that people should use Greek letters, along with Latin terms, as much as possible, and that furthermore there was no excuse for any physicist not to read the Cyrillic alphabet, and realise just how much Russian was comprehensible, especially since modern vocabulary so often resembled French or German.

Then she smiled, remembering Gell-Mann's reputation as a polymath and polyglot who insisted on correct pronunciation of all foreign terms, and decided that she would write her reply exactly as it came to mind.

Earlier today, at half past eight, she had written a one-sentence entry in her diary, after receiving an important phone call – fulfilling the reason she had got the Post Office to install a home telephone in the first place, as soon as she had heard that Carl was an expectant father.

Today I became a grandmother.

It was an echo of the day Carl was born, and more comforting than she had expected, the thought of continuity despite personal mortality.

(She had asked the engineer, when he was installing the phone, whether he had heard of a gentleman called Tommy Flowers. He had said no, then winked, causing Gavriela to smile. Within the next few years, thanks to the thirty-year rule regarding secrecy, the British public would begin to learn how her friend Alan had invented computers and how Tommy built the first, and incidentally shortened the war by two years at least, and perhaps made the difference between victory and defeat.)

The phone rang, one-two, one-two, left-right, left-right as she hurried to the hallway and picked up the receiver.

'Is everything all right?' she said, expecting Carl.

'Most assuredly, old thing,' came a familiar patrician drawl. 'Why ever would it not be?'

'Rupert.' She closed her eyes. 'I thought Carl might be calling from St Mary's.'

'He's in church praying for a miracle?'

'I mean the hospital. Alexander Fleming, penicillin, and now my first grandson,' she said.

There was a short silence.

'That's really most excellent news, dear Gabby.' He would not use her real name on a phone line. 'Most excellent.'

'Yes, it is,' she said. 'And an indication that I'm far too old to work for you, dear Rupert. Assuming you've a little job you wanted me to carry out.'

Another silence.

'I do that, don't I?' said Rupert. 'Ignore you unless I want something.'

That was disconcerting.

'Are you all right?'

'Yes … I was hoping we could meet up, not for work, and have a—'

'Spot of tea,' she said. 'You do that as well. And I'd love to.'

'You would?' He sounded more cheery. 'Fancy a stroll around the British Museum?'

'So one old mummy can cast an eye over the others? I'd be delighted, dear Rupert.'

They agreed to meet in an hour, and then she hung up.

From the outside, the British Museum, like all the other major buildings in London, was a single massive block of soot, black and off-putting. Inside it was airy, calming Gavriela down as she passed the Elgin Marbles – relics of one dead empire stolen by another, whose patrician classes were finally realising they had been trained to rule a quarter of the globe that was no longer theirs – and then stood in front of the dark stone Book of Gilgamesh, realising she was in the presence of the world's first written story, not quite able to process the thought.

Rupert, when he appeared, was wearing a bow tie of lapis-lazuli blue, a touch of startling colour; but his pinstripe suit was as conservative as ever: narrow lapels unlike the modern look, and not a hint of flare to the trousers. His oiled hair was iron-grey, combed from a parting that was geometrically exact.

They strolled around saying little, finally stopping in the Viking room upstairs, where a wide metal bowl hung on chains from the ceiling.

'Cooking-pot,' said Gavriela.

'The inscription says—'

'It's wrong.'

He raised an eyebrow, as if to ask when she had become an archaeologist, but said nothing. Gavriela had been expecting pointed irony.

'How's Brian?' she asked, wondering if that was where the problem lay.

'Shacked up with a dance choreographer in Soho.'

That stopped her. 'Oh, Rupert.'

'The fellow's fifteen years younger than I am.' This was bitterness such as Gavriela had never heard, not from Rupert. 'And here I am among the antiquities. No jokes about old queens, please.'

She slipped her arm inside his. 'I was going to suggest that pot of tea,' she said. 'And perhaps a nice chocolate biccie to dunk in it.'

They sat in a noisy corner of the tea-room, which was better than silence for private conversation. Gavriela was finishing her tea when Rupert said, 'I've other news.'

'What is it?'

'Something best learnt when one has placed the cup back on the saucer, dear Gavi.'

She put it down carefully.

'At least I'm already sitting,' she said. 'I take it you have smelling salts in case I decide to faint.'

'Not an eventuality I thought of, quite frankly. It's just that in addition to becoming a grandmother ... Congratulations, by the way. I mean it.'

She patted his hand.

'Yes, I know you do. And I'm getting nervous. What—?'

'You're also due to become a great aunt,' he told her. 'In three months' time, give or take.'

Several blinks accompanied her search for meaning in his words.

'I don't ... Oh.' It was obvious. 'You mean Ursula.'

Her niece. Step-daughter to Dmitri Shtemenko, defector, for whatever that was worth – the debriefers in the old Wiltshire mansion would have got everything they could from her, but no professional intelligence officer would shared classified material with their family – and living somewhere in Britain, as far as Gavriela knew, for these past, what, sixteen years? That would make her thirty-two or thirty-three, depending on when her birthday fell.

My only niece and I don't know even that.

Or the name that people called her these days. It surely would not be Ursula Shtemenko, or even Ursula Wolf.

'When did she marry?' she asked Rupert.

His answer was a short silence, then: 'A couple of my schoolfriends were bastards, literally speaking. They had a hard time of it, I grant you, bullied every day for years. But they got through it.'

That was not comforting. She wondered if Rupert were annoyed with Ursula out of principle or because – a better thought – he would have preferred to relay a happier version of events to her, Gavriela.

'Carl wasn't exactly born in wedlock either,' she said.

'He was, in the only way that matters.' Rupert meant the legal documentation, forged by his department, that had showed Gavriela, or rather Gabrielle Woods, to be a war widow. 'Sodding Brian, I don't know how you could ever forgive him or me. Especially me.'

She squeezed his pale hand.

'We did what we had to, all of us, dear Rupert. And as for them ...' She gestured to a group of young people dressed androgynously, males and females wearing identically flared pastel jeans, their hair equally shoulder length but without the braids a warrior needed to keep the hair out of his eyes – where had that thought come from? – and ridiculous shoes unsuitable for running or agile footwork. 'They'll never know what we went through, but it doesn't matter.'

Give the young folk their due – they did not look like the kind of people who would care about illegitimacy one way or the other. Perhaps her great-niece or great-nephew would not face the same kind of harshness that others used to.

Or her grandson.

'Anna's not married to Carl either.' She had not meant to tell Rupert. 'I know I call her his wife, but they haven't ever tied the knot, not legally. She's still Anna Gould.'

Rupert sighed. 'You and I ... The people in our lives don't have an easy time of it, do they?'

'Cursed by gypsies, is that what you mean?'

He finally smiled, his face lean, porcelain skin showing lines. 'On the rare times a game gets out of control,' he said, 'I prefer castling as a manoeuvre. A defensive huddle staving off defeat, while I find a way to survive.'

She had always thought of him as playing the chess-game of life, and him a grandmaster, but she had never heard him use the metaphor so precisely.

Then he added, 'Why don't you come round for supper?'

'Um ... You mean to your house?'

'That's what I was thinking of.'

She had never been there.

'And when were you thinking of?'

'Tonight. If you're visiting Anna and the baby in hospital, then a late supper, perhaps.'

Was this what he had meant by castling? Old friends spending time in each other's company as a defence against loneliness?

'I'd love to, dear Rupert.'

'Well, good.'

Over the next few weeks, she became a regular visitor to Rupert's Chelsea home, where listening to Brahms or Bach in his drawing-room (not a term she had ever used outside ironic conversation) became a pleasant habit. At Oxford he had read Greats, which the rest of the world called Classics, and his collection of sketches and old books was fascinating.

But there was another postscript to their meeting in the British Museum that she did not share with him at first, because he did not need the worry. He had officially retired from the Service, and his intention was to write monographs on ancient Troy and the relationship between the early Roman Empire and Greece – echoes of Macmillan's speech in '56 regarding Britain and the States – with the benefit of insight gained from a career spent among the secret strategists and covert machinations of international politics.

In her overcoat pocket, when she had recovered it from the museum cloakroom, there had been a photograph, the second time such a message had been left for her. The other time, the picture had shown Ilse and Dmitri, with the girl who turned out to be Ursula; it suggested that this second photo came from Dmitri also, but the darkness did not leave traces in handled material, so there was no way to be sure.

It was consistent with the location, a photograph of a withered, blackened iron blade that might have come from the museum's Roman room, except that Gavriela could read the pattern that surely no one else could see among the creases and folds.

ᛚᚠᛦ

The sword, more than a millennium old, seemed to be in a display case, no doubt a museum, but the photographer had been careful to exclude any clues as to which museum, or even which country, it might be in. And yet it was not the physical object but the runic word upon it that resonated with Gavriela—

So brave, my Wolf.

—and that was upsetting because it was surely what the anonymous donor intended, and she could not think of anyone but Dmitri Shtemenko who would play with her mind that way. After a day's thought, she decided to share it with Rupert, because she did not like the coincidence of Dmitri's being in the country – him or someone working for him – at the same time that Ursula was pregnant.

'You said he considered Ursula a possession.' Rupert was sitting with legs crossed in his high-backed armchair. 'Not a stepdaughter he loved, but something he owned. That we had stolen from him.'

'I was biased against the idea of him defecting, because I

didn't trust him not to play a double game.' Gavriela was in the matching chair, at an angle to the fireplace, sitting upright because she could not relax. 'It may have shaded my perceptions. But I think I was correct, in terms of how he felt about Ursula.'

The knowledge that Rupert was officially retired hung between them.

'I'll make a phone call,' he said after a minute.

'Thank you.'

There was nothing to do but increase whatever security and surveillance was around Ursula. The details were up to others, far outside Gavriela's purview and even – these days – Rupert's.

'You remember when you sent me to the States?' she said then.

His lean form tightened. He had sent her in wartime across the dangerous Atlantic – pregnant, though no one knew that, not even Gavriela – to visit Los Alamos for legitimate reasons but also to get her away from Brian, her one-night stand, his long-term secret lover.

'The FBI man,' she said, softening her voice, 'called Payne, who showed me around, also taught me some New York slang. Noo Yoik,' she added, 'including "doing a Brody", meaning to take a dive off a bridge, suicidally.'

Rupert shook his head.

'Damnable,' was all he said.

The 'Americanisation' – itself a hated term – of the English language was something he detested, and often said so.

'I think I mentioned it to Anna once,' said Gavriela. 'I'm wondering if that's where she got the name from.'

'Dear Gavi' – he could use her real name here – 'I really am failing to catch your drift.'

'My grandson is to be called Brody Gould. Not even his father's surname, you'll note.'

'Oh, dear.'

'I feel like killing her. Know any decent assassins, Rupert?'

'None that you can afford.'

She let out a breath and sank back in the comfortable armchair. 'Just as well.'

'Speaking of what you can afford ... The rent on your flat is probably quite steep.'

'No more than anyone's. What about this place? It must cost a fortune, so it's lucky you have one.'

Rupert's lean face twisted.

'Not the word I'd use, but I'm comfortably off. As for the house, I own it outright, as did my parents for that matter.'

Without jealousy, Gavriela said, 'Lucky you.'

'Yes, I know. And with all those spare bedrooms that Mrs Hooper keeps spotless and no one ever sleeps in. So I was wondering ...'

This was unusual hesitation for the retired spymaster.

'...whether you'd care to move in, dear Gavi. With all your science books and whatnot, of course. Slide-rules, kind of thing. Broaden my mind.'

She looked at the shelves of books in here – a small portion of the collection scattered throughout the house – then back at Rupert.

'I'll move in tomorrow,' she said.

They stared at each other for a moment, then they both nodded.

'So,' said Rupert, picking up a folded *Times* from the floor. 'Have you seen today's crossword?'

'Not yet.'

He retrieved his fountain-pen and unscrewed the cap. No pencil for him: ink meant getting it right first time.

'Shall we tackle it together?'

'Yes,' said Gavriela. 'I think we should.'

THIRTY-EIGHT

Bad luck hit the mission early. A squadron of Zajinets was heading along the same trajectory, and perhaps for the same purpose; but that was the problem with a war on two fronts – three if you counted the realspace Anomaly of Fulgor and Siganth – against different hostile forces. *My enemy's enemy is trying to kill me*, thought Roger, as comms burst into life with a command from Nakamura:

++Scatter right high. Plan 7 alpha.++

Roger-and-ship sent the *ack* signal – acknowledgement – along with everyone else as forty-five vessels split into nine soaring threads that curved around to avoid the energy beams tearing along the geodesic they had been following, and allowed them within seconds to target the Zajinets.

The first ship to explode was a heavy Zajinet vessel, raked by fire from Rhames and the four Pilots forming her wing. But the chase was on through layers of self-similar spacetime contours, fractal fire forking and branching, like living lightning, and in the next few subjective seconds Roger counted thirteen ships exploding, seven of them Pilots including an entire five-ship wing.

But the Zajinets were tricky, and several vessels broke away and disappeared into mu-space depths. Seeing that, Nakamura sent the break-off signal, and the thirty-eight surviving Pilots disengaged from the fight and tore off onto a near-hellflight geodesic that the Zajinets would find it hard to follow, starting as it did from a hugely non-linear volume of turbulence: only continuous inter-vessel comms allowed the Pilots to keep their ships aligned together and following the same trajectory.

++They might call for reinforcements. Bug-out count-down is now 100 hours from insertion, repeat 100. Copy all?++

Ship-and-Roger were straining with the effort of flight, but they spared the attention to send an *ack* blip, and presumably the rest of the squadron did likewise because they kept formation and flew harder than ever until Nakamura finally gave the signal to disengage and slip into an easier glide mode, ready for the final insertion.

But this was one of the things that made them special forces: the ability to fly hard, beyond the point where most Pilots and ships would break down, and then without recovery to move into a battle zone and operate better there than ordinary com-bat-trained ships and Pilots could when fresh.

Insertion.

And the exit into blazing space, filled with a profusion of starlight from the massive population making up the galactic core.

Quiescent and watching, in a warrior's state of not-thought, of *mushin*, they floated, using passive sensors only – no trans-mission waves to ping against whatever they observed – for their job was reconnaissance, not assault, with the proviso that if they had to fight to get clear, they would bring shock and awe to the renegades, spreading death and confusion as they escaped.

Ordinary Pilots might have seen nothing, but the thir-ty-eight SRS Pilots and their highly trained ships were able, through stillness and hyper-acuity, to observe shapes and movement against the blazing background, to make out pat-terns that others would not perceive, to piece together the nature of the installation existing here, and the vessels that attended it.

In briefing sessions they had referred to it hypothetically

as Target Shadow, and here it was, not just a figment of the planners' imagination but real and still growing, from what they could see.

The extended construction was vast: a sprawling free-floating militarised base, around which a flock of vessels moved, both realspace shuttles and mu-space ships Piloted by renegades. It was that mixture of Pilot and non-Pilot forces that meant the base had to be situated in realspace – that and the fact that the darkness was of this universe, perhaps more so than humanity, with goals that had nothing to do with mu-space and everything to do with the galactic core, and the thousand-lightyear jet that spurted from it, perhaps from the legendary black hole at the exact centre of—

Maybe not.

What do you mean?

Drifting.

No one's been to the very centre, have they?

Not alive. Maybe fragments of wreckage have drifted in.

I wouldn't risk your safety, my love.

Quiet. No signals chatter among the ships.

We're already in danger together, aren't we?

True.

But the countdown continued, one hundred hours steadily diminishing to zero, the bug-out time set by Nakamura acting as squadron leader, while Rhames as commander kept to the rear, relinquishing her right to lead – not the way Roger had envisioned combat squadrons operating, not until he joined one – and made no comment, indicating confidence in Nakamura's decision.

Zero.

Stealth meant exiting to mu-space at such a precise angle and energy that spillover radiation was close to nothing, detectible only to someone who knew where to look and what to look for, with the most sensitive of equipment. One by one, the Pilots' ships slipped out of realspace existence and were gone ...

Ready?

...until Roger-and-ship alone remained.

Ready now.

They blasted into mu-space, creating a transition signature that would have lit up the realspace environment like an explosion, even amid the shining light of a billion suns.

Because they were heading into the true core, and it would take force as well as finesse to prevent them breaking apart in the jagged mu-space reefs corresponding to the titanic gravitational swirls of the black hole at the centre, except, except—

I love you.

Yes.

—they burst out into realspace for a fraction of a second, right at the threshold of obliteration, enough to see what they knew they were going to see, and then they ripped away into mu-space once more, turbulence and chaos as they had never experienced – *so hard to fly* – as they twisted around obstacles like coral reefs formed of folded spacetime, hurtled down through spirals of reality – *very hard, but we can do it* – and finally, finally pulled onto a geodesic that with luck would take them clear – *yes* – and they screamed along a trajectory more extreme than a hellflight, a reality-shearing, self-immolating, agonising way to fly for which there was no word, not even in Aeternum; and then they were through, tumbling into a clear golden void which by the standards they had grown used to was simple mu-space, easy to traverse, though its currents were strong.

They coursed into a crimson nebula.

What year will it be when we return to Labyrinth?

I don't know, I really don't.

Even their superlative ability to track distortions had failed during the ultra-hellflight episode that challenged most of what they had learned in Labyrinth about theoretical limits to ship-and-Pilot performance.

But we'll still be able to find Labyrinth.

That will never change.

Their flight was easier now.

And was it worth it?

The Admiralty will think so.

As of this moment, only Roger-and-ship knew that a theory long held by humanity was wrong, in a way that must be linked to the aeons-long engagement with the darkness that, from the point of view of Pilots and non-Pilots alike, could only be considered an extended act of invasion, of cosmic war.

What lay at the galaxy's heart was not a black hole, and perhaps never had been.

How is it that nobody knew?

Good question.

It was not formed of matter at all.

THIRTY-NINE

EARTH, 793 AD

Morning mist failed to cloak the stench of the dead. Slaughtered villagers and holy men, here and there a whimpering survivor – which meant only that their entrance to Hel's realm was delayed for a while – and soon there would be the buzzing of flies and rustling of beetles, unless more people came to burn or bury the folk of the Holy Isle, whose beliefs and sanctity had so clearly failed to save them.

Fenrisulfr led good men.

A woman was moaning from behind a pig-sty, and someone else was breathing heavily, but there was no reason to investigate. Among the drying blood and hardening gore were fresh shoots of green grass, while sparrows squabbled heedlessly nearby, and the weight of his sword on his hip – he had laid aside his axes for now – with the soft squeak and smell of the leather, were comfortable and pleasing and somehow very new, as if he were seeing the Middle World through a child's eyes.

I lead good men.

It was the thinnest of thoughts, like a dying man's voice.

Stígr felt my vengeance.

And so did all these slaughtered people whom he had never met before, who had never heard of Ulfr's – Fenrisulfr's – home village, or of the poet Jarl slain because of Stígr's machinations, or of Eira, sister to Jarl and *volva* to the clan and everything to the heart of a young warrior and dead, so long dead, because of Stígr's dark sorcery once more, and how was any of this going to bring her back?

It wasn't. Nor would she recognise him, the man he had

become, if she could return, for in a real way Ulfr also had perished a long time ago.

Brökkr and four of his strongest fighters were standing in front of him.

'Chief. Feels like the morning after.'

'It does.'

'Got treasure to take home, but I'm not sure about young Thóllakr's haul. Gold and steel don't eat. Drink blood maybe, but you don't need to carry food for them, is what I mean.'

Fenrisulfr squinted at him. 'Speak plainly, Brökkr.'

'There.' Brökkr gestured with a hooked thumb. 'Got himself a thrall, if you can call it that.'

'Óthinn's piss,' said Fenrisulfr. 'I might have known.'

Two of the fighters chuckled, but their smiles were vicious. This was going to cause trouble, and it amused them. And if they were the ones to spill someone's blood, then all the better – at least that was how Fenrisulfr read their thoughts, and he had been a reaver chief for a long time now.

Too long, by the Norns.

That, too, was a new thought.

Thóllakr's bounty was the girl – young woman – who had been tending his wounds when Fenrisulfr had slain Stígr and triggered the Holy Isle's doom, the destruction of those who lived here. Except that Thóllakr had taken this one for his own, and not by force, to judge by the way she clung to Thóllakr's arm and stared down at the ground, avoiding everyone's gaze and clearly wishing they were not here.

Wishes count for nothing.

If they did, then Eira would still be—

Enough.

He forced himself to speak. 'You're claiming her, is that it?'

'I am,' said Thóllakr. 'Her name is Thyra and she's from an inland village and we're— Well, she's under my protection.'

'Under your hips,' muttered one of the fighters, poking one finger through the fingers of his other hand, and waggling it.

'When we move inland,' said Fenrisulfr, 'I want you to

remain behind with the guarding party. And no trouble, Thól-lakr. All right?'

'Yes, chief.'

'And while you're here, there's a roan gelding by the foundry that I like the look of. I want him looked after for me. Take your thrall, and if she knows how to groom and feed a horse, let her help you. Do it now.'

'Yes, chief.'

Fenrisulfr looked at Brökkr, thought of spinning on the spot and slamming his heel into Brökkr's liver – the kind of kick that drops a man, leaving him conscious and wishing he were not, because of the pain – but an ambush shot was not the way to deal with a feisty former lieutenant who might be considering a challenge for leadership of Fenrisulfr's people, combining two bands into one. Domination for face had to be overt, against a prepared foe, though sneakiness in a fighter was and always would be a virtue.

'Walk with me,' he told Thóllakr. 'Bring the girl.'

The two leering fighters looked at each other, wondering if Fenrisulfr was going to assert his right to take her, either while Thóllakr watched or after Fenrisulfr had beaten him un-conscious, assuming he protested. Fenrisulfr noted this but did not comment further, waiting instead until he, Thóllakr and the girl were far from the others. He pointed at the horse, still tied up where it had been.

'The gelding is strong,' he said. 'Can carry a decent weight.'

'Er, yes, chief.'

Fenrisulfr looked at the causeway peeking through the waves, joining the Holy Isle to the mainland. 'My orders are that you exercise the horse while I'm gone. I'll let the rest of the guarding party know that. When you cross to the mainland,' he added, 'don't even think about heading west inland, because you'll miss the rest of us, since we're turning south.'

'Er ...'

'Then if you carried on riding, deep into Northanhymbra,

you'd find yourself among strangers, maybe even Thyra's people. And if you ended up staying there, you'd have to learn a new way of speaking, earn a living without killing, and all the rest.'

Thóllakr was swallowing, gripping Thyra's hand hard.

'In years past,' Fenrisulfr went on, 'our people ruled here, so they know us. But Erik Bloodaxe is dead these forty summers, and the current king is named Æthelred, one of Thyra's folk.'

Hearing her king's name and her own, the girl stared at him.

'May the Norns treat you well.' Fenrisulfr clasped Thóllakr's shoulder. 'And to Hel's realm with them if they don't.'

Finally, Thóllakr grinned.

'Yes, chief. Thank you.'

Fenrisulfr walked away, pulling his cloak around him.

No looking back.

Brökkr was looking thoughtful when Fenrisulfr returned. Ivarr was with him, in addition to the four fighters from Brökkr's band. Fenrisulfr gestured towards the causeway.

'We'll cross at low tide. Have you decided who's to be left behind?'

'I have,' said Brökkr. 'You want me to run through the names?'

Fenrisulfr shook his head.

'I trust your judgement on this, as in everything else,' he said. 'But I would have private words with you, brave Brökkr. By the holy men's fortress?'

'Er, yes, chief.'

'Come, then.'

Of course Brökkr was suspicious, but Fenrisulfr, not carrying his axes, spread his hands openly as they walked, keeping to Brökkr's right side, and asked a question in an easy tone just before the pivotal moment, so that Brökkr's mouth was open, his mind and tongue forming the reply – the estimated distance the raiding party could cover per day – when Fenrisulfr's body slammed into his. Fenrisulfr grabbed Brökkr's sword-hilt at the same time as whipping his head into the side of Brökkr's jaw – a sideways head-butt, almost getting the knockout – and slamming his knee into Brökkr's thigh – no point in trying for the groin because Brökkr was fast even when surprised – and pulling free, drawing his own blade left-handed, a reverse grip but never mind because he had two swords and Brökkr had none, and as Fenrisulfr swung both blades high Brökkr flinched and tried to duck beneath as Fenrisulfr had hoped and this time he drove the knee in with maximum force, smashing into Brökkr's face, then swung his left hand thumb-first and still holding the snatched sword so its hard pommel drove into Brökkr's temple and then he was down.

There was a water-skin nearby, and after giving Brökkr a few moments languishing in dreamworld, Fenrisulfr splashed the water over his bloodied face, and waited while Brökkr coughed himself awake, then glowered at Fenrisulfr.

'You're already a good leader,' Fenrisulfr told him. 'And capable of leading my men in addition to your own.'

He had both swords in normal grips now, his wrists and forearms loose and ready.

'Huh.' Brökkr pushed himself up to a sitting position, knowing better than to rise any further. 'Not when I let sneaky bastards catch me like that.'

'Thóllakr and his thrall are under my protection. Swear by Thórr you'll leave them unharmed, and tell your men to do likewise.'

'Huh? You only have to give the order and we'll—'

'Swear.'

Brökkr wiped blood from his face with the back of his hand, snorted, then spat a red gob of snot onto the grass. 'I swear by Thórr's balls that Thóllakr and his woman will go unharmed. Good enough, chief?'

Fenrisulfr shook his head.

'I'm not your chief.'

'You're dissolving the alliance? There's no—'

'I'm making you chief of both our bands,' said Fenrisulfr. 'You're more than good enough.'

With care, he placed Brökkr's sword flat on the ground.

'You're not ... You mean it, Fenrisulfr, don't you?'

Fenrisulfr stared at the sea, so huge and uncaring of mortal affairs, and wondered how he could ever have thought his life was so important.

'I'm not sure that's my name any more,' he said, more to the waves than to Brökkr.

Without looking back, he walked down to his longboat, beached among the others. He told the men on guard about Thóllakr, that he and his woman were not be harmed and had orders to groom and exercise the roan gelding, across the causeway if Thóllakr wished. There was no hint in his tone that this was a final order.

Then he fetched the crystal-tipped spear from on board the longboat, slapped the dragon prow and went off to be by himself until night fell and he could slip away and – Norns permitting, and damn them if they did not – never be seen by his reavers again.

He was thirty-three summers old to the best of his reckoning, stronger and faster than ever, as ruthless as he had to be, with no idea how he wanted to live the rest of his life, except that when he found the opportunity that must be out there, no one would wrest it from him.

They could try, of course.

I'll still need enemies.

What else gave meaning to existence?

From time to time Chief Vermundr thought back to the days when Folkvar ruled the clan, and that young whelp Ulfr had shown so much promise that some people thought he would be made chieftain on Folkvar's death, except that Eira had died and Ulfr had grown crazed and that was that: another young man gone to travel far, and by now he might be dead or rich, whatever the Norns decreed.

'She's gone, Father.' His son Vítharr put a hand on Vermundr's shoulder. 'My mother has passed.'

'I know.'

They were in the men's longhall, just the two of them, their words strange in the emptiness.

'I know, my son,' said Vermundr again, his heart hollow.

He stared at the youth, feeling both proud and worried, because Vítharr was taking his mother's death calmly but there was a streak of darkness inside him, and it could surface in cruelty from time to time. And avarice, when wandering storytellers sang of plunder and glory, of warriors founding new domains in the East. Some day Vítharr would take it in his mind to go, and perhaps that would be best for the clan, hard though it was to think so.

In his mind's eye now, Vermundr's beloved Anya came back to him, her spirit reaching out from dreamworld before Hel's dread ship *Naglfar* took her to the Helway, to suffer in Niflheim, Niflhel, for ever.

I love you.

And I you, always.

He had first caught sight of her on entering Chief Snorri's village, as was – on the day Arne became chief unofficially, later to be confirmed ceremonially, for Snorri had been killed in the fighting and only Arne had stepped up to organise the survivors. No one ever raised the subject of how soon Vítharr was born: seven months after Vermundr and Anya began courting, which was two months after they had met. Nor did anyone ever talk about the one-eyed poet who had sojourned in the village beforehand, and tricked them into bloody conflict.

There was a cough from the longhall entrance.

'May I enter?'

It was custom for even a *volva* to ask permission, this being the men's hall, and she was new to the village and therefore still careful, though Vermundr had met her many years back, when they had been travelling to the Thing, and several times years later when she rode with traders. But last winter she had entered the village on foot, leading a daughter who was three or four summers old, and asked whether they had a *volva* she could talk to.

But there had been no one in that position for a long time, and little by little she had made herself useful, healing and counselling, until Vermundr asked her to move in to the old *volva*'s hut, once occupied by Eira, and Nessa before her.

Now she was here to comfort Vermundr's tortured spirit.

'Come in, Heithrún,' he said. 'Come in.'

She came inside and bowed to Vermundr, and nodded carefully to Vítharr.

It was always wise to be careful around him.

FORTY

Jed Goran had never wanted to be a spy – or even a spy's husband, more to the point – but Labyrinth had enemies and backing down from a fight had never been Jed's way. Yet there was bravery and there was foolish unpreparedness, so as his bronze ship orbited Coolth he minimised the external-view holorama and reviewed the briefing holos.

So, Coolth.

Ice-locked continents; oceans where schools of huge balaenae swam, singing songs of epic learning and grandeur, where once every Coolth year, each herd, some two thousand strong, would gather around their vast matriarch whose skin nodules would begin to pulse and finally burst open, tiny forms streaking upward to the surface and up into the sky, for the nymph form soared like birds, a lifecycle discovered by an early explorer called Rekka Chandri, the events of her real life distorted by the popularity of a twenty-fifth century holodrama series called *Chandri, Space Explorer*, which created an extended and improbable mythology of its own, in which Pilots were always mysterious and undefeated in space or hand-to-hand combat.

'True enough,' said Jed aloud, and grinned.

And what about Pilots' ships, in the stories?

He slipped lightly into trance.

They were clueless about you, my love. And about Labyrinth's existence.

Just as well, perhaps.

Jed returned his focus to the briefing material.

*

An hour later, they soared in to land next to Barbourville, an extended series of domes, some large enough to house potentially a thousand people – even though the entire station's complement was no more than eight hundred – sitting securely on the icescape. It was historical coincidence that this, Coolth's largest research station, bore the same name as one of Molsin's former sky-cities that had perished in what people were calling the Conjunction Catastrophe – except that their understanding of what that meant was about to change.

Clara, white-faced, had shared news with Jed before he left Labyrinth, information that was yet to spread among the realspace worlds: Molsin had fallen prey to the Anomaly, and final intelligence reports – before surveillance devices stopped functioning and Pilot ships in orbit transited to muspace before the Anomaly could subsume them – showed the baby sky-cities reaching out to the wreckage of the true cities, such remains as still floated in Molsin's orange skies, and joining quickglass to quickglass, forming one great floating structure that looked to be extending horizontally, perhaps eventually to cover the entire world like a spherical webbed shell.

And there were hints that it was already lowering tendrils to the hydrofluoric acid oceans below, though for what purpose, no analysts were willing to say for sure. What was clear was that Anomalous components like Rick Mbuli – killed fortuitously by Jed, over and over in his dreams and in waking flashes – had succeeded in carrying out the act that Petra Helsen had only faked, in order to get the sky-cities firing on each other out of panic: carrying out the absorption of individual human beings into one giant planetary gestalt, either part of or identical in nature to the original.

Fulgor, Siganth and now Molsin were lost.

This is Coolth and we need to concentrate.

You are so right, my love.

Ice felt cold on their ventral hull as they landed, then Jed and ship slipped apart, their minds disengaging, so the ship could create an opening to the control cabin and use a slender tendril to carry Jed out and lower him to the chilly ground. He blew her a kiss, breath steaming, then trudged across hard-packed snow to the nearest entrance.

His ship watched until he was safely inside, then she ascended, keeping her attitude horizontal, and took up a floating position a kilometre above Barbourville, ready to act should Jed need her, trying not to worry but unable to help it because this kind of operation was new to both of them, and risky enough for those with experience, never mind first-timers.

Once indoors, the smartgel that had coated his lungs began to crawl up into his mouth, and by the time he walked into a grey-decorated concourse, he was able to spit the stuff out as a blue glob, and push it into a small pocket that formed in his jumpsuit for the purpose. His eyes were their natural obsidian with no need for disguise, as he passed research workers who gave small nods and grew quiet until he was past, a reminder that the mythology of centuries-old holodramas remained strong among most of humanity, arguably with good reason.

Ferl Corplane's office was in a section dominated by shiny white ceramic with silver edging, which seemed an unnecessary echo of the icescape and freezing oceans outside. But that was true throughout the building: the floors were stacked like decks in a submarine or sky vessel, with armoured hatches everywhere, all of it hard-looking, devoid of luxury.

Perhaps sheer depression had motivated Corplane to pick up extra money by selling shipment details to Zajinet agents – if not to Zajinets directly – with no thought to the lives of Pilots and passengers who might be killed in stealth raids or ambushes, or the subsequent suffering of colonists unable to receive supplies which in some cases were necessary simply to live.

'I'm Jed Goran.'

'Corplane.' In flat near-monotone: 'Happy to meet you, Pilot.'

He was shaven-headed with implant loops curled around his neck. Jed had met members of the Corpuscular Plasmonad before, although he never entirely understood their philosophical views relating humanity's destiny to homeostasis and apoptosis, the desirability of self-immolation for the sake of the status quo. Those people, he had found unexpectedly good-humoured. Corplane, however, was blank-faced, almost without emotional affect.

Sending you down will be a pleasure, you sour-faced bastard.

No doubt a professional would be more even-tempered, but Jed felt anger rising on behalf of the dead, and had consciously to control his breathing, calming down to get on with the job.

'Here are our shipment requirements,' Corplane went on. 'Some of the required delivery dates are quite tight.'

There were no seats or desks in the office, only work-shelves against the walls. That at least was contemporary, as men and women across the realspace worlds were finally throwing off habits from the sedentary centuries that had had such a deleterious effect on mind-body health. Jed approved, but Corplane was still the enemy.

A sheaf of holos blossomed in the centre of the room.

'Let's see how well we can match up,' said Jed. 'You understand that availability and pricing are determined by technical constraints as well as logistics.'

The secrets of mu-space navigation were not to be shared, but it was occasionally necessary to point out the difficulty or impossibility of a would-be client's request, for example a foray to the galactic core – where the corresponding mu-space region was a turbulent spacetime typhoon – or some mad request such as a voyage to Andromeda, not understanding that other galaxies remained out of reach, if not as unthinkably so as in realspace.

Jed's tu-ring generated branching possibilities, rendered as golden holo streams that fitted in among the sheaf projected by Corplane, and negotiating modules in the displayware found best fits and highlighted them for approval.

There were two main sets of proposal capable of matching the requirements, and after an emotionless inspection, Corplane pointed to one of them. The corresponding holo elements gleamed.

'Done,' said Jed.

The legal notarising took femtoseconds. Holos winked out of existence, leaving only Corplane and Jed standing in the office. Without even a nod, Corplane turned his back on Jed, and gestured to begin working with a his-eyes-only holo.

Charming.

'Nice doing business with you,' said Jed.

Then he left without checking for a reaction from Corplane. As he walked along the white corridor, he reviewed the interaction in his mind, deciding that his own annoyance would have appeared entirely natural, without betraying his secret knowledge of Corplane's duplicity.

Let's see how you handle the outcome, you bastard.

Corplane had just bought his own doom.

The Zajinet attacks had been subtly placed, so that it had been difficult to backtrack to the security leak; but now Clara's people had done just that, there would be counter-ambushes set up and waiting, ready to destroy the attackers while incidentally gaining legal proof of Corplane's guilt, as the Zajinets followed the false data supplied by Jed.

Soon enough, Jed found himself in another concourse, its architecture bare – suggestive of a cargo hold embellished with a series of catwalks – but filled with the bouncing chatter of some three dozen people on a break, the animated energy of those who had been working quietly for hours and had more to do, needing to interact with friends and colleagues while they had a chance.

He bought himself a hot drink and carried it to one of the upper catwalks, where he could lean against the rail, sipping his drink and watching the people, wondering if someone was going to make contact.

There was a local team in place, their job to maintain surveillance on Corplane and detect any contacts he made, and preferably to follow anyone that Corplane met in person. Jed knew nothing beyond that, not even their numerical strength, save for the team leader's name: Shireen Singh. She had a recognition code for introducing herself if she thought it desirable, otherwise Jed would end up leaving Coolth knowing nothing, until such time as Clara or someone else in the Admiralty might share a titbit of information regarding his success or failure here.

The sight of three racks of antlers among the crowd surprised him, until he remembered the rumours, that Haxigoji were travelling to other worlds now, more than just the occasional official delegation to Earth, the previous extent of their voyaging.

Suddenly the antlers jerked.

What have they seen?

Of course he meant smelled, or did he? Either way, something had disturbed the Haxigoji down below, and as far as Jed was concerned they were trustworthy friends, because they had protected him on Vachss Station after he had killed the thing that had been Rick Mbuli, and the reason for their protection was that they had perceived Mbuli's true nature.

So what had they detected here?

Corplane. Must be.

The bastard had been in close contact with an Anomalous component, or more likely a renegade Pilot, and the Haxigoji could detect some echo of that. It was the logical explanation, except that Jed could not see anything of Corplane. Raising his tu-ring, he was about to send a comm signal in the hope Corplane would answer, when a woman appeared beside him and his tu-ring beeped a code-received acknowledgement.

'I'm Shireen.'

'Jed. Corplane is—'

'Still in his office. Whatever they've spotted, it's not him.'

So she had noticed the Haxigoji too.

Her smartlenses were dark brown, enough to make her look like an ordinary human under normal circumstances; but Jed caught sight of tiny golden sparks inside. She was worried and getting ready for action, and if someone were trying to engineer another Anomaly here, the only way to save the research station crew was sudden violence, to kill the once-human component before it could begin absorbing others.

More killing.

The thought made him tremble, because killing Mbuli was already hard enough to deal with. But he would do whatever was necessary now.

You need me, my love?

Not yet. Stay up there.

All right.

His ship's presence, a kilometre overhead, gave him strength, allowing him to centre himself.

'Look there,' said Shireen. 'In the corridor.'

One of the Haxigoji had left the concourse proper, and was pressing his double-thumbed hand against a view window. From here it was impossible to tell what he was seeing.

'Someone outside,' said Jed.

'I'll call in my team.'

'Right. You do that.'

He broke away, jogged along the catwalk to the steps, then threw normal behaviour aside, throwing one leg over the rail and commanding his jumpsuit fabric to become frictionless, as far as it was capable. Like a schoolchild, he slid down fast, hopped to the concourse deck, ignoring the reactions of everyone around, and pelted into the corridor, popping blue smartgel into his mouth because the air outside was impossible to breathe unassisted.

There was an emergency exit and it responded to his tu-ring's signal and then he was in cold air, stumbling across snow, trying to correct his gait and squint against the wind – stronger than before – to make out the man who was staring at him.

Narrow-bodied, brown hair, plain jumpsuit. Nothing special about him – except that when Jed glanced back, two of the Haxigoji were standing in the open exit and pointing. The atmosphere was even less suitable for them, nor were most of them prone to violent behaviour, which was exactly what was needed now.

'Jed?' It was Shireen, calling via her tu-ring. 'Corplane's dead. We just checked his—'

'Shit.'

'I'm triggering the public emergency net.'

The figure ahead was moving away now, his boot-soles elongating to form snow-shoes, moving with an easy-looking gait that drew him further and further away from Jed's awkward pursuit through ever-deepening snow.

A wail cut through the air behind him, followed by a ripping sound – icequake! – but it was not the ice-mass beneath the snow that was splitting apart: it was the research station behind him, the domes and linking tunnels all cracking into segments, sealing themselves into fifty or more modules; and as Jed watched, they began to slide away from each other, their motive power unclear but visibly accelerating, smoothly moving across snow and heading for the cold ocean, because ice-quakes were not uncommon and this was a viable defensive procedure for most contingencies.

Jed was not sure that an incipient Anomaly was one of them.

It's more likely a renegade.

An Anomalous component might have tried to initiate absorption, the process obvious because it was accompanied, as far as anyone had ever observed, by a characteristic spillover glow that was a precise shade of blue. This might be one of Schenck's renegades, but even at this range Jed should have been able to detect the induction neurons and other characteristics of a fellow Pilot. Everything indicated that this was an ordinary man he was chasing.

A man capable of moving faster than Jed, and perhaps heading for a weapons cache or transport, even a submersible flying shuttle, because that was what the researchers used for—

He had stopped, the man, amid falling snow but with an ellipsoidal volume of clear air surrounding him, and it took Jed several stumbling moments to realise what he was looking at: a smartmiasma, no doubt weapon-primed and ready to strike.

I'm dead.

Jed's tu-ring had weapon capabilities and he even had an old-fashioned knuckleduster with embedded grasers tucked inside a pocket, but they needed human action to initiate a strike while the whole point about smartmiasmas and similar technology was that they operated at a trillion times the speed of thought, because organic brains are slow.

The man smiled and raised his arms.

I'm sorry, my—

Something huge and bronze crashed into existence.

What for, lover?

It was a ship, gleaming and beautiful.

Where did you—? I love you.

And I love you.

Which was why she had taken the risk, not descending through air but transiting via mu-space, such a dangerous transition, perfectly executed, and smashing any matter in the way, say a human body, to misty oblivion.

It was not the icy wind that brought tears to Jed's eyes.

Before he left Coolth for good, there was one last event to finish off a very odd day. After the all-clear had been sounded, and the research station modules crawled back together and reformed while Jed's ship hovered overhead, all weapons powered up just in case, Jed had a final meeting with Shireen Singh. Her team had analysed both Corplane's body and the evaporated remains of the unknown man – a man redolent with the scent of darkness, according to the Haxigoji witnesses – along with Corplane's business systems.

'We think Corplane was acting under some kind of compulsion,' Shireen said. 'Which is worrying, but not the most interesting thing. I want you to know this as added back-up to my own report, because the Admiralty need to find out.'

Jed looked into her steady faux-brown eyes.

'Find out what? That I've killed again?'

'It wasn't exactly you this time. Plus' – with a smile – 'the person your ship wiped out was one Petra Helsen, responsible for the Anomaly coming into existence.'

'That bitch.'

'Exactly.'

'But it was a man I—'

'Autodoc,' said Shireen, and shrugged. 'Identity change.'

'Of course. She did it before, on Molsin. Not to that extent.'

He should have thought of it earlier.

Clara was a boy until she was seventeen. You know that.

I know, I know. I'm glad one of us could think clearly in the moment.

Any time, my love.

Shireen raised an eyebrow, as if aware that he was in thought-conjunction with his ship, although of course she could not eavesdrop: no one could.

'You did good, Pilot Goran.'

'Thank you.'

'Give my love to your wife. And belated congratulations to both of you.'

'Cheers. I'll do that.'

His ship, who had been hovering high overhead once more,

took her time descending, and after taking him on board rose slowly. The team of agents, with Shireen at their centre, watched from the ground. There was no hurry now.

Jed-and-ship could fly home in quiet triumph.

FORTY-ONE

It happened on the morning that, over breakfast, Rupert asked Gavriela where cosmic rays came from, and she told him they came from the cosmos – where did he expect? – then after some badinage she talked about radiation from nebulae where stars were born, and the magnetic bow wave thrown up by the galaxy as it hurtled towards Virgo, at which Rupert raised an ironic eyebrow.

She went in to Imperial late, as was fitting for a retired scientist, but young Geoffrey was equally late, and they entered his office together. The room smelled of cigarette smoke and featured a six-foot vertical strip of computer printout on the back of the door: Ursula Andress, bikini-clad, the shading rendered in alphanumeric characters. Or perhaps it was Raquel Welch, from *One Million Years BC*. Embarrassed, Geoffrey hung his overcoat from the door-hook, obscuring Ursula or Raquel, whichever.

'Sorry. I, er—'

A tap on the door was followed by Hannah, one of the administrators, poking her head inside and saying, 'Alex really needs you, Geoffrey, to sort out that budget thing.'

'It's all right,' Gavriela said. 'If that's the meson data over there, why I don't I just poke through it by myself?'

'Oh. Yes, why not?'

She was supposed to be good at this, making sense of columnar figures, allowing patterns to emerge in her mind's eye as easily as a collection of printed characters might be perceived as a movie actress wearing a bikini. But the office was warm and perhaps she was feeling her age, because she jerked her eyes open and realised she had been dozing. At least Geoffrey had not discovered her that way: luckily, his bureaucratic task seemed to be dragging on.

On an A4 pad she wrote, in pencil, some fragments of Fortran code that might group the data in more useful ways, so that the patterns she was unable to see might grow apparent. Why she thought there were patterns, she could not say. Geoffrey could piece the subroutines into a program on the PDP11, and if he spotted nothing in the output, perhaps she might wander in again next week and have another try.

'Er . . .'

'Hello, Geoffrey. I thought you'd been sucked into a bureaucratic hell for ever.'

Geoffrey's expression was the same as when he spotted Gavriela looking at the printout on the back of the door. 'I, um, sort of was. The thing is, some people think we're falling behind King's College – London, I mean – because they're working on new stuff, on black holes.'

'Seriously?' said Gavriela. 'You can't mean that.'

The phenomenon might be allowed by general relativity, yet that did not mean such objects existed, any more than quarks, which to her mind were mathematical figments reflecting the choice of equations in the model, having little to do with what was really there. A meson *might* be a paired quark-plus-anti-quark, but it seemed unlikely.

'Anyway,' said Geoffrey, 'I kind of volunteered to investigate the field. But that means . . .'

'Abandoning this line of research. I understand.' She looked at the stack of printed numbers, and her scribbled lines of Fortran. 'Archive this where I can find it, Geoffrey, and I'll come pootling along to browse when I'm able. No doubt I'm verging on senility, but when I pick up my Nobel Prize, I'll mention you in my speech.'

'You think I'll be working on a flawed theory?'

'I do.'

'And didn't Bohr win the Nobel for his pre-quantum atomic model?'

It predicted the energy spectrum of helium, hence the prize, but his theory was wholly inadequate to a proper understanding of the atom, and in a real sense was incorrect.

'Good point,' said Gavriela. 'When *you* make the speech, maybe you can mention *me*.'

Geoffrey grinned at her.

'More importantly,' he said, 'I hear they've got fresh doughnuts in the tea-room.'

'You mean we're wasting time talking about the nature of the universe when we could be doing something useful. Was that plain doughnuts or jam?'

'Jam, of course. We're not barbarians.'

There were little pings of arthritis when she stood.

'I'll race you,' she lied.

Outside the college, she stood looking at the redbrick grandeur of the Royal Albert Hall, while music drifted from the Royal College of Music behind her, next to Imperial. She smiled and listened: it was the whimsical Bach piece that they used on the telly – *dum, da-da-dum, da-da-dum, da-da-dum; da-da-da, da-dum, da-da-da, da-dum* – as the countdown to educational programmes.

But some forty seconds in, the pleasantness was disturbed by a discordant intrusion – *da, da-dum, da-da-da-dum, da-da* – far off to her right. When she looked, a thin man might have just disappeared around the corner, or she might have imagined it. Her sense of being in the presence of darkness faded.

'Are you all right, Dr Woods?' It was Hannah from Admin, her hair freshly permed, with a silk headscarf to protect it. 'You seem a little pale.'

'Too many doughnuts,' said Gavriela. 'But I'm fine now, thank you.'

Nothing untoward happened on the journey home, and in the end she said nothing to Rupert about her possible brush with the darkness, because what could he have done about it?

That night, in her comfortable bedroom that felt so right, she knew as she was falling asleep that she was going to dream, vividly and in strong colours. Yet she encountered neither crystalline beings nor wolves and swords as she expected; instead, the world in which she found herself was constructed of mathematical metaphor, and in the middle of the dream she had the thought that Lewis Carroll would be proud.

Wonderfuler and wonderfuler, she decided.

Strolling across a meadow of integers, she laughs at the sight of matrices flying in V-formation above, then picks irrational chrysanthemums with florets arranged in infinite recursion, while a row of fractions watches, nudging each other and winking.

An infinity symbol comes bounding across the integers, then stops in front of her, bouncing up and down slowly, like a Lissajous figure trapped upon an oscilloscope screen.

'I'm boundless,' mutters the infinity.

An apparently identical infinity comes bounding into view.

'So am I,' it says. 'Isn't it obvious?'

She waits while they bounce in place.

$$\infty \quad \infty$$

'You look bare and boundless to me,' she says. 'Has Möbius been stripping again?'

The infinities titter.

'What will happen if you divide us?' they say. 'What will happen then? Can you tell, or do we need to swallow you up for all eternity?'

She clears her throat.

'I can tell straight away,' she tells them, 'provided you answer me two questions.'

The infinities, still bouncing, angle inwards to look at each other, then face her once more.

'Ask us,' says the infinity on the left. 'We'll tell you the answer.'

'Anything at all,' says the infinity on the right. 'Really anything.'

'Or imaginary anything,' says Left Infinity.

'As complex as you like,' says Right Infinity.

She lets out a breath, knowing that these two are rascals but bounded by their promise, if nothing else. All around, the meadow of integers stretches for ever, but you can tell that the infinities are different ... though whether from each other, it is hard to tell.

'If you were to twist yourselves into alephs,' she asks thoughtfully, 'what would your subscripts be?'

'I say.' That's Left Infinity.

'That's a little personal.' Right Infinity.

'Do you want to stay bound by a promise for ever?' she asks.

'Oh, dear.'

'Suppose not.'

They bounce a little more, then wriggle into knots, and recommence bouncing in their new forms.

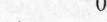

'Unity,' she says.

'We beg your pardon?' they say together.

'You're both aleph nulls,' she points out. 'So you'll divide to produce one, and it doesn't matter which of you is on top.' Which would have been her other question, of course.

'Well ...'

'How risqué.'

'Little people can be so rude.'

'Can't they just.'

She calls up: 'I'm not little!'

But her voice is tiny because she is shrinking, with integers growing large around her. Already they are above her head, and the twin infinities are about to be obscured from sight, which seems hardly fair because she asked only one question.

'You promised two answers!'

'By George, she's right.'

'By Cantor, so are you.'

The integers are so very big, taller than trees and still growing.

'What is—?' She forces her voice to grow louder. 'What's the *pattern* in the *numbers*?'

'Oh, dear ...'

'Hmm ...'

She spirals inwards in endless recursion.

Except that the infinite series of her transformations turns out be convergent, and so she wakes before the end of time, staring at the grey gloom and muttering to herself, 'Too many jam doughnuts,' a second before sleep comes back, this time minus dreams.

When Gavriela woke up, her notebook, closed, was atop the candlewick bedspread, and her fountain-pen, actually borrowed from Rupert, was neatly beside it, cap screwed in place and not an ink-blot anywhere. She had no memory of taking either object to bed.

Senility strikes at last.

Pushing down the covers, she forced herself up to a sitting position, sideways on the bed, wanting to pee but needing to check something first. It was decades since anything like this had happened, but perhaps the notebook contained sentences from her unconscious mind, written while she slept, as on that wartime night in Oxford.

Out in the hallway, the phone began to ring.

The notebook opened naturally at the midpoint, to a pair of facing pages that yesterday had been blank. The left-hand page now bore a blotchy ink sketch:

And the opposite page contained only a handwritten note, a first draft of a message intended to be written by her, not sent to her, although the intent was not obvious.

You will see three. You will be wrong.

G

P.S. Pass it on! $\kappa_\infty = 9.42$; $\lambda_\infty = 2.703 \times 10^{23}$; $\mu_\infty = .02289$

Rupert tapped on the door – it could not be anyone else – so she closed the notebook and pulled her dressing-gown around her, hoping this would not take time because she really did have to pee.

'I'm sorry,' he said when she opened the door, 'but I needed to tell you ...'

He was wearing his dressing-gown with the burgundy lapels, and the new slippers she had bought him to replace the tattered monstrosities he wore when she moved in – less than four months ago, yet already the distant past.

'What's wrong?' she asked.

The lines on his face were deeper than ever.

'Your niece Ursula,' he said, 'must've been further *enceinte* than I realised. Apparently you've had a great niece for the past two months. I had no idea Ursula had given birth.'

'Oh, no.' Gavriela made a guess, hoping she was wrong. 'The baby's ill or even ...'

She did not want to say it.

'Missing,' said Rupert. 'The baby is missing.'

'How could that happen?'

What kind of mother was Ursula if she could not even—?

'—from the house,' Rupert was saying. 'At least three men were involved, in addition to the female decoy. Even I might have opened the door to her, because by all accounts she sounded convincing.'

Some tale of woe, whose details Gavriela could not process because in her mind she was wondering how bloody stupid she could possibly have been, ignoring a clear warning that an enemy was near, almost certainly Dmitri Ivanovitch Shtemenko, who seemed to have some inhibition against killing her – given the opportunities he had passed up – but clearly possessed the capacity to be monstrous.

'One of the men was thin and not young according to other witnesses. Sounds like Shtemenko, though Ursula did not see him, so our people can't be sure.'

Would he have killed the baby out of spite?

It was horrible, but Dmitri might be evil enough to do such a thing.

'The woman,' Rupert added, 'was identified by Ursula from a photograph as one Daniela Weissmann, a young Stasi officer under Shtemenko's command. One rumour says she's his lover also, but that's not known for sure.'

'He's taken the baby,' said Gavriela. 'Taken her home with him.'

'Not even a KGB colonel would mount a team operation purely to snatch a two-month old relative,' said Rupert. 'He must have been here for something else.'

Of course he was, but there was no likelihood of SIS or Five finding out, and if they did, surely there was no reason to divulge the information to a retired spymaster or the equally retired cryptanalyst who shared a house platonically with him.

But Rupert had influence still, it seemed.

'You know the Chester Terrace out-station?' he asked.

'Vaguely heard of it,' said Gavriela. 'I've never been there.'

'Nice place. Georgian mansion, overlooking Regent's Park, ideal for eavesdropping on the Soviet embassy. Stank to high heaven last time I was there, but that was because they were re-lacquering the parquet flooring on the top floor, and half the rest was dug up.'

Gavriela glanced at her notebook.

'They've invited us over,' Rupert went on. 'To talk to Ursula's watch team and find out what went wrong.'

'I had a sense of the darkness yesterday,' she said. 'Not exactly the kind of information I can share with them.'

'No, I suppose not. Maybe *we* need protection.'

Gavriela thought about it.

'I don't think so,' she said. 'But it can't do any harm.'

Rupert would act on his own suggestion, faking a story that suggested the KGB might know his private address and have reason to perpetrate personal vengeance, so that he obtained a permanent watch team to safeguard him and incidentally Gavriela. Whether that was unnecessary, or whether it was the presence of the watch team that prevented the enemy from making a run at Rupert, they would never find out.

Not for as long as Rupert lived, at any rate.

FORTY-TWO

Roger was promoted to captain, with a hint of fast-track advancement to come, on the basis of his intelligence report concerning the dark matter star (to use the newly revived archaic term) that sat at the heart of the realspace galaxy. Roger's ultra-hellflight had become an unofficial legend; and unlike his father, he had not needed to die in order to achieve success. It felt undeserved.

But it was the entire squadron's analysis of the renegades' base, not just Roger's report, that was of immediate interest to the battle planners. Linguistically, the base was again labelled Target Shadow, which gave more than a hint of how they saw it. The combined telemetric data of thirty-eight ships produced a reasonable model not just of defensive resources and their disposition, but also the residential deep-space modules and the massive devices under construction, whose purpose and mode of operation remained conjecture.

This was war, officially so, which meant that personal secrets could not be kept private if germane – hence Roger providing a sealed addendum to his report, the heart of it related as a personal reminiscence of his father's memories: 'After using my tu-ring to defeat the locking mechanism, I opened Greybeard's case to reveal a fist-sized device, purpose unknown. All this while, Greybeard remained in delta-coma, but he wasn't going to stay that way, because his closed eyes were flicking from side to side.

'But when I tried to pick up the device, small though it was, I failed. It was so massive I could not shift it. Yet when Greybeard awoke, he was able to lift the thing easily.'

There were more details, but that was the salient portion, as he pointed out in the covering metadata, in which he also explained the addendum's provenance: 'These are my father's memories, that is Carl Blackstone, from a covert operation conducted nearly twenty standard years before I was born – memories inherited from his ship by mine, but inaccessible to my father due to targeted amnesia applied during debriefing.'

Such treatment prevented memory retrieval during conjunction trance, effectively repressing the ship's memory also ... unless that ship gave parthenogenetic birth to a daughter, in which case the daughter's Pilot might uncover those buried memories, as Roger and his ship had done.

In the final comments, he added his own analysis of the reported memory, highlighting its importance as he saw it: 'Since my father underwent amnesia induction, and since his original report remains archived beyond my clearance level, I cannot tell which details are on record and which were lost. It might be that certain facts which are obviously relevant today, in the light of actions taken by former Admiral Schenck and the other renegade Pilots, would not have seemed significant at the time.

'I note that the human criminals coerced Zajinets into taking them to the galactic core, probably in order to deliver the device to fellow humans living there. That seems to have been their main objective. However, it is the device itself, although I have no insight into its purpose, that I would urge our analysts to consider.

'In particular, I would note that the device appeared alternately massive and light, depending on who touched it. The device was clearly constructed of ordinary baryonic matter. My conjecture is that it was able to interact with *non*-baryonic matter or non-gauge forces under controlled circumstances, a scientific achievement normally considered impossible.

'Could the renegades be using this technology to affect the galactic jet emanating from the core? Or could they be preparing the locale in some other way – perhaps the jet is a side effect – in either case to construct a bridgehead for the enemy we know is coming eventually?

'My recommendation is covert research into the device's origins. However, Greybeard indicated he had covered his traces by murder, so there may be no trail to follow.

'Infiltrating the renegades' base would be highly dangerous, and in any case the base should be considered a primary target for overt, massive assault, with an objective of obliteration rather than capture.

'End of report. Captain Blackstone out.'

The report was professional and he was proud of it; but he had just suggested the violent extinction of probably two thousand people – one in four being Pilots, renegades like Schenck – which under other circumstances would be termed an atrocity. When exactly had he become capable of thinking this way?

It bothered him, too, that his fellow Pilots thought so highly of him, because his ultra-hellflight had been hard but not heroic, more like desperate; and again it was all about ideas more than reality, because it seemed to him that what he had broken was a psychological barrier.

Perhaps it had been physically possible for the last few generations of ships to survive a flight through the mu-space turbulence that matched to the realspace galactic core. Perhaps the real barrier had been sociolinguistic hypnosis, due either to the real limitations of earlier ships or deliberate thought-sabotage by some previous member of the Aeternum language institute.

If this were true, Roger's example would have broken the inhibition, and other Pilots would match the feat soon. Except that there was a war to concentrate upon, fought on two fronts or three, depending on whether you separated the Anomaly from the darkness. While Roger and the rest of his SRS squadron obsessed on the renegade base they had seen, the Admiralty planners had a different view of things, since the

Zajinet numbers were far greater than that of the renegades, and their attacks were growing in frequency and ferocity.

Or so Roger deduced after attending the highest-powered meeting of his career so far.

Admiral Whitwell said: 'Thank you for coming, Captain. I wanted you to see the battle plans, so that you understand why we're asking you to take such a risk.'

A vast array of holos filled the war chamber. Some thirty people, most outranking Roger by far, stood among them.

'Understood, sir,' said Roger.

Commodore Max Gould highlighted a holovolume. What it showed was a simulation, not a recorded image, of something like the renegades' realspace base, but nowhere near the galactic core: it was floating in a region where stars were sparse and space appeared black.

'The segments are under separate construction,' he said. 'In mu-space. Transfer and assembly will be fast, and the location will be here.'

Another holo gleamed. The dummy base would lie on a familiar line, heading outwards from the galactic centre to a distant void: a line on which Earth also lay, at least on a map of this scale.

'Why would Admiral Schenck ...' Roger's voice trailed off. 'Zajinets?'

'Exactly, Captain. They're the enemy we plan to break first.'

Roger examined the dummy base.

'It's convincing,' he said. 'Provided they know what the real Target Shadow looks like, but why should they?'

Whitwell's voice fell flat.

'Certain recordings from your squadron's mission have fallen into the hands of Zajinet agents. The data makes it hard to determine the exact location, but obvious what kind of installation it is. Therefore a new, similar base with known coordinates should form a tempting target.'

'But how could—?'

Max Gould shook his head, as a comment on Roger's naivety. Roger nodded.

So how many poor bastards died this time?

Or ended up in torture chambers, like the one that Clara and Clayton rescued Max Gould from four years ago. Because the best way to leak information to an enemy was to allow it to be captured, in the hands of sacrificial goats who had no idea their own masters had betrayed them.

A senior officer unknown to Roger said: 'Petra Helsen was killed by your friend Jed Goran, or rather by Goran's ship.'

Roger blinked. 'When did this happen?'

The officer frowned while a few other mouths twitched: special forces had a different view of discipline, and lacked subservience when addressing their seniors. Plus Roger had entered SRS from the intelligence service, not the regular fleet, and so had never picked up the protocols of command. Roger had already said *sir* to Whitwell, which as far as he was concerned was more than enough for the sake of politeness.

'During a recent mission' – the officer had clearly decided to ignore Roger's attitude – 'to backtrack shipping route data being passed on to *Zajinet* agents, or so everyone thought, on the basis of earlier attacks on our Pilots.'

'So either the attacks were faked to look like Zajinet weapons-fire,' said Roger, 'or Helsen really was helping Zajinets to attack our people, stirring things up. In either case, a known agent of the darkness' – *the bitch is dead* – 'actively wants us to engage with the Zajinets. My question is, given it's what Helsen wanted' – *dead at last* – 'why would we even consider it?'

And it was Jed who had taken out Helsen! That was excellent news ... although a younger Roger might not have celebrated a friend killing for the second time.

'The easiest way to physically unbalance an untrained person,' said Whitwell, 'is to shove their chest—'

'—and then catch their reaction and whip them forwards. Or pull them and throw them backwards when they jerk back.' Roger smiled at the analogy. 'That's a neat idea.'

'I'm glad we meet with your approval, Captain,' said Max Gould.

It would suit the darkness – assuming the phenomenon could be anthropomorphised that way – to disperse Labyrinth's forces against the widespread Zajinet attacks. But to draw out the Zajinets *en masse*, apparently going along with the intention of the darkness, was like taking an enemy's momentum and subverting it to cause their downfall. If they could cripple the Zajinet fleets in one massive action, there would be less distraction from pursuing Schenck and his renegade force.

'It's a large target that we hope they can't resist,' said the unnamed officer, 'and which they can't attack in the piecemeal way they've been operating in so far. Our xenopsych specialists believe that Zajinets will attempt to operate collectively, possibly to the extent of committing every ship to one massive fleet in order to attack.'

Pinning one's hopes on anticipating Zajinet thinking was risky, but there was no point in Roger's saying so: everyone in the room would know that.

'We want you to aid in planning a series of deception raids,' said Whitwell. 'Counter-strikes that you'll take part in.'

'I see.' Roger glanced at Max Gould.

'And you'd better survive, Captain Blackstone. Because we expect you to lead the enemy to this location.' Whitwell stabbed a finger at the holo showing the decoy base location. 'You understand the objective?'

'I do.'

And it would be subtle in the execution, or it would be unsuccessful, because at every stage the Zajinets had to believe in what they were seeing and learning. Plus there was the possibility of counter-bluff: Zajinets mounting a deception strike of their own against the decoy, while targeting Labyrinth whose forces were committed elsewhere.

Speaking of which . . .

'If the decoy is here in realspace,' asked Roger, 'what is the congruent mu-space location? Is it—? Oh.'

Smiles around the war chamber matched his own, as he examined the infinite twists and whorls in the holovolume he had picked out.

'Mandelbrot Nebula,' he added. 'That is very nice indeed.'

The perfect hiding-place for a battle fleet mounting an ambush.

It'll need more than good topography.

There was also the matter of leading the fleet to victory, and while Roger would have had little idea on how to start organising a fleet, none of the people in the room, not even Max Gould – master of the decades-long covert operation and always as ruthless as he had to be – struck him as being a war leader, a simultaneous strategist, tactician and messianic figure that others would follow.

But this was a personal perception based on incomplete data, and there were limits to what even a special forces captain dared say to senior command. If they must mount this operation, then the primary requirement was to do it right, or they really would be playing into Helsen's hands, even though the bitch was dead.

Later he would realise he had forgotten someone, despite having talked to the legend's own mother in person. Perhaps the battle planners were more astute than Roger had imagined, or perhaps this was simply the unravelling of fate, and sometimes you got lucky.

He could only hope.

Twenty-seven days later by mean geodesic time, two days before the operation was due to commence, Roger was in a hangar deep within Ascension Annexe, looking over his beautiful black ship, her powerful form webbed with lines of scarlet and shining gold, her newly grown weaponry impressive, actually frightening. She was fantastic, and if anyone could get through the dangers to come, it was her.

A pulse signal indicated an authorised visitor approaching. Roger strode across the deck, his beloved ship behind him, and stared at the area of hangar wall about to open. Soon it liquefied and drew apart, revealing a wide-shouldered, strong-looking adventurer. And suddenly Roger thought they might succeed in this insane venture against the Zajinets.

'Admiral,' he said. 'Sir.'

Formality might not be SRS's strong suit, but this was a legend walking towards him with an arrogant grin and easy muscularity.

'Dirk McNamara.'

'Roger Blackstone.'

As Roger held out his hand, an unwelcome image flitted through his mind's eye: Dirk's twin, Kian, face disfigured by the Molotov cocktail, one hand a claw, a mysterious figure who was rumoured to appear from time to time on realspace worlds and nudge people towards peace; while here was Dirk, the twin who had taken immediate vengeance on the mob, left them with eyeballs smoking, and made a daring escape from custody that led eventually to his centuries-swallowing hellflight. Son to Ro, the First Pilot, and in his own right a deadly fighter who could take action while others were only starting to assess the situation.

They shook hands, Dirk's strength and aura palpable.

'If all goes to plan,' said Dirk, 'you're going to have Zajinets on your arse. And they might decide to blast you out of existence, instead of sneaking along to see where you end up.'

'They'll have to be fast to catch me, sir.' Roger could not help grinning.

'You've one hell of a beautiful ship, Captain Blackstone.' Dirk's eyes were assessing her lines. 'Powerful as anything, and I'll bet she tumbles through manoeuvres like nobody's business.'

'She does that.'

'Hmm. Well, good.' Dirk's obsidian gaze was on Roger now. 'That answers my question.'

'Sir?'

'I needed to know you're a fighter.'

The rest had no need to be spoken, because there had been non-verbal recognition between the two of them, at the primate and even reptilian level, the instant Dirk walked inside the hangar.

It takes one to know one.

In this case meaning a warrior who would die sooner than quit.

A soundless message pulsed through the hangar.

=A devil-may-care leader can bring a fleet to victory when even the best of the others would fail.=

Dirk looked up at the ceiling.

'Are you talking about me or him?'

The response came so fast that Roger wondered if Labyrinth had anticipated the question.

=Yes.=

Roger and Dirk laughed together, and then they bumped fists.

Soon enough, the shit and chaos of battle would be upon them, the blood and screaming and awful fear, when desperation and focus and camaraderie would see them through or they would die; and none of that would matter except that Labyrinth herself needed to be safe, because she was the past, present and future of Pilotkind.

And here she had her defenders.

FORTY-THREE

EARTH, 798 AD

The stench of the middens was strong, as the man who had been Ulfr and Fenrisulfr rode past them on the edge of the city. This place was huge, a vast complex of longhalls and other buildings including wharves, and for the first time he believed the travellers' tales were true: Lundenwic contained fully ten thousand folk, living together in one gigantic settlement, constructed around the ruined fortifications that once enclosed Londinium.

A quartet of warrior-guards was extracting tax from new arrivals. He pressed his knees inwards, and his mare walked forward and stopped.

'And you are—?' The warrior stared up at him.

'My name is Wulf.'

He understood the puzzled, careful looks. They would sense that he could fight, and well – though they could not know of his *berserkergangr* ferocity and his ability to control it – and his cloak was of better cloth than theirs. But whether he was *thegn* or *ceorl*, the lowest of aristocrats or the highest of commoners and a freeman, they could not tell.

Wulf leaned over and handed the nearest guard a coin.

'We all piss, shit and fart,' Wulf told him, grinning. 'Even *eorls*. Even kings.'

They laughed at that, fellow fighting men stuck with boring duty. And after five years of working to lose his accent, Wulf-once-Ulfr no longer sounded like a foreigner to beware of. His spear, slung against his saddle, had leather wrapped and tied around its head, and its haft was scarred: an old weapon, nothing special, giving no hint that it was tipped with crystal, not metal.

'King Coenwulf will be shitting out westerners,' said one of them. 'On account of he's chewed them all up.'

'What is that?' asked Wulf.

'Deorwine has the right of it,' said the nearest guard. 'Our boys killed old Cartog what's-his-face, King of Gwynedd. We heard yesterday. Sheep-shagging bastards, the lot of them.'

'That'll be Caradog ap Meirion.' Wulf nodded. 'Biggest sheep shagger of them all.'

The oldest guard shrugged, and Wulf knew exactly what he meant: kings fought kings and ordinary soldiers died, and afterwards what had changed?

'I'll see you men around,' Wulf added.

'Go well, friend.'

Wulf nudged his horse into a walk.

Over the coming weeks, his new neighbours became intrigued by and then accepting of the man called Wulf. With him, to his lodgings where his horse lived at ground level while he slept in the hay-insulated loft, he had brought a rolled cloak full of brooches and torcs, combs of carved bone, and similar lightweight trinkets that he could sell at a profit. He also bought such goods off travellers he met at the local inns and in the nearby market. The reputation he built up was one of fairness, never taking advantage of a wounded soldier down on his luck, nor selling at too high a margin to a love-struck *thegn* eager to impress the maiden of his dreams, or perhaps her parents.

In the mornings he would ride out to exercise the horse, though for half the time he would run alongside her – of all the beasts in the Middle World, none could outlast a man provided he was fit: not a mare, gelding or stallion, neither a dog nor a bitch, not even a wolf.

He missed Brandr, his faithful war-hound, long dead, but would not dream of getting a replacement.

Maybe if I settle.

Even here in teeming Lundenwic, the notion of settling down seemed a strange and distant fantasy for a man who had wandered so far and seen so many things, and carried so much blood on his hands.

Part-way through his daily run, he would work his strength by lifting, pulling and pressing boulders and stones, and by throwing them hard across muddy meadows. And there was weapons practice, of course, for without daily discipline the skills would grow dull, and then he would be unequipped if violence fell upon him. Then he would die embarrassed, deserving to be carried off to Niflheim, ignored by Óthinn's Death-Choosers.

Or whatever gods ruled here.

Perhaps none of the stories are true.

Except that the Norns clearly ruled men's lives, and when he woke in the mornings he sometimes, just for a moment, held on to a fragment of a memory from the dreamworld; and in those times he was convinced that both Valhöll and the preparations for final war, for Ragnarökkr, existed for real.

When his stock of trinkets threatened to become large, too much to carry with him when he left his lodgings, he had a choice to make. Surprising himself, he hired two local men to alternate guard duty on his place. Osmund and Cerdic seemed honest enough, though not warriors he would trust in battle, not comrades; but some twenty days after they began working for him, he returned from his morning training to find Osmund poking around the lodgings, looking puzzled, while Cerdic was gone, along with the lightest and most valuable of Wulf's goods.

'I saw him walking, hurrying' – Osmund gestured – 'and wondered what was wrong, so I came here.'

'Stay on guard,' Wulf growled.

Osmund nodded, fast.

Wolves excel at tracking prey.

*

There were courts for justice, but not in Wulf's world, for men could lie and how could a stranger tell which one told the truth? So Wulf trailed Cerdic, and watched him hide up among stacked coracles on a mudbank, clearly thinking he was safe, and planning to slip out when darkness fell. But Wulf stood in shadow for the remainder of the day, unmoving, until the sun grew large and scarlet, low in the grey sky, and then diminished.

Cerdic headed away from the crowded, muddy alleys, and Wulf followed.

The moon was already high, her light shining stronger as darkness grew, and Cerdic was close to the old Roman walls when Wulf fell on him from behind and that was that: Cerdic's soul was gone to Niflheim.

All you had to do was not betray me.

Wulf had retrieved most of his goods from the body, wrapping them in scraps of leather one by one, and slipping them into the new pouch he wore at his right hip, when a whimper sounded from beyond the walls.

The old stones were the colour of bone in moonlight, and his sword came free of its oiled scabbard in silence as he heard the low laughter of men, and the single cut-off cry that had to be a woman. She would be one of the toothless whores who worked close to the ruins, snatched by a gang who could not be bothered to spend even the pittance she sought.

My reavers did worse.

But he would not allow this, all the same. There was no sound as he slid among dark gaps in the ruined walls, yet still they stopped, six grey figures, though the bundle on the silvery grass continued to struggle; and then Wulf laughed softly, knowing the effect it would have on them.

Six dead men, although they did not know it yet.

Now.

He howled as the *berserkergangr* came upon him, and then it was a turbulence of death, joy in chaos as he whirled through bodies in the night, killing by feel more than sight, blood soaring until it was done, tides of triumph in his veins, chest heaving, as he pushed down the urge to kill because only the woman was left and she deserved to live.

Calm.

And cold, like a dropped cloak as the madness fell away.

There it had been eight of them, it seemed, but the woman had used her daggers to good effect before they subdued her, leaving two corpses in the mud-strewn alley where they trapped her, while at least two of the men Wulf had killed bore wounds from her blades.

'My name is Sunngifu,' she told him, standing straight despite the tremble in her voice. 'My father will reward you, if you see me safely home.'

Wulf had cut the ropes from her arms – they had bound her thumbs together first, not tying her ankles because of what they had in mind. The surprise was that they had snatched her in a decent part of Lundenwic, perhaps believing they might ransom her if she survived the rape, and even if she did not, so long as the family believed her alive.

'I don't need—' Wulf began.

One of the men groaned, and Sunngifu whirled, dropping to one knee as a flash of silver descended to a wet thud, then silence.

'—payment,' he finished.

He checked again, this time making sure they were all dead.

'It's that way.' Sunngifu, pale beneath the moon, pointed out the direction with one of her daggers. 'You won't mind if I keep my blades unsheathed?'

The first thing she had retrieved after Wulf cut her bonds had been her pair of daggers.

'So long as you don't sheathe them in my liver' – Wulf grinned at her – 'I'll be happy to have you guarding me. My name is Wulf, by the way.'

Sunngifu stared at him, then: 'Good name.'

Which did nothing to prevent her from keeping a dagger

in each hand as they walked, but that was fine by Wulf. He talked softly, telling her where he lived now, and a little of his travels over the years, minus the killing. As they drew close to her home, they were clearly among rich folk, for rush torches burned in iron holders set on staves in the mud, bringing light to those who walked in the night.

Wulf's thump on the door, and Sunngifu's calling out: 'It's me,' prompted the sound of two heavy beams being hauled sideways, and then the door swung open, a heavyset woman standing there, gaping. Then she turned to one of the young men further inside, grasped his tunic in her substantial fist and said: 'Run and tell Swithhun she is found. Run fast and do it now.'

'Er ... Yes, mistress.'

'*Now.*'

Then she turned to Wulf and added, 'You have brought our daughter home, warrior.'

'Er, yes.'

She dragged both of them inside, then hugged Sunngifu hard, raising her off the ground.

'Your husband is out searching?' asked Wulf.

'With half the city guard.'

That was impressive. Wulf liked the guards he knew, but had not thought them dedicated enough to search Lundenwic at night, not with the manifold dangers that darkness brought, especially to someone who had already worked through the daylight hours.

Then he saw Sunngifu's face properly for the first time.

She's ...

His heart stopped, just for a moment. Her face was long and evidently strong, her eyes were pale grey and staring at him without fear or shyness, and he could not take his gaze from her. The big woman, Sunngifu's mother, whose name Wulf had not learned, looked from one to the other, and back.

'Well.' She crossed her arms, her bare forearms huge and strong. 'Well.'

Sunngifu ignored her, being too busy returning Wulf's stare.

... *beautiful.*

So strong, that was the thing.

When Swithhun, a bear of a man, came rushing in, it was to hug the women, Sunngifu first and then his wife Eadburga, before clapping Wulf on the shoulder. Then he roared for mead – servants ran for the skins and horns – before turning back to Wulf.

'I did not know whether to think she was dead or eloped and betrothed,' he said. 'And if the former—'

'She would have taken souls to Niflhel with her,' Wulf told him. 'She despatched three men, sir.'

'Did she?'

'Brave Wulf slew five others, Father, and truly, to be honest, a sixth. I just helped that one on his way.'

Her voice was steady now. And Swithhun was looking thoughtful

'You know why Mercia is the greatest of all the kingdoms?' he asked. 'Because we are organised and disciplined. A man of fast decisions and bravery is exactly what we need in the city guard, and I'm getting too old.'

So that was why half the guard had been out looking for Sunngifu: she was the commander's daughter.

'Wulf already makes a living,' Sunngifu said. 'He sells—'

'I'll do it,' said Wulf, and looked at her. 'Join the guard, train them and exercise whatever command I'm given.'

That's right.

Because when evil arrives – evil such as reavers or rapist-kidnappers – someone has to stand up for those who cannot fight for themselves. Someone has to respond, to run towards the danger and not hide themselves away or flee, when the helpless sound an alarm.

I'm a fighter and a killer.

The only question was, what was he fighting for? On whose behalf?

Who would he be willing to die for?

Sunngifu stared at him.

Snow fell on their wedding day, two days before Saturnalia, which was also, handily, the day that the Roman god Mithras was born, along with the Christ-Mass, so that everyone could feast together. Wulf kept his Thórr's hammer beneath his shirt, and was content to join in whatever festivities his new family celebrated.

Two months later, when Sunngifu told him she had not bled for eight weeks, and had thrown up after breakfast that morning, Wulf waited until dark, then slipped from the house, with his crystal-tipped spear in hand, and jogged off into the night.

At the Roman walls where he had met Sunngifu and killed her attackers, he found a spot to bury the spear, close to a stone mask carved upon a wall in the guise of Mithras, and symbols representing the Mithraic Mysteries. Perhaps that old god could watch over a weapon that Wulf had no need of now, for there were no more troll-spirits to be slain, at least not by him. The crystal-tipped spear went beneath the soil, and then it was covered up, not forgotten but no longer relevant, like so much of his past.

'My wise wolf,' Sunngifu told him on his return, after hearing his long explanation. 'My wise and careful Rathulfr.'

Her grandfather had hailed from the Danelaw, and she spoke the Tongue almost as well as Wulf himself. In private, for the rest of their lives and as they raised their many children, that was the name she would use for him: her Rathulfr, her wolf who was wise.

And he would try always, with a warrior's strength, to live up to her image of him.

FORTY-FOUR

It was the first of July, and the four hundredth anniversary of his wife's death. Kian knew better than to visit the place where they had lived so happily: the body of water that he had called The Pond and Kat referred to as their lake was no longer there, and the site of their cottage, the last time he had been in Iowa, was a slow-morphing tower-town formed of slick blue-grey biocrete that looked like intestines. Instead, after his rendezvous with the courier in London, he made his way to Oxford, where back in the mid-twenty-second century, his twin brother Dirk had been a student, here amid the mediaeval sandstone buildings that were so different from Caltech where he, Kian, had studied.

Voluminous greatcoats, designed to billow easily as if they were cloaks, seemed to be in fashion. That made it easier for Kian to walk among crowds without attracting notice, for with the burnt claw that formed his right hand and the silver scar tissue disfiguring his face, along with the trace of a limp, he clearly belonged to the minority who for one reason or another refused (or were unable to undergo) corrective and cosmetic surgery, available in any health booth in any major town.

And yet there was a warrior's grace to his movements, and even among dense clumps of passers-by, he walked without brushing against anyone, always anticipating position and motion, never caught by surprise.

He stayed in a tall hotel overlooking central Oxford, a newish building on the site of an historic tower where Augusta 'Gus' Calzonni had been in residence in 2102, when at the age of one hundred and thirteen, she had instructed her lawyer to book her a shuttle flight into orbit, where she could see with her own faded eyes the success or failure of the first attempted voyage into mu-space.

A floating biographer-globe had recorded her final moments, and the cerebral stroke that occurred just after she heard the famous words of the returning captain, leaving one last legacy: the sight of someone smiling as they died.

'Kat,' said Kian now to the empty room. 'My magic. My world.'

People had called them K'n'K or TwoK, for in the happy years they were inseparable, she with the brash mouth (and ready fists – they had met in Toronto, when an anti-xeno activist had attempted to attack Kian, and while Kian had used a pseudo-hypnotic verbal technique to interrupt the assault, it had been Kat's looping punch out of nowhere that had dropped the man), massive intelligence and ready laugh.

He checked his anti-surveillance motes once more, then opened up the message-seed slipped to him by the non-Pilot courier in a float-hall over the Thames. The sender's sigil would make no sense to anyone but him; he knew it for that of Rowena James, one of his Labyrinthine contacts with only low-level security clearance, yet in a position to deduce much from Pilots' schedules as devised and recorded by Far Reach, along with other unwitting sources of information.

Security measures were tighter these days, but that was all right: they depended, at least partly, on checking for sympathy towards and contact with Schenck's renegades, and neither Kian nor his occasional associates had any love for darkness-controlled Pilots.

He was what he was without need for labels, and most certainly did not require followers; but there was a need for continuity, if he was to carry out his work while continuing to lead the same kind of time-skipping life that Dirk and their mother had gravitated towards. What Kian had founded, the

Tri-Fold Way, was imbued with something of Buddhist philosophy, and a dash of utopian far-sightedness mixed in with practical rhetoric and rigorously applied psycho-emergenics, while he himself was 'a superposition of Mahatma Gandhi and the Unknown Ninja' according to a Labyrinth-based activist back in the day.

The extremes of both secessionist Pilot politics and the let's-control-humanity crowd were anathema to him; but while the middle path meant eschewing violence as much as possible, and he in personal life was normally the gentlest of beings, Kian McNamara was not in the strictest sense of the word a pacifist: he could be as deadly as his flamboyant brother, maybe more so.

Still, when he performed his daily tai-chi-like routines at dawn on Calzonni Meadow, once University Parks, wildlife was unafraid to watch, and this morning a sparrow had alighted on his shoulder during standing meditation, and stayed there chirping until a noisy spaniel came bounding into view.

The situation in Labyrinth was not one to inspire personal calm and oneness with either universe. While there was one disturbing detail in Rowena's report, the bulk of it was straightforward, implying the gathering of militarised forces, and it was no act of scholarship to understand how rapidly Pilot society might change under the pressure of all-out warfare, if things went that far. He mulled over the details as he left the hotel and went on a thoughtful walk around the old town, the sandstone buildings coated with diamond these days, which did not preserve the old look so much as create an entirely new mystique; and he wondered whether he should have come back to Earth at all.

Inside the Ashmolean Museum, a battered, wrinkled, darkened old sword caught his attention. It was displayed among the Roman artefacts, and Kian was no expert, but it seemed to him to have been wrongly dated. Yet the Runic scratches might have been his imagination – they were not mentioned in the descriptive holo – and that might have coloured his whimsical notion that he could somehow know better than the professional archaeologists and curators who stocked and managed the place.

Afterwards, he watched a performance of *Henry V* in the Sheldonian Theatre, a building that had been through much, including a stint as a knife-fighting venue when that was prime-time entertainment and the university was short of funds. The Crispin's Day speech was as rousing as ever, though Kian could not help but think later, as he wandered back to his hotel, how the night-before-battle scene revealed the eternal disparity between rulers and the ordinary folk who die in conflicts they neither instigate nor fully understand, and how hollow were the warrior-king's justifications for his martial aims.

Two days later, in a quaint underground shopping mall in Putingrad, he met up with one Rickson Ojuku, a Pilot who claimed a sort of ancestry from Kian via the Delgasso line, Rorion Delgasso having fathered two children with Maria, Kian and Kat's adopted daughter. Rorion's father Carlos had been a young brat, with an annoying habit of hero-worshipping both Kian and Dirk. Now they had a descendant in common.

'I'm surprised you made contact,' said Rickson, as they walked side by side past gleaming displays. 'With everything that's happening back home, I would've thought political reconciliation was in abeyance.'

He sounded more business-like than necessary, as if overcompensating for the weirdness of meeting his ancestor. Kian sympathised: it was strange though hardly unique among Pilotkind, as ultra-relativistic time-dilating flights continued to occur for one reason or another, mounting up across the centuries.

'Take a look at this.' Kian double-checked the anti-surveillance smartmiasma surrounding them, then zip-blipped a portion of the report he had received in London. 'The silver-and-red ship belongs to *Admiral* Schenck.' His tone turned the rank into an insult. 'Remember, three years ago, when there was an attempted absorption on Vachss Station, the Vijaya orbital?'

'One of Schenck's people tried to plant an absorbed person there.' Rickson blinked his smartlenses, processing the report fragment. 'Is this surveillance footage or computed reconstruction?'

'A mixture of both,' said Kian. 'It seems Schenck picked up a bunch of such people, transferred two to Holland's ship – that's the other vessel in the rendezvous scene, and Holland is the Pilot who went on to Vachss Station – and held on to the others.'

'So how did Molsin fall?' asked Rickson, watching the surroundings as they walked. 'Because of these people, or something else?'

'That would be worrying. The reconstruction is, the failed absorption on Vachss Station caused Schenck to commit all the remaining absorbed people – components – to the Molsin incursion.'

Kian knew only that his Labyrinthine source, Rowena James, had a close contact in the intelligence community there. For the first time, he wondered if that contact knew about the reports that Rowena passed on. Perhaps it would suit the intelligence service's purposes if Kian's people, too, understood the renegades' actions with regards to the Anomaly.

'Good news for the rest of us,' said Rickson, 'and bad news for Molsin. Except that you said *two* Anomalous components were transferred to Holland's ship beforehand.'

'Allegedly. There might have been more. But Holland flew from the Schenck rendezvous directly to Siganth. When he went on to Vachss Station afterwards, he had only a single component aboard.'

The impersonal description could not hide the fact that the Anomaly was built of humans. Among other things.

Rickson's eyelids fluttered as he backtracked through the

report's subsidiary threads. Then he stopped, and Kian knew exactly which portion he had come to.

'That's it,' Kian told him. 'That's what concerns me.'

And made him think that Rowena James really was being fed this information, which was irrelevant provided it was accurate.

'Holy crap.'

'An understatement.'

A mu-space transmission from Siganth had summoned the renegades: a signal picked up and later decoded by the surveillance stealth-sats that the intelligence service had placed around every xeno world. It was awful, and meant that Kian had played a part in enabling the creation of a hellworld.

'The Siganthians are insane,' said Rickson. 'They *invited* the Anomaly to come to them? How could they do that?'

Kian did not consider himself a Siganth expert, except in the sense that virtually every Pilot and human alive knew even less about the place than he did.

'For them, it must have been a kind of transcendence,' he said to Rickson. 'Fitted in with their notions of a hive mind, although different from Earth insects. They feel suffering when they're torn into pieces, but those pieces are remade into other beings. It's ... different there.'

Rickson blinked again, this time purely from bemusement.

'How could you know? Oh—'

'Right. I've visited the place.'

'And the mu-space comms?'

It used to be common for human worlds to rent comms relays capable of transmitting into mu-space, until historic events on Fulgor forced Labyrinth's authorities to rethink the policy. Now it was almost unknown, except under specific, legally constrained circumstances, with constant surveillance in place.

Except—

'It's my fault,' said Kian. 'I gave it to them.'

*

His interest in the Siganthians had been philosophical and scientific, but in cultural and political terms, Kian had believed that engaging more of Pilotkind in realspace xeno research helped to combat secessionism. On a less abstract level, he had observed the growing focus on Zajinets and understood that they were a dangerous enemy only because they belonged, like Pilots, to two universes. For other species, including the wealth of fearsome-looking metallic Siganthian species (to whatever extent the concept applied there, since the organisms tore apart and rebuilt each other all the time), it was easy to avoid possible conflict simply by disengaging from realspace. That disengagement was what Kian wanted to avoid.

Hence, as he explained to Rickson Ojuku, his low-key mission to Siganth two subjective years ago, along with a small team of volunteers from among fellow activists of the Tri-Fold Way, and the comms equipment they had left in situ, for no one had been able (or willing) to remain living on Siganth for extended periods of time. But that had been several time-dilating flights ago, and Kian had little idea what might have happened to those activists or their eventual replacements. As far as he knew, no Pilots had been caught up in the Anomaly, or harmed in any way before the Anomaly's genesis.

'What do we need to do now?' asked Rickson.

Kian smiled. 'I appreciate the *we*. You need to make sure that people in Labyrinth know about Siganthian comms equipment.' It was understood that he, Kian, could never go there incognito – some Pilot would recognise him. 'Just in case. It's too late for Siganthians to lure Pilots to their world with false messages, now that the place is known to be a hellworld. But even so—'

'They can communicate with the renegades, except it's a what, gestalt-thing now, so it's a global *it*, not a *they*, which means it probably won't. Communicate, I mean.' Rickson's scattergun grammar seemed to cover his thinking about two things at once, because he added, 'Admiral? Sir? There's nothing you can do about a hellworld.'

So Kian's guilt had been that obvious, had it?

'I haven't gone by that title for a long time, my friend.'

'You were the Second Admiral,' said Rickson. 'Everyone knows it, whether they mention it to your face or not.'

Which was why Kian had seen, as his mother and brother had not – because of their first century-long hellflight – the fragility of Pilotkind. Mother and Dirk understood the necessity of providing a full, thriving culture that embraced the Shipless as well as those who flew; but it was Kian who lived through the years in which Pilots bound to Earth gradually loosened their ties to UNSA, and looked after their own kind when individuals were unsuitable for flight, and finally grew their own ships in Labyrinth and broke free from the organisation that once ruled their lives.

Part of that time, following Kat's death, had been spent in the elusive, wandering role he still played; but his touch had been sure and all Pilots had known that one of the McNamaras was still looking out for their interests, even before Dirk and their mother reappeared.

'Communicating with Siganthians,' said Kian now, 'was never easy, and getting started was a huge obstacle. What we settled on was a spin-off from LuxPrime tech, adaptive implants that learned to assign similar meanings to different individuals' patterns.'

'Implants? I don't like the sound of that.'

'Reverse that thought. What if we could inject a smart-virus into any Siganthian still carrying implants? Or insert new, ready-coded implants?'

Even if it was a partial success, perhaps freeing a few individuals temporarily, even a tiny victory against the Anomaly would encourage Pilot engagement with realspace, and perhaps spawn tactics other than retreat-and-quarantine to deal with the threat. Anything to maintain involvement, because the worst scenario of all was one in which Pilotkind abandoned humanity to dangers that were irrelevant to mu-space and Labyrinth.

'You want me to do, what?' asked Rickson. 'Gather a research team together?'

As always, after a time-skipping flight, Kian had few personal contacts to call on. The ongoing loose-knit organisation of activists, and the long-lived comms protocols that enabled him to get in touch with each new wave of representatives, was all he had.

'Whoever is the best,' he told Rickson now. 'Whoever can do the work.'

'And then what?'

Kian had a form of low-key charisma involving deliberate psycholinguistic rhetoric, which he employed seldom, but with one hundred per cent of his being when he did so, always and without inner conflict or doubt, when he was certain that his actions were in Pilotkind's best interests. What he said next was a lie, but its intent was to protect, and from what he could sense of Rickson's reaction, the falsehood rang true:

'We hand it over, via an appropriate contact' – Kian thought of Rowena James at this point – 'so that the Admiralty's paramilitaries can do what they do best.'

It would be sensible for Labyrinth's forces to receive a copy of whatever they learned and developed; but Kian would prefer to use a smartvirus in as non-violent a manner as possible – freeing the Siganthians, even if they had initially believed absorption into the Anomaly was a good idea. It was better than, say, holding them in place via virus-induced catatonia, and bombarding their world with destructive weapons, which would be the kind of plan that military minds might hatch, or so Kian believed.

Plus, however the smartvirus were eventually used, the initial incursion would need to be stealthy and low-key, in order to inject the virus into one or two individuals. However well-trained Labyrinth's special forces might be, Kian was a master of elusive movement, and was confident – justifiably, he hoped – that he could do as good a job.

How could he ask anyone else to take a deadly risk arising from his own screw-up? It was his problem to deal with if he could, but not in a stupid way. In case he failed, he would make sure that others possessed the same knowledge, so that they could find better ways to utilise it.

Whether Rickson ever guessed Kian's intentions, he did not discover. But when the results of the investigations among Rickson's extended network of contacts came through – where physical meetings were rare, and never involved more than three Pilots in one place – it was like a military briefing, or what Kian imagined a military briefing to be, a holo session reporting positive results in programming the tiny implant-seeds according to Kian's specifications.

The news regarding Siganthian lifeforms was better than expected, considerably better, and might with luck provide a means of infecting the hellworld without risk to any Pilots who might venture to Siganth system in person, whether or not that Pilot was Kian McNamara.

Seventeen modest-sized planetoids in that system were home to Siganthian colonies or hive-ecologies, while being outside the thousand-kilometre range of Zajinet-style manipulation of the hyperdimensions from the Anomaly dominating their homeworld. How the colonies had been founded was not known for certain – spaceships were not in evidence, now or previously – but the leading guess was this: thousands of individuals re-engineered each other, locked themselves in place to form a composite of deliberate design, forming themselves en masse into spacegoing vessels. Once at their destinations, they had disassembled and dispersed.

And more pertinently, because this had clearly happened a long time ago, those colonies were not part of the Anomaly. Willingly or not, Siganthian individuals bearing smart-virus-spreading implants might be carried to the hellworld via unmanned drones, there to begin a process of counter-infection that might with luck become endemic and lead to the freeing of the Siganthians from a condition that might once have seemed to be god-like transcendence, but would in retrospect feel like slavery.

'We've added meme-vectors to seed that idea,' said one of the speakers in the holo session. 'Regardless of whether it's naturally true, they'll be glad to have broken free of their absorbed condition.'

It was perhaps the least ethical aspect of the whole venture. But from another perspective, this was an act of war that might lead to overwhelming victory with not a single death or even injury. For Kian, it was the least evil, if not best possible, means of ending a conflict and the enslavement of an entire world.

But he was aware that this was the justification for every imperialist venture in history, forcing 'enlightened' change on cultures unaware of their own 'wrongness'; and he would not have proceeded with the plan were it not for the awful threat that Siganth, along with Fulgor and Molsin, presented to humanity.

So I'm no better than anyone else.

Which he had known all along, of course.

His poor ship paid the price for his hubris.

She was no longer the dumb vessel she had been in the early days. Though a second-generation vessel – among the first to bear a natural-born Pilot – her earlier crude AIs had grown and evolved through the care and nourishment of Labyrinth's Ascension Annexe (flying there without Kian aboard, but with his blessing), a place whose name meant what it said. All ships were entangled with their Pilot, and she was no exception, but she had developed the awareness and increased the entanglement over time; and was aware that there was something about Kian that was different from every other Pilot.

A difference that triggered an unexpected reaction among the Siganthians he tried to communicate with.

Floating a hundred metres above a hive settlement on the

farthest colony from Siganth proper, she waited with weapons fully armed while Kian conducted his initial meetings with the metallic, half-organic lifeforms that seemed odd and alien even to her, a spacegoing vessel originally constructed as a mere machine.

They worried her, those Siganthians.

She had deployed eye-seeds for surveillance, stayed ready to act immediately at the first precursor of a threat to Kian, and watched as he stood in the centre of a concave hall decorated with moving metallic flanges, patiently establishing communication with the Siganthians, who allowed him to spray implant-seeds into the air, which they carefully took into themselves through filters and capillaries, and allowed to begin functioning.

'Thank you,' Kian said, when the initial tests and vocabulary-matching sessions were over, and the seven metallic individuals before him – variously like beetles, dragons or tanks, but only in grossest outline – indicated their readiness to begin a first serious negotiation. 'Indicate if you are willing to allow me to transport you to Siganth's surface.'

The hard part of translation was at the deepest neuro-electronic level, and the Pilot researchers had not bothered to add semantic sugar, as it was known, to the system. There remained a level of necessary literalness in speaking to the Siganthians, one aspect of which was this: their language did not allow for questions, only imperative directions to provide information.

To Kian's ship, this was simply one more sign that the venture was inherently flawed and overwhelmingly dangerous. But neither her fears nor her tactical readiness prepared her for what happened next.

The tallest Siganthian's first response was a question, or what passed for it:

{Describe the properties of the brightness in your skull-case.}

From her position overhead, Kian's ship felt a cognitive interrupt akin to a human gasp, because that was exactly how she perceived the *other* entanglement inside Kian's brain, the strange, tiny seed of something that no other Pilot carried, and whose nature, for all the years they had spent in closer partnership than non-Pilots could imagine, she had only just begun to analyse properly.

Kian himself could not have answered the Siganthian's question, even if he had understood it. For she, his ship, had never told him of the thing that glowed inside his head. Perhaps if he had gone to Labyrinth in person, the city-world might have been able to—

'I do not understand,' Kian told the Siganthian. 'My non-compliance is not refusal.'

{Irrelevant.}

And then it happened.

Sapphire-blue light blazed everywhere, and Kian's ship understood the true depth of the Pilots' misunderstanding and miscalculation: they were in fact within range of hyperdimensional manipulation from Siganth's Anomaly, and while the colony here was not part of that gestalt, it appeared to have been in constant communication with it, although that might be a misreading of the situation.

Whether the colony willed it or not, Kian disappeared from eye-seed surveillance, while from overhead, his ship yelled inside her mind, knowing he was gone, and where he was, and what was happening to him.

It was the most awful of tortures.

Kian, my Kian—

And it hurt her more, and for immeasurably longer, than it did him.

FORTY-FIVE

According to legend as well as Kenna's memory, the first of the hellworlds, the former paradise known as Fulgor, a shining beacon of culture as its name suggested, fell to the Anomaly within days, while some of its major battles (as in the fight for control of the global virtual environment called the Skein) were fought on a timescale of milliseconds.

Other dark names from history, like Siganth and Molsin, were less clear in the specifics, but the implication always was that in each case civilisation collapsed fast, soon after the first appearance of the Anomaly. Even less was known about the more recent hellworlds: fourteen in total.

Nulapeiron, the fifteenth world, was different.

Eight centuries after Fulgor fell, the Anomaly manifested in one realm of Nulapeiron after another, taking control of rulers and soldiers, absorbing key humans into its gestalt, but not every human, not yet. Perhaps it was the logotropes in the Lords' and Ladies' brains that made absorption so challenging; or the differences in cognition throughout the populace that arose due to logosophical training; or perhaps it was the greater scale and environment of that population, with billions living in subterranean demesnes, not a few million (or less) on the surface or in the skies.

The final possibility – perhaps with the greater likelihood – was that the far greater distance from Fulgor made the difference. Perhaps it was true that there was only a single Anomaly, increasingly extended each time a new hellworld was born.

Because of the Oracles, well established as tools of the ruling Lords and Ladies, 'Fate' and 'Chaos' had become curse words; yet the undenied truth of every Oracular report had failed to help against the Anomalous invasion. Worse: the lack of reports from further in the future formed a *de facto* prediction of defeat.

For all of those past eight centuries Kenna had been living here: the last seven hundred years in her crystalline form, whose capabilities continued to grow and yet were nowhere near their final development. If she were right in her estimates, every century that passed was like a single day in a human life. She would be entering full maturity – approximately equivalent to a human's thirtieth birthday – a million years from now.

Such a long time in which to keep herself unharmed.

For nearly a century now, in her deep stronghold beneath a subterranean sea, she had been alternately priestess – the word *volva* came from hidden memory – and chieftain to some of the Kobolds who lived in this unofficial realm. They were not the only line of once-humans merged cyborg-like with one or other variant of technology; as a crystalline being herself, Kenna had been instrumental in these blue-skinned part-quickstone beings creating a culture of their own.

The Kobolds had long been allied with the Grey Shadow movement, whose antecedents stretched all the way back to the dissidents first organised by the undercover Pilot, Linda Gunnarsson. Long dedicated to quiet subversion of the status quo, they now – for the first time – began to regard their Crystal Lady as a war ruler. And when they took a special prisoner whose name had featured heavily in the revolutionary movement before such things became irrelevant, it was to Kenna that they brought the man.

He was a commoner turned Lord (for the first time in a century in the region controlled by the Congressio-Interstata Beth-Gamma) who had turned his back on both the incumbent system and the rebels' self-serving alternative; but he was remembered as a figurehead in the revolution.

To many, he was simply Lord One-Arm.

His name was Tom Corcorigan.

Kenna waited in the great hall that was kept cool despite the magma that surrounded it, and watched as they brought him in: a one-armed man in his mid-thirties, with the ascetic look of an endurance athlete. There were fragments of holo footage within the revolutionary movement that showed Corcorigan fighting hand-to-hand, and the significance to Kenna was this: Lord One-Arm was fully human, but he fought like a Pilot.

Clearly there was much to be discovered beyond his reputation. Like most people entering her presence, he stood as if hypnotised, in awe. It would be easy to explore his mind.

The question was, how much should she assist the man?

Around Nulapeiron, armies were fighting back against invading forces which in many cases were almost entirely human, but under the control of Anomaly-absorbed officers. The defenders included fully armed battalions led by General Lord Ygran, a fierce and experienced strategist. His forces boasted fully armoured arachnargoi – near-living vehicles able to carry sometimes hundreds of troops, their forms like huge spiders with strong tendrils, perfectly adapted to both the natural deep caverns of Nulapeiron and the halls and tunnels of human demesnes.

And there were the fringe tribes: wild-riding nomads who practically lived in the saddles of their speeding arachnasprites. Their hard, fierce existence made them cunning, pitiless guerrilla fighters. But however hard the various defenders fought, it could only be a delaying action.

It was not as if the Anomaly cared about any of its components dying.

What Nulapeiron's defence required was something *different,* and every possibility needed to be investigated, including the one-armed man before her now.

—*You are most welcome in this place, Thomas Corcorigan.*

He continued to look awestruck.

'I don't deserve to be here.'

In her presence, he meant. She tried to form her response in an idiom natural to one whose first language was Nov'glin, the contemporary descendant of Novanglin.

—*Your form belongs in this place.* Then: *Tell me of yourself, my fighting Lord.* So he told her of his life.

There was much to tell, and as he related what he remembered, Kenna thought back to another time when she, or rather Rhianna Chiang, allowed one Roger Blackstone's deep subconscious mind to unburden itself of secrets that his consciousness could not be allowed to share; except that in this case, Tom Corcorigan knew exactly what had happened to him, and consciously nursed the stubbornness growing inside him, enabling him to fight back.

The highlights were: aged fourteen standard, he had witnessed an undercover Pilot being hunted down and killed, but not before she had bequeathed him a crystal that told him of Pilot history; then an Oracle called Gérard d'Ovraison predicted the death of Tom's father – who subsequently wasted away for no good medical reason – after d'Ovraison carried away Tom's mother; later, the amputation of Tom's arm as punishment for theft he had been caught up in, not instigated; then servitude and the driven discipline to better himself, to become a Lord in his own right; and the need to kill an Oracle, up close with a blade, even though the Oracle foresaw his own long and peaceful life, lasting well into undisturbed old age.

But Tom Corcorigan, once a boy who had dreamt of being a poet, sometime Lord One-Arm and revolutionary icon, had accomplished his vengeance, and more.

Kenna mulled over this while Corcorigan waited, standing in peaceful trance. There were two pieces of information she could give him, to remain perhaps within his subconscious yet available to his intuition. The first was a logical thing to share.

—*The Grey Shadows have Pilot agents among them.*

Corcorigan's long involvement with the revolutionary movement, now part of the increasingly scattered resistance, meant that he had contacts among the disparate, loosely allied organisations that comprised the Grey Shadows. The point was that Nulapeiron's resistance was doomed unless someone managed to get external allies, powerful allies, involved. In the past, Pilotkind's response to nascent Anomalous incursion had been to get clear at the first sign of trouble, and quarantine the planet.

But the situation here was different, the timescale longer, and the continuing presence of undercover Pilots, however sparse their numbers, gave Kenna some hope.

The second piece of information, though ... That was a wild thought, half rational. The Pilot history that Corcorigan had immersed himself in, the crystal that he still carried inside a stallion-shaped talisman around his neck, had focused on the McNamara clan, and was in fact a copy of a tale that Rhianna Chiang had owned as a girl in Labyrinth. It meant that Lord One-Arm knew almost as much Pilot history as Kenna did, and so this would make sense to him:

—*Ro McNamara lives still, hidden within the Logos Library.*

There was a question concerning the relevance of the First Admiral's continued existence, which strictly speaking, Kenna could not be sure of: it was now eight centuries since she, as Rhianna Chiang, had been in Labyrinth.

But her own intuition had told her to share that information.

A message from my *subconscious?*

Because this was it: she skated on the edge of paradox, and sometimes reality appeared to shimmer, alive with the possibility of breaking causality and all that made sense, threatening dissolution and disaster; and this was one of those moments.

Call it a memory of a future dream, inaccurate though the analogy was, for the simplest of reasons.

She never slept.

After the Kobolds removed the stunned Corcorigan from the chamber, she gave further instructions to Griell, one of her Kobold lieutenants.

—Trevalkin's people must learn that Corcorigan is a worthwhile ally. Get word to them via the usual cutouts.

'Straight away, ma'am.'

There were others who might usefully ally themselves with Corcorigan, and support his efforts.

—The Strontium Dragons Society have a pak tsz sin *called Zhao-ji among their senior ranks. He knew Corcorigan in childhood. Get word to him also.*

The resistance needed heroic figures, and Lord One-Arm was a potent symbol in their mythology.

'Ma'am.'

Alone then, she sank into meditation, considering her own life in relation to Corcorigan's, that mix of contingency and determination, so turbulent; and her greater goal that she could never share at risk of being thought insane: to fight a war that would make this conflict seem insignificant, a battle on behalf of every baryonic-matter lifeform in the galaxy, in a final confrontation a million years from now.

Even though the world she lived in seemed doomed to fall, very soon indeed.

FORTY-SIX

The feints and deception were over. Five members of Roger's squadron were dead, in four cases along with their ships as they exploded beneath Zajinet weapons fire. Now it was all about the waiting: as it had been for every soldier across history, from legionnaires trekking across dusty plains to mech-armoured grunts at the Siege of Mare Tembrum; nerves and boredom, with nothing to do but train and joke and brood on cruelty and mortality.

Shoals of shuttles moved around the pseudo-base they called the Grey Attractor, automated craft that employed random motion and delays to simulate human behaviour, as if they were crewed and engaged on construction work. However, the seventeen huge complex volumes that seemed capable of housing thousands were pure façades, constructed of thin, fragile shells in which lurked twenty squadrons of battle-trained Pilots, including Roger Blackstone and his black, red-and-gold-webbed ship.

They kept their wits about them by playing strategy games, and their reflexes in place by working out with combat gymnastics in their ship's holds or cabins, against gravity created by virtual singularities induced by their ship's drive cores. Meanwhile the ships pulsed in their equivalent of isometric training, flexing their weapon systems and honing their focus.

Corinne, Roger's on-off lover since Tangleknot, was number two in command of Scimitar Squadron. He was a wingman in Sabre Three. All five Sabres were SRS squadrons, not just harder and more ruthless than the others, but trained to fight effectively as individuals as well as in coordination, able to switch modes in a way no other Pilots could.

Sabre Three Leader was Roland Havelock, one of the trio who had quizzed Roger on his first arrival at Tangleknot, and a veteran of one of SRS's intelligence detachments that were now rolled back into the main regiment. In training manoeuvres, he had shown a practical lateral-thinking approach to taking out enemy vessels that had changed Roger's entire way of thinking about military engagements.

It was interesting that none of Schenck's renegades had come from special forces. Admiralty psych specialists had determined that being subverted by the darkness ruled out a Pilot from passing the cognitive-behavioural tests during selection; unfortunately there was no obvious way to use this knowledge against renegades in battle. For now, it was the Zajinet main fleet they were hoping to draw out and engage; but soon enough, it would be time to take the war to former Admiral Schenck and the Pilots who followed him – assuming he was still in charge.

On the ninth day standard, they came: an attack fleet of Zajinet vessels, mean and angular and armoured, reconfigured for war. And their attack mode was even more daring than Roger had expected: bursting in and out of realspace like a storm of stones skipping across black waves, the vacuum blazing as weapon fire cracked it open, magnificent in its violent beauty, if only you were not scared for your life and your comrades, Pilots and ships alike.

Then it was time.

A thousand hidden ships trembled with the need to release their built-up power.

Explosives blew the shells apart, the seventeen deep space fortresses that were merely laminar shells containing the hardest-bitten Pilots of all: five squadrons of SRS, fifteen more from long-range reconnaissance and other élite bands. Now they swooped like arrows, spiralled around incoming fire, and drove towards the attackers, letting their weapons rip. During the first three seconds some thirty Zajinet vessels took fatal hits, fully half of them exploding in spherical detonations, bright and sudden and silent.

++Three dexter, Stone.++

It was a warning to Roger, and he-and-ship whipped through a clockwise helix, avoiding incoming at the same time as firing, the timing *ai-uchi*, strike and simultaneous counter-strike, one of the attackers blowing apart as the other two peeled away.

++Thanks, Ferenc.++

Twenty squadrons, outnumbered three to one, and a part of Roger's awareness assessed this as failure, because three thousand Zajinets were a massive enemy but surely not their main fleet, not unless the analysts were wrong in everything, but there were more immediate things to think about as a Zajinet fighter blasted into existence from mu-space, letting loose on Ferenc whose warning had saved Roger; and comms stayed up long enough to hear Ferenc's scream. Then he and ship detonated their seppuku singularity, the ovoid blast just failing to take their attacker with them into death.

Roger-and-ship killed the attacker.

++Stone wing target two one.++

It was Havelock, identifying the objective as an angle on two orthogonal circles, each divided into twelve: a handy code rooted in mediaeval sun-dials, just as the shuttle boosters even now remained integer multiples of the width of a mediaeval horse's buttocks, which determined the width of carts and subsequently trains and bridges constraining the transport of spaceship components from the factories that built them. Someone who had never been in combat would have been puzzled by such extraneous thoughts, but strange things run through a person's mind during mortal danger.

Then trivia evaporated as Roger-and-ship attained the state called *mushin* where nothing exists but the moment; and this particular moment meant death.

Twelve Zajinets exploded, ripped apart as Roger led the

eight ships in his wing to cut across them, because Zajinets on the whole might manoeuvre better than Pilots but not when it came to Sabre Three Squadron. Havelock had trained them to the point where they were beyond outstanding; and they had all been in combat before, enough to intuit the swirl of battle.

Roger commanded:

++Follow me, curl ura nine.++

Ura meant reverse, and *ack*-blips sounded from his wing as they hauled back through the demanding trajectory, but the payback was there: some twenty Zajinets coming in from the flank of Scimitar, and Roger's wing broke through the enemy formation, killing only one but disrupting their attack, and that was enough to—

++Thanks, lover.++

—let Corinne focus a counter-strike and lead her Pilots around to outflank the Zajinets in turn—

++Anytime, sweetheart.++

—and she took out two of them single-handed and then Roger was busy with another flight of Zajinets hurtling this way. Just as he was beginning to wonder if they were being strategically overwhelmed despite individual success, a signal blared in every Pilot's ship, the code they had been waiting for.

++BUG OUT NOW.++

Time to go.

Golden space burst into being.

Now they flew hard, eight hundred and two surviving ships, the tally automatic amid mutual signal-pings, and Roger was appalled because he had not realised they had lost so many, and the Zajinets would pay for this.

Those two thousand and more Zajinets that tore into mu-space behind them, accelerating.

Faster.

There was no need for a command because every Pilot-and-ship knew exactly what they had to do, which was pull ahead of their pursuers, and never mind that this was not the full fleet they had intended to face, because this was dangerous enough, with far too many of their comrades dead already, and Roger-and-ship put everything they had into simple flight, because the only way to achieve revenge was to live.

Their pursuers were holding fire but gaining on them.

Ahead, through the analogue of visual sensors, they could see the growing, infinitely complex form of Mandelbrot Nebula, crimson and violet and magnificent. Soon enough the Zajinets would realise—

++Scatter now!++

It was an all-squadrons command that might have come from any of the Pilots because that was how they operated, hierarchies abandoned at convenience, a mode of operation once more proven right because without that signal many of them might have died.

Their formation spat apart as if exploding into a sparse cloud.

Enemy!

I see them.

The realisation howled through ship-and-Roger.

They're everywhere.

The visual illusion was this: in the reaches of golden space, clouds of tiny dots were growing, while from the flanks came shoals of vessels on arcing trajectories, and huge ships tore into place above and below; but this was illusion, born of the multiple layers of reality the Zajinets came in on, self-similar spacetimescapes whose scales differed by orders of magnitude, and to navigate so many vessels to come together at the same time was a magnificent feat.

Then there was only awe as the massed Zajinets showed themselves in normal scale, a huge curving face that dominated a third of golden space, an image whose every pixel was a massive warship, their configuration a shallow bowl: a concave whose focus was the eight hundred surviving Pilots and their ships.

The Zajinets must have numbered millions.

++Oh, crap.++

It was an open signal, but not the kind that anyone would reprimand. The answer came from Havelock.

++Nebula. Now.++

The expanding cloud of Pilots-and-ships arced towards the nebula, desperate now, and in the first few seconds the rearmost died; but then they were into their hellflight geodesics, and no one was going to target them during hellflight unless they accelerated to a significant percentage of the Pilots' velocity: a huge task for an immense fleet, and not an order that a Zajinet admiral would give, not that anyone knew how their command structure operated, or even if they had one in the sense that humans would—

They're following.

Unbelievable.

That vast mass of Zajinet vessels, a million armoured ships, was on the move.

And look how fast they are.

Oh, shit.

Once the signal was given, the Zajinet fleet clearly had no problems with inertia, because they were already accelerating hard, and the question was whether they could attain hellflights from such a formation, and the answer was probably no but they were pursuing hard, and it would take only a percentage of their number to forge ahead onto hellflight trajectories and the Pilots would be overwhelmed; but then space went crimson and the nebula was open and Roger laughed aloud because the rules were about to change.

Ver nær okr, berserkrinn!

Vit erum berserkr.

Blood trickled from mouth and ears and eyes as ship-and-Roger pulled into the hardest turn they had ever attempted because there was no way they were going to flee from the next part and never mind the millions of vessels now face-on and approaching fast because this was the moment.

Nine bursts of activity around branches of the nebula, and perhaps the Zajinets had time to wonder what was happening before nine attack fleets, fifty thousand vessels in each, came streaming out of Mandelbrot Nebula intent on destruction.

The vanguards were veterans, hardened by combat, drawing the first-timers in their wake, heading for the kill; and though they were outnumbered, the Pilots had an advantage the Zajinets could never match.

Dirk McNamara commanded them.

They tore through the Zajinets like swords leaving wounds of burning fire, lines of exploding vessels, and the quantum mentality that enabled the xeno fleet to handle spacetime ambiguity did not allow decisive reaction to the deadly geometry of the Pilots' attack.

The enemy configuration tumbled to a relative halt, firing in confusion and hitting their own kind as much as Pilots, maybe more; and Roger grinned, somehow understanding the overall picture even as he-and-ship fought their own war – *there* – as Zajinet after Zajinet – *again, yes* – died before them; and while duration became relative neurochemically and geometrically, the whole thing seemed both slow and fast, so that the reversal was a sudden surprise.

The Zajinets turned away.

Just like that: every one of them.

++Take them all.++

Dirk wanted no survivors. But why had they made themselves so vulnerable? Hundreds, maybe thousands of the Zajinet fleet perished by the simple act of turning, but there was no way this could be a trap to draw the Pilots in because there was nowhere for the mass of Zajinets to go, not without Dirk's ships hunting them down and destroying them all.

So why?

Doesn't matter.

Roger-and-ship let loose with everything, killing two more Zajinets from the rear.

Then a massive comms signal resonated inside every Pilot ship.

<<We leave you to your darkness.>>

Ship-and-Roger continued firing because this had to be a trick, for no Zajinet had ever communicated in such a singular way before; but then hundreds of thousands of Zajinet vessels revolved *inwards* in a way that later no one could ever recreate, not even the Admiralty's most prominent scientists; and the Zajinets slipped out of sight.

Every one of them.

Roger-and-ship, though it was dangerous in the outer reaches of the nebula, dipped out of mu-space, black realspace shivering into existence all around but devoid of ships, other than the few Pilots doing the same. They transited back and broadcast their news of what they *hadn't* seen.

The Zajinets were gone.

To neither known universe.

Holy shit.

How could they do that?

It was a question every Pilot would ask themselves and each other, over and over in war rooms and bars and private homes of Labyrinth, for years and decades to come. The debate would be enduring and never entirely resolved, and kept secret, like so much else, from the ordinary humanity of realspace who would question, from time to time, the non-appearance of Zajinets upon their worlds.

Dirk McNamara had confirmed for ever his reputation as a war admiral *par excellence*, the greatest in Pilot history. If it were not for the renegades assumed to be under Schenck's command, the populace of Labyrinth would have assumed that peace would reign in mu-space for a very long time.

The Chaos Conflict was over.

But the mystery of the Zajinets' destination remained.

FORTY-SEVEN

EARTH, 1989 AD

Chilly sky and green grass: morning on Hampstead Heath, dogs running and playing with tongue-baring joy, and a man in a tweed overcoat walking past, shamrock in his lapel. It was the 17th of March and three years since Rupert's death, and Gavriela missed him dreadfully. She watched the dogs and the people, hoping their lives felt fulfilled.

For herself, Carl visited seldom – she got on better with her grandson Brody, in many ways – and her friends were mostly books, in the elegant Chelsea house she had inherited with surprise from Rupert. Rupert's collection was in many ways the greatest gift he could have given her, in lieu of his continued presence on the Earth.

She hoped Brody was revising with diligence for his O-levels.
Where did the years—?
Something ripped inside her skull.

After the stroke, learning to write again was hard. She had been one of the first to use a Compaq, however, revelling in the concept of a suitcase-shaped computer whose bottom end detached to form a keyboard and reveal a phosphor screen. Apart from the PDP11s in Imperial, she had grown used to the idea of plumbed-in mainframes with water cooling, and air conditioned atmosphere to ensure no dust-particle could ever slip between a disk and its read-write head.

It had got to the stage where ordinary consumers were buying computers, though what they intended to do with them, Gavriela had little idea. Most people did not appreciate what a universal Turing machine actually was, never mind possessing the expertise to program it. To own a computer yet be unable to code seemed like illiteracy.

But hunt-and-peck on the keyboard enabled her to write, slowly at first, and then to participate on BBSs for the first time, discovering pen-pals in this new medium, no programming involved. In real life, her speech and thought remained clear, which was a blessing; but her legs were weak, and her new best friend was the electric wheelchair she steered with a joystick, and which Brody informed her was brilliant, like a pilot flying a Spitfire: he always cheered her up.

Then there was Ingrid, her live-in nurse, on whom Gavriela depended, at first without seeing her as a friend – Ingrid's manner could be brusque – while being grateful that Rupert continued to look after her from beyond the grave, because she could never have afforded Ingrid otherwise.

There was something liberating in accepting one's own helplessness, in recognising that however self-focused she had been in her life, it was all right for her to depend on someone else. She would have liked to explain this to her exuberant grandson, but it was not right that Brody should know of such things: let him be optimistic and blind to his mortality, while he was young.

In the summer, when Brody's exams were over, he came to stay for the full six weeks of the holiday. With her, he could discuss his obsessions – with physics and physical culture (as Gavriela thought of it), the former approved of by his father, the latter remaining secret. Gavriela talked to Ingrid, who told her that the old notion of muscle-bound introverts was untrue. The upshot was Gavriela's purchase, via Ingrid, of a set of weights for her grandson: blue plastic things and a shining chrome bar that nearly gave the delivery man a hernia, or so he said.

What neither Gavriela nor Brody talked about was Carl's impending marriage – at the age of forty-seven, for pity's sake – and the way he had cut Anna Gould out of his life, and appeared to be doing the same to their son, Brody. No doubt

Carl had his own story and justifications, but in the absence of explanation, Gavriela was treating his actions as unforgivable.

Or perhaps it was simply that Gavriela was a better grandmother than a mother, getting it right the second time around. Either way, she smiled at the huffing and puffing that came from Brody's room every day, the occasional thump of weights on the floor, and the vast quantities of milk he drank.

More significantly, the day after Brody received his O-level results, mostly grade 1s, Gavriela despatched Ingrid to Foyle's – at some point, Ingrid had become more than nurse, simply by setting no boundaries on what she was willing to do to help – to buy the three-volume Feynman lectures, the famous red books which she warned Brody would be too hard for him at first, but inspirational.

'There's, er, something else,' he said one night in the drawing-room – a term he found as amusing as she did – while the credits were rolling on the Conan movie. 'You know those letters . . .'

Gavriela touched the joystick on her wheelchair, rotating a little to face him. Of course she had wondered about the letters arriving three times a week or more, but she had patience.

'Her name's Amy,' he went on. 'Amy Stelanko and she's from Iowa and Dad doesn't like her but I do. Her dad, she calls him Pop, works over here, except they'll be going back when I'm in the Upper Sixth.'

Gavriela's friend Jane from Imperial had married the boy she went out with at school, and remained happy. So Gavriela took Brody seriously, instead of dismissing a teen romance.

'Things will be tough,' she said. 'When she goes back.'

And at a time when Brody would be concentrating on his A-levels, or should be.

'I *do* want to go to Uni, Gran,' he said. 'Mr Stelanko said that if I apply to Cornell or somewhere, then he'll help me.'

'Living in a foreign country, that's *really* tough.'

'Oh.' Brody sank in on himself. 'Right.'

For the first time he looked like the sulky teenager his father had been.

'Which means you'll need my help,' said Gavriela. 'And you get that under one condition.'

Brody's face cleared.

'You need to bring Amy round here,' Gavriela went on. 'I want to meet the thief who stole my grandson's heart.'

Blushing and laughing, Brody agreed.

Amy turned out to be a wonderful girl, pretty and smart and interested in psychology, and who listened, wide-eyed and riveted, as Gavriela told her about meeting Sigmund Freud a long time ago. Then she told Amy she was welcome to come back any time, and she meant it.

When the end of summer came, Gavriela's sense of heartache grew large as she realised just how much Brody's presence had brightened her world. With a shock, as he came into the drawing-room dressed in T-shirt and jeans on the evening before leaving, she realised he had turned from a boy into a muscular young man during just six weeks.

'I'm over two stone heavier,' he told her. 'Fourteen kilos, and hardly any fat.'

Clearly the weights and the milk had come at just the right time in his development. They talked over the logistics of getting his boxed-up weights sent home, then the conversation trailed off, until Gavriela found herself saying. 'We've talked about your future, but there are some things I'd like to tell you about. I mean my past.'

'Dad says ...' Brody shrugged his now-bulky shoulders. 'He says you had a tough time of things, and won't ever talk about it.'

Gavriela guessed Carl had worded it differently.

'There's a great deal I've never been able to share,' she said. 'My war work was classified, but people are starting to learn about Alan Turing and Enigma, though much of it will stay secret for a lot longer than—'

'Bletchley Park?' said Brody. 'You mean you *worked* there?'

'We called it BP, and I certainly did ...'

It felt good to pass the memories on.

Gavriela stayed away from Carl's wedding at the start of October. Brooding more than usual, she wondered if Carl might have another child, and if so, whether he would treat this one more kindly. That night in bed, as she closed her eyes, her hands wrapped around her book, she saw in her imagination the note she had written while asleep on a previous notable night, when she learned of her great-niece's abduction.

That was when dear Rupert was still alive, and he had taken her to the SIS outstation on Chester Terrace, the mansion overlooking Regent's Park. Its parquet flooring was dug up during renovation, allowing her to hide the note and photograph intended for an unknown future recipient.

You will see three. You will be wrong.
G
P.S. Pass it on! $\kappa_\infty = 9.42$; $\lambda_\infty = 2.703 \times 10^{23}$; $\mu_\infty = .02289$

That was the note, she remembered as she descended into sleep, which she had wrapped around an old photo of herself with Ilse, to act as a form of identification – to the extent her actions made rational sense. It was Ilse's granddaughter that Dmitri had kidnapped, and it seemed right to use that picture, though the name would likely mean nothing to whoever read it in the future.

The next morning, Gavriela realised she had done it again.

She awoke with the same notebook open atop the bedspread, and a new message written inside. The cruel thing was, the handwriting looked as if she had penned the letter prior to her stroke.

Dearest Lucas,

How wonderful to have a grandson! My words will seem very strange, since we do not know each other and I speak

*from your past. Still, I must ask you a favour, and be assured
it must be this way. Even banks can fail over time, although it
is to be hoped that some familiar names survive, so I am forced
to contact you in this indirect way, with the hope that you will
feel curious enough to investigate as I tell you.*

*Please, my grandson, look under the parquet flooring, in
the right-hand outer corner as you look out the window at the
park.*

> *Love,*
> *Gavi (your grandmother!)*
> *X X X*

If Carl named a future son Lucas, then that would be the
final indication, to Gavriela's satisfaction, that she was not
insane, that this phenomenon of information propagating
backwards in time was real. This letter seemed to be a logical
piece in a very illogical puzzle.

She had hidden the previous note and photograph, information that might prove useful against the darkness, beneath
the floor in an out-station of the Secret Intelligence Service. It
was the safest of locations, yet it had also seemed insane – how
would the intended recipient even find the thing? This new
letter was more explicit, to the extent of naming an unborn
grandson.

It carried other implications: that she might never see the
new baby, and in any case would never get to know him as
an individual.

Should I have gone to the wedding?

Somehow, this unknown Lucas – he would be Lucas Woods,
she presumed – would need to receive this letter, which in
turn would enable him to retrieve the secreted note and
photo. Not knowing what else to do, she folded up the new
letter and tucked it inside *Zen and the Art of Motorcycle Maintenance*, the book she had been reading when she fell asleep.

How do you send a message to the future?

Runes could be carved in stone with relative ease, the

advantage of such angular *futhark*s, the alphabets. But what was the modern equivalent of scratched lines?

'There's nothing simpler than a bit,' she muttered.

There was a tap on the bedroom door, and Ingrid looked in.

'I thought I heard you say something.'

'Nothing important, but I am awake.'

'Let's get you to the bathroom, then.'

Accepting Ingrid's assistance was better than using a bedpan or commode. It seemed so unfair that you could fight for so long and life would come to this; but fairness was not a characteristic of the universe, only of humans at their best.

Philosophy while you go to pee.

When the humdrum details were finished and she was settled in her wheelchair, wrapped in her dressing-gown and ready for breakfast, Gavriela made a detour into her ground-floor study – Rupert had called it his writing-room – where her Compaq lay switched off.

During operation, at any instant, every location in the computer's memory register would be either true or false, one or zero. Right now, while it was off, the state was what Pirsig, in *Zen and the Art of Motorcycle Maintenance*, called *mu*.

It was nothingness; it was neither-nor.

And it struck Gavriela as more profound than she had first thought.

'Gabrielle? I've poured your tea.'

'*Ich komme jetzt, Ingrid.*'

'*Also gut, Frau Doktor.*'

Gavriela smiled. It was not just Ingrid, it was both of them: speaking in the old language brought the old habits of courtesy. The Inuit might not in truth have thirty words for snow – *Schade*, such a pity – but Whorf and Sapir were surely correct in pinpointing the constraints of language on intellectual concepts, witness Pirsig's borrowing from Japanese to come up with—

'Gabrielle?'

Natürlich. Of course.

'I need to make a phone call.' She steered her wheelchair out into the hallway. 'Could you fetch the phone book, please?'

Ingrid pulled it out of the occasional-table drawer.

'Let me find it for you. Whose number do you require?'

Gavriela looked up at the old grandfather clock. Ten to nine. Edmund Stafford, who as a young man had brought her books to read in Oxford while she was largely housebound after Carl's birth, still went in to work every day, despite his *emeritus* status.

'The Computing Laboratory at Oxford,' Gavriela said. 'It's written as Comlab in the book.'

'*Also gut,*' said Ingrid, flicking through pages. Then she went to the phone, dialled the number for Gavriela, and held out the handset.

'*Danke sehr, Ingrid.*'

Edmund had known Turing before the war. If anyone had a notion of how to transmit electronic runes into the future, he was the man.

She smiled, glad that life still offered interesting challenges.

FORTY-EIGHT

It might be infinitely long, but Borges Boulevard appeared to be packed with revellers. The Battle of Mandelbrot Nebula had ended the Chaos Conflict in one sudden phase transition to peace, at least for now, and that was worth celebrating.

Meanwhile, Roger and Corinne knew, the Admiralty Council members were engaged in a series of secret planning sessions, as if the current festival meant nothing. The reason was simple: direct war against the renegades was inevitable at some point, but it might not be for decades yet, even centuries. The urgent administrative question was whether to maintain a war-ready fleet, using the command structure they currently possessed, or to stand down the combat squadrons and revert to a normal mode of existence.

Of the most senior officers, only Dirk McNamara, war leader extraordinaire, was required to leave those Admiralty sessions in order to appear in public. Every population needs a figurehead as a focus of communal triumph, even among Pilots.

'We're still primates.' Roger held a goblet of something fluorescent that fizzed and popped like fireworks. 'When it boils down to it.'

'Damn,' said Corinne, leaning against him. 'You mean like primitive emotions overruling logic, kind of thing.'

A thousand Pilots were jumping in time to pounding music on the stretch of boulevard before them.

'Doomed to enjoy stuff like wild, uncontrollable sex,' Corinne went on, sliding her hand down Roger's abdomen, while the pandemonium of celebration continued. 'How awful, that we just can't help ourselves.'

'Bloody hell, Corinne.'

'Simply tragic.'

'People can see—'

'Jealousy' – she licked his ear – 'won't help them.'

'Ayee-ah ... Probably not.'

Kissing her deeply, he tumbled them both through a fast-path rotation into an isolated pocket of reality, a slowtime layer with respect to mean-geodesic, which meant they could take for ever and still be back in moments. And afterwards they were, back in the victory festival, in the midst of celebration, satisfied and exhausted.

Perhaps a few among the crowd noticed their reappearance and grinned for a moment.

Roger kissed Corinne softly. 'You're pretty wonderful.'

'Likewise.' She tapped her tu-ring, and frowned at a her-eyes-only display. 'Listen, we've been committed to non-commitment, or something like that, since Tangleknot. Do you think we could ever—?'

Scarlet flashing light overlaid Borges Boulevard and the dancing crowds, and for two or three seconds it appeared to be part of the triumphal pageant, but then the low throbbing of alarm tocsins caused the music to die away. For those who could hear, there was the voice of Labyrinth itself, more urgent than ever before.

=An invasion fleet approaches.=

How many thousands of Pilots exchanged stunned looks in that moment? How many cursed the trickery of Zajinets, those alien betrayers that should have been fought against since the first contact with Earth, before they gained a foothold in the human dominions ...?

=They are Pilots. Renegades led by Boris Schenck.=

Corinne shut down her private display.

'There can't be more than two hundred of them,' she said. 'If Schenck thought our fleet would still be occupied with the

Zajinets, he's going to have one hell of a—'

=Half a million ships at least. And there may be many more.=

Schenck was no fool, then.

Roger took Corinne's hands in his.

'Fuck it,' he said. 'I'm not ready.'

Had he realised this was farewell, he would have chosen different words. But he was summoning a dangerous rotation, and as he released her hands and looked into her jet-on-jet eyes for the last time, the fastpath engulfed him, spacetime swirling; and then came ejection – so very dangerous – into mid-air above that most beautiful hull, strong and black, webbed with red and gold. She was already responding to his presence.

I'm—

Falling through the chill air of the great docking bay, several thousand ships inside its concave expanse. Falling towards the dark opening melting into existence in her hull.

Caught you.

Tendrils had snapped out to slow his descent and guide him inside. Then she was sealed back up, ready to fly.

We don't know where to engage the—

That's not where we're going.

They plunged into full conjunction trance, more deeply than ever before. Roger's first thought had been that he was not ready; but together, as one, ship-and-Roger were clear on what they needed to do.

Ultra-hellflight, then.

More than that. The graveyard.

Already they were turning away from the docking promenade and tumbling towards the vast cliff-like wall that led outside. It might have appeared dangerous, but Labyrinth knew everything. An opening appeared as Roger-and-ship began to soar.

I love you.

Golden space burst into being all around, the infinitesimal-point energy of the continuum itself providing power for glorious flight, magnificent and infinite. Distant black stars were inky fractal snowflakes, elegant and fine, while curlicued nebulae were strewn like fresh rivulets of blood. This was existence at its most beautiful, magnificent and heartbreaking.

They had done it once before, Roger-and-ship, making a more-than-hellflight near the insertion context of the real-space galactic core, a dangerous place from which to enter mu-space. This time the destination was less critical, granting more freedom in their choice of geodesic; but duration was everything, the effort awful and agonising, and if they survived they would be forever changed, while if they died it would be simply one more Pilot and ship lost, and in the imminent fight there would be so many deaths: that was obvious.

I would give my life for Labyrinth.

Once that had been Roger's thought alone; now it belonged to both of them.

Half a million renegades, and maybe more.

The past four years, or perhaps ship-and-Roger's entire existence, led up to this.

Time to prove ourselves.

Hellflight, and more.

Schenck's timing was better than first appeared, for the fleet was depleted: exhausted from battle, some gone to recuperate on realspace worlds, most celebrating in Labyrinth, their determination low. At the same time, their ships remained massed together, one of the very few occasions when such a huge number would be located in the same place, therefore a target for a single, massive, all-out strike from nowhere.

Sen sen no sen: seizing the initiative.

It seemed Schenck was a better war admiral than anyone had reckoned. Far better. And with half a million ships! Even more, if the approaching force was just a vanguard ...

Ships fled from Labyrinth in panic.

Abandoning her.

Dirk McNamara was disadvantaged by the stupid ceremony

he was engaged in, on a floating platform surrounded by ho-lostreamers in the midst of several thousand revellers, cele-brating one victory while innocently setting themselves up for defeat by Schenck and his unexpected all-out strike, and with a fleet that was *at least* thousands of times larger than it should have been, perhaps even greater, and how the hell had the bastard managed that?

Not far from the ceremony's location, some five subjective years previously – though decades by mean-geodesic time – Dirk had killed a previous Admiral Schenck: that odious, treacherous fucker who had not been able to back down from a duel, and had nearly won through the most devious of tricks.

Covert femtoscopic weapons had been floating in mid-air, set as booby-traps by Schenck inside hidden layers of reality, programmed to take out Dirk by manifesting directly inside his heart and brain while he fought; but Dirk's perceptions were finely tuned to danger always, and he had read deception in the bastard's eyes and outmanoeuvred him, before taking his revenge in the most appropriate way: causing spacetime to slide apart in shards, wrenching Schenck apart, while twisting the maze of rotations hard, to the mathematical limit.

The duration of Schenck's dying was infinite, literally for ever.

Too bad Dirk had not thought of killing the entire family.

He tapped his tu-ring.

Calling for my mother. Some hero.

But Ro McNamara was the true and legendary First Pilot as well as First Admiral, and if she made an appearance, she could be a figurehead to rally morale, not to mention an ag-gressive tactician who fought just as he did, though perhaps without that edge of madness that took him through when rational tactics failed.

There was no reply to his ping, though, which meant that even Labyrinth had not thought of – or was not capable of – rousing Mother by reaching into whatever layer of reality she was using to skip through time, dipping into mean-geodesic timeflow like a skipping stone touching a lake. She and he both, of course, but by now she might be biologically younger than her own son.

Sons, if Kian still lived, the soft-hearted bastard. Silly fucker wanted everyone to love each other. Once, he had even said *we should spend time among the Siganthians, getting to know their ways* – that was a long time ago, before the place was declared a hellworld – because the aliens might be strange but they were robust and in their own fashion spiritual: fearsome to non-metallic lifeforms, but not to be shunned out of fear, rather embraced in mutual enlightenment.

Enlightenment! Silly fucker.

What had happened to Kian, on the day he was burnt by the mob, had helped to make Dirk the consummate fighter that he was. No other response was logical.

And now, a new and unexpected battle.

His platform continued soaring above the crowd as these odd, irrelevant thoughts swirled through Dirk. They were almost welcome: a symptom of the mind under combat stress. Below him, Pilots were disappearing into fastpath rotations. But he stayed on the platform, soaring over people's heads, because he wanted to be seen.

Heading for the fight.

'We need a battle plan.' This was Admiral Whitwell, his words sounding in Dirk's ears, his face a tiny virtual holo. 'Formations to be—'

'I have one,' Dirk told him.

Accelerating harder now, the platform, with the docking bay in sight, his bronze ship awaiting him.

'What is it?'

Dirk grinned as he soared towards her, his ship.

'We kill the fuckers.'

Her hull was open for him.

Dirk-and-ship flew.

Hard-lined and old school, from a time when every flight

was intrinsically a mortal risk, they had every confidence in taking down soft-living, younger Pilots, however corrupted they might be, however strong this phenomenon, this so-called darkness.

All military commanders study history. Once, Dirk knew, an admiral called Yamamoto struck with a fleet out of no-where; and if the place called Pearl Harbor had contained the whole military and civilian population of the targeted power, the war would have ended there.

Then, they had merely woken a sleeping giant. But Schenck had the opportunity to destroy Labyrinth in a single attack; and if she perished, who would mourn or take vengeance?

Even the Zajinets were gone.

To me, Pilots.

They flew out to face the invaders.

Chains of explosions blossomed around Labyrinth.

Whipping from side to side, Dirk-and-ship avoided weapons fire – others were perishing all around, some destroyed as they exited docking-caverns – making their assessment: the first objective was to take out the vanguard, Schenck's long-range attackers. Failure meant too few defenders would get clear of Labyrinth, and the attackers' main fleet would be upon them, and that would be it: the end.

Those who had flown clear were scattered without for-mation, victorious in simply surviving so far, but more was needed. Most were fighting one-on-one battles, except nota-bly for nine Sabre squadrons, who had not hung around to rally others but simply soared into clear space, before turning to observe and wait until they could make a difference.

Which was now, with Dirk McNamara in command.

Here and here. All Sabres to attack together.

Their *ack*-signals came back as fleeting blips.

Do it, while I gather up the rest.

Dirk switched to max-power broadcast, aiming to reach the scattering ships that were not special forces and needed specific commands. Some might think of personal survival, but if Labyrinth fell then renegades would rule, and isolated fugitives would live in fear until they were hunted down. They had to understand what was at stake here.

The SRS squadrons came hurtling in, taking out a leading rank of renegades in simultaneous firebursts, while Dirk blared his message to the largest concentration of survivors:

This is Dirk McNamara. I need you, Pilots.

There was incoming fire, but Dirk-and-ship twisted away.

Labyrinth needs you! Come to me now.

Something burned across the leading edge of ship-and-Dirk's starboard wing, enough to hurt but not to slow them down.

Time to fight, Pilots.

He curved back towards the battle.

And, miraculously, the other Pilots and their ships accelerated, following their admiral.

Inside Labyrinth, Pilots were still running or fastpath-rotating to their ships. Escape tunnels were forming as Labyrinth reconfigured to provide maximum exit capability, needing the vessels to get clear, as many as possible, before weapons fire started to—

=I'm taking hits.=

This was Labyrinth under direct attack.

While thousands made their panicked way to the docking bays, public broadcasts direct from Admiral Whitwell kept them appraised of the situation outside. There was a pause in that commentary, Whitwell's voice trailing off, before coming back strongly through every Pilot's tu-ring.

'Roger Blackstone is promoted to brevet-Admiral.'

Corinne received that signal as, cursing, she-and-ship flew clear of Labyrinth into a rain of weapons fire that took all their concentration to dodge. Only when they were clear of immediate danger could a part of her mind ask two very obvious questions.

First, what the hell was Whitwell playing at, with such a battlefield promotion for someone so young, even if it was her Roger?

And second, where the bloody hell *was* Roger?

Up ahead, a makeshift squadron, one of many, was forming: some two dozen ships coming together as directed by Dirk McNamara – now there was a real admiral! – so Corinne-and-ship flew to join them. The backdrop was a vast wall of approaching renegade ships, a hundred thousand in the first plane, four times as many crowding behind, eager and menacing and simply overwhelming in their numbers.

Three ships in the nascent squadron of defenders blew up.

Shit.

Ship-and-Corinne hurtled through to take command, leading the survivors along a helical escape trajectory, an avoidance manoeuvre designed to give them time, but doing nothing to immediately hurt the enemy.

This is bad.

Two more ships exploded, either side of her.

We're going to lose.

Corinne sent a determined signal to the survivors.

With me, everyone.

Her squadron turned to face the enemy.

FORTY-NINE

EARTH, 1989 AD

Gavriela used the joystick to position her wheelchair under her rosewood desk, then opened up the terminal emulation session on her Hewlett Packard while the modem blinked furiously.

She had written code back when most people thought that a 'computer' was a woman with a calculating machine. To her, 'data transmission' still evoked images of tape reels and motorcycle couriers; but here she was, at home in Chelsea and talking to a mainframe in Kensington, itself allowing passthrough to CERN.

Using her Imperial login, she accessed the astrophysics server that she needed, typing with her frail, blotched hands. Despite her eighty-two years, she had felt herself to be an old woman only since the stroke.

But she still had her mind, and the richness of memory.

```
$ cd /astro/geoff/heimdall
$ grep 'meson' *
```

A wealth of occurrences of the word 'meson' appeared. Using the cat command, she examined the contents of the archived research files.

The surprise was that some of the dates were recent, and she realised that her no-longer-young friend Geoff – some of his former PhD students were now supervisors in their own right – had resurrected the old project, or at least the name, while consolidating new cosmic-ray data with the old. She checked, but there were no new readings from the direction of the galactic anti-centre. No one besides her, then, had seen significance in the old data.

Message in a bottle.

Edmund Stafford had brought her up to date, and helped her obtain the necessary permissions on the necessary machines. In the world of computing, everything seemed to change so fast; but it was Stafford's musing over the new edition of *The Selfish Gene* that verified her thinking on the best way to send a message into the future.

'Dawkins is absolutely right in the new foreword,' Edmund told her. 'The book became the replacement orthodoxy *without* controversy among scientists. It was the theme's *reputation* that later aroused irate discussion, mostly among the clueless. But I heard a visiting biochemist in the Bird and Baby' – he meant the pub where Gavriela first met Rupert – 'call Dawkins a genetic determinist, which is nonsense.'

Ingrid had kept them supplied with coffee and Bourbon creams, not joining in the conversation, but giving approving looks at the increasingly feminist tone of Edmund's diatribe, as his thoughts leapt from Dawkins to Sagan, then the groundbreaking work of Sagan's ex-wife Lynn Margulis, who first described the origins of mitochondria, the in-cell powerhouse organelles common to all animal life, and likewise the chloroplasts occurring in plants.

Those organelles, Margulis argued, were the remnants of archaic symbionts, separate bacterial species absorbed but not digested, instead continuing in mutual cooperation.

'Species can work together instead of fighting,' Edmund said. 'Maybe if a man had said it, people would have taken the idea more seriously right from the beginning. Like Beatrix Potter proposing that lichen is a symbiotic pairing of two species.'

'I didn't know that,' Gavriela told him. 'Is it?'

'It absolutely is, but the Royal Society didn't think so at the time, which was why she ended up writing children's books instead of becoming a scientist.'

Gavriela might never have applied that thinking to computers, but Edmund made the analogy explicit. 'In a few years, people won't remember languages like Algol or RPG,' he said. 'But bits will still be ones and zeros, and characters will be encoded in EBCDIC or ASCII, or a superset thereof, with TCP/IP at the root of comms. And don't be too surprised if C continues to run, for decades, if not centuries.'

'To be fair, some things deservedly die out,' Gavriela had said. 'Remember those one-hand card punches? They used to give me cramps.'

'I hated the blighters,' Edmund had said, and laughed. 'And when you only had one chance a day, most likely overnight, for your program to compile ... These youngsters with their interactive debuggers and the like are just so *spoilt*.'

And there the conversation took a new direction, but his provocative advice remained; and when she later needed practical hints, Edmund helped in that regard as well. Because new technology would retain its primitive ancestors deep inside, like the chemical powerhouses in every human cell, and if mitochondria could survive for six hundred million years, surely a few words in plain English could last for decades.

Four days later, Gavriela's handwritten note was now a .JPEG file, cocooned in self-replicating code that would someday send a POP message to a recipient not yet born.

As always, she had dozed off from time to time during her work. It seemed inevitable that late in the third evening, she came awake to find that she had typed while asleep, hardcoding the message destination in the source code (based on a nonexistent URL, with a *device* name-value pair that made no sense with current technology), along with the trigger timestamp.

If this code survived, the *send* routine would activate on the ninth of September, 2033, at 07:30 Universal Standard Time, meaning half past eight if they still put the clocks forward in summer, thirty-four years from now.

Or else the stroke made me insane, if I wasn't already.

She opened the image one last time to check.

Dearest Lucas,

How wonderful to have a grandson! My words will seem very strange, since we do not know each other and I speak from your past. Still, I must ask you a favour, and be assured it must be this way. Even banks can fail over time, although it is to be hoped that some familiar names survive, so I am forced to contact you in this indirect way, with the hope that you will feel curious enough to investigate as I tell you.

Please, my grandson, look under the parquet flooring, in the right-hand outer corner as you look out the window at the park.

Love,
Gavi (your grandmother!)
X X X

Then she closed down everything apart from a monochrome console window, and fired off a shell file that would send out the first generation of her code package. Like organisms, some would survive to propagate while most would die; but it took only one copy to persist in order to count as victory.

Madness, of course.

The Christmas holidays rolled around, and with them came Brody. Her grandson had put on a little more muscle in addition to the massive increase over the summer, extra mass that suited him, and he had grown a first patchy attempt at a beard, which didn't suit at all.

It gave Gavriela and Ingrid something other than the fall of the Berlin Wall to talk about. '*Es ist nicht möglich,*' Ingrid would mutter, '*dass die Mauer zerstört ist,*' while Gavriela would declare it the death of Communism: '*Das Kommunismus ist ja kaput.*' Brody's first term of A-level physics had been too easy, he said, which worried Gavriela a little, because everyone needs a challenge.

He and Amy had joined an astronomy club, which was perhaps an excuse for being together late at night, but seemed also to have sparked a genuine interest in cosmology.

'I'll give Geoffrey a ring,' she told Brody, wanting to encourage him. 'Perhaps he can get one of his students to show you the particle accelerators.'

It was a well-established principle of labour and autocracy: pharaohs had slaves, academics had grad students. But when she rang him, Geoffrey surprised her. 'I'll show you around myself,' he said, taking it for granted that she intended to accompany Brody.

'Um, I'll need to use the goods ramp,' she told him. 'Because of the wheelchair.'

'For you, anything. You can have a dozen chaps bearing you aloft on their shoulders, if you prefer.'

'Grad students, of course.'

'Well, yes. Nice to get some use out of the buggers.'

His touch of East London coarseness had the same effect as Ingrid's formality when speaking German: both caused Gavriela to smile, both made her feel at home.

'I'll spare them the effort,' she said. 'But I'll see you tomorrow.'

Next morning, they disembarked carefully from the taxi – Ingrid and Brody helping Gavriela in the wheelchair – and went inside with the college porter's assistance. They rode up in a lift with Geoffrey, and as a group of four they poked around inside one of the labs, chatting to a researcher who seemed glad to share his enthusiasm for the work. Brody looked fascinated.

Gavriela drifted away, having a 'senior moment', before realising she needed the bathroom. Remembering the way, she steered her wheelchair out into the corridor, accompanied by Ingrid.

'When you die,' Gavriela told Ingrid for the twentieth or the hundredth time, 'they'll make you a saint. You know that, don't you?'

'Let's put off the moment for both of us,' Ingrid replied. 'This door here?'

'That's the one.'

Afterwards, they found Brody in a different lab, left temporarily by himself (which he seemed proud of) after a departmental secretary had dragged Geoffrey away to deal with something.

Brody grinned, showing Gavriela several large colour monitors atop a lab bench.

'They're running pattern recognition over *your* work,' he told her. 'And they've found a rare astronomical event of some sort. See?'

To prevent people from switching off the processors in mid-run, someone had put a felt-tip-written label beneath one of the monitors.

Property of Project HEIMDALL. Please leave running.

But this was bad. Someone *had* found her old data of interest. No one was supposed to know what Gavriela had spotted amid the cosmic-ray data. Or did it not matter at this time?

'Tell me.' Her voice came out as a whisper.

'Sure, Gran. See here?' He pointed at the leftmost monitor, where among scattered white dots, three scarlet points glowed brightly, forming the vertices of an equilateral triangle. 'There's the event.'

'Finally,' whispered Gavriela.

To see them rendered like this ... It meant she had not deluded herself about the pattern in the data; and if that were true, then perhaps the strangest of her thoughts and actions were founded in reality also.

'What do you mean, finally?' Brody looked puzzled.

'Never mind,' she told him, her voice a little stronger.

Then a hard woman's voice sounded from behind her wheelchair: 'No, I'd like to know. What did you mean by that, Dr Wolf?'

Gavriela used the joystick, rotating her chair. The woman was a stranger, with twists and shards of darkness encircling her head

And death in her eyes.

'I've led a long life,' Gavriela told her.

But Brody must live.

'Hey,' he said. 'What's happened to the screen?'

The image was randomised, just electronic noise.

'Not the device.' The stranger smiled in a way that made Gavriela shiver. 'The data's corrupt, including the backups.'

Gavriela had wrinkled hardcopy pages of numeric data in her study at home, but this bitch could not be allowed to learn of it.

'Too bad,' the woman continued, 'that you didn't—'

But the door creaked as Ingrid stepped inside, and Ingrid's knuckles cracked as she formed fists, something Gavriela had thought was Hollywood invention. Then Brody was at Ingrid's side, chest swelling as he inhaled, and his newfound muscular strength was obvious.

My guardians.

The woman looked at them, then made a wide semicircle around Ingrid, avoiding her, and left through the doorway Ingrid had entered by.

'*Scheisse*,' said Ingrid.

'What was that about?' asked Brody.

Gavriela told him she had no idea.

When Geoffrey returned, he frowned at their description of the woman, having no idea who she might be.

'She gave me the creeps,' said Ingrid.

'Because you're a saint,' Gavriela told her. 'And she was the devil.'

But the informal tour ended without disaster, and at the end, when Geoffrey asked Brody what his plans were, Brody answered: 'To do research just like you,' and everybody smiled.

Good enough.

Whatever else spun off from today, her grandson – her *first* grandson, the only one she would ever know – was on the right path. She could wish for no more.

That night she woke to see a silhouetted figure standing by her bed.

'I have your papers,' the woman whispered. 'The meson data.'

'It does not matter,' Gavriela said, her old-woman voice devoid of fear.

'You know this is the end, don't you, Dr Wolf?'

The stranger raised her hand, a shadow in the darkness.

'Everyone dies,' said Gavriela. 'A hundred per cent. The question is, how much do you live?'

A pinprick accompanied the hand's pressing against Gavriela's neck.

Poison.

Perhaps the woman was KGB – this was their kind of technique – or perhaps she was something else. No matter.

It felt like stone inside Gavriela's heart.

No …

The colour of nothingness was black …

FIFTY

LUNA, 697006 AD

... until she woke again, this time in an airless hall with shining walls, with Kenna's crystal form bending over her.

—*Greetings, brave Gavriela.*

—*Kenna! Am I here for good?*

The answering smile was like diamond, beautiful and shining.

—*You are.*

—*Finally!*

Gavriela stretched her own living-crystal arms.

Time for real life to begin.

387

FIFTY-ONE

It lasted minutes. It lasted centuries.

And it was awful.

In a metallic fastness, a Siganthian hive, this was what happened to Kian as he writhed in the suspension field where spacetime at the smallest scales could twist, distort and rip reality. First, the flaying, as his skin peeled back into nothingness. Revealed, the red glistening strips of muscle and sleek grey fat were removed and vanished in turn, leaving the disembodied web of capillaries; and then, when the blood vessels too were gone, the fine black tracery of nerves, along with the unprotected eyeballs and the suffering brain containing the mystery seed of entanglement whose nature confounded Kian's Siganthian captors.

It was cyclic, the torture, as his body reformed and the iterative vivisection started up once more. But for Kian, it was a total quantum reset, a return to the initial state for every traversal of the analytic loop, leaving no memory of the previous cycles of agony, because pain was not the point of the procedure.

But for his poor ship, it was endless hell, endured remotely but intensely as if she herself were being dissected, over and over. What she wanted to do was dive to the planet's surface and blast her way in, but that was impossible without triggering Kian's death. Fleeing to Labyrinth for help would have been her other option, were it not for the thing inside Kian's head, which was perhaps the sole reason for this predicament.

And the reason she could not flee.

Because that seed of entanglement appeared to reconfigure

slowly over time, but in a shocking, negentropic way. She was reading the effects of causes that were located in the future, not the past; and that should have been impossible, but there was no other interpretation to fit the analytic data.

While the Siganthians kept the torture cycle running for centuries, presumably long after Kian had been forgotten – after the first mean-geodesic weeks, they stopped visiting his cell – his sorrowful, raging, tortured ship followed that chain of reverse causality, deducing that its origin was a profound state-change, derived from the future freeing of Kian from the vivisection field. She needed to be there when the field collapsed.

Hence the awful, ultra-relativistic geodesic that she flew, undergoing agony that was bearable only because it matched Kian's pain. And because of hope, because whatever state Kian might be in when that future release came, he would be alive, at least initially.

And she would fight to keep him that way.

FIFTY-TWO

MU-SPACE, 2607 AD (REALSPACE-EQUIVALENT)

Everywhere, ships were exploding and Pilots were dying. Fractal firebursts blazed across the golden void. They sold their lives dearly, those Pilots, but still they perished: in the larger picture, they were losing.

Dirk McNamara, like the legendary leader that he was, led strike after strike against the advancing wall of the enemy, all five hundred thousand renegade vessels headed for Labyrinth. As more and more vessels exited from Labyrinth, they flew to join the formations that Dirk had decreed; but their losses at the front exceeded the number joining at the rear.

Soon the invading mass of renegades would simply overwhelm the arcing lines of defenders, to fall upon the city-world itself.

=I could stop them.=

Labyrinth broadcast a message to those who could hear.

=But I would need a thousand years.=

It was a bizarre, morale-sapping litany for desperate Pilots to listen to.

Of those who could hear, while they raced for their ships in the docking-bays or cowered with their families inside Labyrinthine apartments whose wonder and luxury they had never appreciated fully until now, most kept Labyrinth's words to themselves, rather than spread the fatalist comment.

No one expected a city-world to be anything but an armoured refuge at best, a target at worst; but why say anything at all? And even worse, why the hell did Labyrinth keep sending out the same message over and over and over again? Had some kind of computational virus affected the city-world's mind? Was this another aspect of Schenck's attack, even as his renegades smashed the Pilots who flew against them?

Dirk's personal squadron tore through renegade ships with practised accuracy, but they were tiny against an enemy fleet that was even stronger than they—

Incoming message:

A second wave approaches.

—had expected, while in the absence of effective resistance, Schenck threw his remaining vessels into the attack, their numbers hard to estimate, but at *least* two hundred thousand more, with the total armada now numbering anything up to a million renegades heading implacably for Labyrinth.

We defeated the Zajinets.

But Dirk-and-ship knew they had outplayed the Zajinets through superior preparation: long planning and prior calculation in addition to aggression and daring in the moment of battle. This time it was bastard Schenck who had performed the strategic planning and, unlike the Zajinets, neither Labyrinth's Pilots nor Labyrinth herself possessed a secret escape route.

An entire line of Pilots-and-ships blew up.

Renegades cut at the defenders from all directions, using finite-range weapons that meant they could fire even when one of their own was in the line of sight, provided it was far enough away.

Smart. Very smart.

But you didn't ask for our surrender, you fuckers.

As ship-and-Dirk raked fire across another renegade, they knew that Labyrinth's Pilots had only one advantage: Schenck had left them no way out, leaving a binary choice.

Fight or die.

Or both, of course, because there was always a third choice: it was axiomatic. Dirk yelled with rage and pain as something cut across their dorsal hull, but his squadron took the bastard out – *die, you fucker* – making him or her pay for shooting at their commanding admiral, fighting hard in order to avoid examining the truth.

Labyrinth and her Pilots were lost.

They were about to die in a single act of genocide no real-space human would ever get to hear about. Behind Dirk, three of his squadron went up in flames, and beyond them arcs of fire swept across the other makeshift squadrons of defenders, and he wept to see them die because this was it, the end.

If only he knew which one was Schenck, he could at least—

Admiral. Admiral!

He pulled back from his suicide run into the heart of the renegade armada, straining hard to swing into clear golden space so that he could process the priority signal, because he could always die later, but if there was any chance to be taken, he would seize it.

It's Roger Blackstone, sir!

Dirk blasted back an immediate reply.

Who? What are you talking about?

But then he saw it: a black ship powering out of nowhere, webbed with red the colour of blood and gold the colour of mu-space; and in recognising the ship, he took a moment extra to realise what else was coming into view.

Reform!

Dirk's order was desperate, sent to every squadron.

Attack the armada! Now! Everyone, with everything you've got!

Anything to divert the renegades' attention from the new force on the scene.

Brevet-Admiral Roger Blackstone was back.

And those ships—?

Dead ships.

Leading thousands of reinforcements. Hundreds of thousands. Perhaps more.

No. He can't have …

Clearly, he did.

Inside his ship, Dirk laughed his buccaneer laugh.

Well done, lad.

Ship-and-Dirk turned back to the fight.

Had anyone chosen to and been able to measure Roger Blackstone's biological age inside his powerful ship, they would have found he was forty-three standard years old, aged decades since beginning his more-than-hellflight less than two hours ago by mean-geodesic Labyrinth time.

Time of course had lain at the heart of his desperate calculation, because if Schenck's force had grown in strength by three orders of magnitude beyond expectations, there was only one way he could have achieved it: by taking some or all of his renegades into some slowtime layer of mu-space, there to live and propagate, increasing their numbers and leading their darkness-corrupted lives, building an attack force as Genghis Khan had once created a marauding army that swept across a continent without effective opposition, for they were fierce and trained to a single purpose, led by a very particular kind of genius.

Roger did not believe Schenck possessed that kind of flair, instead relying on a single pre-emptive one-strike, one-kill attack – *ikken hisatsu* – coming out of nowhere.

For himself, Roger had spent his subjective decades in a single-minded honing of his own skills by simulation, incorporating his real combat experience, while his ship upgraded herself, using the infinitesimal-point energy of mu-space to power and feed them both; and finally they had reached their destination, a place whose pull could be felt by his beautiful ship, but only by exquisite sensitivity to her subconscious perceptions, because in her current state, that urge, that drive, had yet to be awoken.

It is in the nature of a blindspot that people remain unaware of its existence, even when logic dictates it must be there.

So Roger had wept with new knowledge, and his ship also, in her own way, when they broke through at their ultra-hellflight's destination after a subjective decade of straining effort in which their very real madness – for in their obsession, Roger-and-ship could no longer be counted as entirely sane – might all have been based on illusion.

Until, that is, the moment they exited their hellish geodesic and burst into violet-tinged space through which the golden void could barely be glimpsed, while all around them ships were floating, serene and linked together in permanent comms, inhabiting a collective mental state unimaginable to any Pilot, even Roger Blackstone.

Thousands upon thousands of Pilotless ships.

For this was the Graveyard Nebula.

I greet you all, and come to ask for help.

Every ship whose Pilot had ever died, in four centuries of Pilotkind's existence, floated here. Senescence could not affect vessels powered by the energy of spacetime itself; only violence, accidental or intended, could kill them.

Labyrinth is about to fall.

They were old in their minds, most of these ships, and they had not been trained to fight. A significant number would bear no weaponry at all; few would have combat capability against latest-generation renegades raised for battle. There would be time to prepare during the return flight, but that was irrelevant.

His plan did not rely on weapons.

Only suicidal courage.

And when, a subjective decade later, they burst out in the vicinity of Labyrinth, it was clear the city-world had read Roger's intention from the start, because this message was blaring out repeatedly to those capable of sensing it:

=I could stop them. But I would need a thousand years.=

Inside his ship, Roger smiled.

You'll have your millennium.

There was no need to signal his fleet of dead Pilots' ships.

They knew exactly what to do.

*

Unconstrained by the fragility of Pilots' bodies carried within, the graveyard fleet flew hard in synchrony, tearing through mu-space, leaving what at first appeared to be a wake, a churning of vacuum; but Dirk McNamara had once wrought vengeance on a different, earlier Admiral Schenck, leaving him to die for all eternity in twisted spacetime on Borges Boulevard, and Dirk recognised straight away what Blackstone and the ships from nowhere were attempting to do.

It's impossible.

But he broadcast the retreat to his squadrons nonetheless.

Fall back! Get clear!

Of course the renegade armada moved on without deviation, stately and evil, assuming sheer momentum would carry it to Labyrinth where the city-world's destruction would follow.

But the fleet of Pilotless ships, perhaps as big as the renegade armada – it was not obvious from the way they flew in each other's wake, not at first – was on a course that was equally inevitable. No Pilots-and-ships, Labyrinthine or renegade, could hope to fly that fast or hard, not without crushing the Pilots.

Dirk sent one last direct message in the hope that Roger Blackstone might receive it.

Respect, my friend.

And Roger's mouth pulled back in a smile just as he-and-ship bent into the final geodesic along with all those dead Pilots' ships: such a multitude of courageous vessels.

Then everything was gone.

Golden void twisted into an envelope, surrounding the renegade armada, slowing it down and capturing it within an impenetrable event horizon, topologically symmetric: no renegades could escape; neither could Labyrinth's fleet poke inside to observe or attack.

It was a vast distortion in the continuum that drew exactly upon the techniques Dirk had used in his duel with that other Schenck, but the sheer collective mass of the renegade armada, the best part of a million vessels, along with that of the dead Pilots' ships who had trapped themselves inside along with the enemy, meant the duration of the stasis was finite.

But it should last a thousand years, which was all that Labyrinth had asked for: the opportunity to prepare and unleash destruction in the instant time unfroze.

When the renegades and Roger and his fleet of graveyard ships would perish.

Together.

FIFTY-THREE

Watched by Kenna's secret surveillance motes, Tom Corcorigan, otherwise Lord Corcorigan, Lord One-Arm, ex-revolutionary, in a demesne far from the conflict, enjoyed his honeymoon accompanied by his new wife, naturally, and rather unnaturally by an old friend, the severed but still-living head of a Seer (one of occasional such mistakes in the ongoing programme producing Oracles) called Eemur.

Not just alive, but flensed, that head: glistening, blood-wet facial muscles exposed to the air, life processes maintained by transfusion via spacetime distortion – hyperdimensional blood-sucking – the closest an almost-human might come to possessing the abilities once characteristic of Zajinets.

Corcorigan made odd friendships.

There was no vicarious pleasure involved in Kenna's watching the one-armed Lord at the start of his marriage, but there was every fascination in observing as Tom disappeared from the plush chamber in which he faced Eemur: teleported in a flash of sapphire light, unnaturally far, in a way that provided evidence of the Anomaly's true nature.

It was in fact a single extended Anomaly, Kenna deduced, extended across the hellworlds just as she had once comprised distributed components in Palace Avernon. The proof was this: the impossibly long hyperdimensional route that Corcorigan rode, tapped into by Eemur in a massive mistake – the teleportation had been intended as a playful gift – sending her Lord and only friend to a distant world.

There was nothing Kenna could do to help.

But when Corcorigan reappeared, falling to the floor and

gasping, bleeding, she knew for sure that she had done the right thing in encouraging the resistance to see him as a war leader. This was an unpredictable man, and no one could fight the Anomaly by performing the obvious.

He thanked Eemur wearily for the unexpected present, and hauled himself to the bathchamber and finally to bed. There, in his sleep, he muttered in pain, fragments about flensing and vivisection that Kenna first took to be references to Eemur, then realised were a description of something he had seen: a man being stripped of flesh and then rebuilt, over and over again, using hyperdimensional manipulation as horrific torture.

From afar, she directed some of her surveillance motes into Corcorigan's ear, there to whisper the posthypnotic trigger-words that caused him to relate what he had seen.

Subvocalising, he talked of the prisoner who, in the brief seconds when he was physically whole, was nevertheless claw-handed, facially disfigured and obsidian-eyed, a Pilot. And from Corcorigan's description of the metallic beings who chased him when he appeared on the world, and the mechanical architecture in which they lived, the location was Siganth: it had to be.

All of which made it more urgent to do something here in Nulapeiron. For the first time, Kenna had a notion of tracking down one of the undercover Pilots inside the Grey Shadows and getting them to take her offworld, simply fleeing; then she quelled the idea.

Dropping the surveillance link, she sank inside her thoughts.

The war against the Anomaly's forces progressed incrementally towards defeat. Corcorigan became Warlord Primus and directed his forces from a floating terraformer, the same stone sphere that once was home to Oracle d'Ovraison, dead at Corcorigan's hand. Closer to home, in the subterranean ocean above Kenna's headquarters, her Kobold warriors crewed armoured mantargoi and fought metallic intruders out of nightmare: Siganthians, transported here along the hyperdimensions.

Only her surveillance of Corcorigan's secret efforts gave Kenna hope, in particular his use of the current Lord Avernon, who – as Kenna watched from deep inside Nulapeiron – flew with Corcorigan's personal guard, his fierce carls, to the orbital shell where the spinpoints were normally harvested for the Collegium Delphinorum, whose logosophers and technicians continued to create new Oracles for the nobility's use, although predictions from the future were now absent.

Aboard his skyborne terraformer, Corcorigan opened comms with the shuttle. 'Avernon. Are you there?'

'Oh, Tom.' The voice was high, shaking. 'Yes.'

'What happened? What went wrong?'

'Those orders of magnitude ... I misjudged a single factor in the equation, approximated it as a constant when I should have known ... Should have.'

'How do we fix it?'

'We can't. We just ... can't.'

(Kenna thought: *If this effort fails, it is the end.*)

Neither the shuttle crew nor the equipment could work with the precision Avernon needed to translate his ideas into practicality, to turn a shell of singularity seeds into a shield that would cut through the hyperdimensional links and with luck sever all of the Anomaly's influence.

'Send me the equations,' ordered Corcorigan. 'Send it now.'

This was desperate.

From deep within her magma-shielded chambers, Kenna searched through her distant surveillance nets among the Grey Shadows resistance forces, looking for a Pilot, realising she had been wrong: wherever the Anomaly was to be defeated, it was not here.

Escape, now, was all that was left.

Her search was a tour de force of surveillance analysis that she could never share: using her own no-longer-human brain in lieu of pattern-recognition engines, scouring through image after image after image, looking for what she—

There.

They were in stone chambers among heavy, dumb-fabric hangings, surrounded by cots filled with wounded and dying fighters. Two men: one shaven-headed, Brino by name, an asset of Labyrinth's intelligence service but not a Pilot; and one Janis deVries, his obsidian eyes disguised by smartlenses, either highly skilled or desperate, because his ship was in a cavern nearby, ready to transit directly to mu-space.

Kenna had the escape route she needed, provided she could find a location for this deVries, whose presumed forebear had played such a role in her genesis, to materialise his ship close to her current location.

She would be sorry to abandon Nulapeiron, her home for eight centuries: as Kenna rather than Rhianna Chiang, the only home she had known.

Regret caused her to take one last look, via remote surveillance, at what was happening inside the headquarters of Warlord Primus Corcorigan, the last war leader of humanity before the Anomaly engulfed this world, like the others, and turned it into hell.

What she saw changed everything.

The terraformer was a floating stone sphere under attack by flying Siganthians; but dart-shaped flyers belonging to the Strontium Dragons were fighting them off, along with Corcorigan's commandos, battling hand-to-hand on the terraformer itself against the implacable metallic warriors.

Meanwhile, Corcorigan himself was crucified on the sphere's exterior – so like a one-eyed wanderer out of legend, Kenna thought, forcing himself into the most extreme of mental states – and assisted by two beings: a cyborg embedded in the sphere – a feeling of kinship welled inside Kenna – and the flensed head of Eemur, the Seer, who was searching through the hyperdimensions, trying to find the help that Corcorigan needed.

Trying to find a Pilot.

He needs deVries.

So much for Kenna's escape; but Corcorigan's headquarters was about to fall unless he gained the help he needed.

Very well.

She directed her motes closer and closer to glistening, blood-red flesh.

And whispered coordinates inside the Seer's ear.

Kenna was not privy to what happened next. Whatever response the Seer made, spillover energy destroyed the surveillance motes in the terraformer, and when Kenna tried to re-establish contact with her motes in the field hospital where deVries was working, a similar massive distortion had broken every link.

She linked to her surveillance motes in orbit.

And waited.

FIFTY-FOUR

MU-SPACE, 3427 AD (REALSPACE-EQUIVALENT)

For the first time in centuries, the First Admiral was back, openly standing in the Admiralty's Great Hall, waiting for the rescue team to return. The greater fleet – moving out of Labyrinth's docking halls and taking up formation immediately, under Admiralty Council authorisation, as soon as Ro McNamara appeared and made her wishes clear – was standing by, ready to carry out a mission involving immense precision, intended to disrupt the Anomaly's current attempt to add another hellworld to its collection.

Whether it was feasible, Ro did not know for sure. Already, strategy analysts had indicated that even if worked to free Nulapeiron, it was not a technique they could extend to other hellworlds. There was no point in even trying to free them: whatever had happened to the once-human Anomalous components over the generations, nothing of humanity could remain. The best that could be done was the same as always: to quarantine every known hellworld and stay as far away as possible.

The most recently created hellworlds, apart from the yet-to-be-freed Nulapeiron – and if it worked, it would only be by interrupting an incomplete process – were not even human originally. Saving xeno ecologies was far beyond anyone's remit.

These thoughts were Ro's attempt to distract herself, since the current crop of admirals seemed too awed to speak to her, while all she could think about deep down was her poor, tortured son, and what the Siganthians had done to him – all this time, so very, very long – and the suspended comms session featuring a strange, one-armed bare-chested man who had appeared to hang in space before her, riding a mu-space comms-beam all the way from realspace Nulapeiron, to beg for her help in saving his world from the Anomaly, and offering a very special gift in return.

The location of her son Kian.

And the description of ongoing vivisection-torture inflicted on him by his captors. How Corcorigan had been teleported to Siganth, to witness what he related, was a mystery for Admiralty analysts to unravel later. What mattered now was—

=They are here.=

Ro looked up.

'Is ...?'

=Kian is aboard the squadron leader's ship.=

She had always been a fighter. For the first time, a sudden loss of stress was threatening to make her faint.

=And his own ship is flying alongside.=

Ro turned away.

'Thank you,' she whispered.

It would not do for her fellow admirals to see her cry.

After a minute, she spread her hands apart, manipulating reality, restarting the comms-session she had frozen, though to the disembodied Corcorigan the delay might have been only seconds.

He hung there, a bizarre image, desperate for her help.

'They're back,' she told him, meaning the special-forces squadron despatched to Siganth, taking Corcorigan at his word. 'My ... Kian is safe.'

The expression in Corcorigan's eyes did not change. He had been confident in the gift he had offered. Clearly what he needed was her response to his plea.

'We will help,' she said.

At her command, ten thousand ships commenced a hell-flight for Nulapeiron.

*

At the same time, aboard a fast special-forces vessel, a claw-handed, scar-faced Pilot, lying exhausted on a passenger couch at the rear of the control cabin, smiled despite his trauma.

I love you.

She was flying in parallel with this vessel, his own ship, having arrived with beautiful precision alongside the rescue squadron, fighting alongside them, though she was no combat vessel. They laid down covering fire while the Pilots descended in drop-bubbles direct to Kian's location, wreaking destruction everywhere, killing every Siganthian in sight as they fought through to the hive-cell where he had been left, a forgotten, tortured captive, and destroyed the hyperdimensional field that held him.

And I love you.

It was all that mattered.

We're flying to Labyrinth.

Perhaps it's time.

To go home?

Yes. Home.

To be among their own kind, at least for a while. Outsiders no more.

An end to isolation.

FIFTY-FIVE

From the shuttle that had carried Avernon into orbit, Kenna's surveillance motes drifted into a wide array allowing her remotely to see perhaps the most beautiful sight of her life.

Ten thousand mu-space ships, every one of them shining silver and bronze, materialised together.

Brutal warfare might be unfolding on the world below, but here in orbit what happened next was a stately, elegant dance. Avernon's drones dispersed, to be taken on board – with exquisite, gentle control – by the Pilots' fleet. Then the shining ships dispersed, and pulsed like a single spherical wave around Nulapeiron, resonating as they harnessed the shell of spinpoints that burst into life, forming an unbroken, shining, spherical shield.

Severing the Anomaly's links.

Labyrinth had responded to Corcorigan's call for help, and that was that: victory.

In the aftermath, it took Kenna some time to realise what Corcorigan almost certainly deduced straight away, or perhaps knew in advance, back when he set Avernon on the path to creating the planetary shield out of spinpoints that were already there, harvested in order to create Oracles ... but had not existed when Kenna, as Rhianna Chiang, first approached this world.

It was not the finite duration of the spinpoints' lives so much as the *direction* that held significance. When Avernon's drones appeared to destroy those distributed seeds of negentropic timeflow, he was of course creating them – almost as a sideeffect – their deaths having already occurred, centuries before.

In a real sense, Corcorigan, whose identity had been built upon hatred of Oracles and the political system they empowered, had in fact created them.

It was Kenna's first true lesson in paradox.

FIFTY-SIX

NULAPEIRON, 3498 AD

Alexa Corcorigan deVries, her obsidian eyes glistening with grief, stares down at her aged grandfather's death-bed. They are on a tall, open-topped tower formed of quickglass, overlooking rolling heathland. A peach-coloured sunrise hovers above distant purple mountains.

Her grandfather, Tom Corcorigan, loves the open air, so different from the tunnels of his youth. This is where he has said he wants to die.

Beside Alexa, her grey-eyed half-brother, Samson Gervicort, is as distraught as she is: they equally adore Grandfather Tom, who may be legendary to others, but to them is the most warm-hearted of real people, always gentle, and missing Elva dreadfully: Alexa and Samson's grandmother, dead for almost a decade.

On Grandfather's rug-covered lap, a neko-kitten with soft amber fur lies curled up, sleeping.

'Grandfather,' asks Samson. 'Do we have things right?'

The old man is nearly gone, unable to open his eyes; but he raises a single finger slightly.

'He means yes,' says Alexa. 'It is as it should be. This' – blinking away tears – 'is his moment.'

She takes his fragile hand—

You've done so much.

—and, as Samson turns away for a moment to blink away tears, she places her hand upon his forehead, and her turing gleams. A virtual holo, her-eyes-only, shows the winking-out of a tiny point of light, deep inside Grandfather's brain.

A spinpoint has just ceased to exist, from the viewpoint of ordinary time.

Or been created, to live all the way back to Tom Corcorigan's conception, from a different way of considering things.

'I love you, Grandfather,' she says, and it is the truth.

'I love you, Grandfather,' says Samson, placing his hand on the dying man's shoulder.

There is no mistaking the final breath, the last release of pressure, as life leaves the body.

Grandfather.

He is gone.

From a distant chamber, well appointed in smartmarble, two figures watched a giant holo of Corcorigan's final moments, respectful and solemn, while approving of the finesse with which Alexa carried out her task.

'It had to work out all right,' said the claw-handed Pilot, his face half-covered in scar tissue. 'It's predestined, isn't it?'

'Careful,' said Kenna beside him. 'We skirt on the edge of paradox, and it's so very, very dangerous.'

'I know. It's strange, to think of Tom Corcorigan and me, entangled in that way.' He looked up at the holo. 'We never talked, yet he was in a sense more a brother to me than Dirk.'

'Never that, Kian.' Kenna placed her crystalline hand upon his burnt one. 'Your real family love you, even if they don't understand.'

After the rescue from Siganth, thanks to Tom Corcorigan's signal to Labyrinth, direct to Kian's mother, Kian and his ship had remained in Labyrinth for several contiguous years, getting to know Dirk and Mother once more. But Kian's political-philosophical effectiveness had depended on his time-skipping nomadic ways, while all three of them were infected by that same need to skip relativistically across the decades and centuries, to see how Pilotkind turned out. They were getting restless. With luck, they would see out the next three or four hundred years, until the Aeternal language, along with technology and culture, had changed so much that not even they could adapt to it.

As for Kenna, Kian had met her some seven decades earlier, two years after the Anomaly's defeat on Nulapeiron, when official celebrations had declared the rescued planet part of the allied realspace worlds of humanity. Kian had hovered at the edge of a celebration that Tom Corcorigan had declined to take a starring role in, when ambassadors had gathered, and *Ode to Victory* had been played, and so on: the usual mix of solemnity and parade. When Kian, hooded and cloaked, had sneaked away, another hooded figure followed and she introduced herself to him.

Of course he had paid attention. 'It's not every day you get to meet a woman of living crystal,' he told her later.

For all that, he was the only non-Kobold not to fall into awed trance in her presence, and she treasured his friendship, and the infrequent visits that followed.

Plus, there was a mystery that no one had resolved, and had been only deepened when Labyrinth herself had given Kian a piece of information that he understood was confidential, not to be shared, no matter how little information he extracted from the words.

=There is a bright seed in your brain.=

It was Kenna who deduced the implant's nature: a spin-point entangled with one other, an identical counterpart. And that partner was in Tom Corcorigan's brain.

How else could Corcorigan's journey along the hyperdimensions have deposited him precisely in the location where Kian was being held? Unexpected events had crowded upon everyone, and the Seer-mediated teleportation was known to have been directed to Siganth along the hyperdimensional channel used by the Anomaly, joining Siganth to Nulapeiron. Bizarre as the events might be, there was no mystery in Corcorigan's destination being the hellworld; but no one had questioned the deeper coincidence, that he had ended up near the one hive-cell containing Kian.

The hidden entangled spinpoints had played a role in the fine details of hyperdimensional navigation, drawing one towards the other.

Now, a realtime holo showed the interior of Kian's brain. As he and Kenna watched, smartbeams projected from the walls – like the ones generated by Alexa's tu-ring – caused the shining white point inside his head, the other half of the entangled pair, to wink out of existence.

It was gone.

Except of course it was not extinction – it was the moment of the spinpoint's birth, beginning its life backwards in time, all the way to Kian's conception, when it would collapse. Dirk had grown from the same initial cell in the womb, but when the growing cells divided into two separate clumps, the spinpoint would have had to go along with the proto-Kian, not Dirk.

Was this a form of gross mechanical motion induced by future goals, teleology instead of cause-and-effect? Was it a veridical paradox, one that would be resolved by looking at it from a different perspective, with new knowledge? Or was it the real thing, an antinomy?

Even with the old aristocratic system on its knees if not extinct, such logosophical questions were a natural thing to ask here on Nulapeiron. Kenna and Kian smiled at each other, aware of how odd their friendship was, and the weirdness of the events that indirectly linked them.

'What do you think happens eventually?' asked Kian. 'Do we win?'

In so many ways, they were both outsiders, with very different viewpoints. Though he was not trapped in hypnotic awe of Kenna, the way most people were, he thought she might be wisest being alive right now.

'I don't know,' she said. 'I hope so.'

There was nothing more to say then, as they watched the realtime holo showing a former Warlord's grieving grandchildren, Alexa with the neko-kitten in her arms, and the flyers arriving at the quickglass tower, where soon enough the funeral would be held.

A good death, then.

If there could ever be such a thing.

FIFTY-SEVEN

MU-SPACE, 2608 AD (REALSPACE-EQUIVALENT)

Autohypnosis is part of every Pilot's education, but this is a key moment, important, so Corinne is glad to have medics around her for every minute, with Clara nearby – a close friend since peace came to Labyrinth and Corinne got to celebrate Roger's memory with those who knew him, Jed Goran included. For over twenty tendays they have been close, and particularly supportive recently, not just because of the weight inside her and the aching back and all the rest.

And when it happens, it is just as everyone said: using trance and hypnotic time-distortion and breath control to hold back the tremendous impulse to push; and then in the second phase to do exactly that when the medic says: 'Now, push now!'

Soon enough, it comes: the final yelling shove, and the sound she was dying to hear: a thin crying, the most beautiful sound in any universe, and those frequent yet never-to-be-forgotten words:

'It's a boy.'

FIFTY-EIGHT

LUNA, 703017 AD

Kenna remembered her era of involvement with human affairs, at the beginning of her existence in this form, seven *hundred* centuries earlier, and the Anomaly's defeat on Nulapeiron, a defeat never replicated elsewhere, except for a handful of absorption attempts interrupted at an early stage. The twisty complexity of humans plotting and engaging in treachery were not the only things that came to mind, when it came to multitudinous lives intertwined and conflicting, but they became foremost during the dream awakenings, when she induced past-mind resonances in this particular crystalline body.

It was the same recruitment process she had employed for the other members of the Council, but this individual was different, though he might be their salvation. In admitting the Trickster, the risk was awful.

Knowing this, she awoke him in private, away from the others, on every occasion. In his earlier organic life as he dreamt, he was in his later years. Those who fully belonged to the darkness never heard her call across the aeons; those who were strongly affected *yet also fought it* were paradoxically the most sensitive to the possibility of resonance. Of that number, one stood out above the others in his dark, twisted strength. His was the subconscious call that she answered, and drew him forward across time from his dreams, and talked to him.

In the vast majority of other destinies, she avoided recruiting any hint of chaos, and in doing so met eventual defeat – assuming her pseudo-memories had any basis in reality, and were not imaginary workings-out, in her vast computational

413

subconscious, of different paths through the events she perceived.

The slumbering crystalline form was thin in appearance, and the first symptom of resonance engaging was the twisted smile, even before the transparent eyelids opened and he sat up.

—*Kenna. Nice to see you again. Particularly since I was already dreaming, before I fell into this dream. It was very strange.*

This was the Trickster, with whom no conversation could be taken at face value. Nevertheless, she asked him to elucidate.

—*Tell me more about that, since it is on your mind.*

Her name meant one-who-knows, but she did not know everything, though others often acted as if she did.

—*I tore my own eye out, and then I crucified myself. It was not pleasant.*

—*Punishing yourself for the things you have done?*

She knew much about the atrocities that were part of his original life.

—*That is a pretty thought, Queen Kenna, but the dream is one I have encountered before, and it is not fantasy but memory.*

—*I understand.*

—*Truly? Then enlighten me, please.*

He was always polite to her.

—*You understand music.* She knew this about him. *Call it a subharmonic in the standing wave that is your mind. Or consider two wires alongside each other, one slightly longer than the other, vibrating together when plucked.*

—*I am not just me, is that what you mean?*

Kenna regarded him with stillness, as only a living-crystal being could.

—*In this place, we are all more than we once were, Dmitri Ivanovitch Shtemenko.*

—*But not necessarily better, is that it?*

—*To what are you alluding?*

—*You wake me away from the others, every time. Until I wake permanently and the transformation is complete, you do not wish them to—— Oh!*

The Trickster's eyes widened, and his body shuddered. Kenna knew him to be capable of practical jokes, but this was not one of them.

——What is happening to me, Kenna?

Their previous sessions had on occasion been filled with rage, or calm, chilling descriptions of the darkest needs that drove him in his younger years, and any number of devious debates, games that he played because he was yet to make a final resolution, the commitment to join the Council for real. This was the first time his thoughts had sounded small with fear.

——It just happened, Kenna told him.

——I do not understand.

She smiled, knowing that he was fighting against the knowledge inside him.

——In your sleep, as you dreamt this dream, you——

His face showed horror.

——No!

——Yes. You died, my Loki-Óthinn, my Dmitri-Stígr.

Even as they were talking.

——That is not possible.

But of course it was and, after a moment, that familiar self-mocking, universe-mocking smile appeared.

——I appear to have made my decision, he added. *And accept you as my war-queen.*

She held out her hand.

——Welcome to the Council.

He took her fingers gently, and went down on one knee, head bowed. It was a graceful gesture of obeisance, a promise of fealty, performed with such feeling that a human leader might have been taken in by emotion alone. But Kenna knew that what bound him was logic and self-interest, for his resurrection was by her machinations; and only the Council and the forces they commanded were of his kind, now that he lived in this form (for not even he could live totally alone for ever); and when the darkness came, its goal would be to obliterate them. The only special treatment that the Trickster might receive would be a more agonising destruction, suitable for one who had betrayed the betrayer.

Thus would he fight hard and craftily and well, loyal to Kenna as a side effect of loyalty to self, hoping that through victory he might survive the Final Days.

The Trickster was nothing if not adaptable.

While the touch of chaos he brought to their armies might be the edge they needed against the enemy. Or it might be their ruin.

She led him in to meet the others.

FIFTY-NINE

A thousand years had passed since The Trapping of Schenck's Armada, and it was almost time.

The evacuation of Labyrinth was complete.

Fleets of ships, hundreds of millions of shining vessels, hung at a safe distance from the city-world, also keeping far away from that region of shining nothingness soon to collapse and reveal the massed enemy ships. All of the Labyrinthine ships were armed; but none expected to use those weapons.

This was Labyrinth's moment.

=It has been an honour, Pilots.=

The moment of her death.

We love you.

Every ship conjoined in sending Labyrinth that message.

Then she split apart—

We love you!

—becoming a thousand fragments as she died.

Giving birth.

To a thousand daughters.

Much had occurred during that millennium, including the Stochastic Schism that so divided Pilots. Many aimed for secession as the darkness had wanted, but for different reasons, seeking to divorce mu-space, which seemed cleansed, from the home universe where the darkness still manifested and would one day come in strength.

Others argued for increasing involvement, citing the success in using Haxigoji allies to root out those who were corrupted by the darkness, realspace allies who were literally

417

incorruptible – who died if the darkness started to take hold – and in the spacetime shields that prevented several new hellworlds from forming, though the Anomaly did gain new worlds from time to time, and no existing hellworld was ever freed.

Both sides of the Schism evoked the legendary image of Dirk McNamara in their rhetoric; but there was also the mysterious, crippled figure who appeared from time to time as a moderator, and was supposed to have lived in semi-secrecy in Labyrinth for a while, before returning to his wanderings; and whether it was truth or fiction that Kian McNamara originated the Tri-Fold Way, what was certain was the success of that philosophy in eventually merging both views, both halves of Pilotkind, once more.

They had forged unity and peace, in full view of a blatant symbol showing how important and how fragile such concepts remained.

The event horizon that enclosed Schenck and his renegade armada.

Each of the thousand new city-worlds was magnificent, infinite in her complexity, able to steal as much time as required to grow and get ready ... to become strong. Each honoured their mother, each loved the inherited memory of her, the first Labyrinth; and each knew well the circumstances that had forced her to produce another generation, and in the process, die.

Spacetime rippled.

It's starting.

Signals flitted among Pilots, but the daughter-Labyrinths had no need of comms. They knew what was about to happen.

The event horizon around the renegade armada and the graveyard ships, along with Roger-and-ship frozen in the instance of their death, collapsed, revealing the ships within. There was no hesitation as, in their wrath and sorrow, the thousand new Labyrinths poured their infinitesimal-point energies upon the captive ships, obliterating spacetime within that horizon.

It blazed, so that even the shining golden void appeared momentarily in shadow.

Then they were gone, the millennium-old enemy, along with the selfless allies who had trapped them, held them in place for the kill.

Victory.

Almost a billion Pilots and ships took part in the remembrance ceremony that followed; and when it was done, they convened among their new homes, their extended realm of a thousand Labyrinths that in future would grow even greater. As the region of mu-space in which they dwelled was now vast, they recognised it was time to choose a name for their realm: a name for the ages, if not for ever.

They chose to call it Ásgarth.

SIXTY

In realspace orbit around the cloud-creamy world, Amber Hawke's ship drifted. Rekka was in the control cabin with her, some twenty minutes out of delta-coma. They were drinking fragrant tea, taking time over their farewells.

'Things are coming to a head in UNSA,' Rekka told her oldest surviving friend. 'Too much, too soon, your people are asking for.'

'Maybe,' said Amber.

Her eye sockets looked scratched around the edges, but the metal was bright as ever across the contact surfaces where the cables plugged in.

'Jared's generation might be the last to take ships for granted.' To Rekka, this was the urgent point. 'I know they can survive here in realspace, but to be without ships ...'

'You mean' – Amber tapped a fingernail against one of her eye sockets – I/O sockets – in a gesture that Simon, blast his memory, used to describe as scrotum-tightening – 'they didn't sacrifice their sight for the organisation.'

They were two old women, looking back across the years; and although both had taken time-dilated journeys, they were not that much younger than they would have been on Earth: Rekka herself was born seventy-eight years earlier, five years before the height of the Changeling Plague, eight years before her adoptive parents rescued her from the Suttee Pavilion.

'If mu-space is as wonderful as you say, as you've always said,' Rekka told Amber now, 'then you can't deny it to the next generation.'

'Because we need UNSA to build ships.'

'Well, of course you do ... er, not. Oh, Amber!' Rekka found herself grinning. 'You haven't, have you? Found a way to—?'

'If we had,' said Amber, smiling, 'we wouldn't be able to tell anyone, would we? Not even old friends.'

'No. No, you probably wouldn't.'

Rekka sipped from her tea, closed her eyes, exhaled.

Good for you.

As for herself, today was surely the beginning of her last big adventure. Relocation at UNSA's expense was a benefit that few people in her position would have taken, preferring the cash option to add to their pension at home.

That Jared had turned out bad, or at least estranged from both Amber and Rekka, was a festering memory that lay between them, not to be discussed today. For herself, Rekka had occasionally wondered whether the boy would have turned out a better man had he gone to Zurich, when Karyn McNamara still ran the place.

Nowadays only the grandson, Kian, remained alive, as far as anyone knew. He was married to an acerbic American scientist, and had consistently refused plastic surgery, preferring to wear his injuries as a reminder of the way that fear and ignorance produce intolerance.

'I could still take you back.' Amber's voice pulled Rekka into the present. 'And hang the schedule.'

'That kind of thing can get you in trouble.'

'Like I should care, at my age.'

Rekka squeezed Amber's hand. 'I'm where I need to be. Nulapeiron. The world with no borders. It's a good name.'

'Also ironic, given how they plan to live.' Amber hesitated. 'I have a contact for you. Someone who's ex-AAC. She'll give you a consulting job if you want it.'

'XAAC? I've never heard of it.'

'I mean she used to be with the Altair Adventurers' Combine, the neurocomp division, before they relocated to Fulgor and called themselves LuxPrime.'

All these new colony worlds. It was hard to keep track of them.

'Her name's Claudette d'Ovraison,' Amber went on, 'and she's working on a concept called logotropes, which should be right up the alley of a smart person who can make an autofact sit up and beg, never mind force-evolving new proteins on a whim.'

'Unfortunately,' said Rekka, 'that smart person got replaced with a tired old woman who falls asleep easily. But I'll talk to this Claudette.'

Rekka was going to Nulapeiron to live out her remaining days – and that did mean *living*, not slowly dying. A challenging job, no matter how little she might contribute in the end, was exactly what she needed.

'She lives on one of those floating terraformer spheres,' said Amber. 'Could probably make room for you to stay on one, if you've problems finding a place to live.'

'I'd rather take my chances living below ground,' said Rekka. 'But it's nice to have another option.'

'So. Good.' Amber reached out to the side, and a narrow robot arm delivered a package to her hand: a slim box the length of a person's forearm. Amber held it out and said: 'A present for my sister.'

No court would recognise the relationship, but they *were* sisters: the last two members of the *de facto* family they had chosen.

'Shall I unwrap it?'

'If you like. I inherited the thing when Aunt Adele died. I'd rather you owned it, you and not a museum.'

'Er ... Amber! Is this some kind of replica? Because if it isn't, it's far too valuable.'

It was in the shape of a spearhead, but formed of crystal.

'Heirlooms should be kept in the family, don't you think?'

'Oh, Amber.'

They hugged then, the gift forgotten amid the greater significance of the moment.

An hour later, in the cargo hold, they embraced for the last time. Then Rekka stepped into the drop-shuttle that already contained her belongings, everything she needed to begin her new life on a new world, settled back in the tiny cockpit that flowed shut and vitrified into solidity.

She glanced back at Amber standing there with her blind silver eyes, then felt the sudden jerk and the stomach-dropping freefall that followed as her drop-bug took her out into space. It headed down towards the cloud-filled atmosphere, below which a nascent, perhaps superior, civilisation was being brought into existence.

As on the day she learned of Simon and Mary's betrayal, and later when Jared was orphaned, with Amber unable to cry for the lack of tear-ducts, Rekka bit her lip and wept enough for both of them.

But when she reached the surface, her crying stopped. She would not feel so deeply, had there not been love in her life. That being so, what was there to be sad about?

The drop-bug descended slowly inside a vertical shaft, to a bright reception area below ground, with smiling people waiting to greet her.

A new world!

For a moment Rekka was young again, alone on the surface of EM-0036 before it became Vijaya, on the verge of changing her life and becoming the person she was meant to be.

I'm in the right place, at the right time.

This would be a good ending.

SIXTY-ONE

The crystalline man twitched on the silver bier. He opened his transparent eyelids as he came awake, seeing a woman, equally of living crystal, asleep on a bier like his. At that beautiful sight, he smiled.

—You're so beautiful, and I know you.

For now he remembered nothing more, but confidence was strong in him, and soon everything would come back. He swung himself to his feet, onto a polished floor; a shining hall of sapphire and glass surrounded them. This was a fastness, a place of power, and his body thrummed with it.

Shields hung on the walls, decorative and war-like simultaneously, some ancient and battered, others new and formed of exotic matter, each marked with a rune; and each of the runes glowed a soft blood red. A sign of some kind. There was deep history here, a sense of the glory involved in sheer survival across time.

In an archway, he paused at the threshold of an even larger hall, this one star-shaped with nine annexes, while sapphire dots of light shone overhead, soft and elegant, a sign of great powers tamed. Another man was lying here asleep, his name almost available to memory; but another mental image came crowding in.

The galactic core, the light of a billion suns, and the fifty-thousand-lightyear jet arrowing outwards, stretching from the dark-matter centre to the outer halo, the bridgehead of ... what?

Darkness.

Peaceful vitality filled him, but this was not a time of peace.

There was an enemy invading from beyond the void, and the warlike glory of these halls reflected long preparation for the Final Days. He understood that conflict was, is, and always would be awful; that pride and camaraderie are born of necessity, without which defeat will follow; but there was the possibility of moving beyond fear, of finding the best within a person when the universe was at its worst.

From the wall, he took down one of the heavy spears, and runes flared upon the haft.

He walked through to a long, gleaming corridor of crystal, and followed it to an external balcony set upon an outer wall of that shining fortress, overlooking the grey landscape marked with sharp black shadows, beneath a black and airless sky.

This was the homeworld's moon.

And there it was, the planet that gave birth to so much: her disc full, revealing blue oceans and green land, beneath the ribbons of crimson and silver that girded the globe.

−Hello my love.

The words had formed inside his head. He smiled as he turned.

−My beautiful Gavi.

More than beautiful: wondrous.

−Is that my name?

He took her hand.

−I am sure it is. If you remember mine, let me know.

Hand in hand, they looked out upon the moonscape for a long time before she asked a question:

−How long have we slept?

Looking at the stars, he shook his head, then stopped. Three stars formed a distinct row.

−See Orion's belt. What colour is the central star?

−It seems … red. Does that mean something?

He had remembered the constellation's name, and she recognised it. Full memory was about to come flooding back, but he answered her question nonetheless.

—It means a million years have passed.

She squeezed his fingers, crystal upon crystal.

—So much time.

Emanating from behind but sounding in their heads, a feminine, commanding voice manifested:

—You remember what we've always known to do. Observe what the enemy does, deduce what the enemy intends, and then prevent it.

Without turning, the man sensed Gavi asking:

—And now we fight the darkness?

—Now we fight.

He raised his spear in salute to the banded Earth, as everything came back to him.

And laughed, though the vacuum was hard.

For Ragnarökkr was imminent.

Rathulfr joined them in the Council conference hall, straight from the star-shaped chamber in which he had lain. Sharp was waiting, their watcher who could see the darkness more clearly than the rest, with pinpoints of reflected light sliding along his living-crystal antlers; along with Harij the Seeker, around whom sapphire light billowed and blazed, for Harij embodied the talent of mind-talk and hyperdimensional severance, their defence against absorption.

Kenna, Roger and Gavriela stood near the great table.

Magni teleported into existence, smiling.

—This may turn out to be exhilarating.

Of them all, only he had not known death and crystalline resurrection. He represented humanity of the past half-million years, and those of his kind who had not fled the galaxy were preparing to fight.

They could entangle their minds, the Council, the linkage mediated by Harij. When the crystalline fortress blazed at full energy, slamming orthophotons backwards through time (to use a primitive metaphor) to recruit their masses of warriors, such conjunction was necessary to maintain control; but when the need was over, they were individuals once more.

But the coming fight was not just theirs.

—We need to inspect our Valhöll that is Earth, suggested Rathulfr.

Awoken from the conjunction-trance, for the ninth and final time, they were not just recovered – they were energised, and Rathulfr's thoughts gleamed with power.

—Roger and I will go first. That was Gavriela. *To check they have absorbed what they need. If that sits well with you all.*

The others smiled at her.

A feminine reply hummed through the hall, vibrating with gentle humour:

—Time for young lovers to be alone?

Another Council member.

Freya her name, a slender crystalline woman who looked a lot like Roger, her brother. In her pre-resurrection existence, she had not required a name: she had been a ship, uniquely Roger Blackstone's. Now, in their present forms, it would be truer to label both Freya and Roger as superpositions: she partly her Pilot, he partly his ship.

—Not so young, sister. Roger was smiling. *For the rest, we plead guilty.*

Rathulfr was scanning the hall.

—We are eight, war-queen. Perhaps the Trickster will not come.

Kenna shook her crystalline head.

—It's unlikely he . . .

Shimmering sapphire light brightened then attenuated, revealing the kneeling figure of a living-crystal man, the last of their number.

—Trust him to turn up like that.

That was Roger, primarily to Gavriela. Long-range teleportation in this manner – Dmitri reeked of ancient, distant stars – was natural to Magni and his modern ilk, something of an affectation to those of the old kind.

Dmitri the Trickster rose without effort to his feet, and his smile was sly.

—Waiting for me, brothers and sisters?

His presence altered the Council's dynamic in a manner that

kept them on their toes. He was insightful regarding the ways of the darkness, his cunning wisdom occasionally disturbing. Roger believed that Kenna recruited him in part because the inherent risk kept everyone else alert – *don't step in any causal loops*, she liked to remind them – and remembered a conversation from half a million or a million years ago, depending on viewpoint:

—*This is not the first Ragnarok Council*, Kenna had told him.

—*If we're the second, what happened to the others?*

—*They perished in paradox.*

Roger's former naivety made him smile.

At some point, half a million years ago, Kenna had pushed through a transcendent reworking of her physical and mental self – again – to become exquisitely conscious of causal history and the sheaves of possible paths not taken; and if she had some awareness of those other destinies, then why just *one* other?

To be aware of an infinite number of disasters, and yet face this reality with confidence and courage: the more he understood of Kenna's nature, the more awed he became.

Now, he took Gavriela's hand, glanced at Dmitri, and turned to Kenna.

—*Perhaps we should all fly together.*

—*To Valhöll?*

—*Exactly.*

Dmitri smiled his Trickster smile.

They walked through the shining halls, all nine war leaders with Kenna in the lead, each taking a shield and some other weapon en route, until they came to a great gleaming ramp that led outside to the stark lunar landscape beneath ink-black sky.

As they placed the shields horizontally two centimetres above the ground and released them – the shields vibrated and hung in place – Magni seemed embarrassed.

—*Must we travel this way?*

Kenna touched his arm.

—For show before our armies, it is best.

In vacuum, soundlessly, Magni sighed.

—I'd rather be fighting.

—Soon enough, you will be.

Magni was not the only one to nod, accepting Kenna's words. Resurrection and a million years of preparation were about to boil down to that most ancient phenomenon, an army of one species throwing itself against another, all the wonders of civilisation reduced to the need to fight, and do it well.

It was a bitterness that Magni, of all of them, had found hardest to swallow, while Rathulfr – and perhaps Dmitri, in a less wholesome way – experienced a kind of fulfilling joy, even vindication, in preparing for war, leaving the others to commit themselves out of duty and necessity.

Each of the nine stepped upon a floating, quivering shield. Then, as one, they looked up to Earth's disc, banded with silver and crimson, serene in the night.

Kenna gave the command.

—We fly.

They rose amid invisibly roiling vacuum; and then they soared, heading for Valhöll.

To a battle-ready Earth.

They flew the skies, made speeches that were beamed across all nine armies within this, the ninth wave of Einherjar, of resurrected warriors. Battalions stood to attention as the exhortations rang in their minds, and the strategic pictures unfurled: the visual representations of that which could not be seen, the darkness, and its journey comprising hundreds of millions of lightyears across a cosmic void and onwards to this galaxy.

It had a bridgehead established at the core, weaker than it had intended but existing nonetheless, and it had continued its advance, for it was almost here, almost at the galaxy's edge.

In the inevitable aeons to come, when two trillion years

have passed, baryonic matter will cease to dominate the universe, and each galaxy will be alone, the others receded far beyond an impenetrable black horizon. That will be the epoch of darkness.

—But we will not allow it to hasten that victory.

To fight a holding action that would last two trillion years was the greatest victory that ordinary, baryonic-matter lifeforms could hope to achieve.

Across the Earth, billions of humans and Haxigoji of living crystal shared those broadcast thoughts and images and grew fierce, because this was their reason for existing now: to beat back the enemy's advance, to hurt it enough that it would never try again.

The earlier waves were in final preparation, having fought training campaigns in the depths of Jovian oceans and interstellar space; soon the greatest deployment the galaxy had ever seen would begin.

When the initial speeches and briefing were over, the nine war leaders split their mid-air formation and flew to their respective armies. Gavriela chose to walk among her troops as an individual instead of addressing them from on high, so she glided across the metallic crimson expanse of a continent-sized arsenal, in parallel to one of the silver regions where the crystalline warriors grew.

At random, she picked a spot and swooped down to land on metal.

Among her warriors, standing at ease now, were humans of the modern kind like Magni, born to this form, and those who were grown for the battle, Haxigoji and human alike, their neural patterns laid down via cross-temporal resonance: some personalities copied many times over, to varying degrees of fidelity.

Each possessed true warrior spirit: they were grown that way, absorbing from the very start paraneural crystal shards analogous to archaic logotropes, whose purpose was only to awaken natural potential. Any individual is the descendant of billions of years of ancestors who fought and survived: the son, daughter or clone of champions.

Gavriela stopped before a strong-looking crystalline woman.

—*I am Gavriela. What was your name, originally?*

Diffractive spectra shifted as the woman smiled.

—*My name was Rekka, War Leader.*

—*And do you remember your first life?*

The woman shook her head.

—*Vague dreams, is all. Though I have spirit-sisters who remember more, some of them clearly.*

—*And your thoughts on the war? Or on the way we resurrected you?*

Again, the Rekka-echo shook her head.

—*If you hadn't resurrected me, I wouldn't exist, and that would be a shame. And as for the darkness, whether the hatred comes from the training or just from being me, who can tell?*

This was the moral question faced by every commander:

—*Is it worth fighting against?*

—*With respect, War Leader, you know it is.*

Once, Gavriela would have been unhappy at being addressed as a military commander, but half a million years had hardened the notion inside her.

The other warriors in the platoon nodded agreement.

—*Good luck,* Gavriela told them.

She stepped upon her shield and soared upward.

So many weapons. So many warriors.

But against an enemy like the darkness, was even the population of Earth-turned-Valhöll enough?

Perhaps they were like children playing with toy guns and mock-heroic fantasy, to be brushed aside and killed when the real invaders came.

When the war leaders reconvened, eight of them floating in a circle surrounding Kenna at the centre, they raised their arms and tuned their minds to the crystalline armies standing to attention on those silver and crimson pseudo-continents banding the globe, to the eight waves floating ready across the solar system, and for a time they became one being, unifying their purpose: protecting life, protecting the galaxy.

We fight until we win.

Or die.

It was thought and emotion combined, shared and uniting them all. Then every warrior raised a weapon and transmitted a single intention:

Win.

Nine times nine billion warriors were ready for the fight.

For Ragnarökkr.

SIXTY-TWO

The galaxy had continued to rotate, but the jet had not, relative to distant stars: it still pointed in the direction of Auriga, though Valhöll-once-Earth no longer lay exactly on that radial line. The enemy's bridgehead linked the dark-matter star at the galactic core to the intricately structured dark-matter halo enclosing the galaxy like an eggshell.

A black bridge from intergalactic space stretched from beyond a distant void all the way to the galactic core: so long that it would take photons hundreds of millions of years to travel from end to end. Beyond the galaxy's halo, it was thick and intricate and strong; inside the galaxy proper, its narrower presence could be sensed only by the spotter squadrons, deep space reconnaissance groups composed of Haxigoji warriors, their crystalline bodies resonating with the zero-point energy of spacetime itself, needing no ships to fly, no more than fish needed assistance to swim.

Among the living-crystal Haxigoji were crystalline Seekers, entangled in constant communication with their brothers and sisters, remaining alert for hostile feelers along the hyperdimensions, for the Anomaly had also enjoyed a million years in which to prepare: the darkness was not without allies among the baryonic-matter entities of the galaxy.

The location where the jet ended was designated Shadow Gate, and unless something unexpected occurred, this was where the battle would begin. For all the timescales involved in reaching this moment, no one expected this to be an extended campaign: this was a single confrontation, with everything at stake.

When Schenck's renegades of distant memory had tried such a strategy in a different universe, they had failed and died; luckily they were the enemy. Here in realspace, Kenna and her fellow war leaders intended to do better.

The first test was upon them.

It was darkness with structure: a three-dimensional moving maze of invisible matter and energy falling upon the spotters and the lead warriors of Roger's army: phalanxes of crystal-line fighters floating in space, some in human form, others morphed into dart-like shapes, all trained to lay down devastating fire by cracking apart raw vacuum, by letting rip with zero-point energy.

The greater darkness was here.

—*Now.*

Warriors attacked.

Explosions and death were everywhere.

Around the fiery end of that great spindle, the galactic jet emanating from the core, spacetime burned, and gamma- and X-radiation spurted like blood, while squadron after squadron threw themselves against the dark, complex structures of the enemy: a ghost creature or creatures wide enough to devour stars, crawling along its black bridge from who-knew-what dark-matter hell, pushing implacably on into the precious galaxy, advancing despite its wounds and losses, for the squadrons *were* damaging it, that was certain, even as they died.

An honourable death is still extinction.

—*Fall back.*

Roger had delayed as long as he dared, but to lose his entire vanguard was not his purpose. A huge mass of darkness, all right angles and hollows, was growing large before him; standing on his shield, he focused along his spear and used it to direct his vacuum-splitting beam, gamma-rays and sapphire light spilling everywhere. Then he tipped back, whirling through a vertical half-circle, crouched on his shield as he accelerated hard.

Angular dark extrusions grew on either side, soundless yet seeming to clatter into place, attempting to enclose him; but he swung his glowing spear and spacetime shimmered and the darkness shrivelled back, unable to touch him as he flew to rejoin his retreating army.

Angular extensions of darkness were expanding to follow but that was all right because they had hoped for something like this.

—*Having fun, brother?*

—*Wonderful, sis.*

Freya's death squadrons came hurtling in from Roger's left, screaming out of spacetime distortions like sapphire starbursts, and they tore through the darkness-extrusions, breaking them apart. Complex angular structures of non-matter tumbled off, twisted and bent, apparently inert.

Suddenly they returned to life, those fragments; but Freya had foreseen the possibility and a hundred more squadrons followed, taking the smaller structures apart, wielding zero-point energy with exactitude, obliterating the enemy offshoots.

A partial victory, so early on, built confidence.

But the greater mass of darkness was still advancing.

Magni's people materialised then, glowing blue and directing destructive energy back along the length of the darkness, but still it came. And then space was glowing the colour of sapphires, and the best part of a hundred worlds shivered into existence, transported by an unimaginable spacetime distortion.

It was all the hellworlds, linked together and teleporting into place.

The Anomaly joining the fight.

And it reached out through the hyperdimensions into the

crystalline warriors' minds, eager to absorb them. It was Magni who sent the desperate call.

—*Harij! We need your army now.*

Seekers were everywhere among the squadrons, but this threat was something that Harij's people needed to face together. In his original life, Harij had been the first to break Anomalous links; now his Seeker battalions fell upon the hellworlds, disrupting the distortions that were subverting human warriors and killing Haxigoji.

They died in their millions, those diving Seekers; but in doing so, they split apart the links, separating hellworld from hellworld. Finally, they reached a critical phase transition in the Anomaly's destruction, like a neurotoxin preventing the chemical flow of thought; and every one of those planets exploded in time, but at such a cost.

The Anomaly was dead for ever.

And so were five million Seekers or more. Kenna sent out her questing thoughts with increasing desperation, but no answering resonance occurred, no response to the ping.

No trace of Harij.

Around the glowing line of the galactic jet, Roger and Gavriela and Magni's forces were falling back, retreating towards the galactic centre, employing ever more frequent hyperdimensional jumps as the great mass of darkness chased them: somehow the dark vanguard dragged itself faster than lightspeed towards the core.

—*Break off now*, Kenna commanded from a distance.

She turned to her massed battalions: nine billion crystal warriors blazing with reflected light, floating in formations like quivering arrowheads, close to the centre of the galaxy they were sworn to defend, while a billion suns shimmered all around.

—*This is our time, warriors.*

Nine billion hands raised nine billion spears.

—*Now.*

They streamed out along the galactic jet.

Warfare is fractal, self-similar at every scale, a truth Kenna and Roger, as one-time Pilots in the ancient past – and Freya, given her own mu-space origin – had always known, deeply and intuitively.

To follow a skirmish or a continent-wide campaign is to understand geometry and weakness, aggression and failure, in a way that translates to two creatures fighting with claws and teeth, all the way up to a battle whose field is a galaxy, the fate of billions of stars and baryonic-matter life itself the prize.

But simulation and practice, even across a million years, were not the real thing: this was many times worse and more horribly exhilarating than any had imagined, even Kenna with her knowledge of other destinies, of infinitely many modes of failure.

The battle raged along the fifty-thousand-lightyear length of the galactic jet, and it was magnificent as much as it was tragic; because everybody dies, but how many get a chance to spend everything in a cause and setting such as this? Forget mythology: they *were* gods, and they knew it; and everything boiled down to this: defeat the vastest of enemies or let the galaxy perish.

Kenna would not allow that to happen, and neither would her warriors.

They gave their lives by the million, by the billion.

But still it came, the darkness.

—*Fall back. Disperse.*

No ruse this time: not the order Kenna had wanted to give.

It advanced like a galaxy-devouring worm along the pathway defined by the glowing jet: the titanic darkness that was angular and complex, perhaps infinitely so, pouring onwards towards the centre. Legions and battalions of Kenna's finest warriors were beaten back and fell away, meaning only one thing: the beginning of the end.

Shimmers of blue grew around the darkness, surrounding it. Then new, unexpected forces spilled out into view:

crystalline creatures with jagged wings, angular and strange, a billions-strong army great enough to change the momentum of the battle, led by the war leader who had been missing from Kenna's awareness since Roger's vanguard engaged the enemy at Shadow Gate.

Kenna's prismatic face split into a rainbow smile.

—*Dmitri-Stígr. You* are *the Trickster.*

The reply came resonating back.

—*More than you know, War Queen.*

Kenna had believed that the darkness would reserve its worst horrors for any who betrayed it. Could this be the critical miscalculation leading to her armies' defeat?

Perhaps Dmitri had waited until now in order to be sure of which way the battle's momentum went. To determine which side was the more likely winner, having devised some way of avoiding destruction by the darkness. Now, as he directed his forces to the attack, his analysis would be the same as Kenna's: that *likelihood* was a weak term for the virtual certainty of victory that now obtained.

His Siganthian-derived warriors fell upon Kenna's forces, killing multitudes.

I trusted the Betrayer.

Kenna bent her head and concentrated, linking to her six war leaders that remained: to Roger and Freya at the galaxy's periphery, to Magni and Gavriela halfway along the jet's length, and to Sharp and Rathulfr, whose forces were still standing off, ready to swoop at the opportune moment – except that Kenna no longer believed the moment would come.

—*We are lost*, she shared with them.

Overwhelming desolation suffused her: the pseudo-memories of all those other realities, that infinity of failures; and now this, here in the only physical reality, the only true life, that she would ever know.

Failure, bitter and total.

While the galaxy and every lifeform in it paid the price.

SIXTY-THREE

Rathulfr moved through space, making distance between himself and his personal squadron, then bent down upon his floating shield, concentrating hard, creating total focus. In a moment, his questing ping was answered; and the tone of Dmitri's reply was mocking:

—*How goes it, brother mine?*

Rathulfr's crystal face hardened into diamond.

—*I killed a poet once, Trickster. He reminded me of you.*

Again, sneering amusement coloured Dmitri's thoughts:

—*Poetry? I'll give you a poem. Listen to my saga of death, my epic of destruction.*

—*Wait, Dmitri . . . The darkness will kill you. You must know that.*

—*Actually, that's not our agreement.*

In vacuum, Rathulfr snarled without sound. So one touched by darkness in a previous life could communicate with it now. It followed from everything that Rathulfr knew of Dmitri's nature, and of Stígr before him, long dead.

—*Kenna trusted you*, he told Dmitri. *She trusted you, the Trickster.*

—*That's her fault, brother, wouldn't you say? Why would anyone who knew me actually believe in me?*

There was a smile on Rathulfr's face now, and it was grim.

—*Why indeed, brother? Why would anyone?*

—*What do you . . . ? You bastard!*

Rathulfr, floating in vacuum, laughed.

—*Meet my* berserka *regiments. And give my regards to Hel.*

His secret force of carls, trained to fight as only he could teach them, burst out of their hyperdimensional hiding-places and fell upon the Siganthian-descended creatures of Dmitri's army. Those carls were strong and skilful, fast and courageous, able to fight as units or individuals, commanding zero-point energy with a daring no others could match; yet that was not what brought them victory.

It was *berserkergangr*, pure and simple, controlled at will, that rendered them superlative killers. They flew to contact, they fought, and Dmitri's demonic army died, and that was that.

Rathulfr gave the command to his personal squadron.

—With me.

The rest of his army would remain in place, ready for the signal to commit. But he would need to fly himself to the galactic jet where the Trickster's forces were dying, because there was one task Rathulfr needed to carry out in person.

Dmitri's head was his.

It bought them time, no more. Gavriela and Magni were deep in conjoined analytical thought, keeping track of their swirling forces around the mid-point of the jet, fighting not just the great extrusions of the darkness, but something new: split-off extensions, hard to perceive in their angular complexity, fighting like soldiers in their own right.

Dark hordes upon hordes, though whether they were individuals or cell-like components, as the dead Anomaly had once subsumed organic beings, it was impossible to tell.

Gavriela's resurrected warriors, her beloved Einherjar, and those of Magni's people who had remained in this galaxy to fight, did their best against the growing force. But the darkness was increasing in strength, pouring ever more strongly along the bridgehead.

Roger and Freya were still in the midst of fighting, though they had fallen further back again, too busy for the greater strategic picture. Sharp, whose warriors could most clearly perceive the shapes of the darkness, led the only army holding back; but soon enough, lacking a clear target, he would have to let his fighters loose regardless.

They might at least damage the enemy, just a fraction, before succumbing.

—*We're losing,* Gavriela told Magni.

—*I'm afraid you're right.*

Her crystalline face grim, Gavriela said the thing she had been holding back.

—*Your people should get away, Magni. Join the others who've fled the galaxy.*

For a long moment, Magni seemed to think about this; and then he smiled.

—*That would be sensible, wouldn't it? But the sensible ones left long ago.*

Finally, Gavriela smiled back.

—*I've had enough of directing from afar. Time to fight?*

—*Now I know what Roger sees in you. Yes, time to fight.*

From their commanding positions, they soared towards the main battle. After a split second to react, their personal squadrons followed, some of them smiling their hard, crystalline smiles.

This was what they had lived and trained for.

But ninety per cent of their fellow warriors were dead already: none of these fighters retained delusions about what they were flying into. This was death. The question was, how much damage could they inflict before they were done?

Now they would find out.

Then Gavriela and Magni were in the midst of it, blasting with zero-point energy in all directions, destroying creatures or extensions of the darkness, whatever the dark warrior-things were: killing them and killing them, while still the darkness poured onwards like a torrent. It was implacable, and when it finally reached the centre of the galaxy, it would lock in place and strengthen, and the black bridge would be in place forever.

Now, for Gavriela, there was only the fight.

As she became the death-bringer.

Fight. Then die.
So simple, in the end.

Dmitri, flying free of his demonic legions to face Rathulfr alone, began a mocking challenge:

—*Well met, brother. What do you hope to*—?

But a warrior who fought like a wolf knew that conversation was a distraction, that the Trickster intended to elicit a reply and then strike while he, Rathulfr, was attempting to communicate in return. Instead, he fell upon Dmitri, cracking space apart with the energy of his swings and thrusts, and when Dmitri dodged through the trickiest of trajectories, Rathulfr simply followed, implacable and focused.

Hairline fractures webbed Dmitri's right arm.

—*Wait, my*—

Rathulfr knew that in an epic duel against the Trickster, in which the momentum of violence swept back and forth, that devious bastard would eventually win. Among Rathulfr's resurrected forces, his Einherjar, were humans who had needed to be stripped of culturally induced fantasies regarding fair fights; but his élite carls had no such illusions, and neither did he.

Dmitri's torso crunched, white and opaque like sugar, hammered glass that has not yet given way, and he screamed without sound.

Of course he had his own final trick, as a myriad diamond death-lizards swarmed out of hyperdimensional folds in space, Rathulfr's own strategy turned against him. But the wolf did not care about a thousand cuts when the blood-enemy was there before him with defences that could not last much longer.

Now.

Vacuum bled sapphire light as Rathulfr cut it open.

And the Trickster's living-crystal body exploded.

Thórr's blood, at last!

It was done.

Laughing, Rathulfr spun around in space, ready to bring slaughter upon the death-lizard horde – who squirmed back into their hyperdimensional folds, keening with fear. The wolf was no stranger to others fleeing before him, and he bared his crystal teeth at the sight.

And turned back towards the greater battle, making ready to swoop.

In the absence of victory, it was time to fall in glory.

Kenna, too, fighting amid the blaze of a billion suns, was hand-to-hand against dark forces, chopping with and firing incandescence born of zero-point energy, destroying the enemy that fell on her piece by piece. But all the time the enemy's momentum overwhelmed her, and it could not be long before she made a slip and that would be it: everything over.

Roger and Freya at the vanguard; Magni and Gavriela; Rathulfr in the aftermath of killing Dmitri, now up against the main dark forces crawling along the jet; Harij lost; and only Sharp hanging back from the final battle: none of them could stop it, the enemy.

Sharp's forces suddenly moved, diving towards the greatest mass of darkness travelling along the galactic jet, and Kenna wailed as she fought because it was too soon, far too soon, there was no point of vulnerability. But of course Sharp knew this, and had determined the inevitable: neither Kenna nor the others could give him the best chance, so his warriors were going to do what they could before the end.

—*I'm sorry, my friends.*

Sorrow howled inside her as she slew the darkness but the flood kept coming and this was it: the final defeat.

—*I'm so very ...*

Golden light exploded everywhere, surrounding the galactic jet, all fifty thousand lightyears in length, with a great cylinder of brilliance, from which complex, living shapes emerged.

Such strange, beautiful, wonderful beings, or perhaps divinities.

At the same time, with a strange outpouring of energy that caused the innards of every crystal warrior to shake, a scarlet blaze enveloped the Shadow Gate, and lanced along the darkness beyond the galactic edge and the dark-matter halo that imprisoned it.

Gold from one direction, red from another.

Two new forces upon the stage.

=We are here, humanity.=

From golden mu-space they came: huge entities that once had been Labyrinths and ships and Pilots, long transcendent, long combined, long become something greater.

<<We tried to warn you. Now we help.>>

Emerging out of scarlet fire around Shadow Gate and the black bridge beyond, newly returned from whatever unknown universe they called home, came a second force. These were glowing lattice-beings, vast and wonderful and powerful: the distant descendants of Zajinets.

Gold, the lightning that gleamed like mu-space.

Red, the fires that shone like blood.

Both forces of newcomers fell upon the darkness, attacking together.

And the darkness split apart beneath their joint attack.

—Now, my warriors!

Kenna's yell reverberated inside three billion crystal bodies: all that survived of her armies. Blue was the glow illuminating space as they and the surviving war leaders brought the zero-point energy to bear.

All of them, getting ready to fire together.

—NOW.

Cataclysm engulfed the darkness.

The galactic jet burned as the black bridge beyond exploded, spinning off into the depths of intergalactic space, shrivelling and dying. Countless parts tumbling, crumbling, becoming dust. The darkness shattered, it tore, it dissipated; and perhaps in ways that no one left alive could hear – not with the Trickster gone – it screamed.

Dead and sundered, its connection to the bridge-head useless.

Beyond Shadow Gate, the darkness split away from the galaxy's dark halo, unravelling, perhaps all the way back to its beginning, to its origin beyond the cosmic void. Its route was destroyed, and perhaps the darkness itself was dead or dying; but either way, it could no longer reach the galaxy.

Baryonic-matter life was safe.

The darkness was defeated.

EPILOGUE

The gods that were Roger and Gavriela floated free near the galactic core, watching the greater beings that were Labyrinth and Zajinet descendants as they worked together, repairing damage to the galaxy: refurbishing suns and tidying up their configurations.

Multitudes of crystal humans also watched, though many had returned to Valhöll-now-Earth, or made other worlds their home for now. This was the aftermath of victory.

It was no surprise when Kenna and Rathulfr flew towards them; the surprise was that the former war queen and warrior held hands as they did so. They smiled as they drew close and hovered.

—*We did it.* Kenna gestured to the greater gods at work. *Thanks to our friends, fulfilling prophecy.*

—*Prophecy?* asked Gavriela.

—*Nine realms on three levels of reality,* Kenna told them. *There was always a third universe, not to mention glowing Múspellheim, which always fit badly into the scheme.*

Was that a hint that the darkness, mediating through Stígr a million years ago, had seen in his half-believed myths the possibility of its demise?

But Rathulfr had a different question to ask.

—*Sharp still believes he can resurrect Harij, Magni is headed for Andromeda to fetch his people back, and Freya seems determined to personally thank every one of three billion people that fought alongside us. Kenna and I wish to learn from our omnipotent friends.* He gestured towards the great beings at work, fixing the galaxy. *But what of you two? What are your plans?*

446

Gavriela and Roger looked at each other.

—*We have other questions*, said Gavriela.

—*Like whether war is the only way to interact with darkness*, said Roger.

So, even Kenna and Rathulfr could look surprised.

They floated in space, mulling this over.

—*You think we could have avoided all this?* Kenna gestured at the fading jet, among which crystalline corpses floated like clouds of tiny diamonds. *You think if there had been another way, we would not have taken it?*

Roger and Gavriela shook their heads.

—*Ragnarökkr was inevitable*, said Roger. *It's the aftermath that's negotiable.*

All four turned their gazes away from the galactic centre, to the greater universe beyond.

In a trillion years, two trillion years, as Kenna had told her warriors, the distant galaxies would no longer be visible: the cosmos would have expanded so far, pulling galaxies apart by such unimaginable distances, that no light from any galaxy would ever reach another.

Then the darkness would rule.

—*What if the darkness*, said Gavriela, *wanted to link galaxies for good, so they would not be sundered apart?*

Kenna blinked.

—*For good?*

So great a power might simply crush baryonic-matter life-forms because such life seemed too trivial and worthless to care about, as humanity once treated microbes.

—*And your intentions?* asked Rathulfr. *Your specific intentions, my friends?*

Roger smiled, and took hold of Gavriela's hand.

—*We're thinking of travelling.*

They looked along the ruined jet, in the direction of Shadow Gate where so many fell. And Gavriela smiled.

—*It will be an adventure, if nothing else.*

Kenna looked at Rathulfr, then back at Roger and Gavriela.

—*That much is certain.*

—*You mean,* said Roger, *it's predestined?*

The four of them laughed, floating in vacuum.

And Roger and Gavriela turned away, still holding hands, as spacetime whirled around them, lighting up with a brilliant sapphire glow.

—*Go well.*

—*And you.*

They flew towards the void.

ACKNOWLEDGEMENTS & FINAL NOTE

When it comes to using recent historical figures in fiction, I agree with Barbara Kingsolver: an author does not have free rein. My depiction of Alan Turing, in this and the previous volume, relied heavily on the superlative biography by Andrew Hodges. It is my interpretation, a fictional rendering and not the real person, transformed to serve the needs of the narrative. The world owes the real Turing an immense debt, not to mention an apology.

Peter Hennessy's analysis of 1950s Britain, *Having It So Good*, was particularly helpful. The savagery of continental Europe following World War II, as hinted at in Chapter 2, was too brutal for me to detail here. A conversation with historian Keith Lowe prior to the publication of his *Savage Continent*, followed by the book itself, formed a shocking eye-opener.

In Chapter 30, the descriptions of termites and weaver ants (including the phrase, 'sending their old women to war') come directly from E.O. Wilson's essay *In The Company Of Ants*. The Chapter 12 quotation regarding gastrulation comes from the biologist Lewis Wolpert.

The Bach piece mentioned in Chapter 41 is Badinerie from his Orchestral Suite No.2 in B Minor.

My depiction of the galactic centre as something other than a black hole comes from a speculation by Nobel laureate Robert B. Laughlin. Not from the Laughlin book cited below, however – that belongs here because of its emergent-properties perspective on fundamental physics.

In the previous volumes, the Absorption scene in

Berchtesgaden contains a nod to Roald Dahl, and Gavriela's homecoming after the US trip in *Transmission*, though it came into my head fully formed, is *homage* to Nicholas Monsarrat for *The Cruel Sea*.

The fictional SRS's pre-deployment antics are inspired by a description in Robin Horsfall's book, *Fighting Scared*.

For long-lived academic supervision, encouragement and friendship, infinite thanks to Professor Jim Davies. And thanks to everyone else at Oxford's Department of Computer Science, previously the Computing Laboratory.

Thank you to physicist/writer Dave Clements for organising the *Science for Writers* conferences at Imperial College, and giving me Imperial as a setting.

Many, many thanks to Fluffy Mark for reminding me about Kian.

At my redoubtable publishers, enormous gratitude goes to the magnificent Marcus Gipps (thank you for the insights, which made this and the previous book so much stronger), the stupendous Simon Spanton, and jolly Jon Weir.

Thank you to Bonbon and Nutmeg, for putting in an appearance in Labyrinth, and being wonderful.

As always and ever, love and gratitude to Yvonne, who puts up with it and gets me through it all.

While I was writing this, the third and final volume of Ragnarok, researchers reported definitive evidence that in the eighth century, *during the year 775 or 776*, Earth experienced a blast of gamma radiation. (Note that Stígr was corrupted over a year before Ulfr encountered him.)

Several days before I submitted the completed book, news from the Fermi Space Telescope came to my attention: patterns in the data suggest some of the gamma-rays emitted from the galactic core are produced by dark-matter interactions.

It seems the darkness is on the move ...

Mid Glamorgan, Wales, January 2013

BIBLIOGRAPHY

Barnes, M., *A New Introduction to Old Norse*, Viking Society for Northern Research, University College London, 3rd Edition, 2008

Bloom, H., *The Lucifer Principle*, Atlantic Monthly Press, 1995

Booth, M., *The Dragon Syndicates*, Doubleday, 1999

Cohen, J., *The Privileged Ape*, The Parthenon Publishing Group Ltd., 1989

Copeland, B.J. et al., *Colossus: The Secrets of Bletchley Park's Code-breaking Computers*, Oxford University Press, 2006

Crossley-Holland, K., *The Norse Myths*, Pantheon Books, 1980

Dawkins, M.S., *Living with The Selfish Gene*, an essay in *Richard Dawkins* (ed. Grafen, A., Ridley, M.), Oxford University Press, 2006

Dawkins, R., *The Selfish Gene*, Oxford University Press, new edition 1989

Gribbin, J., *Science A History 1543–2001*, Allen Lane, 2002

Hawkins, J., *On Intelligence*, Holt, 2004

Hennessy, P., *Having It So Good*, Allen Lane, 2006

Hodges, A., *Alan Turing: the Enigma*, Vintage, 1992

Horsfall, R., *Fighting Scared*, Cassell, 2002

Jeffery, K., *MI6: The History of the Secret Intelligence Service*, Bloomsbury, 2010

Kaku, M., *Quantum Field Theory*, Oxford University Press, 1993

Kynaston, D., et al., *Yesterday's Britain*, Reader's Digest Association, 1998

Laughlin, R.B., *A Different Universe*, Basic Books, 2005

Lerwill, S., *Running Manual*, Haynes, 2012

Lowe, K., *Savage Continent*, Penguin, 2012

Magnusson, M., *The Vikings*, Golden, reprinted 1985

Margulis, L., Sagan, D., *Slanted Truths*, Copernicus, 1997

McKee, M., Revelations from the Body Electric, *New Scientist*, 213, 2855, March 2012

Miller, D., *The Tao of Muhammad Ali*, Vintage, 1997

Miller, R., *Chiron Training: vols 1-5*, Rory Miller, 2011

Page, R.I., *Chronicles of the Vikings*, The British Museum Press, 1995

Page, R.I., *Runes*, The British Museum Press, 1987

Parker, A., *Seven Deadly Colours*, The Free Press, 2005

Pert, C.B., *Molecules of Emotion*, Simon & Schuster UK Ltd., 1997

Pettas, N., *The Blue-Eyed Samurai*, Global Friends Communications Co. Ltd., 2011

Popper, K., *The Logic of Scientific Discovery*, reprinted by Routledge, 2002

Rennie, J., *The Operators*, Pen and Sword Books Ltd., 2007 (first pub. Arrow Books, 1997)

Richards, J.D., *The Vikings: A Very Short Introduction*, Oxford University Press, 2005

Roberts, J.M., *Shorter Illustrated History of the World*, Helicon, 1993

Sanmark, A., Sundman, F., *The Vikings*, Lyxo, 2008

Stafford, D., *Spies Beneath Berlin*, John Murray, 2003

Strogatz, S., *SYNC*, Hyperion, 2003

Syed, M., *Bounce*, Fourth Estate, 2010

Taylor, P.B., Auden, W.H., *The Elder Edda*, Faber and Faber, 1969

West, N., *GCHQ: The Secret Wireless War 1900-86*, Coronet, 1987

Wilson, Edward O., *In Search Of Nature*, Penguin Books, 1998

Yourgrau, P., *A World Without Time*, Basic Books, 2005